FIELD RULES

ROMANCING THE RUINS #1

CARLA LUNA

MOON MANOR PRESS

First paperback edition: July 2022

Cover Design: *Bailey McGinn*
Editing: *The Editing Soprano*
Proofreading: *One Love Editing*
ISBN 978-1-7368661-7-7 (paperback)
ISBN 978-1-7368661-6-0 (ebook)

Published by Moon Manor Press
Cedarburg, Wisconsin
carlalunabooks.com

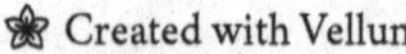 Created with Vellum

For all the girls who dream of being archaeologists.

CHAPTER ONE

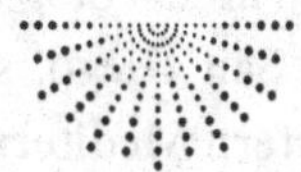

Olivia Sanchez adjusted the straps of her enormous olive-green backpack. She felt like a giant turtle. Scratch that—she felt like a tiny turtle with an oversized shell. When she'd hoisted the heavy pack off the baggage carousel, the weight had sent her staggering sideways.

Clearly, the pack had been designed for someone who might be classified as "tall," whereas Olivia measured a mere five foot two. Still, with the backpack on, her messy, dark brown curls pulled into a ponytail, and worn hiking boots covering her feet, she looked ready for adventure. Like a *real* archaeologist.

True, she had minimal field experience, but when it came to the ancient world, she knew her stuff.

After a final glance in the restroom mirror of the Larnaca International Airport, she gave her ponytail a toss, hoping to convey a sense of bravado. Even if she was thousands of miles from home, she wouldn't let her anxiety derail her.

That's right, people. Olivia Sanchez isn't messing around. She's a badass archaeologist and doesn't take shit from anyone.

Then she snorted with laughter. No one would ever mistake her for a badass. She was a doctoral student of classical history at UCLA, most comfortable in the library surrounded by ancient tomes. Not a rugged explorer accustomed to roughing it in the great outdoors.

But at least she looked the part.

She wished she'd had more than two weeks' notice to prepare for this trip, but the unexpected opportunity was too good to pass up. For the next six weeks, she'd be here in Cyprus, working as a teaching assistant at an archaeological field school. Instead of spending her summer in San Diego, she'd be living on a sun-drenched island in the Eastern Mediterranean.

Not only would this job give her academic resume a boost, but it would also give her a chance to redeem herself for the mistakes she'd made seven years ago on her first—and only—dig, back when she'd been nineteen.

With a little strut, she left the restroom and cleared Customs in the blink of an eye. All that remained was securing a ride. She scrolled through the slew of texts she'd received from her friend and fellow graduate student Frida Gallego, who'd worked in Cyprus last year.

Frida's last message dampened a little of Olivia's enthusiasm. *Don't count on getting picked up. Go to the taxi stand outside Arrivals and find a group taxi to the Paphos area.*

Despite her friend's warning, Olivia secretly hoped someone might be waiting for her. Someone with an air-conditioned ride and an ice-cold bottle of water. She headed for the Arrivals area of the Larnaca airport. All around her were brightly dressed tourists and lively families eager for the start of summer vacation. Cheerful tour guides waving bright blue flags waited for their clients. Sadly, no one held up a sign with her name on it.

Bracing herself for the heat, Olivia exited the sliding glass doors. The sweltering temperature and blinding sunshine hit her like a smack upside the head, and the clamoring noise assaulted her senses. Cars pulled up to the curb and honked. People called out to each other in a babble of languages.

With a swell of pride, she recognized three of them. She was fluent in Spanish, thanks to her father's side of the family, the boisterous Mexican-American Sanchez clan. German was one of the language requirements for a doctorate in Classics. And Greek was a given, seeing as how her graduate research focused on the wine trade in Ancient Greece. Since it was the primary language spoken in the southern half of Cyprus, her fluency put her at an advantage.

At the taxi stand, she took her place in line behind an older couple. As they argued with the dispatcher, their demands escalated into a torrent of foul language.

Countless summers working at El Marinero, her family's Mexican restaurant, had given Olivia little patience for rude customers. She was about to put the entitled tourists in their place when a sharp whistle grabbed her attention. She whipped her head around and caught sight of a battered green Jeep with a faded ragtop idling in front of the line of taxis.

The driver leaned out of the window and beckoned to her. "Hey, Olivia! Over here!"

Yes. Someone had come to get her.

She stepped out of the taxi line but stopped short when she got a closer look at the driver.

Rick Langston.

She had to be dreaming. She rubbed the grit from her eyes. Considering how little she'd slept on the red-eye from LAX to Athens, followed by the flight from Athens to Larnaca, she might be hallucinating.

"Olivia!"

Shit. It *was* him.

Her stomach bottomed out, her emotions churning in a stew of shock, anger, and guilt. After seven years apart, she'd never expected to see him again.

She marched up to the curb. "What are *you* doing here?"

Ignoring the barrage of horns, Rick got out of the Jeep and sauntered over to her.

The last time she'd seen him, he'd been nineteen—a cute, well-built nineteen, but still kind of gangly. A teenager. This was a *man*. Deeply tanned, broad-shouldered, and seriously ripped. Toss in thick, wavy brown hair, a strong jaw, and killer cheekbones, and the total effect was breathtaking.

But even if he was far hotter than she remembered, he was the last person she needed in her life right now. Given her lack of experience as a field archaeologist, she had enough to deal with. Adding an ex to the mix made everything even more stressful.

Not just any ex, but the guy who'd captured her heart when she'd met him on a dig in Clear Lake, California. A dig that ended so catastrophically she'd never been out in the field again.

Rick crossed his arms, revealing impressive biceps. "Nice to see you, too."

"You didn't answer my question. What are you doing here?"

"What do you think?"

She groaned as the realization hit her. "Please tell me you're not working at the UC field school."

"Yep. Up until two hours ago, I thought I was picking up Frida Gallego. Imagine my surprise when I found out you took her place."

Did he think that was her fault? "That's not on me. Frida broke her ankle, so I was asked to fill in at the last minute. I wouldn't have said yes if I'd known you were going to be here."

He scowled. "What the hell, Olivia? If anyone should be pissed, it's me. You're the one who ended things without a word of explanation."

Guilt slammed into her, twisting her stomach in knots. At the time, she'd been so distraught she believed her decision was justified. Now it just seemed callous. "I'm sorry, but I thought it was the right move. After everything that happened, I…"

"You what?"

She struggled to come up with a decent excuse for ghosting him, but she was too frazzled to think rationally. She shook her head in defeat. "Sorry."

"Forget it. I've moved on." Rick's gaze roamed over her. "So, you're working here? Teaching students about archaeology?"

"Like I said, I'm filling in for Frida."

"I heard you. But when's the last time you were on a dig?"

His scornful words brought back the anxiety she'd battled over the last two weeks. Before she could defend herself, one of the taxi drivers yelled at them. She turned around and cursed him out in Greek.

A ghost of a smile flickered across Rick's lips. "Nice comeback. But you didn't answer my question."

"Can we talk about it on the drive?" She wiped her forehead. Five minutes in the broiling July sun and she was already sweating. When he didn't budge, she flashed him her humblest smile. "Please, Rick. All I want to do is offload this pack and crash in that sweet, air-conditioned Jeep of yours. It does have air-conditioning, right?"

"No worries, princess. The AC works just fine."

"Perfect." Maybe the drive would give them a chance to talk things out.

A hesitant voice interrupted them. "Excuse me? Rick Langston?" A lanky guy with glasses and shaggy brown hair, wearing a pack similar to hers, stood a few paces away.

"TJ, right?" Rick said. "Good to see you, man."

TJ grinned. "Dude, I was so pumped when I heard you'd be working this gig. It's been—what—five years since Tel Dor?" He turned to Olivia. "Rick was a square supervisor at the Tel Dor site in Israel. That was an awesome dig. Seriously hard-core."

Whatever, bro. Olivia had endured her share of "hard-core" dig stories from the archaeology students at UCLA. The rougher their experiences, the more they liked to boast.

Not that she was jealous or anything.

Hoping to hide her irritation, she pasted on a welcoming expression. "Nice to meet you. I'm Olivia Sanchez."

"TJ Mayer, Harvard University. I'm here as a lithics expert, focusing on Stone Age settlement patterns in the Eastern Mediterranean. ABD and kicking ass. Not to brag, but I should be done with my doctorate by this time next year. Then I'll be Dr. Mayer."

ABD. All but dissertation. She was in the same boat, though less inclined to flaunt her academic status. "That's great. Congrats."

After another driver honked at them, Rick pointed to the back of the Jeep. "We'd better head out. Find a place to stow your gear, and hop in."

She walked with TJ behind the Jeep. The tiny space was crammed full of wooden stakes, buckets, pickaxes, and bales of plastic rope. TJ shrugged off his pack, wedged it between some ropes, and got into the Jeep.

When Olivia tried the same thing, her pack wouldn't stay put. It thudded onto the road, bringing a plastic bucket with it. She crouched to pick up the bucket, but it rolled under the Jeep. Even when she knelt and stretched out her hand, she couldn't reach it. She made another attempt to grab the bucket, only to have it roll further away.

Rick's shadow blocked the sun as he loomed over her. "What's the holdup?"

She scrambled to face him, heat coursing through her cheeks. From the way he was smirking, he'd enjoyed watching her clamber around on all fours like an idiot. Either that, or he'd been checking out her ass.

"Just get the bucket, will you?" she said.

"My pleasure." He retrieved it with little effort. Then he hefted her pack—as if it weighed five pounds instead of forty—and crammed it in. "There. All set."

Did he have to sound so smug about it? "Thanks," she muttered.

He placed his hand to his ear. "What was that? Didn't quite hear you."

She gritted her teeth. "Thank you."

"No problem. If you need to cool down, there's water in the Jeep. You'll need to ride in the back because the passenger seat's full of supplies."

Still fuming, she climbed in the back seat next to TJ, grabbed one of the stainless-steel bottles, and chugged the ice-cold water. As she leaned her head against the seat, a wave of exhaustion crashed over her. A quick nap might recharge her batteries, but if she drifted off now, she might snore. Or drool. She'd humiliated herself enough for one day.

Rick pulled away from the curb and exited the terminal area. He zipped through a series of complicated roundabouts, then merged onto the highway. Though he was driving on the left side of the road, he seemed comfortable behind the wheel.

Of course he's comfortable. Everything comes easy for him.

Not like her. At age twenty-six, she'd worked damn hard to get this far in her academic career. She'd taken out student loans, worked multiple jobs, and applied for every scholarship under the sun. No one had ever handed her anything.

Turning her focus away from Rick, she peered out the window, curious for her first glimpse of Cyprus. Rolling green hills, scraggly brush, and scruffy pine trees dominated the landscape. Atop one of the hills was an array of tall windmills, but they resembled the stark wind turbines she'd seen in the Midwest rather than the iconic old windmills found on the Greek islands. Billboards along the side of the road advertised real estate companies and luxury villas. They passed a highway sign listing the distance in Greek and English. Seventy miles to go.

That gave her a little over an hour to recover from her shock at seeing Rick. Not only was he back in her life, but she'd be working with him for the next six weeks.

Remorse washed over her as she recalled what she'd done to him. After they'd left Clear Lake, she'd cut him off completely. She hadn't meant to hurt him. But the fallout from their mistakes had been so devastating she wanted to put the whole summer behind her.

That didn't mean she'd forgotten him. Or the passionate memories they'd made. But if she wanted to succeed at this job, she couldn't let those memories tempt her into losing control of her emotions again.

She couldn't let anyone knock her off course.

Not even Rick Langston.

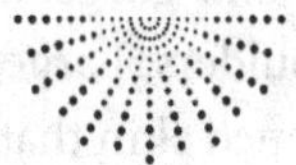

Picking up Olivia had been a true test of Rick's patience. Five minutes with her and he wanted to leave her at the airport. Better yet, book her a one-way flight back to California. Sure, he'd caught her off guard, but when she'd first spotted him, she acted like she hated him.

Which was grossly unfair.

She was the one who'd ghosted him after they'd been sent home in disgrace from the Clear Lake dig. Now she was treating *him* like the bad guy?

To think, he'd been looking forward to seeing Frida again. He'd met her two years ago on a dig in Greece. She was a hardworking, hard-partying grad student who loved a good challenge. Rock climbing, scuba diving, spelunking—she was up for all of it.

Why hadn't she warned him Olivia was taking her place?

Probably because she knew how you'd react.

To say he'd been stunned was putting it mildly. Especially since he hadn't known about Olivia until two hours ago, when the assistant director had pulled him aside to talk to him. "When you get to the airport, you'll be picking up Olivia Sanchez instead of Frida Gallego," he said. "Do you need me to send you her photo? So you'll know what she looks like?"

Rick had stood there in shocked silence, unable to form a coherent response. Olivia was coming to Cyprus? Today?

Once he'd recovered, he shook his head. "Nah. I can find her."

Even if seven years had passed, he'd never forget what she looked like. Short, curvy, and gorgeous, with dark brown curls that cascaded past her shoulders. Large, expressive eyes the color of rich chocolate. Olive-toned skin that burned first, then tanned beautifully. A rainbow of freckles across the bridge of her nose.

He'd seen her naked, under the light of a full moon. He knew she loved pistachio ice cream, hated spiders, and had a beautiful singing voice. Like him, her favorite movie was *Raiders of the Lost Ark*. She'd seen it numerous times and had most of the lines memorized.

Finding her had been easy. Working with her? Another matter entirely.

TJ leaned forward to catch his attention, jolting him back to the present day. "Hey. You were at Berkeley, right?"

"Good memory. Yeah. Graduated four years ago." Rick had done so much traveling since then he could barely remember what it felt like to be in a real classroom.

"I haven't seen you at any conferences or caught your name on any publications," TJ said. "Where are you doing your graduate work?"

There it was. The usual questions. *Where are you getting your doctorate? Who's your adviser? What's the subject of your dissertation?* Rick always got them at the start of any project, especially if it was affiliated with a university. By now, he'd learned to shrug off the judgment.

"I'm not in grad school. This is a job."

TJ gave a derisive chuckle. "Oh, a shovel bum, eh?"

Rick's hands tightened around the steering wheel. Though the term didn't sting as much as it once had, he didn't appreciate it.

He glanced in the rearview mirror to gauge Olivia's reaction, but her gaze was focused on the scenery outside her window.

"You can't go far without a graduate degree, you know," TJ said. "It's all about making connections—who you know, where you've been, that kind of thing."

Even if Rick had spent the past four years busting his ass in the field, he suspected he wasn't the type of connection TJ wanted. Not that he gave a damn. He'd worked in projects all over the Mediterranean and was fluent in Greek and Italian. He had his scuba license and had helped uncover the ruins of an underwater shipwreck. But to people obsessed with academia, he was a grunt without a degree.

"Hey, Olivia," TJ said. "You're one of the teaching assistants, right?"

"Huh?" she said. "Sorry. I was spacing out. Yeah, I'm here as a TA. I'm getting my doctorate in classical history at UCLA."

Rick's ears perked up. Even if he wasn't thrilled to be working with Olivia, he was curious about her. Clearly, she'd gone the full academic route in her passion for ancient history. But why hadn't he crossed paths with her sooner? The world of classical archaeology was so insular he should have run into her—or heard of her—at some point in the past four years. He suspected it was because she'd confined her studies to archival research rather than venturing back into the field.

Not that he had any right to judge, but the Olivia he'd known had been passionate about hands-on archaeology. She wouldn't have traded the adventure of fieldwork for the tedium of poring over musty tomes in some library.

TJ snapped his fingers. "Now I remember where I heard your name. You're writing a dissertation on the wine trade in Ancient Greece during the Hellenistic era."

"How'd you know that?" she asked.

"I heard you speak at the AIA meetings in San Francisco last year. Killer presentation. Did I mention I'm at Harvard? I'm working with Dr. Preziosi. He's phenomenal. Did you go to his talk when you were in San Fran? It was mind-blowing."

Blah, blah, blah. TJ rambled on about the American Institute of Archaeology meetings, making sure to name-drop every prestigious professor he'd encountered. Naturally, Olivia was familiar with all of them.

Another thirty-five minutes to go. The drive couldn't end soon enough.

As the city of Limassol came into view, Rick was irked by the proliferation of high-rise buildings under construction. In the short time he'd been away from Cyprus, more condos, luxury villas, and expensive hotels had cropped up on the island. A newly erected billboard advertising Starbucks made his hackles rise. Though he had nothing against the chain, he didn't want it to crowd out the local coffeehouses.

"Hey, Rick," TJ said. "Once we get settled, I'm gonna need recs for authentic places to eat. I've never set foot inside a McDonald's or a Starbucks, and I don't plan to start now. I figured you'd have the inside scoop since you worked here last year."

"You've been here before?" Olivia asked. "What were you working on?"

Her question filled Rick with a twinge of satisfaction. Nice to know he wasn't the only one who harbored a little curiosity. "I spent a couple of months as a project manager on an archaeological survey for the Department of Antiquities. Most of the time, I was based in Paphos, which isn't far from where we'll be working."

Once Rick passed the turnoff for Limassol, the high-rises were replaced by a sprawling expanse of buildings bearing the familiar red-tiled roofs so common to the Mediterranean. He imagined how liberating it would feel to drive into the city and drop off TJ at the nearest Intercity bus stop. Maybe if the guy wasn't around to dominate the conversation, Rick could find out more about Olivia.

For the moment, however, TJ was still holding court. "Whenever I take on a project, I like to know where everyone's worked to make sure they can hack it. Olivia, where's the roughest place you've ever dug? For me, it would be excavating the ruins at Humayma in the Jordanian desert."

"Um…fun fact about me." Olivia's voice wavered. "I don't have any field experience. None worth mentioning, at any rate."

She wasn't even going to mention Clear Lake? The omission rankled Rick.

"First time in the field, eh?" TJ smirked. "I hope you like rough conditions, because this isn't going to be a luxury vacation."

"Damn," she muttered. "I was hoping for a spa and a heated pool, at minimum."

"Wait—you thought that?" Before she could reply, TJ burst out laughing. "That was a joke, right? Good one."

Rick held back a groan. Could the drive be any more excruciating?

For a blessed few minutes, TJ was silent. Rick fiddled with the dials of the Jeep's ancient radio until he found Viva FM—an English-language station playing a cheesy mix of '70s and '80s pop. When "Take A Chance on Me" started up, he wondered if Olivia was itching to sing along. ABBA had always been her go-to on karaoke nights.

TJ's nasally voice rose above the song's chorus. "So, Rick, on a scale of one to ten, how rough is this project gonna be? And by ten, I'm talking hard-core, like my experience in Jordan."

Rick turned down the volume on the radio. "Dunno. Maybe a five?"

"Oh, so there's running water? And flush toilets? Should be a breeze."

As TJ regaled them with tales of his desert adventure, Rick stayed quiet, keeping his focus on the road. He could have spouted equally impressive horror stories—he'd been on digs with scorpions, blistering heat, grumpy camels, and droves of mosquitoes—but he was too tired to muster up the effort. His lids drooped as he fought back a yawn. When the Jeep swerved to the left, he shook himself awake.

"Rick? You okay?" Olivia's voice was laced with concern.

"I'm wiped." He rubbed his eyes, willing them to stay open.

"You can take a break if you want. We're not in a hurry, right?"

"I'm supposed to get you back to camp by six. There's a staff dinner at six thirty."

Olivia pointed at the turnoff for Pissouri. "Can you take that exit? You could stop and grab some caffeine."

"Good plan. I need to get gas anyway." If he brought the Jeep back with less than a quarter tank, he'd get an earful from the assistant director of the field school.

He exited the highway and pulled into the nearest Petrolina station, then turned to face TJ and Olivia. "Do you want anything to drink? It's on me."

"Sure," she said. "Diet Coke, please."

"I'll take a Mountain Dew," TJ said.

"Got it." Rick eased out of the Jeep and asked the waiting attendant to fill it with gas. Above him, the sky was a brilliant blue, the heat shimmering off the road in waves. He took a deep breath, grateful this was his last round of airport pickups for the day. Though he hated playing the role of errand boy, he'd kept his complaints to himself. In a few days, he'd be out in the field, doing what he loved best.

Olivia climbed out of the Jeep and caught up to him. She smoothed her hair, as though trying to tuck the wayward curls back into her ponytail. "Rick? Just so we're clear…no one knows about us."

"What do you mean?"

"I never told anyone about Clear Lake. Since we didn't finish the dig, I didn't put it on my resume. My family knows about it, but otherwise, I don't talk about it. Ever."

His earlier irritation returned. Even if they'd screwed up

royally, they'd also made some fantastic memories. But she'd chosen to block all of it. "You were that ashamed of what we did?"

Her mouth gaped open. "Weren't you? We were *expelled*. I wanted to put it behind me. No one at UCLA knows."

"Not even Frida?"

"She's heard the basic story, but I never told her your name."

He raked his hand through his hair. "No wonder she didn't warn me."

"In hindsight, I wish I'd mentioned you, then I could have bailed. Now it's too late." She gnawed on her lip. "Anyway, it might be best if we keep the past a secret. I want to come across as professional, and the students might not respect me as much if—"

"If they knew you'd fucked your coworker?" As soon as the words were out, he regretted them. *Way to sound like an asshole, Rick.*

She flinched as though he'd struck her. "Don't be a jerk. Besides, we didn't actually…"

No, but they'd done damn near everything else. And if he recalled correctly, she'd enjoyed it as much as he had. He blew out a long breath, annoyed at himself for reacting so crudely. "Sorry. That was a low blow."

"It was." She closed her eyes and released a drawn-out sigh.

Was she remembering? Or trying to stop the memories from returning?

"Anyway, it's ancient history," she said. "So, can we please keep things quiet?"

As much as he hated to concede, her request worked in his favor. After his disastrous slipup two months ago, his reputation didn't need another hit. "Works for me." He cast a glance over at the Jeep. "We should get going before TJ comes looking for us. He's probably wondering what the hell's going on."

"Do you think if I paid him twenty bucks, he'd shut up? I'm getting a headache."

"You and me both." When she laughed, the pressure lifted just a little.

He went inside the station's convenience store and headed for the refrigerated section. After grabbing three bottles of soda, he joined Olivia at the counter, where she was perusing a small display of tourist trinkets—key chains, sunglasses, magnets, pens, and blue glass charms meant to ward off the evil eye. Off to one side, a small rack held a meager selection of postcards.

He pointed to the rack. "You still collect postcards?"

When she smiled at him, it was like the sun breaking out of the clouds. He'd forgotten how powerful her smile could be. "Yeah. My sister sends me a new one every month."

"Does she travel for work?"

"Sort of? She's an Instagram influencer and has a foodie-travel account. Maybe you've heard of her? SoFood SoFia?"

"I'm not on Instagram or Facebook. Not a big social media guy. Half the time, I'm working in places where I'm off the grid." After flipping through the postcards, he found one displaying an ancient Roman amphitheater. He paid for it, along with the gas and the drinks, then passed it to her. "Here you go. This place should be right up your alley."

She looked over the inscription. "Kourion. Is it nearby?"

"Just outside of Limassol. It's one of the sites we'll be visiting during field school."

"Thanks. And thanks for agreeing to keep things quiet."

"Sure." What else could he do? If she didn't want anyone to know they'd ever met, he'd do his best to play along.

Like she said, their fling was ancient history. It didn't need to be dug up again.

CHAPTER THREE

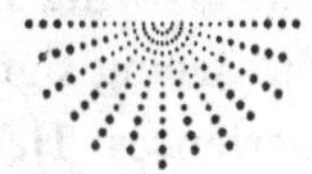

T hough TJ continued talking for the rest of the drive, Olivia tuned him out. She traced her fingers over the photo of the Roman amphitheater on the postcard Rick had given her.

As a kid growing up in San Diego, she'd barely traveled anywhere outside of Southern California. Running a restaurant meant her family couldn't pack up and leave town for a week. Holidays, weekends, and summer vacations were all times when the restaurant was at its busiest.

Even so, she'd caught the travel bug early, after getting hooked on the National Geographic Channel. When one of her friends sent her a postcard from Yosemite, she tacked it to the bulletin board in her room. Others followed—from friends, family members, and teachers. By the time she met Rick, she'd covered the entire board and had started on a second. "Once I really start traveling," she'd told him, "I'm going to fill up that board with postcards from all over the world."

Some traveler. In the seven years that had passed, she'd only been to Greece once. Thanks to a generous scholarship, she'd spent two months at the American School of Classical Studies in

Athens, doing research for her dissertation. But she'd barely ventured outside the city, other than a few organized day trips.

Even if she hadn't been living her dream, her life had been safer that way. More predictable. Things didn't go off the rails when you stuck close to home and followed the rules.

But now that she was actually *in* Cyprus, she couldn't deny the tiny seed of excitement growing inside of her. There was something so thrilling about seeing signs in a different language and anticipating new experiences. Her desire to travel might have diminished over the years, but it hadn't vanished completely.

When the road curved, she caught a glimpse of the coast. They drove past a long stretch of beach where large, craggy rocks jutted out of the water. The Mediterranean was a stunning swath of turquoise, more vivid than any photograph.

She broke into TJ's monologue. "Check out that view."

"The Mediterranean is the bomb," TJ said. "As soon as we have a free day, we need to hit the beach."

"That would be great," Olivia said.

"I take it you like to swim, *Olivia?*" Rick asked her.

Wiseass. He knew damn well she loved the water, because she'd been the first one in the lake when he'd dared her to go skinny-dipping. As a blaze of heat rose in her cheeks, she tried to keep her voice even. "I...I love swimming. In lakes *or* oceans. Anywhere, really."

TJ seemed oblivious to her discomfort. "Awesome. Where's the best beach in the area?"

"Coral Bay," Rick said. "We can go there on Sunday for our day off."

As it was, their schedule left little room for relaxation. The six-week field school was split between three weeks of ground surveying and three weeks of excavation. The students spent weekdays in the field and the lab, with Saturdays reserved for visiting museums and historic sites. If not for the Sunday breaks, they'd have no time off at all.

At a sign pointing toward the town of Kouklia, Rick headed inland. He took them along a narrow road, past palm trees, cream-colored buildings, and a small village square containing a cluster of shops and restaurants.

When he stopped the Jeep, Olivia was at a loss. Frida had said a local school would be providing their accommodations, leading Olivia to envision a boarding school, with dormitories and actual beds.

At best, this place resembled a rural elementary school. It consisted of several one-story buildings, a few smaller outbuildings, a gravelly parking area, and an open field. Scattered around the grounds were gnarled olive trees providing small pockets of shade, but otherwise, the landscaping was minimal. Next to one of the buildings was a flagpole bearing a faded black flag that read "Camp Kouklia." The logo was a skull and two crossed shovels.

Where were they supposed to sleep? The buildings didn't appear large enough to house any bedrooms. She didn't see any tents, either.

At this point, she was so tired she'd settle for curling up under one of the olive trees. After getting out of the Jeep, she retrieved her pack and hoisted it onto her shoulders. "Where should I put my stuff?"

"Over there." Rick pointed to a one-story building with a wide porch. "We set up the women's quarters in those classrooms."

"Thanks. I can help you unload after this."

He waved her away. "Don't worry about it."

Though she didn't want special treatment—not when she was meant to be pulling her weight as a staff member—she was too exhausted to argue. She hauled her pack over to the porch and let it fall onto the wooden boards. What she wouldn't give for a shower, followed by a long nap. As her lids fluttered shut, she willed herself to stay upright. She still had to get through the staff dinner.

At the sound of footsteps, she forced her eyes open, praying TJ hadn't come to share another story. The sight of a familiar face gave her a burst of energy. "Stu! Great to see you."

Like her, Stuart Carlson was a graduate student. She'd known him since their freshman year of college when they'd bonded in Latin class over their love of old-school gladiator movies, like *Ben-Hur* and *Spartacus*. Despite their shared passion for the ancient world and the fact that Stuart was pretty hot—tall, sandy-haired, and well-built—she'd never harbored any romantic feelings for him.

Stuart joined her on the porch. "I can't believe you're here. What a wicked surprise."

"I know, right? I'm so glad you're the other TA."

"How'd Frida convince you to take her spot? I didn't think you were the outdoorsy type."

"The school offered me a lot of incentives—a plane ticket here, a stipend, and…" She threw in some jazz hands. "As long as I do a decent job, Dr. Roth agreed to be the fourth member of my dissertation committee."

As the director of the field school, Dr. Albert Roth was the lead academic in charge of the entire project. In addition to his years of experience in Cyprus, he was a tenured professor who'd published four books on Mediterranean archaeology. For Olivia, getting him to serve on her committee would be a huge coup. She needed four professors to approve her dissertation—a technicality she'd taken care of last year, until one of those professors took early retirement.

Stuart gave her a high five. "Nice work. Roth's name carries a lot of weight in the classical world."

"Thanks. I really lucked out. Now I have to make sure I don't screw up. Which might be tough because I'm way out of my depth."

And I'll be working with my ex. Not that she'd share that tidbit of information with Stuart.

"You'll catch on quickly. Our biggest challenge is making sure those undergrads stay out of trouble."

"No kidding. I reviewed the school's code of conduct on the plane ride over. The rules about underage drinking were unbelievably strict."

Stuart rolled his eyes. "It's kind of a joke. Even if the students can't bring booze into camp, they can still head into Paphos on Saturday night and hit the bars."

"We're not expected to stop them, are we?" Her anxiety clawed its way to the surface. Since the harbor town of Paphos was only twenty minutes away, the students could easily get there by taxi.

"Don't worry about it. We're here as teaching assistants, not camp counselors. Though we should warn them digging in the hot sun while recovering from a massive hangover is a hellish ordeal."

"Speaking from experience?"

He barked out a laugh. "We've all had our share of drunken shenanigans in the field."

"Are we contemplating shenanigans?" a snarky voice asked. "If so, then I want in."

A petite woman with short dark hair, dressed in a tank top and faded cargo shorts, joined them on the porch. One of her bare shoulders bore a tattoo of a stylized pyramid. The other displayed a set of crossed shovels, like the ones on the Camp Kouklia flag.

She nodded at Olivia. "Nice to meet you. I'm Dusty."

"I'm Olivia." After a beat, she turned to Stuart. "Wait. Is this the Dusty you told me so much about?"

Dusty gave a little bow. "The one and only."

Over the years, Olivia had heard a lot of stories about Dusty Danforth. Her parents were Egyptologists whose passion for ancient Egypt had made them legends in the field. Since Stuart's parents were also archaeologists, he and Dusty had grown up together, spending countless seasons on their parents' digs.

"Dusty's here as our illustrator," Stuart said. "She'll be drawing the finds and teaching the students the basics of archaeological illustration. When Dr. Roth said he needed someone, I persuaded her to join us."

"It wasn't hard," Dusty said. "What's not to love about spending the summer in Cyprus?" She pointed to Olivia's pack. "You trying to figure out where to put that monstrosity?"

"Yeah. After I unload it, I don't want to lift it again until I leave."

"Good plan. Come on." She pushed Stuart in the direction of the Jeep. "Go help the guys unload while I get Olivia settled."

Olivia hefted her pack and followed Dusty into one of the classrooms. Sunlight streamed in through a row of tall windows, illuminating tiny dust motes. Desks, tables, and chairs were stacked along one wall. Six dark green camp cots were spread across the remaining floor space. Beside each one was a wooden produce crate, presumably for storing personal items. The room gave off a musty odor, and the air was so heavy and thick Olivia immediately broke into a sweat.

"There are two classrooms like this set aside for our cots and our stuff," Dusty said. "You'll be in here with five of the female undergrads. I'm in the next classroom over with the other three students."

"Is this where we'll be sleeping? It's so stuffy." As soon as the words were out, Olivia wished she could take back her whiny tone, but Dusty nodded.

"Yeah, these classrooms are the worst. They don't have AC or ceiling fans, and the windows barely open. Rick said we'd be better off dragging our cots outside to sleep. Did you see the big soccer field when you came in? We can set them up there."

"We're sleeping outside? In the open?" A tent was one thing.

But if all they had were camp cots, they'd be exposed to the elements. "What if it rains? And what about predators?"

"You mean the bears? There've only been a few brown bear attacks this year, and they weren't on this part of the island."

Bears? How was she supposed to sleep if there was a remote possibility a rogue bear would creep into camp?

Dusty burst out laughing. "Sorry. That was totally out of line. No bears in Cyprus. But you should have seen your face."

"Fuck, you had me going there." Olivia's tension released in a short burst of laughter. "I'm already on edge after spending the drive listening to TJ brag about his 'hard-core' experience battling scorpions in the Jordanian desert."

"The guy never shuts up, does he? But he's the only one obsessed with being hard-core. Obviously, Stuart's not. Neither is Rick. He's had some wild adventures, but he's not trying to one-up everyone."

Olivia's stomach dropped. "You've met Rick before?"

"Yeah. Last fall when I was in Turkey illustrating the artifacts from a shipwreck. He's a lot of fun."

A powerful surge of jealousy flooded through Olivia. Had Dusty and Rick hooked up when they'd worked together? She could imagine someone as adventurous as Dusty being his type.

Not that it was any of her business, because she was completely over him.

"Um…sounds like Rick has a lot of experience." The minute she said it, she cursed her choice of words.

Dusty chuckled. "In more ways than one. The guy gets around. I'm sure you know the type."

Only too well. Except when Olivia had fallen for him, she'd thought she was special. But maybe he hooked up on every dig, and she'd just been the first in a long series of women.

As if sensing Olivia's inner turmoil, Dusty spoke quickly. "Don't get me wrong—he's a great guy. He's been working in the field for years, and he's got a knack with students."

Then why didn't he go on to grad school? Back when they'd been nineteen, Rick had told Olivia he wanted to get his doctorate in archaeology and teach at the college level. But from the skimpy details he'd revealed on the drive, it was evident his life had followed a different route.

"Anyway—about sleeping outside," Dusty said. "It doesn't rain here in the summer, so we won't get drenched. There's no dangerous wildlife, and the mosquitoes aren't bad if you use bug spray. *Thank God,* because the evil buggers tried to eat me alive at my last job in Tunisia." She shuddered. "The local workers gave us this ointment called 'Moustiquecalm' that was supposed to drive them away. If anything, it made my skin tastier."

Dusty's candid humor was easier to take than TJ's bragging. Olivia's shoulders loosened as she let down her guard for the first time that day. "Everyone here has so much experience. Especially you and Stuart. I can't imagine what it must have been like, spending all that time in Egypt on your parents' digs."

"Sometimes, I felt really lucky," Dusty said. "Because of my folks, I got to explore sites tourists never visit. But other times, the days dragged, and I wanted to be back in the States, hanging out at the beach with my friends."

A sharp whistle drew their attention. An actual whistle, like the type referees used in basketball games.

"How delightful," Dusty muttered. "Grant's at it again with the whistle. I told him earlier we're not dogs."

"Grant?"

"Dr. Grant Nilsson, Dr. Roth's second-in-command. The blond, Swedish dude with a stick up his ass. I think he's summoning you."

Olivia battled a rush of trepidation as she went back outside. When Frida had worked at the field school last year, she'd described Dr. Nilsson as a joyless control freak. Though his rank as assistant director placed him below Dr. Roth, he wielded a lot of power since he oversaw the day-to-day logistics.

Just as Dusty said, Grant was so tall, pale, and blond that he gave off a chilly Nordic vibe. He stood on the porch, arms crossed, impatience radiating from every pore.

Hoping to hide her uneasiness, Olivia fixed a bright smile on her face. "Hi. You called for me?" Was this a Captain Von Trapp thing where they'd all end up getting their own whistle signals?

"I did. I believe a whistle is an effective way to call people to attention." He extended his hand. "Welcome to Cyprus. I trust you arrived all right?"

She shook it. Maybe he wasn't *that* bad. "I got here just fine. I appreciate Rick taking the time to pick me up."

He gave a dismissive grunt. "Rick's good at the little jobs."

Ouch. Was that a jab at Rick? It seemed uncalled for.

"I'm Dr. Grant Nilsson, the assistant director of the University of California Archaeological Research Practicum in Cyprus. You may call me Grant if you wish, though I'll be insisting on academic formality around the undergraduate students. You are not yet Dr. Sanchez, I take it?"

"One more year." She shot him an eager grin. "If all goes well."

"Let's hope for that, shall we? Despite your stellar academic record, I'm a little disappointed Dr. Roth wasn't able to find someone with *actual* field experience to serve as the female teaching assistant. I trust this won't be a problem when it comes to leading the students?"

His words cut into her, bringing back the doubts she'd harbored when she first agreed to take the job. She struggled to recall her accomplishments. "I...I don't think it should. I spent three years as a TA at UCLA, so I'm good with students. I'm well versed in the history of the Eastern Mediterranean, from the Bronze Age to the early Byzantine era. I speak Greek. And..."

She couldn't think of anything else. Not a damn thing.

Grant nailed her with a frosty gaze. "There are at least twenty other graduate students who could make similar claims, and they all know their way around an excavation site."

But they weren't available.

Should she remind him of that? Or would she come off as impertinent?

"I assume you took this position in the hopes of gaining favor with Dr. Roth?" he asked. "Since you still require a fourth member of your dissertation committee?"

His contemptuous tone unsettled her stomach. "It's not the only reason. I've been wanting to get back into the field ever since—"

Shit.

"Get *back* into the field? Your resume didn't mention any field experience."

She scrambled for a response that wouldn't reveal anything about Clear Lake. "I took a summer class when I was in…high school. For a few weeks. It got me excited about archaeology."

A blatant lie, but he seemed to buy into it. "A high school class? Hardly what I'd call experience. I hope you won't be a burden. If so, I'll have no qualms about informing Dr. Roth you're not up to the job. He won't want you here if you can't pull your weight."

"Of course. I understand." *Please let this conversation be over.*

"Good. We're having dinner in the village of Kouklia at six thirty. It's a short walk, so I suggest you clean up and be ready to go in ten minutes. You'll meet Dr. Roth there."

"Great. Thanks." As she watched Grant walk away, all Olivia wanted to do was retreat to the hot, stuffy classroom, crash out on a camp cot, and sleep for the next ten hours. If it wasn't stressful enough that she had to deal with Rick, now she was stuck with a supervisor who acted like a judgmental prick.

The next six weeks weren't going to be easy.

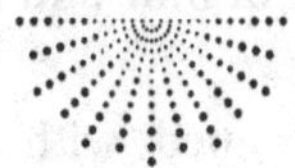

CHAPTER FOUR

y the time Rick finished putting away the supplies he'd picked up in Larnaca, he was sweaty and exhausted. He'd done two round-trip drives to the airport, spent hours searching for all the crap on Grant's list, and still had a heap of tasks to accomplish. All of which needed to be finished before the undergraduate students arrived the day after tomorrow. Given how much Grant hated him, Rick wasn't surprised to be stuck with the most grueling work imaginable. For example, item five on the list—*construct the camp showers*—was a beast of a job.

Don't let Grant get to you. Dr. Roth's the one who matters.

Since Dr. Roth was the dig director, his opinion counted far more than Grant's. As long as Rick did his job and stayed on the professor's good side, he'd get the recommendation he sorely needed to secure his next gig. In this field, word of mouth was everything, especially for a guy like him without a graduate degree. Unfortunately, Dr. Roth was so busy with his own research that he let the assistant director oversee the everyday workings of the field school. That meant Rick would be dealing with Grant constantly over the next six weeks.

Rick washed up and hustled to join the others, who'd started walking toward the village. Grant led the way, followed by Stuart, Dusty, and TJ, but Olivia lagged behind. Head down, she appeared to be lost in her own world.

Though Rick wanted to ask if she was all right, he wasn't sure she'd welcome the intrusion. Even if they'd reached an agreement at the gas station, they weren't exactly friends. He slowed his pace, letting her get ahead of him, and took his time to savor the view.

The quiet street was lined with a mixture of old stone cottages and newer homes, most with balconies and red-tiled roofs. Orange and lemon trees shaded the front yards, and colorful bougainvillea adorned a few of the older buildings. With the sun slowly making its descent, the day's heat faded, bringing the faintest hint of a breeze. He passed a few stray cats and stopped to pet a friendly calico that rubbed against his legs.

Further up the road, a pack of kids kicked a ball back and forth. One of them waved at him. "Kalispera, mister!" he called out.

Rick waved back. "Kalispera!"

Olivia stopped as though waiting for him. "Rick?"

He caught up with her. "Hey. You get settled okay?"

"I'm good. Thanks."

Her flat tone and slumped shoulders didn't inspire confidence. "You sure?"

"Not really. I just had my first meeting with Grant. Have you ever worked with him?"

Talk about a loaded question. He glanced down the road, but Grant was too far ahead to hear them. "I've worked with everyone. Except *you*, apparently, because we've never met."

That got a faint smile out of her. "Nice. But seriously, have you?"

"Yeah. He's an asshole." Rick didn't sugarcoat it. Grant might have serious academic chops, but the guy was terrible with people.

A sleek tabby cat came up to them. Olivia cooed until the friendly feline wove its way around her legs. She bent down to pet it. "Are there a lot of stray cats around here?"

"Yeah, they call them 'the cats of Cyprus.' But don't worry—the tourists keep them fed."

She straightened up. "Good. I wouldn't want this guy to go hungry. So…about Grant. He's mean to everyone?"

"Maybe not everyone. Just those of us working beneath him."

"Oh, thank God. Frida warned me, but sometimes she has issues with authority figures and—"

"And you don't?"

"Not usually. But Grant didn't seem to like me. It's too bad, because for someone who's only thirty, he's ambitious as hell. He's already published a ton of articles. But he acted like I was this huge liability." She released a ragged breath. "Shit. Why am I burdening you with this?"

"Because you know I'll be honest? You heard what TJ called me. A shovel bum. I don't care about all that academic bullshit."

"You did once. You told me you wanted to be an archaeology professor. Remember?"

Of course he remembered. But nineteen-year-old Rick had been a naive idiot. "Yeah, and you wanted to be a big world traveler. Right? So, tell me, Olivia, how many of those postcards on your wall are from places *you've* visited?" He made no attempt to hide his bitterness. She was no better than TJ, calling him out on his decision to forgo graduate school.

Her face fell. "You don't have to be so mean about it. I don't know why I confided in you for a second." She strode on ahead, leaving him feeling like a complete prick.

Why couldn't he have shrugged off her question? Why had he felt the need to reply in anger?

Maybe because he hadn't shared that dream with anyone since college. It had died four years ago, when he'd left home and started traveling full-time. He didn't need her reminding him that he'd failed to live up to his potential.

He joined the others, keeping quiet while Dusty and TJ got into an impassioned debate about venomous snakes. Though he wanted to apologize to Olivia, he couldn't do it without arousing their suspicions.

When they reached the village square, Dusty peered up at the sign for Kouklia. "Population 698. This place is tinier than I thought."

"The actual population's higher in the summer because of all the tourists," Rick said. "A lot of Europeans rent homes here in July and August. It's still quiet compared to Paphos. That place is nuts on the weekends."

Given that Rick wasn't a fan of overcrowded tourist towns, Kouklia suited him fine. The village square included a small grocery store, a few shops, a traditional coffeehouse, an old church, and a handful of restaurants with outdoor seating.

"I don't suppose there's a good bar in town?" Dusty asked.

Rick gestured to the restaurant on their right. "You can get a drink here at Spyros Taverna. It's where we'll be eating dinner during the week."

Their group had a reserved spot on the taverna's patio at a long table covered with a blue-and-white checked tablecloth. Dr. Roth was already there, along with Juno, the sole staff member from Cyprus, who was finishing up her doctorate at the University of Cyprus in Nicosia. Rick had worked with her last year, and they'd gotten along well.

Before he could ask Olivia if she wanted to sit beside him—so he could make amends for his shitty comment—Stuart turned to her. "Olivia? You met Dr. Roth last year, right?"

"Yeah, at the AIA meetings in San Francisco. Thankfully, it was *before* you convinced me to join you on that ill-advised bar crawl. But since he's your adviser, you can introduce me again if you want." She beamed at him.

As Stuart led her over to Dr. Roth, Rick fought back an irrational pulse of jealousy. Evidently, Olivia and Stuart were old friends. But had they ever been more?

He plopped down beside Juno, who greeted him with a fist bump. She was in her late twenties, lean and toned, her long, dark hair caught back in a braid. Unlike many of the women he'd worked with, she was more likely to call him on his bullshit than swoon over him.

"All done playing taxi?" she asked.

"Thankfully." He waved over one of the servers, a boy who couldn't have been more than twelve or thirteen.

"Hey, Mister Rick," the boy said. "Do you want a beer?"

"Yes, please. A nice cold Keo, thanks."

Juno laughed. "Two days here and the servers already know your name?" She passed him a basket of thick peasant bread and a bowl of tzatziki, and he loaded up his plate.

He grinned at her. "When you're as charming as I am, everyone knows your name." He dipped his bread in the tzatziki. It was creamy and delicious, laden with chunks of fresh cucumber. "Mmm. Best tzatziki on the island."

"Have you eaten anything since breakfast?"

"Barely. Grant's been working me like a dog. Tomorrow won't be much better."

"At least you'll have me, plus the rest of the grad students, to pitch in with the setup." She eyed them warily. "What do you think of them?"

"Stuart and Dusty should be a huge help. TJ's experienced, but he might be a pain in the ass. And Olivia…"

He stared over at her. She was now engaged in a lively discussion with Stuart and Dr. Roth, her hands moving in excitement. It was the happiest he'd seen her all day.

Juno nudged him. "What about Olivia? Please tell me you're not planning your next conquest."

Though it was a fair question, he tried not to reveal how much it irritated him. "Nah. I'm not about that."

"Is this the same Rick Langston I worked with last year?"

"Not exactly…"

"What's that supposed to mean?"

He waited a beat to answer. Though the incident had happened two months ago, the humiliation still haunted him. "You know what happened. I messed up at the Palaikastro dig."

She gave a dismissive wave. "It'll pass. You made a bad judgment call. That's it."

"I've made a lot of them. So, I'm trying to stay out of trouble."

She smirked. "Good luck with that. You know a leopard never changes his spots, right?"

Maybe because she'd learned English as a second language, Juno loved peppering her speech with idioms. But her words hit the mark.

During his four years in the field, he'd always liked jumping from project to project. Six weeks here. Three months there. Not only was the short-term commitment a perfect fit for his restless nature, but it had enabled him to travel all over the Mediterranean. It had also allowed for a lot of fun, no-strings hookups. He was always honest about what he could offer the women he met. Which was to say, nothing. Once a project was over, he packed up and left. He hadn't had a fixed address in years.

But lately, he'd felt like he was missing something. No strings meant no real connections. The passion faded as quickly as it sparked. While the short-term flings might shield him from heartbreak, they often left him feeling empty. But it was hard for him to open his heart to anyone—or to believe they'd truly want him, just as he was—when his own father had disowned him. Still, he'd never have a shot at lasting relationship if he put up walls every time he got close to someone.

So, he'd decided to stop fooling around until he figured out what he wanted. Only to get lured into the dark side while working in Palaikastro, where he'd made one of the biggest mistakes of his career.

~

AFTER BEING PUT IN HER PLACE BY BOTH GRANT *AND* RICK, Olivia's mood was bleak at the start of dinner. Fortunately, Dr. Roth's enthusiastic welcome set her mind at ease. Unlike Grant, the professor hadn't disparaged her lack of experience but viewed it as a learning opportunity. "Just think," he said, "after all those years of using archaeological reports in your research, now you'll be contributing to them. Experiencing ancient history firsthand."

That was why she'd been so passionate about archaeology as a kid. She'd been eager to uncover the relics of past civilizations. She'd read every archaeology book she could get her hands on, watched every movie and documentary. For years, becoming a professional archaeologist had been her dream until she'd screwed up at Clear Lake.

She could have tried again. Gone back into the field and given herself a fresh start. But she'd never had the courage. What if she messed up a second time? Archival research was a much safer option, and it was risk-free.

Stuart uncapped a bottle of beer and passed it her way. "Want a Keo? It's a local brand."

"Thanks." She pressed the cold glass against her cheek, then took a drink. After the long day she'd had, it tasted like heaven. She could have chugged the entire beer, but she slowed down so she wouldn't get light-headed.

Dusty raised her bottle. "Here's to us and six weeks of shenanigans."

Olivia lifted hers in solidarity, as did TJ and Stuart, but Rick was too engrossed in his conversation with Juno to join in. He appeared so comfortable with her that Olivia wondered if they'd worked together before. Or done more than just work.

How many women had he charmed during his years in the field? If Dusty's gossip was to be believed, this version of Rick Langston—the twenty-six-year-old archaeological stud—was popular with the ladies. No surprise there. Even when he'd been nineteen, he'd won her over far too easily. She'd fallen for him so hard she'd willingly followed his lead when he suggested breaking the rules. But their reckless behavior had cost her dearly.

Stop dwelling on the past. You need to move on.

When Dr. Roth stood to excuse himself for the night, he gestured for all of them to stay seated. "There's no need for you to rush back to Camp Kouklia," he said. "Why not indulge in another drink? The real work starts tomorrow, so have fun while you can."

She liked his attitude. Regardless of what tomorrow's job list entailed, they'd probably have to toil in the hot sun getting camp ready for the undergraduate students.

Dusty had just ordered another round of beers when Grant called them to attention.

"Before I turn in, there are a few things I'd like to make clear." He frowned at the beer bottles. "We let you drink tonight, but after that, no alcohol is allowed in the presence of the students. If you want to come here after hours for a drink or go to a bar on your day off, that's acceptable, although I expect you to use discretion.

"Second thing. I know how life in the field is. Less boundaries. Fewer restrictions. But I'd like to discourage all of you from… inappropriate relations."

Inappropriate? What did that mean?

Stuart spoke up first. "You mean sexual relationships with the students? That seems kind of obvious, from an ethical standpoint."

"That goes without saying," Grant snapped. "I was referring to the rest of you." He waved his hand to encompass their group of six—Stuart, Dusty, Rick, Olivia, TJ, and Juno.

"Can I ask why?" TJ said. "We're all consenting adults."

For the first time that day, Olivia appreciated TJ's pushy manner. Not that she was contemplating a steamy fling with anyone, but she didn't understand why Grant felt the need to exert this much control over their personal lives.

"You need to serve as good examples," Grant said. "While I can't prohibit you from indulging in this kind of behavior, your actions could impact the type of reference you get after the field school ends."

Was he threatening them? Frida was right. The guy *was* a joyless control freak.

The entire table went silent until Grant stood and wished them good night.

The minute he was out of earshot, TJ spoke up. "What's his deal? Hasn't he ever heard of field rules?"

"Field rules?" Olivia asked. She almost didn't want to know. Especially since it might lead to a lengthy story.

"Yeah, what happens in the field stays in the field. Like in Vegas. No harm, no foul, no consequences. It's definitely a thing." TJ grinned at Rick. "Right? You know *all* about that."

Do you, Rick? Is that your thing?

Rick had the good graces to look sheepish. "No comment."

"Come on," TJ said. "Lots of digs means lots of women. You must have some juicy stories."

Dusty held up her hand. "Enough. I don't need to hear hookup stories from either of you. I've put up with too much of that misogynistic bullshit."

"Fine," TJ said, "but I can't believe Grant's being such a killjoy. Why's he so tightly wound?"

"Maybe because of his dad? It couldn't be easy growing up in his shadow." At the group's curious looks, Dusty added, "You've heard of him, right? Dr. Olaf Nilsson, distinguished professor at Princeton? He's not an archaeologist, but he's huge in the world of Classics."

"He's supremely arrogant, too," Juno said. "I met him once and was not a fan. I can see where Grant gets his sparkling personality."

"I didn't even make the connection. That's a lot for Grant to live up to." Olivia's graduate seminar on ancient Roman literature had featured two of Dr. Nilsson's publications.

"It's still no excuse for being a dick," TJ muttered.

"Whatever the case, let's try to stay on Grant's good side," Stuart said. "He's not someone you'd want to piss off."

"He hates being challenged," Rick added. "And he's not the type to let go of anything."

Rick's words sparked Olivia's curiosity. What had happened to cause so much animosity between him and Grant?

As the others complained about Grant's expectations, Olivia kept quiet. Though she wouldn't have admitted it out loud, she liked the idea of setting boundaries on their personal lives. This way, she wouldn't be at risk of temptation. While following the rules was a lot less exciting than breaking them, fewer risks meant fewer repercussions.

CHAPTER FIVE

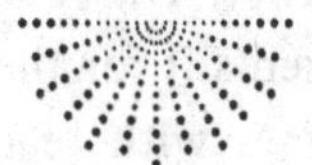

As Olivia made her way back to camp, the cool night air washed over her, bringing the faint aroma of honeysuckle. Her earlier tension had ebbed away, thanks to the beers she'd consumed with dinner. Though she was still smarting from Rick's jab, she was determined to keep things civil between them. If they were going to be stuck together for six weeks, she didn't want to fight with him the entire time. She'd already spent too long mired in guilt and resentment after they'd parted.

Dusty fell into pace with her. "Ready for your first night outdoors?"

Olivia grinned. "I hope I don't get eaten. I should have packed my bear spray."

"There are bears here?" TJ loped over to join them. "I didn't read about them in my research. That might push this dig to a six on the hard-core scale."

Olivia held back a laugh. "Just kidding."

"No venomous snakes either," Dusty said. "But we *are* sleeping outside, so that's more rugged than a tent."

"Is Grant going to bunk down on the field with the rest of

us?" Olivia asked. She'd have to place her cot as far from his as possible.

Dusty snorted. "That bastard gets to sleep in the field house."

"Wait. There's an actual house available?" Had a field house been one of the choices? Olivia wished she'd been given that option.

"Rick mentioned it earlier," Dusty said. "It's a cottage near the village square. Dr. Roth rents it for the summer, and Grant gets one of the rooms. It comes with real beds, hot water, and an Italian coffee maker." She gave a dramatic sigh. "Must be nice."

Compared to camp cots on a field, it sounded like heaven. Then again, sharing a house with Grant might be hell on earth.

As they approached Camp Kouklia, Olivia hit a wall of fatigue. She had no idea how many hours she'd been awake, but it was too many. She went with Dusty into the women's quarters, changed into a tank top and shorts, and dragged her cot outside. The so-called soccer field, located on the east side of the school grounds, was little more than a long stretch of packed dirt, interspersed with clumps of grass. At least it offered ample room for them to spread out.

She set down her cot, grabbed her toiletries bag, and headed for the communal bathrooms that occupied a small outbuilding next to the field. They reminded her of restrooms she'd seen at public campgrounds—cramped, slightly grungy, illuminated by harsh fluorescent lighting. The smell of pine-scented disinfectant was so strong it made her eyes water.

Midway through brushing her teeth, the realization hit her. This was like *camping*. The longest she'd ever been camping was five days. Now she was spending six weeks living and working outdoors on an island where the summer temperatures often hit ninety degrees or more.

Why had she ever thought she could handle this?

When she got back to her cot, she tried lying down, but the stiff canvas chafed her bare shoulders. She sat up and grabbed the inhaler she'd brought with her in case of an asthma attack. Her usual triggers were allergies and exertion, but stress could also set if off. And right now, she was stressed as hell. She took a puff from her inhaler, held it in, then let out her breath in a long, slow exhale.

Get yourself together. It's only six weeks.

The buzz of her phone made her drop the inhaler. She picked it up and set it on her cot, then glanced at the screen.

Her sister, Sofia, had sent a text: *You around?*

Usually, Sofia didn't give her any warning. She liked to talk at all hours of the day or night, regardless of the time zone. Olivia had gotten calls from her while teaching class, during dinner rush at the restaurant, and at three in the morning. When her phone rang, she stood and speed walked to the far end of the field, putting some distance between her and the others. If anyone had already fallen asleep, she didn't want to wake them.

"Sofia?" she said.

"Liv! Did you make it? Are you on the island of love yet?"

"Did you just call Cyprus the 'island of love'? Is that even a thing?"

"Of course, silly. It's the birthplace of Aphrodite, the Greek goddess of love and sex. I'm surprised you don't know that."

Olivia plunked down on a scraggly patch of grass. "I'm fully aware of Aphrodite's reputation. Classics student, remember?"

"Then you should appreciate how special Cyprus is. Don't you think an island dedicated to Aphrodite is unbelievably romantic?" Sofia's voice was so bubbly Olivia couldn't tell if she was drunk, high, or being her usual exuberant self. "Just imagine, you could be back at home for the summer like always, working at El Marinero and serving up your millionth platter of shrimp fajitas, but you're in the Mediterranean. Where life is good and the partying is nonstop." She sounded like she was about to burst into song.

"Are you drunk right now?"

"Liv!"

"Are you?" Not that Olivia had any right to judge, seeing as how she'd had two beers.

"Maybe a little tipsy. I'm about to hit the town for a night of clubbing, so I did some pre-gaming. But I only had two cocktails. Okay, three, but who's counting?"

Considering Sofia was built like Tinkerbell, three was a lot. But she knew how to hold her liquor.

"Are you still in France?" Olivia usually tried to keep up with Sofia's Instagram feed, but the last two weeks had been so busy she'd fallen behind.

"I left last week. It was *so* fun. I spent a couple of days in Paris with Rafael and his girlfriend, Victoria, and we visited all these *incroyable* bakeries. The pastries were to die for."

Olivia could only imagine. As a chef, her cousin Rafael was a total foodie, not unlike Sofia. If anyone could find the best patisseries in Paris, it would be him. "Where are you right now?"

"I'm on Mykonos, so kinda in your neighborhood. I did a photo shoot today at a fab fusion restaurant, and then I was a guest on a foodie show about Greece. I'm taking the night off to party, but I thought I'd check in with my big sis first."

A photo shoot, a TV show, and a night of clubbing. Truly, Sofia was living the sweet life. Or, as she would put it, #goals. Her life had always been like that. Sailing through school with mediocre grades but having a blast. Never lacking a date or a posse of friends. Cute, adorable, and utterly irresponsible. As teens, they'd both been expected to work at El Marinero, but half the time, Olivia had ended up filling in for Sofia, who rarely turned down a social opportunity.

"Liv? You okay? Did I lose you?"

Olivia plucked at a blade of grass. Now was not the time to envy her little sister. "I'm fine. Just tired. This place feels more like a campsite than a school. I have to get ready for the students, so I need to get in the right mindset."

"They're gonna have a fabulous time. Six weeks on a Mediterranean island? It'll be so much fun."

Olivia fought back the urge to snap in frustration. "It's a class, not a cruise. I'm supposed to be teaching them the basics of archaeology."

Given the exorbitant cost of the field school, she didn't take her responsibilities lightly. She wanted the students to feel as though they'd learned something.

"Ooh. Maybe one of them will dig up a lost treasure. Wouldn't that be exciting?"

"It's not like that. Archaeology is about using the scientific method to uncover ancient civilizations and study how people lived. The students are supposed to be learning valuable skills, not chasing dreams perpetuated by the Hollywood media."

"Is that what you're going to tell them? You'll be like the worst TA, *ever*. Why kill their dreams?"

"I just want to give them realistic expectations." Why was she arguing with Sofia about this? Though her sister hustled constantly to maintain her social media presence, she was completely self-focused. She couldn't imagine what it was like to oversee anyone, let alone a group of students.

"You're supposed to make this fun, spoilsport." Sofia's voice took on a pouty tone. "Don't you think it's going to be fun?"

"It's going to be work, Sof. That's how most of life is. It's hard work and a lot of stress."

"It doesn't have to be. Not all the time. Promise me you'll try to have fun. You used to get so excited about traveling. Remember when Dad got you that globe for your birthday? It was just a boring old globe, but you were so freaking excited about it."

Olivia remembered. She'd loved spinning the globe and letting her finger fall on a random country. Uzbekistan. Fiji. Malta. Then she'd look up the place to learn more about it.

Sofia's voice broke into her memories. "Are you stressed

because of that dig you went on in college? The one with the hot guy who got you in trouble?"

Olivia winced. For all of Sofia's cluelessness, she sometimes hit the nail square on the head. "Maybe. That experience messed up everything."

"Only because you let it."

"But Mom and Dad…" Olivia broke off, not wanting to remember. Worse than the shame and the money she'd owed them was the fear she'd disappointed her father so badly he'd never forgive her. He took responsibility seriously, at least where Olivia was concerned. Sofia, on the other hand, usually got a free pass because she was the "baby" of the family.

"Mom and Dad are over it," Sofia said. "Everyone's moved on except you. And maybe Mr. Hottie. I'll bet he *never* got over you."

"He's over me all right. He hates me."

"How do you know?"

No sense in hiding the truth. "Because he's here."

"What? Seriously? Ohmigod, is the spark still there?"

Olivia could only imagine how Sofia might be reacting. Jumping around in excitement. Mixing up another cocktail. She loved relationship drama.

"No. Like I said, he hates me."

"That seems kind of extreme. Maybe he was just shocked to see you again."

"Maybe." Even if he'd snapped at her tonight, he'd shown her a different side when he bought her that postcard. "But I can't deal with him right now. I'm already under enough pressure."

"Do you need my support?" Sofia's voice perked up. "I could come to Cyprus in a heartbeat. I've never been there."

"That's okay. I'll be fine." As much as she adored her little sister, Olivia couldn't handle any distractions. Not when Grant was just waiting for her to mess up.

"Okay. Well, let me know if you change your mind since I'm

only a teensy plane ride away. I'd love to get some new sponsors and do a series about Cyprus."

"Thanks. Right now, I need to get settled."

"I think my ride is here. Have fun, okay? Like actual fun, not Olivia fun. And don't let Mr. Hottie get to you."

With that, she signed off. Still seated, Olivia slowly released the air from her lungs. Seeing Rick again had brought back a host of powerful memories. For years, she'd tucked them into a corner of her mind and locked them up tight. But tonight, that was no longer possible.

So she let them back in.

The summer before her sophomore year of college, she'd participated in her first dig—a two-month archaeological field school in Clear Lake, California. She'd been with sixteen other undergrads, bunking in army tents and learning excavation techniques. She loved everything about it. The thrill of uncovering artifacts. The camaraderie and inside jokes. The satisfying exhaustion she felt at the end of each day.

She'd bonded with Rick right away. Like her, he'd just completed his freshman year of college and was passionate about archaeology. He didn't just want to travel; he wanted to have adventures. She fell harder for him than she'd ever fallen for anyone, and he felt the same way. Even though he was returning to Berkeley after the dig ended while she'd be back in San Diego, they both believed they could make their relationship last.

When she was with him, she felt like a different person—someone who wasn't afraid to let loose and take chances. One night, after everyone else had gone to sleep, he convinced her to sneak out with him. He borrowed one of the staff trucks and took her to the lake, where they went night swimming, kissed under the stars, and shared a bottle of brandy he'd smuggled into camp. When they returned at one in the morning without getting caught, Olivia had felt like a badass.

The next few weeks followed the same delightfully wicked

pattern. More swimming, more late-night conversations, more swoony make-out sessions. Until the night they were caught in a powerful storm. As the rain hammered down and the lightning flashed, they waited in the shelter of the truck rather than risk the roads. Lulled by the steady rainfall, they fell asleep in each other's arms until the sun streamed in through the truck's windows the next morning.

By the time they made it back to camp, everyone knew what they'd done. Given that their crimes included underage drinking and "borrowing" a camp vehicle without permission, the dig director could have involved the police. Instead, he'd expelled them from field school and called their parents. Rick's father arrived first, but Olivia waited all day for her dad, her apprehension growing with each passing minute.

When he arrived, he was more upset than she'd ever seen him. No matter how many times she apologized, he refused to listen. It was months before he forgave her.

She couldn't believe how stupid she'd been. She'd put her whole future in jeopardy—all because Rick had sweet-talked her into breaking the rules. The toughest thing to accept was that he wasn't entirely to blame. He might have provided the lure, but she'd taken the bait like a lovestruck idiot.

Her adventures ended there. Though she'd been tempted to go out in the field again, she was too afraid to take the risk. What if other archaeologists got wind of her epic failure? They'd never respect her. And how could she trust her own judgment after the mistakes she'd made?

After she and Rick had parted, he'd reached out to her for weeks, but she wouldn't answer his calls or his texts. Even though she missed him, she couldn't let him back into her life. Not if there was any chance she'd be tempted again.

Up until now, she'd never considered how much her actions must have hurt him. No wonder he hadn't been pleased to see her again.

The sound of footsteps startled her back to the present day. With a jolt, she peered up, only to see Rick standing over her. Having him appear after her deep dive into their memories threw her heartbeat into a wild cadence.

"What's up?" she said.

"I was out looking for you. What are you doing all the way over here?"

He was looking for her? If he was trying to stir up shit, she wasn't having it. Today had been enough of an emotional roller coaster. She stood and brushed dirt off her bottom. "My sister called to check in on me, and I didn't want to wake the others."

"Must be nice. I haven't talked to anyone in my family in weeks."

She didn't recall him being at odds with them. "Why not?"

"It's not important." His scowl suggested her question wasn't welcome.

Fine. Let him keep his secrets.

A wave of tiredness washed over her. After everything she'd been through, she didn't have the strength to keep fighting with him. "Look, I'm exhausted. Is there something you wanted?"

He rubbed the back of his neck. "Yeah. I came over here to apologize. I was a dick today. Sorry."

His words eased the tightness in her chest. "It's okay. I wasn't much better."

"I'm ready to move on if you are."

She wanted to step back and put some distance between them, but she couldn't make herself move. As she fumbled for a reply, the words dried up on her tongue.

He put out his hand. "Friends? For the next six weeks?"

When she took it, his grip was so warm and solid she didn't want to let go. If anything, she was overcome with the desire to nestle against his broad chest and feel his arms around her. After the day she'd had, she could use a hug.

Instead, she merely nodded. "I can agree to that."

"Good." He released her hand. "We should get some sleep."

"Right. Good night, Rick."

"'Night, Olivia."

She watched him walk away, unsure as to what had prompted his gesture. Maybe he wanted a fresh start as much as she did.

Could she do it? If she relegated their memories to the back of her brain and tried to regard him as a colleague rather than an ex, they might be able to survive the next six weeks together.

After returning to her cot, she lay on her back and looked up at the stars. Whether it was due to the lack of clouds or the thin crescent moon, the night sky provided a stunning panorama. The speckled band of the Milky Way was visible.

When was the last time she'd seen stars like that?

Not since Clear Lake. Sitting out at the lake with Rick at midnight, looking for constellations.

Stop.

Even if they weren't enemies, she could *not* allow herself to fall for him again.

She was over him. She had to be.

CHAPTER SIX

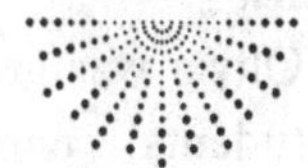

After a restless night's sleep on the world's least comfortable camp cot, Olivia hoped her first day of work wouldn't be too arduous.

She was wrong.

While she was spared the physical labor of helping Rick and Stuart construct the outdoor showers and tables, she was put to work with Dusty and Juno preparing the lab classrooms. All the rooms were hot, stifling, and in need of a deep clean. The heavy layer of dust sent the three of them into sneezing fits and triggered Olivia's asthma. When nightfall came, she was too tired to do anything but collapse on her cot.

The next day was much the same but with the bonus of the undergraduate students, who arrived in groups over the course of the afternoon. Fifteen in all—seven men and eight women, ranging in age from eighteen to twenty-three. Despite their obvious exhaustion, the students had been forced to sit through a lengthy welcome dinner at Spyros Taverna. Halfway through the evening, they'd started to droop. Olivia didn't blame them.

Now it was up to her to make them feel comfortable without

being a total downer. Or, as Sofia had put it, without killing their dreams.

Olivia led the eight female students to the wide wooden porch that ran the length of the sleeping quarters. They scattered themselves around her, waiting for her to begin. She cleared her throat. "I'll keep this quick since I'm sure you're tired. Before I start, are there any questions?"

Three hands shot up. Olivia was grateful Dr. Roth had sent her files with the students' names, photos, academic backgrounds, and health issues. She pointed to a tall, blonde girl who looked more suited for six weeks at a luxury resort, what with her flawless makeup and perfectly manicured nails. Designer sunglasses perched atop her lustrous mane of thick, golden hair.

"Okay, Courtney, what's your question?" Olivia asked.

Courtney let out a pained sigh. "I heard we're supposed to be sleeping outside? Like, in the open? What's the deal with that?"

"Sleeping outside is optional, but it's cooler there than inside the classrooms," Olivia said. "Just drag your cot onto the field when you're ready for bed and bring it back here in the morning."

"That sounds totally rustic, and not in a good way," Courtney said. "No one warned us ahead of time."

No one warned me, either. "Sorry about that."

Courtney let out a huffy breath, leading Olivia to suspect she might be one of the more demanding students. Beside her, another blonde spoke up. Brynn. From the way she'd been glued to Courtney's side, Olivia assumed the two women knew each other or had bonded during the flight from Los Angeles.

"I heard the legal drinking age in Cyprus is seventeen," Brynn said. "Does that mean we can drink?"

"Sorry, but no," Olivia said. "Since the field school is affiliated with the UC system, we have to stick to the legal drinking age in the US. For that reason, there's no booze allowed at camp. Getting caught with it could result in expulsion."

Trust me, you don't want that to happen.

Brynn gave a giant eye roll, then whispered something to Courtney, who snickered.

Fine. Olivia couldn't please everyone. Time to move on.

A woman with her hair woven into a series of box braids raised her hand. Unlike Brynn and Courtney, she seemed easygoing. All through dinner, she'd entertained Olivia and Dusty with her sly asides and off-color jokes. "Two questions. One—are there actual showers? Because I'm not a fan of bucket baths."

"Good question, Alisha. The guys on the team built the outdoor showers yesterday. If you're modest, you might want to wear a swimsuit while you shower since the curtains aren't completely opaque. The water's cold, but it'll be a welcome relief after a hot day in the sun."

Liar. Olivia had tested the showers yesterday. At first, the water wasn't too bad. A little lukewarm but bearable. Within five minutes, the spray turned brutally cold. Like diving into an icy pool headfirst. But she hadn't complained. According to TJ, they were lucky to have running water at all.

"Second question," Alisha said. "The curriculum said we'd each have to do a presentation at an archaeological site, and I got assigned Sotira-Katta-Nudey or whatever. Never heard of the place."

Olivia couldn't help but laugh. "Sotira-Kaminoudhia. It's not a well-known site outside of Cypriot archaeology. Fortunately, the camp library is stocked with books and articles. You'll also have access to all the online journals in the UC system."

"That sounds like a lot to wade through."

"It is, but I'll be glad to help you. Same goes for the rest of you. We can set up times to meet and work through the material until you get what you need for your presentations."

Alisha's nod boosted Olivia's confidence. If there was one thing she was good at, it was helping students wade through the sheer mass of data and articles about the ancient world.

But if there was one thing she *wasn't* good at, it was talking about sex. "So…I was asked to address this issue by Dr. Nilsson. I realize you're all legal adults, but if you…um…"

If you what? Want to sneak off and have sex?

Alisha laughed. "Is this about hooking up? There aren't any rules, are there? Other than making sure we have consent?"

Thank you, Alisha. Olivia wiped her forehead. "Right. The UC system has a zero-tolerance policy on sexual harassment, and we'd hate to send any of you home early. Also, if you get involved with someone and it goes badly, you'll still have to see them every day until field school ends."

A few women nodded like they were taking her seriously. Good. Even if she wasn't bringing down the hammer like Grant would, she wanted them to understand their actions had consequences. Maybe then, none of them would behave as foolishly as she had when she was their age.

For the next fifteen minutes, she reviewed the rules, the schedule, and the course expectations. She didn't want to overwhelm them, not when they had a full day of lectures and training tomorrow. When she was done, one of the students asked to talk to her privately. At eighteen, Marisol was the youngest of the group, but her petite stature and round, cherubic face made her look even younger.

Olivia took her aside while the others went to get their cots. "Everything okay?"

Marisol's light brown skin glistened with sweat. She twisted her jet-black braid between her fingers. "What if I mess up? Or do a bad job? I'm way out of my comfort zone."

You and me both. "I won't lie—the first week might be rough, but I think you'll adapt quickly. By the end of this class, you might even feel like a real archaeologist."

Marisol scuffed her sneaker along the wooden porch. "Right now, I feel stressed-out. Like I don't belong here."

"That's normal, but even if you're nervous, you belong here as much as anyone else."

"Thanks." Marisol managed a faint smile. "Can I come to you if I have any problems?"

"Absolutely. If I'm not around, Dusty or Juno can help you out, too."

As Marisol went to join the others, Olivia wished she could offer more reassurance. But even if she felt more grounded than she'd been on her first day, she was still struggling to adjust to the conditions.

Quiet time didn't start for another hour, so once the students set up their cots, they were free to talk, play cards, or read. If they kept the noise down, they could stay up as late as they wanted. But they'd soon learn that wake-up was a bitch, thanks to the nearby farm filled with animals that woke at the crack of dawn. On Olivia's first morning, an overly zealous rooster had roused her at 5:30 a.m. with his nonstop crowing.

The soft strum of a guitar caught her attention. She stood stock-still, listening as the guitarist played a few bars of Pink Floyd's "Wish You Were Here."

Rick.

She'd always had a weakness for musicians. At Clear Lake, when Rick had brought out his acoustic guitar, she'd been drawn to him like a moth to a flame.

Following the strains of the music, she walked over to the small outbuilding that housed the camp kitchen. Next to it were two long picnic tables, shaded by a couple of olive trees, that served as the eating area for their morning and afternoon meals. Rick sat on one of the benches, strumming his guitar. At the sight of her, he smiled knowingly, as though fully aware of how much his music was affecting her.

You don't have to join him. Just smile and walk away.

But the lure of his guitar was impossible to resist.

~

RICK SET HIS GUITAR ON THE BENCH BESIDE HIM. HE HADN'T BEEN sure how Olivia would respond to his music. Would she feel a touch of nostalgia? Or be annoyed at him for resurrecting old memories? Back in Clear Lake, she'd been the first person to join him when he'd played for the camp. Once he'd heard her incredible singing voice, he'd been a goner.

"Is…that the same guitar?" she asked.

"Yep. Kind of a pain to haul around, but I take it everywhere."

"I wasn't sure…you didn't play it before, so…"

"I wanted to wait until the students got here. The first day of field school is always stressful, but sometimes music helps."

Usually, his music brought people together. Some wanted to hang out and listen; others wanted to sing along. Over the years, his repertoire had expanded to include popular tunes from Greece, Italy, and Turkey. When in doubt, he fell back on the classic rock standards so many people seemed to know.

He patted the bench. "Sit with me a sec?"

Still wary, she gnawed on her lip. "Um…"

"Come on. I don't bite—much."

That got her to laugh. It was the same line he'd used the night he coaxed her into joining him.

She sat down beside him. A simple gesture, yet the familiarity of it pleased him more than it should have. He suspected they wouldn't be alone for long, but he'd take what he could get. She'd been on his mind a lot over the past two days. Which made no sense because whatever passion she'd felt for him must be long gone by now. But that hadn't stopped him from revisiting old memories.

"Are you doing any better?" he asked. "That first day was rough."

"Yesterday wasn't much easier. Those classrooms were in terrible shape. But now that we've set up a research library in one of them, I'm getting excited. It's going to be a great resource for the students." Her voice rose with enthusiasm. "We also got all the computers online, the site forms loaded, and the database program up and running. It's an awesome setup." She bubbled with laughter. "Listen to me. I sound like a total geek."

"You sound excited, which is what students need from a TA, especially when they're thousands of miles from home. Seems to me like you're ready for anything." This was the Olivia he remembered, the woman who wanted to take on the world.

"It's all going well, except…" She dug a groove into the bench with her fingernail.

"Except what?"

"Right now, this is all setup. Going out in the field is a much bigger challenge. I'll be out of my element."

"You know you can ask any of us for help, right? Except maybe TJ, because that might be more advice than you need."

"Thanks. I'm usually not this anxious about teaching."

His attitude probably hadn't helped. He wished he hadn't questioned her lack of experience when he'd picked her up at the airport. "Sorry if I implied you couldn't handle it. I was being a jerk. But you know your stuff. I read one of your articles last night."

Her glowing smile confirmed he'd given her the exact boost she needed. "You did? Which article?"

"The one TJ mentioned—the paper you presented at the AIA meetings about the wine trade in Hellenistic Greece." He'd been blown away by the depth of her research and the meticulous way she'd supported her thesis. She'd taken her passion and used it to craft a compelling argument. "If that's the subject of your doctorate, it's going to kick ass."

Flushing slightly, she broke his gaze. "Thanks. You didn't have to read it."

"I wanted to. But I couldn't help but wonder…"

"What?" Her voice took on a defensive tone.

Don't ask. Not when things are going so well. But the words tumbled out before he could stop them. "Why didn't you go back into the field? You haven't been on a dig since Clear Lake. Library research is great and all, but wouldn't you rather uncover the evidence yourself? You used to love getting your hands dirty."

"You really want to go down this path? After everything that happened?"

Not really. But he wanted to know what had stopped her from following her dream. "Maybe I do. I realize we were stupid and reckless, but no one got hurt. I'm sorry we got kicked off the dig, but in the grand scheme of things, it wasn't a big deal."

"It was a huge deal to me." Her voice trembled. "Maybe you got away with a slap on the wrist, but my dad was furious. Did you know he paid for half the course because I couldn't afford it? When I didn't get credit for it, how do you think he felt, knowing he'd wasted over a thousand dollars? It's not like he had that kind of cash lying around. I spent the rest of my summer waiting tables so I could pay him back."

Guilt washed over him. Though he'd known her family wasn't as wealthy as his, the subject of money had rarely come up during their conversations. "I'm sorry. But you should have told me you needed money. I could have gotten it from my dad and helped you out."

She rubbed her hands over her face. "It wasn't just about the money. It was about me screwing up and letting my parents down."

"Olivia—" He tried placing his hand on her shoulder, but she shrugged it off.

"You have no idea what I went through." She clenched her fists. "For the next two months, my dad barely spoke to me. But I still had to show up for work every day at the restaurant and live with the shame."

The pain in her voice cut into him. She'd suffered for months because of what they'd done, and he'd been oblivious the whole time. "Why didn't you tell me? I tried to reach you. I tried for *weeks*."

"Because you wouldn't have understood. You didn't care about the consequences. Why should you? I heard your dad when he came to pick you up. He just laughed and said, 'Boys will be boys.' My dad's not like that. His parents came from Mexico with nothing. If he wanted to succeed, he had to make it happen. He taught me the value of hard work and responsibility, and he always thought he could count on me. It was a long time before he trusted me again."

"I wish you would have told me." If nothing else, he could have offered sympathy. Even if he couldn't relate, he could have listened to her.

He braced himself for another tirade, but her shoulders slumped in defeat. Like the very act of unburdening herself had taken too much out of her.

She let out a ragged breath. "Maybe I should have, but I wanted to put it all behind me. That's why I never attempted another adventure. I was too afraid I'd mess up again. When my adviser asked me if I wanted this job, I almost didn't say yes."

He tried to lighten things up with a smile. "And then you found out you'd be working with me? Hardly the ideal scenario."

She met his eyes but wouldn't return his smile. "It's not your fault. But I can't screw up when so much is riding on this job. Unlike last time, I can't afford another huge mistake." She got to her feet. "I should go. Good night, Rick."

He watched her walk away, too numb to respond.

After everything she'd told him, he shouldn't have been surprised she considered their fling a mistake, but the words still stung.

Had she forgotten about the passion they'd shared? Or the long conversations where they'd bared their souls? Up until they'd gotten caught, it had been one of the best summers of his life.

But she didn't feel the same way. To her, it was just a big mistake.

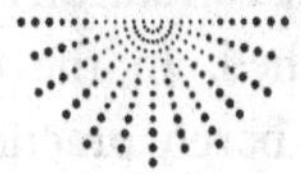

Fighting back a yawn, Olivia shuffled into the classroom the next morning. She couldn't have gotten more than five hours of sleep, all because of her anguished conversation with Rick. It had left her so unsettled that she'd lain awake for hours.

She wished she'd stayed and talked with him a little longer. She should have explained that she didn't consider *him* a mistake, just their reckless behavior. But she'd felt too vulnerable after exposing so much of herself.

According to today's schedule, the students were expected to attend a three-hour presentation on the history of Cypriot archaeology. Not the easiest start to the day when most of them were still jet-lagged. As they filed into the classroom, Olivia tried to summon up a little pep in the hopes of hiding her exhaustion. But as the minutes crawled by, she wished she were anywhere else. More than once, she had to pinch herself to stay awake. It didn't help that Grant was a dry speaker with a monotonous voice.

Two hours later, when the door opened and Rick poked his head in, Olivia startled back into full consciousness.

"Hey, everyone," Rick said. "We're ready to review survey techniques."

Grant pursed his lips. "We won't be done for a while. You'll have to wait."

"Got it." Rick scanned the room. "Is there anyone who didn't give me their GPS unit this morning? I've been uploading the area maps onto them so we can start training for the survey."

Olivia's stomach lurched. In the short time she'd had to prepare for her trip, she'd barely practiced with the Garmin GPS that Dr. Roth had sent her. Even after watching a series of instructional videos, she hadn't gotten the hang of it. Now that zero hour was approaching, she didn't want to look like an idiot in front of the students.

Rick turned to leave. "I'll be out by the picnic tables whenever you're done."

She leapt from her seat. "Rick? Can I talk to you for a second? About the training?" Before he could stop her, she made her way over to him.

"Sure," he said. "If you're not needed here?"

"I'm not, right?" It wasn't as though she was contributing to Grant's talk by sitting and listening. The one time she'd tried to ask a question, he shut her down.

"You can go," Grant said. "But I'd prefer no further interruptions."

"Got it. Sorry." She all but pushed Rick out the door and closed it firmly behind them.

"What was that about?" He didn't look pleased. No surprise, given the guilt trip she'd laid on him last night.

"Just walk with me, okay?" She led him outside, not saying anything until they reached the picnic tables they'd sat at last night. He eased down onto one of them, but she remained standing.

As anxious as she was, she couldn't help but notice how his faded Berkeley t-shirt stretched across his broad chest or how his sleep-mussed hair begged for the touch of her fingers. Why did he have to look so damned good? She, on the other hand, felt like a hot mess.

Focus, damn it.

"Dr. Roth sent me a GPS before I left, but I didn't have much time to practice using it," she said. "Now I'm worried because I've never had to survey in uncharted terrain before. Could you help me get up to speed? I don't want Grant to find another reason to criticize me."

He raised his eyebrows. "You sure you want my help? Given that you consider me one of the biggest mistakes of your life?"

Her cheeks heated, and not just because it was ninety-eight degrees outside. "I'm sorry. I didn't mean to imply that you were a mistake, just that—"

"No need to take it back. I appreciate the honesty. Though I would have appreciated it more if you'd told me seven years ago instead of letting me twist in the wind."

A painful ache pinched her heart. In the process of unburdening herself, she hadn't considered his feelings. Though she didn't regret telling him the truth, she hadn't meant to hurt him. Now she'd torched any goodwill they'd built up between them.

"Sorry," she muttered. "But I'm in kind of a bind right now. Do you know where Dusty or Juno went? Maybe one of them could help me."

"They went into Paphos to get supplies for the lab. I wouldn't worry about it. You'll catch on fast." He waved her away. "Go back to the classroom. You can't afford to piss off Grant."

No. She couldn't give in that easily. If she left now, she and Rick would be back to where they started three days ago, resenting each other as much as ever.

She forced herself to stand her ground. "It's not just about the GPS. I'm worried about leading a survey team. Have you forgotten what a terrible sense of direction I have?"

When he didn't respond, she kept going, hoping she could get him to crack a smile. "You used to tease me about it, remember? I've gotten on the wrong freeways before. I've come out of a store in the mall and started walking in the wrong direction. I even get lost in San Diego, and I've lived there almost all my life."

Rick granted her the faintest of smiles. "That tracks. The one time I let you drive to the lake, you got us completely turned around."

"Right? That's why I love maps. Not just for my research but in real life. I don't even like relying on my car's GPS. I need to plot out my route ahead of time, so I know exactly when to turn and which exit to take. I sound like I'm eighty, but...I have developmental topographical disorientation."

"What? Is that even a thing?"

"It is. I looked it up online."

"Of course you did." But he didn't seem quite as angry. Instead, he released a jagged breath.

"Please, Rick?"

His shoulders sagged. "I'm tired of fighting with you."

"No fighting. I promise. No more bringing up the past."

"First, answer me one thing. But do it without getting mad, okay?"

She swallowed, trying to clear the knot from her throat. "Okay."

"I know you were upset last night, but do you really regret everything that happened at Clear Lake? Was it all just a big mistake to you? If the answer's yes, I'll accept it, but I've been wondering for years."

She was surprised at how much that summer meant to him. After all the experiences he'd had, he could have dismissed their fling as nothing more than a youthful diversion. But he'd been as powerfully affected by it as she had.

If he was making himself vulnerable, then so could she. "Most of it wasn't a mistake. Those nights at the lake were incredible. I loved being with you. I've never felt like that with anyone." She drew in a shaky breath. "But the fallout was terrible."

Her pulse rate quickened out of fear she'd admitted too much. Even after all these years, being around him still played havoc with her heart.

The warmth in his gaze eased her worries. "Thanks for being honest. In return, I'll help you out."

A huge weight lifted from her shoulders. "Thank you so much."

"Sure. Since you're already out here, I can give you an overview. But the bigger issue is whether you should be leading a survey team at all. I know you're meant to be taking Frida's place, but this is a huge challenge. We'll be crossing rough terrain—not just farm fields but deep valleys and steep hills with nothing to guide us but our GPS units and our topo maps."

A growing panic spread through her. Frida hadn't gone into much detail when she'd described the survey unit. "Once I've practiced, I should be able to handle it. Right?"

"Maybe, but there's another issue. The team leaders have to drive the rental cars. You'd be driving on the left side of the road, finding the start point for each day's survey in unmarked territory, and then driving back."

She groaned and looked up at the sky. "Are you serious?"

He laughed, but it wasn't mean-spirited. "I'm totally serious."

She was sunk. At most, she figured she'd have to drive into Paphos to get supplies. Not traverse the country's back roads looking for random markers. She twisted her hands together. "What should I do? I don't want Dr. Roth to be upset that I'm not leading a team."

"You won't be doing him any favors if you can't figure out where you're going. You can still supervise the students during the lab sessions, and you'll have no problem leading a trench during the excavation unit. Providing you can remember what you learned at Clear Lake?"

She nodded. Despite the way the dig had ended, she'd learned a ton in the six weeks she'd spent excavating. "It'll come back to me. But what about the survey teams?"

"We've got enough leaders. I'm in charge of a team, and so are Grant, Juno, and Stuart. It wouldn't be a stretch to put you with one of them." He gave her a sly smile. "Unless you want to join my team?"

Did she? No doubt he'd be an encouraging leader but avoiding temptation would be easier if she wasn't working with him directly. "You sure that's a good idea?"

"No, but I'd like to work with you again."

"You would? After everything I said last night?"

He raked his hand through his hair. "Don't be so fucking stubborn. Just say yes."

If she was being sensible, she'd tell him to put her with someone else. *Anyone* else. But she couldn't do it. Now that they weren't at each other's throats, she wanted to spend more time with him. "Okay. Yes. *Please.*"

CHAPTER EIGHT

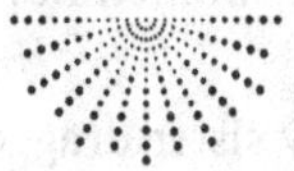

Have you lost your damn mind?

What happened to the Rick who was trying to stay out of trouble?

Questions Rick asked himself as he considered what he'd offered. To have Olivia by his side rather than keep her at a distance. To work with her constantly over the next three weeks. To place temptation right in his fucking path.

Idiot that he was, he couldn't stay away from her.

As much as her confession had gutted him, he now understood why she'd ghosted him. In his opinion, her dad sounded like an unreasonable hard-ass, but Olivia was close to her family and cared what they thought. He couldn't fault her for that.

"Let's get started." He took a GPS unit out of a box and passed it to her. "Most people use GPS technology to get places, like when they're driving or hiking. But when you're surveying, you don't just use the map feature. You need to record your finds and mark them. This way, if you discover a major site, one of us can go back to the area and investigate it further.

"Each GPS unit contains topographic maps of the area. That's what I was doing this morning—uploading these maps to everyone's units. They come in handy when we survey in the mountains. There aren't many buildings or roads to serve as markers."

"Are we talking actual mountains?"

"Not like the Sierras or anything. More like hilly areas, but they're tricky to navigate. Sometimes we have to rely on goat paths."

"Aww. I love goats. My sister dragged me to a goat yoga class once, and they were so adorable."

Goat yoga? He snorted with laughter. "Mountain goats aren't that docile. Neither are the mouflon—the wild mountain sheep native to Cyprus. Even though they're shy around humans, you don't want to mess with the males." He pulled up a photo on his phone and passed it to her.

She stared at the image in horror. "Fuck me. Those are serious horns."

Maybe he'd gone too far. He took the phone back. "Didn't mean to frighten you."

"The hell you didn't." But the teasing glint in her eyes hinted at amusement rather than anger. "You wanted to play up your prowess as a fearless mountain man."

"Maybe so, but most of the time, surveying isn't that treacherous. It's a great skill to have in your back pocket. Most field schools focus on excavation, but this course also teaches students how to conduct a ground survey. A lot of people don't realize it's a fundamental part of archaeology."

She offered up a playful grin. "Look at you, being all teacher-y and everything. But you're right. Surveying is like a real treasure hunt. There's no telling what you could find."

"I love working on digs, but when you excavate, you're usually stuck in one location. When you survey, you get to explore places off the beaten track."

Though there were a lot of high-tech ways to survey, like

using drones and aerial footage, he loved hiking in the hills and finding the sites for himself.

Rather than make her wait until the students came out to join them, he reviewed the basic instructions and let her practice on the soccer field. After a half hour of baking in the hot sun, he led her back to the picnic table. The shade of the olive trees made the heat a little more bearable.

"That's enough for now." He sat and gestured for her to join him. "Let's take a break."

She plopped down beside him. "But I don't know all the features yet."

"Don't worry about it. I'll review everything once the students come out for their lesson."

She pulled off her hair tie and ran her fingers through her dark-chocolate curls. He watched her with barely disguised longing. During their nights at the lake, he'd spent a lot of time tangling his hands through those wonderfully messy curls.

When she caught him staring, he broke his gaze, ashamed he'd been ogling her. What was wrong with him? Last night, she'd left him feeling frustrated and angry, but now that he wasn't mad at her, he could barely keep his eyes off her.

From day one, you've never been able to resist her. Why should now be any different?

It should be. The stakes were higher this time. Neither of them could afford to mess up. But he still couldn't deny how strongly she affected him.

"You're staring," she said. "It's my hair, isn't it? I know it's a giant mess. Sometimes wearing it up gives me a headache."

"Why don't you leave it down?" *For my sake.*

"It's too damn hot." She gathered it back up and secured it with the hair tie. "Any chance I could steal a drink? I left my water bottle in the classroom."

"Sure." He passed her the bottle. "Take as much as you need. You don't want to get dehydrated."

"Thanks." She took a long swig and passed it back to him. Glancing over at the classroom, she gave a full-body shudder. "I really don't want to go back in there."

"Why? Is Grant's riveting lecture technique not doing it for you?"

"What's the story with you two? Are you archaeological rivals like Indy and Belloq from *Raiders*? Did you steal a priceless treasure from him?"

He nudged her. A slight nudge, but the feel of her bare shoulder against his was more tempting than it should have been. "You're such a geek."

She stuck out her tongue. "Takes one to know one. But seriously, what's the deal, Indy? Unless it's a deep, dark secret. Were you competing for the same woman?"

"Nothing like that. It happened about three years ago. After I graduated from Berkeley, I left home. Started traveling through the Mediterranean, going from dig to dig."

"But why—"

"Let me tell the story, okay?" If she was planning to ask him why he hadn't gone on to grad school, his tale would take a different turn, and not one he wanted.

"Sorry." She stole his water bottle and took another drink. "Continue."

"I'd been traveling for about a year when I got a job working at a field school in Crete. Grant was one of the TAs there, and— no surprise—he was a grumpy, controlling dickhead. During the last week of the course, one of the undergrads messed up when he was entering his field notes into the database. The system crashed, and we lost a lot of data. Rather than wait to see if we could recover it, Grant went off on him. Like, totally lost his shit. The student ended up filing a formal complaint. Said Grant was verbally abusive."

The memory still infuriated Rick. The poor kid had cowered

in shame as Grant chewed him out in full view of the other students.

"That's awful," Olivia said. "I can't imagine treating a student like that."

"Same here. I stood up for the kid, only to have Grant ream me out for questioning his authority. But three weeks later, he had the balls to contact me. He asked me to write a letter on his behalf, vouching for his character."

Olivia drew in a breath. "You didn't, did you?"

"Nope. I told him he shouldn't be supervising students—not until he'd taken an anger management course or whatever. He was so furious, he said he'd ruin my name in the field."

"What a dick. I hate him even more now." She aimed a glare toward the classroom.

Rick derived immense pleasure from seeing her anger directed at someone other than himself. "Maybe I should have played his game, but I wasn't trying to get ahead in the academic world. I wanted the students to enjoy themselves, and Grant didn't make that possible."

"I always thought you'd make a great teacher."

Nope, not going down that road. "I'm not sure about that. I'd rather be outside than in a classroom. But now you know why Grant hates my guts."

"He needs to get his comeuppance. Like Belloq." She smacked her fist into her palm. "Though in a less violent way."

"True. We don't need anyone's head exploding."

Though he could joke about it, he still hadn't forgotten how shitty Grant had made him feel when they'd worked together. Like he was worthless because he wasn't in grad school. Even now, after he'd spent three more years working in the field, Grant still treated him the same way.

Olivia's voice snapped him back to the present. "Got any food? I'm starving?"

"Hang on." He went over to the kitchen outbuilding, rifled

around in the pantry, and brought back a bowl of figs. "Here. Leftover from breakfast but still good."

He sat with her in the shade as they munched on ripe figs and passed the water bottle back and forth. Though he tried not to drift into inappropriate fantasies, he couldn't resist sneaking a few glances at her.

Dressed only in a tank top and shorts, her sexy figure was on full display. The swell of her breasts underneath the thin cotton, the curve of her bare shoulders, the expanse of thigh peeking out from under the hem of her shorts. He wanted to touch it all.

She turned abruptly. "You're staring again. What is it? Do I have something on my face?"

"Nah, you're just…"

"What?"

You're really cute. And way sexier than I remember.

He was tempted to tease her, but all thoughts of joking evaporated when Grant emerged from the classroom and charged over to them like an angry bull.

Shit. If the guy had come out fifteen minutes ago, he would have seen them working. Instead, they were relaxing and eating figs. Not a good look. Rick braced himself for a blistering takedown.

But Grant directed his fury at Olivia. "Miss Sanchez. Is there a reason you're still out here with Rick?"

She sat up straight and cleared her throat. "He was helping me with the GPS unit. Even though I've had some practice, I don't have the years of experience Frida does. I wanted to make sure I was up to speed before we train the students."

Grant narrowed his eyes at her. "I assumed you were up to speed already."

"She had less than two weeks' notice to prepare," Rick said. "Cut her a break."

Grant kept his focus on Olivia. "Given your experience, it

might be best if you worked with me on my survey team. That way, I can keep an eye on you."

Asshole. If that bastard assigned her to his team, he'd make her miserable and chastise her for every mistake.

Knowing he was digging himself deeper into a hole, Rick spoke quickly. "Dr. Roth is aware of Olivia's lack of expertise in this area. That's why he put her on my team."

"On *your* team? The one person on the staff who isn't working toward a graduate degree?"

"I've been on more surveys than anyone here." Not only had Rick traversed mountainous territory in three different countries, but he also had an uncanny sense of direction. "Besides, Dr. Roth made the assignments yesterday. Unless you want to rearrange his entire setup, you should leave things as they are."

Rick sustained a calm facade, hoping to hide his growing tension. If Grant called his bluff and insisted on retrieving the list himself, then Rick was sunk.

After staring him down, Grant threw up his hands in frustration. "Fine. I'll be bringing the students out in fifteen minutes. Go grab the list of teams from Dr. Roth." He stalked back into the classroom, shutting the door loudly behind him.

Once he was gone, Olivia let out a whoosh of air. "Shit. You didn't have to do that for me."

"You'd rather be on Grant's team?"

"Hell, no." Her mouth quirked up in an adorable smile. "I'd rather work with you. But you have enough issues with Grant."

"I can handle it." He stood up. "I should go to talk to Roth. Make sure the list is…exactly how I said."

She grinned. "Thanks. I owe you one. Remind me to buy you a drink at Spyros some night."

Gladly. As Rick walked over to the lab, he swallowed back his uneasiness. Despite what he'd told Olivia, he shouldn't be pushing Grant's buttons. The guy didn't need any more excuses to hate him. Even if he didn't have the power to fire Rick, he could still make his life miserable.

Rick found Dr. Roth in the largest of the classrooms—the one they'd set aside as the main lab for processing their finds. The professor was setting up three tables with artifacts from last year's survey. The tables were laden with broken bits of pottery from every era, as well as a smaller selection of stone tools, like grinding stones, arrowheads, and scraping rocks.

In Rick's mind, Roth perfectly fit the image of a stereotypical male archaeology professor—sturdily built, bearded, giving off the faint aroma of pipe smoke, his skin weathered from countless summers spent on dig sites.

"Dr. Roth?" Rick asked. "Do you have a minute?"

The professor moved a few pieces of pottery into a larger pile. "Certainly. First, can you look over the display and make sure I haven't left anything out?"

"Is this for the afternoon session?"

"It is. I thought the students might appreciate a hands-on demonstration so they can see the types of artifacts they'll encounter when they're on the survey."

Rick examined each table. "Do you have any more Cypro-Geometric ware? It's not as common, but you mentioned wanting to find sites from that era."

"Good call. I'll see what we have in storage. Anything else I should add?"

"Nope. Looks good," Rick said. "I'm here to get the list of the survey teams."

"Right. I have it made up. Was Grant asking for it?" Dr. Roth went over to a desk at the front of the classroom, piled high with papers. He shuffled through them until he found a sheet of lined paper filled with hand-written notes. "Kind of a mess, but I was still fiddling with it this morning. Can you give it a once-over?"

Rick's shoulders tightened as he took it, only to loosen in relief after he scanned it. Purely by chance, Olivia was on his team. He kept his voice casual. "You're not having Olivia lead a group?"

"Do you think she'll be insulted? Frida told me she hasn't done this before, so I didn't want her to be out of her depth. I figured I'd put her with you because you know the area so well. Is that all right?"

"It's perfect."

In addition to Olivia, Rick's team included TJ. Not ideal. No doubt the guy would use the long drives to regale them with more of his dig stories. The other two team members were Brynn and Marisol, neither of whom he knew very well.

"This looks good," he said. "I don't see any potential for conflict. Then again, people reveal more of themselves when they're out in the field."

Dr. Roth chuckled. "Too true. But since the list meets your approval, can you take it over to Grant?"

With pleasure.

CHAPTER NINE

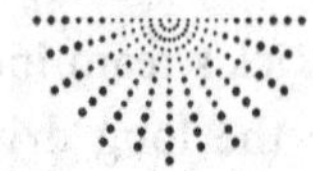

At six thirty on Monday morning, Olivia waited by the cars in the parking area, eager to get started. Eager or anxious? She wasn't sure. More than anything, she wanted to get her first day of surveying over with. Even if she'd been spared the agony of working on Grant's team, she was still worried about screwing up. The last two nights, she'd been plagued by disturbing dreams in which she'd gotten hopelessly lost.

She checked over her daypack to make sure she had all the essentials: GPS unit, spare batteries, water bottle, granola bar, field notebook, two pencils, and her inhaler. She'd also tossed in a paper copy of the topographic map for backup.

Rick strolled over to meet her, appearing more rugged than ever with his sturdy hiking boots, faded t-shirt, and wide-brimmed hat. His calves were so firm and muscular he looked like he could climb an entire mountain without breaking a sweat.

Stop ogling his legs. He's your team leader, not your high school crush.

"Hey, Rick." She gave him a casual wave, hoping he hadn't noticed her staring.

"Morning," he said. "You ready to go?"

"Yeah. I'm kind of nervous. But also excited? Maybe?" She tugged on her ponytail. "Does that make sense?"

"It does, coming from you." He gave her a warm smile as if to reassure her.

She looked away, feeling awkward. All of a sudden, she wasn't sure how to act around him. If they were just friends, why did she feel so self-conscious? And why couldn't she stop gawking at him? By now, she should have adjusted to his hotness.

She turned her attention to the row of vehicles in the parking area—five compact cars and a pickup truck. "Where'd the Jeep go? Isn't that our ride?"

"Hate to disappoint you, but we don't get the Jeep."

"Why not?"

"It's Roth's. He borrows it from the Department of Antiquities every summer. He lets us use it for errands and airport pickups, but not for the survey. Instead, each team gets one of these crappy rental cars." He pointed to a drab gray Kia. "That's our ride for the next three weeks."

"Bummer. I'd feel more like an archaeologist if we could use the Jeep."

"Another time." He gestured with a sweeping movement. "Hop in. TJ, Marisol, and Brynn should be here soon."

She opened the door to the front passenger side, but a snotty voice interrupted her. "You'll need to get in the back."

Excuse me? She turned to face Brynn—a student best defined as high-maintenance. So far, she'd bitched to Olivia about the cold showers, the uncomfortable cots, and the heat. All of which were fair criticisms, but it wasn't like Olivia had any control over the conditions.

Olivia tried to keep her irritation from showing. "Any particular reason?"

"If I don't sit up front, I get carsick." Brynn brushed past her and plopped down in the front seat. "That's how it is."

Fine. If riding shotgun would make Brynn happy, Olivia wasn't about to argue. But as she got into the back, she realized how truly compact their rental car was. For once, her height—or lack thereof—put her at an advantage. A minute later, TJ settled in beside her, carrying an oversized daypack and an enormous water bottle, as though prepared for a lengthy expedition.

When Olivia's phone buzzed, she pulled it out of her pocket. Marisol had sent her a text. *Not going to survey today.*

Olivia texted back. *Sorry to hear it. You okay?*

Marisol replied quickly. *I'm fine but not up to surveying yet. Dusty said I could work with her instead.*

Of all her students, Marisol was the most anxious about the course. Olivia had hoped to offer reassurance by showing her surveying wasn't that scary. But maybe Marisol needed to ease into it. All the students were allowed to miss a few days of the survey, providing they used the time to learn the basics of archaeological illustration from Dusty.

"Marisol's not coming," she said, "so we can get going."

"Is she all right?" TJ asked.

"Yep." Olivia didn't want to reveal too much, especially since TJ didn't seem like the empathetic type. "She's going to help Dusty today."

By now, the other students were waiting in the parking area for their team leaders. Rick put the Kia in reverse. "First ones out."

"And we'll be the first ones back." TJ thumped the roof of the car. "We're going to kick ass."

"I assume you all have survey experience?" Brynn asked.

Olivia groaned inwardly, knowing TJ had been waiting for an opening.

"Of course," he said. "In much harsher conditions. We're talking real mountains, not these piddly hills. Crossing streams and hiking up cliff faces. Taking on wildlife and battling giant bugs."

Then he was off, regaling them with one of his lengthy stories. Olivia wasn't eager for another TJ saga, but if he dominated the conversation, she wouldn't be put on the spot about her lack of experience.

The drive to the survey location took fifteen minutes. They parked alongside the road, seemingly in the middle of nowhere. Stretched before them were rows of plowed farm fields, dotted with the occasional scrubby tree.

Olivia, TJ, and Brynn followed Rick out of the car and gathered around him. Even at seven in the morning, the blazing sun promised another scorching day.

"Any questions before we head out?" Rick asked.

Though Olivia could have used a quick refresher, she didn't want to slow down the group. Fortunately, Brynn spoke up. "Could you go over the basic parameters again?"

"That would be great," Olivia added.

"Okay," Rick said. "We're mainly looking for pieces of broken pottery, known as potsherds. Bonus points if you spot any stone tools, like arrowheads, harvesting knives, or grinding stones, because they're older and might indicate a Stone Age settlement. If you can find one of those, I guarantee Dr. Roth will be thrilled."

Olivia smiled as she remembered the professor's enthusiasm during the hands-on display in the lab. Unlike Grant's lecture, his presentation had been lively and energetic.

Rick continued. "If you find a cluster of artifacts, record it. The cluster might indicate the presence of an archaeological site. But it might also mean the debris was churned up when the farmer plowed his field. Either way, we need to know where it is." He cast a pointed look at Brynn, who was scrolling through her phone. "Got it?"

Brynn put her phone in her back pocket. "Courtney said her team's already started. We're going to fall behind."

"It's not a race," Rick said. "But if you're ready, we can get going."

"No, you can finish your explanation," Brynn muttered.

Olivia itched to chastise Brynn for her rudeness, but she held her tongue.

Remember, Rick's the one in charge. Let him handle it.

Rick gestured to the field in front of them. "This is where we'll start today's survey. Each transect is a mile long and ten feet across. We'll be walking parallel to each other, with a slight gap between us. Walk in a zigzag, and scan the ground as you go. Artifact clusters should be marked on the GPS as waypoints, then photographed and written up in your field notebook. We'll meet after the first transect and take a break. The second transect will bring us back—more or less—to our starting point here. Okay?"

Brynn rolled her eyes. "I guess. It seems *so* complicated."

"Think of it like one of those police shows where people fan out to search for someone who's missing," Rick said. "We're doing that with artifacts."

"Piece of cake," TJ said. "We'll whip through it in no time."

Brynn glared at him. "It won't be that easy, *Teej.*"

"Finding pottery in cultivated fields is a snap. It's not nearly as tough as surveying in the mountains, like when I—"

"Enough with the stories," she said.

Rick held up his hand. "Let's get going. Is everyone ready?"

Anything to ward off an argument between TJ and Brynn. Olivia took a final drink from her water bottle. "Ready."

Once they began walking, Olivia's jittery nerves gave way to excitement. Though the odds of finding a significant site were slim, the possibility still existed. What if she discovered one of those elusive Stone Age sites? She could imagine the thrill of coming back to camp and showing everyone what she'd found. *In your face, Grant.*

She kept her eyes on the ground as she walked her route, but nothing of interest came into view. All she saw were small rocks, churned-up earth, more rocks, and more dirt. Until she spotted something that wasn't a rock. Small pieces of pottery were scattered by her feet.

She crouched down, picked up the largest piece, and wiped off the dirt. *Nice.* It was a burnished red color, but she couldn't tell what era it was from. She'd snapped photos of the samples they'd studied in the lab with her phone. But even with the close-ups she'd taken, she couldn't distinguish whether the pieces she'd found were from the Roman era or much older. She pawed around in the dirt and unearthed a few more potsherds.

Sitting back on her heels, she reviewed her photos again. What would it hurt to mark this spot and make a few notes? Better to record her finds than overlook something important.

When she stood to brush off the dirt, she couldn't spot anyone. How was that possible? The terrain was flat, allowing her to see far in the distance. The only explanation was that she'd fallen way behind. She was tempted to pick up her pace but didn't want to miss anything. Either she was exceptionally slow, or her path was laden with archaeological goodness, because she couldn't catch up with the others. Sweat soaked through the back of her tank top, and her legs ached from squatting every few minutes, but she kept going.

Her heart sank when she reached the end point. The rest of her team sat waiting under a grove of almond trees.

"Took you long enough," Brynn said.

Olivia slumped onto the ground. "Sorry. I needed to mark down a lot of pottery." Maybe the others had moved so fast that they'd missed a few spots.

"Your area couldn't have been that much different from ours," TJ said. "Let's see what you got."

With a growing sense of dread, she passed her phone over to him. Even before he scrolled through her photos, she suspected she'd screwed up.

"It's the same stuff I saw," he said. "Early Roman era, maybe first century AD. Dr. Roth said a lot of those pieces are usually churned-up debris and don't require careful attention. I doubt they indicate a site."

Her face prickled with heat. "I was just trying to be thorough. I didn't want to miss anything."

Rick looked up from his field notebook and offered her a quick smile. "Nothing wrong with taking your time. That's how we've found some of the best sites."

Though his words made her feel marginally better, she wished she didn't look like such an amateur in front of Brynn and TJ.

"Make sure to drink enough water," Rick said. "And have some grapes. They'll help you stay hydrated." He passed around a bag filled with an enormous cluster of grapes. Olivia grabbed a handful and popped them in her mouth. They tasted sweeter than any grapes she'd ever bought at the supermarket.

On the second transect—the one that would bring them back to their starting point—her route took her through an area filled with dense, knee-high plants. They obscured her view of the ground and twined around her legs, like they were attacking her for invading their territory. The sharp leaves stung her bare calves. She tripped over a root and sprawled forward, catching herself before she fell on her face.

Already, her legs had started tingling. She leaned over to scratch them, but when she stood up, she was hit with a powerful head rush. Whether it was from the blistering heat or her near fall, she couldn't be sure, but she took a break and drained the rest of her water bottle.

With no shade to offer protection, the sun beat down without mercy. Under her sun hat, her sweaty hair was plastered to her head. Her arms and shoulders felt sensitive to the touch, making her wish she'd worn something with more coverage than a tank top. SPF 40 was no match for hours of bright sunshine and ninety-five-degree weather.

This sucked.

She hadn't made any real discoveries. She didn't feel adventurous, just hot and frustrated.

When she got back on track, the others were beyond her line of sight. She ran until her breath hitched, forcing her to stop. She leaned over, hands on her knees, and sucked in air. Once she used her inhaler, she was out of danger, but she couldn't risk running again. That could lead to a full-blown asthma attack, and the recovery time would take much longer.

Ten minutes later, she reached the start point. Guilt crested over her in waves as she approached TJ and Rick, who were leaning against the car and spitting grape seeds into the field. "All done. Sorry to make you wait."

Rick popped another grape into his mouth. "No worries. I'm glad you made it back all right."

Brynn came around the side of the car. "We've been waiting forever. I thought we'd have to send out a search party." She narrowed her eyes. "What's wrong with your legs?"

Olivia winced. "I think it's an allergic reaction to those tall plants."

"You also have a wicked sunburn." Brynn snickered. "Nice going."

Could you be any more of a bitch? Olivia fought back the urge to lash out at her. She was supposed to be serving as a good example, not snapping at the students.

Rick's brow pinched in concern. "You sure you're okay? Did you have enough water?"

"I'm fine, thanks." She didn't want to call any more attention to herself. Not when she'd performed so pitifully compared to the others.

"All right, then," he said. "Let's head back."

"Shotgun," Brynn called out, "Because I—"

"Get carsick?" Olivia said. "Yeah, I remember."

She tensed as they approached camp, praying they weren't the last ones to return. According to Grant's schedule, the teams were expected back from surveying no later than one in the afternoon, so that they wouldn't delay lunch. He'd made arrangements with a few women in the village to supply the camp's lunchtime fare—peasant bread, salads, and local dishes like moussaka and pastitsio.

Olivia's fears were confirmed when she counted the cars in the parking lot. Everyone else had already arrived. Brynn and TJ got out of the car and headed for the camp restroom. Olivia was about to join them but stopped when Grant strode over to them, bristling with anger.

"Is there a reason you were so far behind?" he asked. "You're late for lunch."

Olivia checked her watch. Though it was a few minutes past one, no one was seated at the picnic tables yet.

"We're not that late," Rick said. "Looks to me like lunch isn't ready."

"That's not the point," Grant said. "You arrived a good twenty minutes after the other cars. There must be a reason."

Pushing past her trepidation, Olivia forced herself to speak up. "It's my fault. I was overly thorough and slowed the team down."

Grant scanned her from head to foot. "You're looking a little worse for the wear, Miss Sanchez. That's quite the sunburn. And what's that on your legs?"

Why was everyone obsessed with her legs? Glancing down at them, she shuddered. In the space of half an hour, they'd grown worse, all red and bumpy from her spreading rash. "I think I was allergic to some of the plants on my route."

He shook his head in disgust. "Are you sure you can handle this job?"

"Don't be a dick," Rick muttered. "It's her first day."

"What did you call me?" Grant said.

"You heard me."

The two men stared each other down like a pair of vicious

dogs. Olivia wanted to grab Rick's arm and pull him away, but she worried her interference might make things worse.

Grant broke first. "Go clean up. Lunch will be here soon."

As she watched Grant leave, Olivia hoped Rick would stick around so she could apologize. But he took off quickly, leaving her alone.

Some archaeologist.

Her first day of survey and she was a giant failure.

CHAPTER TEN

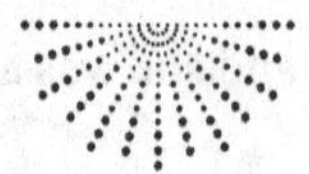

As exhausted as Olivia was, sleep proved impossible due to the brutal combination of rash and sunburn tormenting her skin. Her shoulders throbbed. Her legs itched with the fury of a thousand mosquito bites. And her churning stomach added to the misery. Whether it was from their dinner at Spyros or her general state of discomfort, she wasn't certain.

After two agonizing hours, she couldn't take it any longer. Using her flashlight, she crept over to the sleeping quarters to locate her Benadryl and her bottle of Tums. But as she looked through her pack, she realized she'd forgotten to bring a tube of aloe vera.

Rather than go back to her cot, she walked over to one of the picnic tables and plopped down on the wooden bench. When she turned off her flashlight, the inky darkness enveloped her, making her feel more alone than ever. She wanted to be strong. Resilient. A true badass. But she couldn't hold back the tears. What started as a few self-pitying whimpers turned into a flood of uncontrollable sobs.

Why had she messed up so badly? No one else had gotten

brutally sunburned, attacked by hostile plants, or made their team glaringly late.

How was she going to survive the next few weeks?

She could offer to work with Dusty instead of surveying, but her drawing skills were mediocre at best. Plus, she was supposed to be accompanying the students and helping them. Some help she was. The people on her team would have been better off without her.

As always, when her anxiety got the best of her, her mind spiraled into a series of worst-case scenarios. If she couldn't hack it on the survey, Grant would report her to Dr. Roth. Then the professor would regret hiring her. He might even send her home early. Forget about getting him on her dissertation committee. If the word of her pitiful failure got out, her name would be mud in the world of classical archaeology.

She was doomed.

At the sound of a brusque voice, she tensed up. *Rick.*

"I'm not reaching out to Dad again," he snapped. "If he wants to talk, he can call me himself. I'm sick of trying." After a pause, he spoke in a gentler tone. "I'm sorry, but I'm sure he'll be fine. It's just a biopsy."

Was he on the phone with his mom? His sister? Either way, his conversation sounded serious. Definitely none of Olivia's business. If she was quiet, she could sneak back to her cot before he noticed her. Before she could slip away, he ended the call abruptly.

She held her breath, waiting for him to leave, but a tiny sniff gave her away. *Stupid tears.*

He turned toward her. "Is someone there?"

"It's me. Olivia."

"Were you listening to me?" he demanded. "That was a private conversation."

Her voice wobbled. "I…didn't mean to."

"Wait—are you crying? What's wrong? Where are you?"

She turned her flashlight back on. "Over here. But I'm a huge mess."

He joined her on the bench and placed a hand on her shoulder. The gentlest of touches, but it made her wince in pain. "Calm down. I'm not upset."

"It's not you." She wiped her eyes, feeling more like six than twenty-six. "Today was awful. I got sunburned, picked up a weird rash, and made our team last. I'm a total failure."

"You weren't that bad."

"I was terrible. Go ahead and hand me over to Grant if you want." Even as she said it, her apprehension ramped up to an eleven. For all the mistakes she'd made today, Rick hadn't gotten mad at her. Grant wouldn't have been as compassionate.

"Nope. I refuse to torture you that way."

She managed a weak smile. "Thanks. But I don't understand why I was slower than everyone else. I've spent years using archaeological reports in my research. I know the material better than most people. Not that I'm trying to sound like TJ, but—"

"That's your problem. You're trying too hard to be perfect."

"What do you mean?" Aware her voice had risen, she cast an uneasy glance toward the soccer field, hoping she hadn't woken anyone. An owl hooted in the distance, but otherwise, Camp Kouklia was quiet.

"You're used to being meticulous in your research. Right?"

"Of course. I want to make sure my evidence backs up my arguments. I don't just skim over my source materials—I read them carefully and look for inconsistencies."

"That's great for library research when you have a lot of time, but when we survey, we're getting an overview. Is it a perfect technique? No, but the idea is to get the lay of the land. If we find a site, then we'll dig some test pits to explore it further. But do you remember what Roth told us during the hands-on demonstration? When he showed the students the Roman pottery?"

"Yes. We're not supposed to spend too long examining every pile of Roman garbage." She should have taken his words to heart, but she'd been too afraid of missing something.

"Right. You should take note of the pottery, but since most of that stuff has been churned up over the centuries, it doesn't tell us much about settlement patterns. What we're trying to do here is map out the big picture."

His explanation made sense. When she used survey reports in her research, they weren't micro-focused. Instead, they contained months of data and covered a broad swath of territory.

"You just need to pick up the pace," he said. "Don't rush too much, though. Brynn might have been fast, but she did a sloppy job. When I reviewed her notebook, she'd barely written anything down." He gave her shoulder a gentle squeeze. "You'll catch on soon, I promise."

When she flinched in pain, he drew back his hand. "Sorry. I didn't mean to hurt you."

"My shoulders are killing me. Do you have any aloe?"

"Sure. Hang on a minute." He leapt up from the bench.

She scanned the field again, looking for signs of movement. She didn't want anyone to catch the two of them together. Even if she hadn't done anything wrong, meeting up with Rick in the middle of the night hardly looked innocent. But the camp remained quiet. Everyone was probably dead asleep, wiped out from the first day of survey.

When Rick returned, he sat beside her and handed her a large bottle of aloe vera gel. "Take as much as you want. Grant asked me to buy a few bottles when I was out running errands."

"For the students?" She squirted aloe onto her palm and kneaded the gel onto her arms.

"He's not that thoughtful. It's for him because he burns so easily. Normally, he uses SPF 100, otherwise he turns bright red, like a big, angry lobster."

The image of Grant as a lobster made her laugh. She rubbed

the gel onto her shoulders but strained to reach her back. Rick took the bottle from her. "I'll do it."

With gentle fingers, he massaged the aloe into her overheated skin. The cooling gel sent shivers down her spine, making her recall a long-dormant memory. He'd administered the same treatment when they'd been together at field school.

As if he knew what she was thinking, he chuckled. "I seem to remember doing this at Clear Lake. You got so fried during that first week of excavation."

"It's completely unfair. You'd think my Mexican heritage would come in handy. My father never burns. Neither does my sister. And my mom's half-Italian, so she tans beautifully."

"So do you—it just takes you a little longer." He continued rubbing the aloe on her back and shoulders, his movements slow and gentle. "After a few weeks in the field, you had an incredible tan. I should know since I'm the one who saw those tan lines."

Like the first time he'd seen her naked, when they'd gone skinny-dipping together. He'd stared at her in awe and told her she looked beautiful. No one had ever made her feel that way before.

Stop it. No more delving into the past.

But she couldn't help it. Now that they'd grown closer, it wasn't merely the memories that were returning but the powerful feelings as well. Not just affection, but stirrings of lust. She wanted him to keep touching her. To brush his lips against her bare shoulders until she quivered with delight.

What would happen if she turned and faced him? A rush of desire surged through her as she imagined claiming his lips and reigniting the sparks between them.

She needed to pull away before she melted into a puddle of longing.

But she couldn't find the will to move.

~

RICK CONTINUED SMOOTHING ALOE OVER OLIVIA'S SKIN. THE longer he touched her, the more he wanted to keep going. To caress her everywhere and make her whimper with pleasure. The more he thought about it, the more aroused he grew.

Hardly an ideal reaction, considering she was in pain. He was supposed to be comforting her, not giving in to inappropriate fantasies.

"Are you feeling any better?" he asked.

"Much better. Thanks."

"Do you want me to stop?"

When she didn't respond, he took that as a no. Good, because he didn't want to. He lifted her ponytail, moving the thick mass of curls out of the way so he could touch her neck. Though her sunburn didn't reach that far, he dabbed the gel on it anyway. It was all he could do not to bend down and kiss that sensitive patch of skin, just to hear her gasp.

She let out a groan of relief, then went rigid and pulled away. "Thanks. I'm good now."

What the hell was he thinking? He set the bottle on the bench and adjusted himself. "Great. If you need more aloe tomorrow night, hit me up."

"Rick?" Her voice caught, like she was fighting back a rush of emotion. "Why are you being so nice to me?"

"Why shouldn't I be? I thought we were good. Right? Unless there's more stuff you need to get off your chest. About Clear Lake or whatever." Not that he wanted to make her angry, but he'd rather hash things out than have her resent him.

"No. We're good. But now that you've seen me in action, wouldn't it be easier to hand me over to Grant? You have enough shit going on with him."

He gave a casual shrug. "What's a little more? If he gets on my case because our team's too slow, I can take it. I don't have anything riding on this gig, not like you do. Don't you need Dr.

Roth's endorsement when this job is over? For your dissertation?"

"How'd you know that?"

Busted. After that first day, he'd brought up the subject with Stuart when they were building the showers. He'd asked because he still couldn't understand why Olivia had agreed to take Frida's place, since she was clearly out of her element.

"Stuart mentioned it. He said this field school is important to you, in terms of getting Roth to serve on your dissertation committee. I get that."

"You do? I thought you weren't about academia?"

"I'm not into all the bragging and name-dropping like TJ. But I admire anyone with the persistence to pursue a doctorate in a field they love. Especially the ones who'll end up teaching. Students need professors like you who are passionate about this stuff."

"But not you? You aren't interested in following that route?"

He drove out a harsh sigh. "Olivia, don't."

"Sorry. I'm sure you have your reasons. But if you ever want to talk about it, I'm here."

"Now who's being extra nice?"

She laughed. "I'm a nice person. Most of the time."

"Yeah. You are." He picked up the bottle of aloe but didn't want to leave. The Olivia he'd once known had changed a lot, and he wanted to learn more about her. Had she enjoyed grad school so far? Was she still close to her family? What did she dream about at night?

Without thinking, he placed his hand over hers. Rather than pull away, she twined her fingers with his. His breath caught as he leaned in closer, hoping to steal a kiss.

Until the sound of someone coughing instantly doused his desire.

Olivia turned off her flashlight, casting them back into

darkness. After waiting a beat, she spoke softly. "I'm not sure if we woke anyone, but I'd better get back to my cot."

He wished he could convince her to stay, but they'd already risked enough by talking this long. If someone saw them, the rumors would spread like wildfire.

He stood up. "'Night, Olivia."

"'Night. Thanks for the aloe. And…um…everything."

Back on his cot, he'd almost drifted off when he recalled his conversation with his sister, Cassie. She'd left him a series of texts, begging him to call their father. *He's going for his biopsy soon. What if it's cancer? You'll regret it if you don't reach out to him.*

What was the point? After Rick had left home, he'd tried contacting his dad—he'd called, texted, and even emailed—but the old man never responded. He was still too pissed that Rick had chosen archaeology over law school. His mother called about once a month—usually when his father wasn't around. Only Cassie had stayed in touch consistently. She'd tried to get their father to forgive Rick but with no luck.

Though Rick hadn't been back home in four years, at times the longing struck him like a physical ache. Especially during the holidays. He loved traveling, but he missed feeling grounded. Having a place to call home. But who would he be if he went back to California? What would he do for a job? His whole life was tied up with traveling and working. Who was he if he wasn't Rick the freewheeling shovel bum?

All questions he shouldn't be pondering at two in the morning. Maybe he'd feel better if he talked them over with someone.

Like Olivia.

CHAPTER ELEVEN

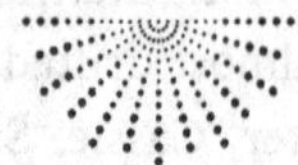

Olivia sat in the lab classroom, supervising her students as they sorted and labeled their finds and uploaded the data from their field notebooks. Occasionally, someone came to her with a question, but so far, the afternoon lab sessions had been a breeze. As she finished reviewing her notes, she couldn't dispel the nagging fear she was being too detail oriented. Even after four days of surveying, she was still slowing her team down.

Fighting off a bout of drowsiness, she stood and stretched. If she sat still for much longer, she'd doze off. Not a good look for a TA.

After telling the students she was taking a break, she walked over to the adjoining classroom, which served as Dusty's illustration studio. Most of the chairs had been pushed against the wall, and the small space was dominated by six long tables displaying a variety of artifacts. Dusty's table was set up with drawing equipment and measuring tools, as well as a laptop and a tablet for the digital aspects of her job.

Dusty was drawing a large piece of Geometric ware—burnished red pottery decorated with a series of dark, concentric rings. Beside her, Marisol appeared deeply focused, her head bent over her paper as she sketched a stone projectile point.

"Hey, there," Dusty said. "How goes the survey?"

"We haven't found much yet," Olivia said. "None of the teams have, other than churned-up Roman pottery. But it's going all right."

Marisol cast a hesitant gaze up at Olivia. "I'm sorry I didn't make it out there today."

Olivia tried to imbue her voice with patience. "It's okay, but you'll need to join us soon. The survey counts for part of your grade."

"I want to, but it sounds so daunting." Marisol blinked rapidly, as though fighting back tears. "You got a nasty rash and a terrible sunburn."

Wincing at the memory, Olivia glanced at her shins, which still bore traces of the red bumps. "Only on my first day, and I wouldn't have gotten a sunburn if I'd worn protective clothing."

"But Brynn said…" Marisol bit her lip.

"What?"

"She…she said our team's not doing very well. We keep coming in last."

Olivia struggled to keep her irritation in check. Four days in, and Brynn was still whining as much as ever. "Even if we've been slower than the others, it won't impact your grade."

"That's not what Grant—I mean Dr. Nilsson—told us," Marisol said. "He warned us our grades could suffer if our team couldn't keep up. He doesn't want anyone throwing off his schedule."

Why was he so intent on intimidating the students? "I'll talk to him about it tomorrow," Olivia said.

Or not, depending on his mood. Asking Grant for anything when he was riled up was like poking an angry bear.

"I'll be there tomorrow morning. I promise." Marisol stood

up. "Right now, I need to work on my site presentation. Can you help me after you're done here? I'll be in the library."

"Absolutely," Olivia said. "I'll stop by in a bit. Take a break if you need one. There's water and lemon squash in the kitchen fridge." She'd never heard of lemon squash before but was slowly developing a taste for the sweet concentrated syrup that made a half-decent lemonade when mixed with water.

After Marisol left, Olivia plunked down on a wooden chair across from Dusty and allowed herself a moment to wallow in self-doubt. "Some teaching assistant I am. Thanks to my incompetence, I'm pissing off Brynn and making Marisol too scared to go on the survey."

Dusty brushed eraser shavings off her drawing. "Marisol was anxious from the day she got here. Why not let her keep working with me? She's a good artist."

"I'd love to, but the survey component makes up a third of her grade." Olivia picked up the projectile point Marisol had been sketching. "Where'd you get this?"

"Last year's survey. They found a couple of sites on the last few days but didn't have time to deal with all the artifacts. They'll keep me busy until one of you makes a major find."

"It won't be me. I'm not exactly crushing it." Olivia twisted the projectile point between her fingers, still finding it awe-inspiring she was touching a stone tool someone had made thousands of years ago. "How am I supposed to convince Marisol to join the survey if I keep messing up?"

"Rick's your team leader, right? Could she shadow him for a few days? Walk beside him when he covers his transect? Then he could show her what to look for."

The solution was so obvious Olivia mentally chastised herself for not coming up with it on her own. "Great idea. I'll ask him later."

Dusty grinned. "Besides, who wouldn't like shadowing Rick? Walking behind him and checking out that ass? Yes, please."

Olivia's stomach dropped. She was torn between wanting to know if Rick and Dusty had ever hooked up and wanting to remain oblivious. "Well…thanks. I should probably get going."

Dusty narrowed her eyes. "You okay? You look kind of annoyed. Is this about Rick? If you want him, then go for it. You won't have any competition from me."

Why was her face so flipping transparent? Olivia's cheeks prickled with heat. "What? *No.* I'm not going after him. That would be unprofessional."

"Oh, please. Nothing unprofessional about a little late-night action once the workday ends. Grant's fooling himself if he thinks he can stop it. I've been going on digs my whole life, and this shit happens."

"But not between you and Rick?" Olivia cringed at the blatant neediness in her voice.

"Nope. Despite his obvious hotness, he doesn't do it for me. But if Stu ever pulled me aside and wanted to take things to the next level, well…"

"I thought you guys were just friends. Isn't he dating someone?" In all the years Olivia had known Stuart, he'd never mentioned Dusty in a romantic way.

Dusty let out a deep sigh. "Shelby. I'm sure he'll propose once he gets his PhD. But idiot that I am, I've been crushing on him for years." She cast a furtive glance around the room, as if she suspected someone might be listening in. "No telling, okay? You keep this quiet, and I won't rat you out if you want to get with Rick."

"But I don't…"

Who was she kidding? Though she hadn't been alone with him since the night he'd soothed her sunburn, he'd been on her mind a lot. Not that she wanted to fry her skin again, but she longed for an excuse to bask in his touch. To feel his warm hands, massaging her shoulders. The powerful memory made shivers dance along her spine.

Stuart poked his head into the classroom. "Hey, ladies. What are you up to?"

Now it was Dusty's turn to flush. She cleared her throat. "Ah…nothing. Just talking."

"About the survey," Olivia said. "How it's been kind of slow. No big discoveries yet."

"Yeah, my team's disappointed about that." Stuart wandered over to their table and glanced at Dusty's sketch. "Nice drawing. I hope we find something half as good." He placed his hand on her shoulder. "I think we need a break. Later tonight, you two want to walk into town and get a drink at Spyros?"

Now that Olivia knew Dusty liked Stuart, she couldn't miss the way her friend reacted to his touch. Her hand trembled as she fiddled with her pencil.

"Shouldn't someone stay here with the students?" Olivia asked.

Stuart gave a casual shrug. "They're adults. I can't imagine they'll get into too much trouble. Grant said he'll be working in the lab tonight, so he'll be around." When Olivia hesitated, he flashed her an affable grin. "Come on. One drink. Maybe two. Juno said she'd be up for it. Same with TJ, though I told him to limit himself to two stories, max."

"I'll go," Dusty said. "Did you ask Rick?"

Stuart nodded. "He's in."

"I'm in, too." Olivia replied so quickly that Dusty shot her a side-eye. She sprang to her feet, wanting to leave before she started blushing again. She'd already revealed far too much about her feelings for Rick. "I'd better go help Marisol with her presentation."

She found Marisol in the research library, a classroom outfitted with bookshelves and study tables. Along one wall was a shelf holding four computers and two printers. Marisol had covered an entire table with printed articles, books, and pages of scrawled notes.

"Thanks for coming," Marisol said. "My talk's kind of a mess right now. I have too much source material."

"We can go through it together if you want. What site were you assigned?" Dr. Roth had given Olivia a list of all the assignments, but she couldn't remember them offhand. Once the survey unit ended, the undergrads would spend a few days visiting the archaeological sites in the area. Each student was responsible for preparing a talk on one of them.

"Kition. The site was occupied from the late Bronze Age through the Roman era, so there's a ton of history. How can I possibly cover it all in twenty minutes?" Marisol placed her head in her hands. "Why is Dr. Roth making us do this? I suck at public speaking."

"It can be hard if you're not used to it. Even if you're a dynamic speaker, some people still won't pay attention. You can't take it personally." Olivia cast her mind back to her first year as a teaching assistant, when she'd learned not every student was going to be as passionate about ancient history as she was.

"I know that in my head. But in here"—Marisol placed her hand across her heart—"it still stresses me out."

"Most of the others will probably be as nervous as you. My advice would be to keep your talk short, hit the highlights, and infuse some excitement into your voice."

Basically, be the exact opposite of Grant.

"You've taught before, right? Was it hard when you first started?"

The memory coaxed a laugh out of Olivia. "It was *so* hard. The week before I started teaching, my sister let me practice on her. Not only did she call me out whenever I was too boring, she insisted on recording me. You can't imagine how painful it was to watch all those videos."

"But now you're confident?"

Though Olivia wanted to encourage Marisol, she didn't want to lie, either. Not after her humbling experience with surveying.

"Sometimes. Other times, not so much. But it helps when I know the material well or if I'm excited about it."

She scanned through the articles Marisol had printed out and set two aside. "I'd start with these to get a basic overview. For your talk, you only need to hit the high points in Kition's history. Why don't I help you figure out what to include? Once you've drafted an outline, you can expand it. When you're done, you can practice on me anytime you like."

"Thanks. That would be great."

As they worked together, Olivia's spirits lifted. Even if she was still struggling on the survey, she needed to be as patient with herself as she was with the students.

Hadn't Rick told her she'd catch on soon?

If he could have faith in her, then she could, too.

CHAPTER TWELVE

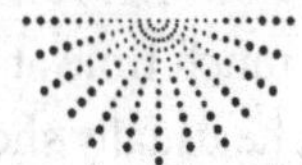

Rick was in the camp kitchen, making up a batch of hard-boiled eggs. Since his team was on breakfast duty tomorrow, he wanted to lighten their load by preparing a few things ahead of time. When Stuart popped in and suggested going for drinks after dinner, he agreed without hesitation. A couple of beers might ease the pressure building up inside of him.

For the past three nights, he'd been mulling over his late-night chat with his sister. When they'd talked, he'd dismissed their father's health scare as if it wasn't worth worrying about. But what if it was serious? Did Rick want to risk losing him before they had a chance to reconcile?

He'd toyed with the idea of going home before. Despite his painful estrangement from his dad, he missed his friends and the rest of his family. But each time he was on the verge of returning, he found another job to sustain him for the next few months. Each gig gave him a reason to keep moving forward rather than go home and deal with the past.

Maybe it was time he stopped running. If he went back to California, he could try convincing his dad—yet again—that his passion for archaeology was as worthy as a career in law. Just because Rick wasn't following in his old man's footsteps didn't mean he was a failure or a slacker.

Before Rick could book his ticket back, he needed a game plan. He couldn't wing it and hope the job opportunities would magically appear.

His best bet was to seek out Dr. Roth and ask for his help, but the professor didn't spend much time at camp. Since he didn't join the students on the survey, he usually showed up around two, once the lab work was underway. He'd talk to each team, examine their finds, and confer with Grant. By four thirty, he headed back to the field house to work on his own research until dinner. Though the house was only a short walk from camp, it felt distinctly off-limits, as though it were the professor's private sanctuary.

After setting the hard-boiled eggs in the fridge, Rick tracked down the professor in Dusty's illustration studio. Dr. Roth pulled a large bin out of storage, filled with bagged and labeled finds.

"If you want to look through these and see if there's anything worth illustrating, have a go," he said to her. "Once you're done, the museum will take them off our hands."

"Will do. Thanks." Dusty fixed her gaze on Rick. "What's up?"

"I was hoping to talk to Dr. Roth." He caught the professor's eye. "Unless you're busy here?"

"I'm good. As a matter of fact, I wanted to have a chat with you. Let's head outside."

His serious tone set Rick's nerves on edge. "Sure. See you later, Dusty."

He followed Dr. Roth out of the classroom until they were standing beneath the largest olive tree on the grounds, which stood adjacent to the kitchen. He spoke calmly, trying to conceal the unease growing inside of him. "Is everything all right?"

Dr. Roth uncapped his stainless-steel water bottle and took a drink. He had a large collection of them, all with different logos.

Today's was bright orange with the words "Cyprus Rocks" written in a giant font. He smiled as he caught Rick staring at it. "A gift from one of my students last year. A bit garish, but it does the job." He screwed the lid back on and waited a beat before speaking. "Grant came to me earlier. He said you're having problems with your survey team."

Less than a week in and Grant had the knives out already? Rick drew in a slow, steady breath, willing himself to answer calmly. "I wasn't aware of any problems."

"He told me your team has been consistently late returning to camp. One of the students complained to him about it."

Brynn. Who else could it be? Marisol hadn't joined the survey yet, and TJ was happy as long as he had an audience for his stories. "Sorry, but other than the first day, our team hasn't lagged that far behind the others. I'm trying to make sure we're as thorough as possible."

"I understand, but Grant's concerned about sticking to the schedule."

No, he was trying to get Rick in trouble. If anyone else's team had struggled to keep up, Grant would have let it go without reporting the issue.

"Is Olivia doing all right?" Dr. Roth asked. "I know she's out of her element. I hope I didn't make the wrong decision, choosing her to replace Frida."

"She's fine." Even though she was the main cause of the delay, Rick refused to throw her under the bus. "But I can talk to my team tomorrow if that would help."

"Good. Is there anything else?"

Asking for a favor now wasn't a good look, but Rick plowed on ahead. "I recently learned my father could be dealing with a serious medical issue. I've been traveling for years but might be needed at home this fall."

A white lie, but easier than explaining his complicated

relationship with his dad. Or elaborating on the real reason he'd stayed away for four years.

Dr. Roth's expression softened. "I'm sorry to hear that. What can I do to help?"

"After field school ends, I was thinking of going back to California and looking for work there. A job in cultural resource management would be ideal. You once mentioned having a colleague who runs a rescue archaeology company. Is there any way you could put in a good word for me?"

Rick clammed up when a couple of students walked by—Brynn and her friend Courtney, the two most high-maintenance members of the field school.

Dr. Roth turned on the charm, beaming at them. "How are you ladies this afternoon?"

"Hot," Brynn muttered. "It's always hot."

"We're going into Kouklia to get something to drink," Courtney added. "There's nothing good in the fridge. That lemon squash is full of empty calories."

"There's a suggestion list tacked up to the bulletin board in the kitchen." Rick struggled to keep his voice even. He'd been mentioning the damn list since the first day. "If you write down what you want, I can look for it the next time I get groceries in Paphos."

"Thanks, but that doesn't help us now." Courtney sighed. "Let's go, Brynn."

Rick waited until they left before speaking again. He didn't want to appear too pushy, but if he didn't keep the conversation going, Dr. Roth might forget about it. "So…about your colleague?"

"Right," Dr. Roth said. "He works in Southern California. Based in Ventura County. But that might not be ideal. Aren't you from the Bay Area?"

"I am, but I'd be fine working anywhere in the state. I could visit my folks between jobs." Whether or not this would happen, he couldn't say. But at least he'd be employed. As he waited for Roth's answer, he tried to control the churning in his stomach.

Dr. Roth gave a slow nod. The fact that he hadn't agreed to the request immediately was a bad sign. "I'd like to help. You have a lot of experience in the field, and you clearly know what you're doing, but…"

Rick swallowed, his throat suddenly dry. "Is this about the Palaikastro dig?"

"Exactly. When you applied for this job, I wasn't sure whether to hire you, based on what I'd heard. But since Frida endorsed you, I decided to give you a chance. I'd like to get through this season without any issues, so let's see where we are in a few weeks. If all goes well, then I'd be happy to recommend you. I could even make a few calls."

Rick forced a bright smile on his face, not wanting to reveal how gutted he was. He'd foolishly assumed the professor's recommendation would be a slam dunk. "Thanks. I won't let you down."

"Good. I need to head back to the field house. There's a cold beer calling my name."

After he left, Rick sat in the shade of the olive tree, fighting back a surge of frustration.

For years, he'd been a dependable worker. Someone who showed up on time and took any jobs he was assigned. But because of a stupid judgment call, he was now viewed as a liability. If he screwed up again, he'd be lucky to get a job anywhere.

AFTER DINNER, RICK CONSIDERED BAILING ON DRINKS AT SPYROS. Given his rotten mood, he didn't want to drag everyone down. But when Olivia asked if he was going, he didn't have the heart to say no. They'd grown closer since the night he'd treated her sunburn, though not so close that she'd asked him to do it again. Probably for the best because he'd gotten too aroused touching her bare skin. He didn't need that temptation.

When he got to Spyros, she was already there, seated at a table on the patio. To his delight, she was wearing her hair down, her wild curls cascading past her shoulders. Seeing her in such a relaxed state raised his spirits.

Dusty sat across from Olivia, cocktail in hand. "Come join us. We're trying our first brandy sour. Juno told us it's the national drink of Cyprus."

Olivia lifted her glass in a salute. "Kalispera."

"Kalispera to you, too." He pulled up a chair and ordered a brandy sour for himself. The sweet cocktail—made up of brandy, lemon squash, bitters, and soda water—went down far too easily. During his last gig on the island, he'd enjoyed his fair share of them.

"What do you think?" he asked Olivia.

"Delicious." She gave him a cheeky smile. "I was only going to have one, but I don't know if I have that kind of willpower. Not where brandy is concerned."

He bit back a grin as he remembered how uninhibited she'd gotten at Clear Lake after a few shots of brandy. Was she recalling the same thing?

Stuart, Juno, and TJ arrived, pulling up chairs around the table. After ordering drinks, they took turns venting about their survey experiences.

"I don't envy the lot of you, having to traipse around outdoors at the crack of dawn," Dusty said. "I can stumble into my studio still wearing my pajamas while you battle evil plants." She shot Olivia a look.

"That only happened on the first day," Olivia said. "I haven't had any more carnivorous plant encounters since then. Though I'm probably the worst surveyor in the whole field school, which is embarrassing as hell, considering I'm a year away from getting my doctorate."

Rick caught her eye, hoping to reassure her. "None of that. You're doing fine."

She sighed. "Thanks, but Brynn doesn't seem to think so. She came to me after lunch and bitched about our team's performance. I told her if she wanted to switch teams, we could make it happen." She glanced over at Stuart and Juno. "Would either of you like her?"

"No, thank you," Juno said. "She is, quite literally, a piece of work. I don't need that piece anywhere near me."

Stuart laughed. "I'll trade her for Logan. He's a decent guy but a total slacker. Four days in and he hasn't written a damn thing down. I'm worried he might accidentally stumble across a site but be too lazy to record it."

"I'd pay serious money to off-load Brynn," Rick said. "Thanks to her, I'm on Grant's shit list again. After she complained to him, he went to Roth behind my back and claimed I'm doing a crappy job."

"Shit." Olivia rubbed her forehead. "I didn't think she'd go to Grant. I should have warned you."

"Don't worry about it," he said. "I wouldn't care except I needed a favor from Roth, and Grant had already gotten to him."

"What do you need?" Stuart asked. "Could any of us help?"

"I might be able to," TJ said. "I have friends in high places. Seriously, bro, I'm connected."

For once, Rick didn't mind TJ's bragging. As much as the guy liked to flex his networking prowess, he wouldn't hesitate to help a fellow archaeologist. "Thanks. I might take you up on that, but what I really need is Roth's recommendation once this project is done."

"Why wouldn't Dr. Roth support you?" Olivia asked. "You have a ton of experience." She scanned the group. "What am I missing here?"

No sense in hiding the truth. She'd find out eventually. "Palaikastro," Rick said.

"That's the dig where you screwed the pooch," Juno said. "That's right? Yes? Screwing the pooch? Except you didn't screw a pooch."

"Nope. Just Thea, the dig director's daughter." He winced as he said it, waiting for Olivia to react in disgust. But she merely regarded him with wide eyes.

"I don't see the issue, as long as Thea was of age and it was consensual." Dusty's expression hardened. "If it wasn't, then I might have to hate you."

He held up his hands. "Nothing like that. She was twenty-four, and the fling was extremely consensual." She'd started flirting with him the moment he arrived. Sending out so many signals he couldn't miss them. Like a fool, he'd given in without thinking of the consequences.

Olivia's gaze dropped down to her drink as she stirred the remaining ice with her swizzle stick. Her reluctance to meet his eyes made his stomach clench with regret.

"What's the issue then?" Dusty asked. "Did Thea claim sexual harassment?"

Rick shook his head. No matter how casual the hookup, he always made sure his partner was completely on board. "Her father caught us together."

"No way," TJ said. "Like, *actually* together?"

Now Rick wished he hadn't brought up the subject. Olivia didn't need the details. Then again, better she hear it from him instead of Grant.

"It wasn't that bad, but he spotted me leaving her tent—after, you know. He was this old-school Greek archaeologist. Very patriarchal and overprotective. He would have beaten the shit out of me if Thea hadn't intervened. But he fired me with two weeks left to go on the dig. Worse than that, he spread the word about me to all his colleagues."

"How did his daughter feel about that?" Dusty asked. "I mean, she was involved, too."

Rick gave a short laugh. "He kept her out of it. Instead, he told everyone he'd fired me because I'd acted unprofessionally. That I drank too much, showed up for work hungover, and couldn't be trusted with responsibility."

"You didn't defend yourself?" Stuart asked.

"I didn't want to drag Thea's name through the mud. Bad enough her dad treated her like she was sixteen instead of twenty-four." When Rick had first learned of the accusations, during a phone interview for a job on a site in Sardinia, he'd been devastated. Four years of hard work, undone by a vindictive father.

"That's very gentlemanly of you," Dusty said. "Take it from me, I rarely meet anyone who's a gentleman in the field. There are so many snakes, especially men like Grant who abuse their power."

Rick appreciated the group's support. "Thanks. I'm trying not to screw up this time."

"You won't," Stuart said. "We've got your back." He raised his glass, and the others followed.

But for the rest of the evening, Olivia stayed quiet. As they were heading back to camp, she caught Rick's eye, as though she wanted to talk to him. He wasn't surprised, given the truth bomb he'd dropped about Palaikastro.

He urged the others to go on ahead, then waited until they were out of earshot. He fell back until he was by her side. "Olivia. I'm sorry."

"No. *I'm* sorry." Her shoulders sagged. "I didn't realize you had so much to lose. If Grant is complaining to Dr. Roth about your leadership abilities because of *my* failings, then I need to stop being a burden."

"Wait. That's why you're upset?" From her silence, he'd

assumed she was stewing with anger over his stupidity at Palaikastro.

"Of course. I'm still too slow. I've been trying to hurry, but I'm spending too much time checking out random clusters of pottery. I keep hoping one of them will turn out to be a real site, but all I've done is make you a prime target for Grant. If I asked to be on his team, he might ease up on you."

He stopped, too stunned to keep walking. "You aren't pissed about Palaikastro?"

"Because you had sex with a woman you met on a dig? I don't love the concept of field rules, but it's not any of my business. Although…"

"What?" His spine stiffened.

"There've been a lot of women, haven't there?"

Her tone sounded more curious than judgmental, but it didn't lessen the uneasiness churning in his gut. "Maybe in the past. Not so much this year. Not until I met Thea."

"Were you…um…" Her voice wavered. "Were you in love with her?"

He was surprised it mattered to her. "No, and she didn't feel that way about me either. I was just a diversion—a way to say, 'screw you' to her domineering father." Recalling it gave him a sick feeling. Their relationship had been based on pure lust and nothing else. He didn't want that anymore.

"Has there ever been anyone special? On your digs, I mean?"

He wasn't sure what she was after, but now that they'd grown closer, he had no qualms about answering honestly. "Just one woman. I was madly in love with her, but it didn't go well. After I got her in trouble, she ghosted me for seven years."

"*Oh.*" Her eyes widened. "Wow. That…um…"

He couldn't help grinning. "Too much?"

"No. It…makes me feel special."

"You *were* special. You still are." He placed his hand on her shoulder, letting it linger. What he really wanted to do was take her in his arms, but he restrained himself. "That's why I want you on my team. Don't put yourself at Grant's mercy. Stay with me."

"You sure?"

"Positive. If Brynn's unhappy, we can switch her out next week. But I don't want you to leave. Providing that's what you want?"

She gave him a shy smile. "I do. Thanks. I'd rather work with you than anyone else."

That smile made it all worthwhile.

CHAPTER THIRTEEN

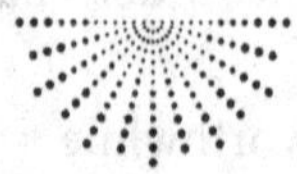

"Time to wake up."

Curse you, Rick. Not only had he invaded Olivia's dreams, now she couldn't get him out of her head.

The voice took on a teasing tone. "I'm warning you. Don't make me tip your cot over."

Her eyes flew open. It *was* Rick. What was he doing? He crouched beside her cot, getting a little too close for comfort.

"What the hell?" she said. "It's only five thirty. I have another half hour of sleep left."

"We're on breakfast duty. Remember? I mentioned it during survey training. The teams rotate every five days." He pointed to the kitchen. "Come help as soon as you're dressed."

"Five more minutes." For once, her nemesis, the evil Crowy McRooster, had decided to sleep in. She wanted to take full advantage.

"I'm serious. I'll tip you over, princess."

She eased herself to a sitting position but refused to meet his eyes. Her thin tank top and tiny sleep shorts exposed too much of her bare skin. She crossed her arms, trying to hide her lack of a bra since the cool morning air had made her nipples perkier than usual. "Go away. I'll be there as soon as I put some clothes on."

He backed away from her, wearing a grin. "You can come as you are. It's a good look."

She tried to muster up a scowl, but instead of being angry, his nearness aroused other feelings. All because last night's dreams had drifted into the erotic zone. Though they were a welcome departure from the nightmares she'd had about surveying, the steamy visions had thrown her off-kilter.

Lately, everything about Rick was throwing her off-kilter. Too often, she caught herself staring at him, admiring his toned physique, his warm hazel eyes, or the way his encouraging smile lit up every part of his face. When she was alone, her thoughts drifted back to those long-ago nights at the lake, when they'd delighted in exploring each other's bodies. What would it feel like to touch him now? To stroke his rock-hard muscles and relish the warmth of his bare skin?

Pull yourself together. It's five thirty in the morning.

By the time she got to the outbuilding that housed the kitchen, Rick was there, along with TJ. The term "kitchen" was generous—the gas stove resembled an antique, the cupboards were missing their doors, and the tiny sink barely held any dishes. Dented pots and pans took up an entire counter.

She reviewed the list of breakfast fare stuck to the bulletin board: *hard-boiled eggs, sliced melon, figs, apricots, peasant bread, Greek yogurt, honey, juice, tea, hot water.* The same breakfast they'd had every morning since she'd arrived. Not that she minded, but she would have killed for real coffee. All they had was a jar of Nescafé.

Rick tossed her a melon. "Can you cut this into slices? Knives are in the top drawer."

"Sure. Where are Brynn and Marisol? Shouldn't they be helping us?"

"This kitchen's small enough as it is. I figured the three of us could handle breakfast without them."

"No fair." TJ filled a kettle with water and set it on the stove. "I can't believe you're letting Brynn slack off."

"You want to wake her?" Olivia asked.

"Hard pass." TJ turned up the heat on the burner. "She's already bitchy enough."

Olivia carved up the melon and arranged the slices in a bowl. The fruit smelled so cloying she suspected it was past its prime. "I can ask her if she wants to switch with someone on Stuart's team. Maybe Logan."

Rick grabbed a bowl of hard-boiled eggs from the fridge. "Let's get through today's survey, and we'll see where we're at."

"Then it's time for the beach, baby." TJ lifted his hand and met Olivia's for a high five.

One more day and they'd get their first break. A whole day off with no agenda other than beach time. She couldn't wait.

THE MORNING'S DRIVE TOOK THEM OVER THE SAME STRETCH OF coastal plain they'd been surveying all week. Since Marisol had decided to join them, the back seat of the Kia was more cramped than usual. Olivia fought back a stab of resentment toward Brynn, who demanded the front seat on every ride. Worse yet, she fiddled with the radio constantly, never able to settle on a station for more than one song.

Rick stopped the car on a small dirt road beside a stretch of farm field. Olivia's stomach knotted as she extracted herself from the back seat. Despite exerting every effort not to hinder their team, she kept coming up short. Yesterday, she'd been so determined to keep up that she pushed herself too hard. When her asthma kicked in, she had to stop until she got it under control.

"Okay, everyone," Rick said. "We're still on the coastal plain, so you all know the drill. I realize our pace hasn't matched the other teams, but none of you will get penalized for it. That being said, if you have a problem with my leadership, please come to me first before going to Grant so I can work out a solution. If you'd like to switch teams, I can try to accommodate your needs starting next week. Any questions?"

Olivia waited for Brynn's response, but she said nothing, keeping her eyes on her phone. Like she didn't give a shit that she'd gotten Rick in trouble.

"All right," Rick said. "Since this is Marisol's first day of survey, she's going to be walking along with me."

Olivia was pleased he'd agreed to her suggestion. Even better, he'd offered to let Marisol shadow him for the next few days.

Marisol went to stand beside him, anxiety etched on her delicate features. At least she was properly dressed for her first day out, wearing a long-sleeved shirt, cotton pants, and a bucket hat. Though she might roast in the heat, she wouldn't end up with Olivia's sunburn-from-hell.

Brynn looked up, as if suddenly aware of what was going on. "Why does she get special treatment? I didn't get to shadow Rick."

"You can shadow me if you want," TJ said. "Since I'm probably the person here with the most experience. After Rick, of course."

She scowled at him. "Hard pass. I'd rather get head-butted by an angry mountain goat."

"Enough chatter," Rick said. "Let's get going."

Olivia's first transect went smoothly. Since it was relatively free of artifacts, she had little to record. She beat Rick and Marisol by a full five minutes, though she suspected he'd slowed his pace to adjust for her inexperience. When the two of them returned, they spent their break reviewing Marisol's field notebook. Watching them together, Olivia admired Rick's patience. Even if he had no aspirations to teach, he had a great rapport with students.

Toward the end of her second transect, Olivia was keeping pace with the team when she spotted a cluster of potsherds. Though she was tempted to ignore them, she squatted down to get a better look. She picked up a handful and brushed off the dirt. Each piece was decorated with black bands; one had a zigzag design. The largest piece displayed a detailed line drawing resembling a duck's head.

A rush of exhilaration washed over her. This wasn't like the pottery she'd found before. Based on the designs, she suspected it belonged to the Cypro-Geometric period, dating as far back as the eighth or ninth century BC. During that time, Cyprus had been divided into city-states, populated by a mix of Greeks, Phoenicians, and native Cypriots. Both Grant and Dr. Roth were interested in finding more sites from that era.

As she pawed through the dirt, her heart pounded faster. She no longer cared about the relentless sun or her growing thirst. All that mattered were the potsherds beneath her feet. Ignoring the dirt lodged under her fingernails, she unearthed more pottery.

She was reluctant to pull herself away but couldn't risk delaying her team any longer. If Dr. Roth wanted the site explored further, he'd send someone back to investigate. She took a series of photos, zooming in on the details, and placed the biggest pieces inside a large Ziploc bag. Fifteen minutes later, she reached the car, panting and dripping with sweat.

The rest of the team stood waiting, their expressions grim. When she checked her watch, her breath hitched. Five minutes to one. No matter how fast they hustled, they'd be late for lunch. Grant would be furious.

Brynn let out a pained sigh. "You took forever. What's wrong with you?"

"I thought you were trying to speed up the pace," TJ grumbled.

Her shoulders tightened as she waited for Rick's reaction, but he didn't reprimand her. Instead, he approached her and placed his hand on her arm. "You okay? I was getting worried."

"Sorry, but I found an artifact cluster. A real one." Her voice shook with a mixture of nerves and excitement. "It could be a site."

Marisol clapped her hands together. "That's amazing."

TJ raised his eyebrows. "You think? I didn't see anything special in my transect."

"Me neither," Brynn added. "Are you sure it wasn't a bunch of churned-up pottery?"

"Pretty sure." Olivia thought she'd made the right call, but now she was second-guessing herself. She thrust the Ziploc bag at Rick. "See for yourself."

He opened it and looked through the samples. His breath caught when he saw the piece with the duck's head design. "This looks like Cypro-Geometric ware."

Yes. She was tempted to do a victory dance, but she didn't want to cross the line from proud to obnoxious.

TJ pumped his fist. "Sweet! Iron Age pottery. The other teams will be so jealous."

Rick handed the bag back to Olivia. "Nice job. How'd you do it?"

"By not rushing and taking a second look." She couldn't help but grin. "I know I made us late, but these finds were worth it. Right?"

Rick locked eyes with her. "Absolutely. Your instincts were spot-on."

"Thanks." She all but melted under his tender gaze.

Brynn let out an exasperated breath. "Can we go? We're going to miss lunch, and it won't taste good if it's cold. That crappy kitchen doesn't even have a microwave."

Rick motioned for all of them to get in the car. Despite driving well beyond the speed limit, they returned so late the other teams were already at lunch. Grant materialized within seconds of their arrival, like he'd been eagerly waiting to chew them out.

As Olivia got out to face him, her heart beat in double time. She brandished the bag like a shield. "I'm sorry I made us late, but I think I found a site."

She braced herself for his rage as he snatched it from her hands. She'd already decided she'd take full responsibility for her actions, no matter how dire the consequences. If she'd made a bad call, she didn't want Rick to suffer.

But Grant smiled at her. Actually *smiled*. He took the pieces out of the bag, inspecting each one with care. "Well done. Geometric ware. That period was the subject of my dissertation."

"Really?" Maybe she'd found a way to win points with him.

"Yes. 'Kingship and Social Stratification during the Cypro-Geometric and Early Archaic Periods.' I'm working on a few follow-up articles, so another site could add to my data. With a Geometric site, there's a chance we'll uncover chamber tombs."

Chamber tombs? Hot damn. Even if she'd taken five days to get into a groove, she'd redeemed herself.

Today's lunchtime casserole—moussaka with ground lamb—was lukewarm at best but still tasted delicious. As did the bountiful village salad that accompanied it, laden with cucumbers, tomatoes, onions, kalamata olives, and feta. Olivia was so ravenous she had two helpings. It didn't hurt that everyone at the table wanted to hear about her discovery.

At two, Dr. Roth came into the lab for his daily visit. When he stopped by her team's table, Olivia showed him her samples, which she'd washed and laid out to dry. He examined each piece, then scrolled through the photos on her phone.

"Excellent work," he said. "You have the location marked on your GPS?"

"It's on my topo map, too." She forced her limbs to relax as she waited for his verdict. Would he deem her find worthy?

"Wonderful. It's hard to judge from a handful of pottery, but

I'd say your discovery merits further investigation. Rick, why don't you head back over there and set up a test pit this afternoon? Depending on the yield, we could do more testing next week."

Once again, Olivia resisted the urge to break out a victory dance.

Grant walked over to join them. "Since this period is my area of specialty, I should be there."

"You're of more use supervising the lab," Dr. Roth said. "Rick can handle it for today."

"But—"

Dr. Roth shook his head. "You'll stay here." He beamed at Olivia. "Do you want to join Rick? Since it's your site?"

My site? If she wasn't careful, her ego would explode.

Before she could answer, Grant spoke up again. "That doesn't seem wise. If Rick's going to be gone all afternoon, Olivia needs to supervise the team. They haven't finished entering today's data or processing their finds."

Spoilsport. But she said nothing, too afraid to challenge him.

TJ looked up from their group's table. "How about I supervise the lab session? I'm a pro at this stuff."

"Thank you, TJ." Dr. Roth said. He gave Olivia an indulgent smile. "Then you and Rick are free to go."

Yes. She was going to check out her site. With Rick. Her heart could barely handle the anticipation.

Until Grant scowled at her. *Damn it.* Whatever points she'd earned from him by finding a site had vanished. If she was being smart, she'd step aside and let him take her place. But she couldn't do it.

Temptation or not, she wasn't passing up a chance to be alone with Rick.

CHAPTER FOURTEEN

When Rick led Olivia over to Dr. Roth's Jeep, she let out a squeal of delight. "We get to use the Jeep?"

Her enthusiasm was irresistible. "You bet. Roth okayed it. If we're going to be digging up lost treasure, we need to look the part."

"Damn right." She climbed into the front seat. "I can't believe Dr. Roth allowed me to go. Grant's got more seniority, and this is his area of study."

"You're the one that found the site. And actually…" As he got in next to her, he hesitated, not wanting to trigger her anxiety.

Too late. She whipped around to face him, her eagerness turning to apprehension. "What is it?"

"Since you're new to this and you suffer from topographic-disorientation-whatever, there's a chance you might not have marked the location correctly." He pulled away from the parking area and headed toward the road.

"Oh, shit. What if I messed up?" She rubbed her hands over her face. "Grant's going to kill me if I can't find the site again."

He placed his hand on her thigh but didn't let it linger. Since she'd changed from her long, baggy surveying pants into shorts, the feel of her bare skin was too enticing. "Sorry. I didn't mean to stress you out."

"I left a tiny pile of stones next to the site. That might help." She was clasping her hands together so tightly he wished he'd kept quiet. But the truth was, Grant would lose his shit if they failed to relocate her site.

Best not to worry about that yet.

Rick flipped through the radio dials until he found Viva FM. Some old-school pop might brighten the mood. As soon as "Dancing Queen" came on, Olivia started singing along.

Even if she was sweaty and dusty from the morning's survey, her hair coming loose from that annoying ponytail, she was as desirable as ever. No matter how hard he tried to resist her, his attraction to her grew stronger with each passing day. Watching her geek out over a handful of eighth-century pottery made her even more appealing. He loved that she still held an unabashed passion for all things archaeology-related.

"Hey." She turned to him. "You're being quiet. Is my singing annoying you?"

"No. I like it. I should bring out my guitar again some night. If you'd be up for singing?"

"Yeah, why not?" She turned down the volume on the radio. "Are you sure there isn't anything else on your mind? Besides the crushing fear that I might not be able to find my awesome cache of potsherds?"

"We'll find it. But I was thinking I was right all along. You weren't a failure. You just needed a little time."

She uncapped her water bottle and took a drink. "I got lucky, that's all. If TJ had been in my transect, he wouldn't have missed that pottery. Same with you."

"Maybe. But this time, the win goes to you. Why not bask in it?"

"True." She leaned her head against the seat. "It's so nice to sit up front. You have no idea how squished it is in the back of that teensy rental car. And I'm not even tall." She let out a sigh of contentment. "Do you think if we pass a town or village on the way back, we could stop for ice cream? I like grapes and watermelon, but they're not real dessert. What I need is ice cream. Cone optional."

"Pistachio, right?"

Her eyes lit up. "Good memory. Wow. And you liked…butter pecan?"

"Be serious. No one likes butter pecan except my grandfather."

She poked his shoulder. "Kidding. You liked chocolate peanut butter cup."

The fact that she remembered made him smile. At Clear Lake, they'd frequented an ice cream stand a mile from their dig site. He'd often teased her about her pistachio fixation—because who preferred pistachio to chocolate?

He parked alongside the road at the exact spot they'd started their survey that morning. All they had to do was retrace Olivia's steps back to the waypoint she'd marked on her GPS. Grabbing the equipment from the Jeep, he passed her the dig bag filled with smaller tools while he took the heavier load—a shovel, a large wooden sieve, two buckets, and a tarp.

As they followed the path of her transect, he hoped Olivia hadn't marked the wrong spot. But even if she had, he was willing to comb the entire area until they got results. He didn't want her to feel like a failure again.

When they reached the waypoint, Olivia rushed forward and knelt next to a small pile of stones. "Found it! I made this mini cairn just in case. This is where I was digging." A few potsherds were visible near the small hole she'd clawed in the dirt.

Rick's chest loosened in relief. Now they could take as much time as they wanted. As long as they brought back samples, Dr. Roth wouldn't care if they were gone all afternoon. For the next few hours, Rick would have Olivia all to himself.

Remember, you're just friends. No messing around.

"We're going to set up a one-meter-square test pit and dig down ten centimeters at a time," he said. "Do you remember when we excavated those first few trenches at Clear Lake?"

"Sort of. It's slowly coming back." Still kneeling, she looked up at him, her eyes bright with excitement. "I realize you've been on dozens of digs, so this is probably old hat."

"It's not old hat."

"Seriously? You must have found more important stuff than broken pieces of eighth-century pottery."

He had. Nothing quite like the Ark of the Covenant or the Holy Grail, but he'd worked on the remains of villas, churches, fortresses, and an underwater shipwreck. But he hadn't been with her. "It's still exciting. More exciting because I'm with you."

As soon the words were out, he worried he'd said too much, but her ardor didn't diminish in the slightest. "Thanks. I'm glad I'm with someone who knows what he's doing."

"I appreciate that. I might not have the same academic credentials as most people here, but—"

"But you have lived experience. That's more important. Honestly, the more I'm around you, the more I'm in awe of everything you've done."

Her words struck a powerful chord that left him speechless. Olivia Sanchez, ABD, kick-ass graduate student, future professor, was in awe of *him*. Damn, if that wasn't an ego boost.

For a moment, he could only stare at her, until he forced himself to focus on the task at hand. He measured the square, then marked it off with four wooden stakes and a roll of twine. Olivia set out the tarp, laid the sieve on it, and took some photos with the digital camera Dr. Roth had loaned them.

"You sure it's okay to just dig here?" she asked. "We're not in someone's backyard or anything, but this has to be private property."

"We'll backfill the pit once we're done. If Roth decides to do a full-scale excavation, he'll make sure to get the landowner's permission first, like we did for portions of the survey. It's all good." He grabbed the shovel. "I'll dig up the top layer and set it in the buckets. Sift the dirt directly onto the tarp and save the pottery in the finds bag. We can switch off after a bit."

Though the sun was as fierce as ever, he barely noticed as they got into a comfortable rhythm. A few times, he peeked at her while she shook the sieve, enjoying the sexy way her hips swayed, as if moving to a silent beat. Occasionally, she stopped to show him the bigger pieces of pottery, including the handle of a jug, decorated with striking black designs.

When it was her turn to dig, she crouched in the pit with the trowel and slowly worked her way through the dirt. By the time they'd dug down thirty centimeters, they'd filled three large bags with samples of pottery, all from the Cypro-Geometric period.

"It's after six," he said. "We should stop."

"Five more minutes? *Please*?"

Like he could say no to her? "Five minutes, but that's it." He continued sifting the dirt but stopped when she let out a cry.

He dropped the sieve and hopped into the pit next to her. "You okay? You didn't get hurt, did you?"

"No. But look." She lifted the edge of her tank top, exposing a tantalizing glimpse of her bare stomach as she wiped off a curved piece of pottery. "I think this was part of a bowl or a larger vessel. No big deal, except those scratches look like Phoenician writing."

He took the piece from her and examined it closely. "Shit. You're right. Do you know how incredible that is?"

She was grinning like a maniac. "Pretty fucking incredible. Can you read Phoenician?"

"No, but I'm sure Roth can." Talk about a major score. The professor would be thrilled.

She placed her hands on her hips. "And you wanted me to stop digging. Good thing I asked for five more minutes."

"I bow to your superior instincts. Let's give it another fifteen. I'll help you."

After twenty minutes, they stopped digging, since they hadn't found anything else of note. Olivia took a final round of photos, then Rick undid the twine and pulled up the stakes. Grabbing his water bottle, he sat on the edge of the pit to take a break.

Olivia joined him, sitting so close her bare thigh was almost touching his. "So, Dr. Jones? What do you make of today's finds?"

He lowered his voice to a growl. "Well, Marion, if the Nazis ever get wind of this treasure, we're in big trouble."

"That important, huh? We'd better be careful."

He laughed. "Seriously, I think we're onto something. We can't tell that much about the site from one test pit, but there's enough here to warrant getting a bigger sample. If we could find structural evidence, we might have a reason to excavate at some point in the future."

She placed her hand over her heart. "I'm *so* glad I didn't lead us out here for nothing. Thanks for having faith in me."

"Anytime." He locked eyes with her but couldn't pull away. When she tugged off her hair tie and freed her wild curls from her ponytail, his desire grew. Even if she was as sweaty and grimy as he was, he wanted her more than ever.

"What? I know I'm a total mess right now." She held up her hands. "I have a ton of dirt under my nails, and my hair—"

"Olivia. Stop." He couldn't take it any longer. Leaning toward her, he cupped her face in his hands. Her eyes caught his, but she didn't shrink away. He kissed her softly, seeking out her consent. When she opened her mouth wider and slid her tongue against his, he was a goner. The taste and feel of her flooded his senses.

He pulled her closer, deepening the kiss, his desire only increasing as she groaned with pleasure. He tangled his fingers in her hair, relishing the feel of it as he devoured her mouth. She placed her arms around his neck and pulled him toward her, kissing him back just as fiercely. He wanted to go even further, to burrow his hands under her shirt and caress her glorious breasts until she cried out in ecstasy, but alarm bells went off in his head.

What the fuck are you doing?

With great reluctance, he pulled away from her, painfully aware of how aroused he was. She stared at him, eyes wide, still breathing heavily. Considering the line he'd crossed, he deserved her fury. Instead, her bemused expression turned to laughter. Real, honest-to-God laughter that was so contagious he couldn't help but join in.

"I can't believe you kissed me now when I'm sweaty and disgusting," she said. "Nice timing."

"I'm equally sweaty, and you kissed me right back."

She grinned and swung her legs against the side of the pit. "Maybe I did."

Neither of them spoke, and he was torn between apologizing and trying to kiss her again. Now that he'd gotten a taste of those lips, he wanted more.

She let out a lengthy sigh. "This isn't a good idea, is it? Grant asked us not to 'indulge' in this kind of behavior. Not us, per se, but you know what I mean. Even if Dusty thought it wouldn't be a problem, she doesn't realize how much Grant hates you. And me, by extension."

He raised his eyebrows. "You talked to Dusty about me?"

"Maybe? Because I thought the two of you were…together last year, and I was…sort of jealous."

"No. We're friends. Same with me and Frida. Or me and Juno. I'm not trying to score with every woman I meet."

"I know. I wasn't trying to imply it, either. I just didn't want any awkwardness with Dusty." She gathered up her curls again. "Have you seen my hair tie?"

"Leave it. I like it down." Even in her grubby state, she was so beautiful with her hair like this, all messy and wild.

"Yeah, I remember that." She let out her breath. "Wow. I remember a lot." She glanced at the pile of dirt on the tarp. "We need to backfill the pit. That should get our primal urges under control."

All he wanted to do was kiss her again. Scratch that—he wanted more than kisses. He wanted to lay her down behind a bush, run his hands over her curves, and taste her everywhere. But she was right. They had a job to do, especially if they wanted to be back in time for dinner. If they were gone too long, the rumors would start flying.

He stood and retrieved the shovel. "If you want to write up a summary in your field notebook, I'll backfill the site."

Filling a pit was hot, dusty, and not nearly as satisfying as excavating it. When he was done, they used the wipes in the dig bag to clean their hands and faces. As they trudged back to the Jeep, he continued teasing her but kept his hands to himself.

Remembering her request, he stopped at the small grocery store in Kouklia, where he bought them each a vanilla ice cream bar coated in a layer of thick dark chocolate. They ate them while leaning against the Jeep, not caring if the chocolate melted onto their hands and the ice cream dripped on their clothes. Seeing Olivia so happy filled him with a warm glow. Whether it was due to her spectacular find, the kiss they'd shared, or the sheer joy of ice cream on a hot day, he couldn't say. But he'd take the win.

CHAPTER FIFTEEN

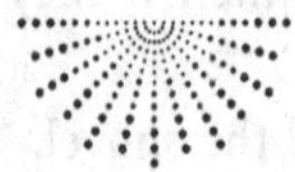

Olivia filled the battered kettle with water and heated it on the stove. After making herself a cup of tea, she walked over to the far end of the soccer field. The sun peeked over the horizon, bathing it in soft hues of pink and orange. She hadn't intended to wake this early on her day off, but Crowy McRooster hadn't let her sleep in. No one else had been roused by his noisy crowing either. Just her. Which suited her fine because she needed some time to herself.

In the ten days since she'd arrived in Cyprus, a lot had happened. She'd survived her first week of surveying, found a legitimate site, and kissed Rick. Not just any kiss but a five-alarm, fireworks-inducing, panty-melting kiss that had sent her nerve endings into overdrive.

She couldn't stop thinking about it. His mouth claiming hers, his hands tangling in her hair, the rush of unbridled lust that had made her toss her precious rules aside. Not only had she enjoyed every minute of it, but she'd wanted more than kisses. If they'd had a blanket, and she hadn't been worried about a random farmer stumbling upon them, she might have kept going.

In the seven years that had passed since she'd met Rick, she'd had a few semi-serious boyfriends and one relationship that had lasted two years. They'd been nice guys. Decent in bed. But she'd never felt the same heart-pounding, starry-eyed longing with *anyone* that she'd felt with Rick at Clear Lake. A feeling she hadn't experienced again until now.

Shit. What was she going to do?

When her phone started buzzing, she jumped. *Sofia.*

She answered in a low hiss. "Sofia. It's five thirty in the morning."

"I know, but I just got home from an all-night party, and I didn't feel like going to sleep. Plus, I needed to give you some awesome news."

"What kind of news?" With Sofia, it could be anything from a smoking-hot hookup to a stunning new travel destination. Olivia had lived vicariously through her for years.

"I know you said you didn't need my support, but I reached out to a few sponsors just in case. Now I'm coming to Cyprus! Isn't that the best?"

Didn't see that one coming. Olivia took a second to respond. "Wow. That's…fast. Who'd you get as your sponsors?"

"One of them is this swanky resort near Kouklia called Aphrodite Gardens. Because it's Aphrodite's island, of course. Speaking of that fickle goddess, how's your love life? Is Mr. Hottie still being an asshole, or did you decide to bang it out of your system?"

"Sofia!"

"*Aha.* You did, didn't you? Was it superhot?"

It would be. Now that she'd kissed Rick, she could imagine going further. A warm flush crept across her cheeks, making her grateful they weren't on FaceTime. "Of course not. But…um…he did kiss me. And I didn't hate it?"

"Didn't hate it? That's a ringing endorsement."

"What do you want me to say?" Realizing her voice had risen, Olivia scoured the field for movement, but no one was stirring yet. *Thank God.* She needed this conversation to stay as private as possible.

"Be honest, you coward. Admit you loved it."

"Okay, it was amazing. If we hadn't been all grimy…" Olivia paused. The dirt and sweat had made the whole experience even more of a turn-on. "If we hadn't been out in the open, with nothing to lie on except a tarp covered with dirt, I would have gone a lot further."

"Yes! Why can't you? Obviously not when you're working, but why can't you sneak out somewhere and do the deed?"

"There's literally nowhere to go, and we can't take one of the cars without permission. Besides, the guy who's in charge—Grant—doesn't want any of us hooking up. We're supposed to serve as good examples for the students." She hadn't forgotten the veiled threat he'd given the staff on their first night in Cyprus.

"These are college students, right? What do you think happens when they're away from home? They're hooking up constantly. That's half the fun. Grant sounds like a dick."

As usual, Sofia never minced words. "He is, but he's got a lot of power."

"Maybe I should have a chat with this Grant." Sofia let out a squeal. "Is he hot? I love a good challenge."

Olivia shuddered, not wanting to imagine her sister with anyone that toxic. "He's okay. Tall, blond, kind of Scandinavian-looking. But more like an icy businessman than a sexy Viking. You'd be better off steering clear of him. He's got too much negative energy."

"Then no, thanks. Good vibes only, please. What are you up to today?"

"We have a day off, so we're going to the beach in Coral Bay." After a hot, grimy week, she couldn't wait to get into the water.

"Did you pack the bikini I sent you? The one I bought at the flea market in Florence?"

As gorgeous as it was, Olivia had been too chicken to wear it in public. Not when it left so little to the imagination. "That swimsuit's pretty revealing. I brought it, but I was planning on wearing a tankini."

"Wear the bikini. You know Mr. Hottie will totally dig it. Get it? Dig it? Because he's an archaeologist?" Sofia yawned loudly. "Damn, the buzz is wearing off. I have to crash. I'll text you more about Cyprus once I know my dates. Catch you on the flip side."

Olivia set down her phone with a lengthy sigh. After two years apart, she should have been thrilled to see her little sister. But field school was demanding enough without Sofia's high-energy, zero-filter personality. She wasn't exactly known for her discretion.

Don't stress. You've got enough to worry about

Besides, today was Olivia's day off. For once, she wasn't going to obsess over what came next.

WHEN THEIR GROUP ARRIVED AT THE PUBLIC BEACH IN CORAL BAY, Olivia assumed they'd have no trouble scoring a spot to lay out their towels. But the place was unbelievably crowded. Lounge chairs with blue and white umbrellas blanketed the area. Families with little kids and teenagers clumped in large groups. Vendors moved through the crowds hawking ice cream and soda. The air carried a tang of salt water mixed with the pervasive aroma of coconut sunscreen. But even if the beach was packed and chaotic, it was still a beach. The sea was a perfect shade of turquoise, the waves cresting in gentle swells.

Though everyone else wanted to sunbathe, Olivia was eager to get in the water. "Anyone up for a swim?"

Rick stood up. "I'll go with you." He pulled off his t-shirt and dropped it onto his towel.

Damn. Though Olivia had seen him shirtless before, that had been years ago. Viewing him now, in all his muscular glory, stirred up butterflies inside her. She licked her lips and quickly averted her eyes.

After a moment of hesitation, she shrugged off her cover-up, revealing the bikini Sofia had sent her. Given that she was on the curvy side, Olivia had never dared to wear a swimsuit this small before. But when she stole a glance at Rick from under her lashes, she was glad she'd worn it. Because he was definitely checking her out. As her cheeks flamed, she raced toward the water before anyone could catch her blushing.

The waves were cool at first, though nowhere near as chilly as the Pacific Ocean. Once she adjusted to the temperature, the water felt heavenly. She treaded water alongside Rick until he suggested they swim out to a large, flat rock just past the breakwater.

When he reached the rock, he hoisted himself up and stretched out on his back, closing his eyes. Water droplets glistened on his bare chest. "Mmm…this is perfect."

She flopped down beside him. As she snuck another peek at his firm muscular body, she imagined leaning over him, tracing his broad shoulders with her fingers and stroking his lean stomach. Or lying back and letting him make the first move. Heat flooded through her as she envisioned those strong, callused hands exploring under her bikini.

Rick's voice jolted her out of her fantasies. "You're so quiet. What are you thinking?"

That I'd like to kiss you. Or run my lips across your chest and taste the salty tang of the sea on your bare skin.

Whoa. She needed to get a grip. "Nothing much. Just glad to be out here. That water feels so good."

He rolled on his side and propped himself on one elbow so he was facing her. She turned toward him, acutely aware he was only inches away and they were both wearing next to nothing.

"I never get tired of the ocean," he said. "If I ever directed my own dig, it would have to be within driving distance of a decent beach."

"Is that why you chose to work in the Mediterranean?"

"Maybe, although I've excavated plenty of landlocked sites. But, yeah, I love it here. The weather's so warm you can work outside almost all year long. The food's great, and you can't beat the scenery. Most of the people I've met have been so welcoming."

"You've had so many adventures. I'm kind of jealous."

He flicked water droplets at her. "No need to be. You still have plenty of chances for adventure, especially if you embrace your inner archaeologist. You're starting to enjoy it, right?"

"Yeah, that site I found definitely gave me field cred." The thought of it made her swell with pride.

"Absolutely. I don't think you'll have any problem getting Roth on your dissertation committee. He was blown away by our samples, especially that piece with the Phoenician writing. He might send us back there to dig a few more test pits."

Her heart started its wild dance. Given what had happened the last time they were alone, she didn't know whether to feel excited or anxious. Too much temptation might be dangerous. "I'm glad he was impressed."

"He should be." Rick leaned in closer and tucked a strand of hair behind her ears. "It doesn't have to end here. If you want to go back into the field again, you could do it during your summers. You'd still have the rest of the year to teach and focus on library research."

For the first time in years, she allowed herself to consider the possibility. To travel and seek out adventures. To not be so focused on playing it safe that she missed her chance to embrace the unknown. "What about you? Do you think you'll stay in the Mediterranean indefinitely?"

"I'm not sure. Remember the night you caught me on the phone? That was my sister, Cassie. Our dad's having a biopsy next week, but she's worried it might be cancer. She wants me to come home. So I've been thinking about flying back to San Francisco once we're done here. I wouldn't want to live in the city, but I could see myself putting down roots in California again."

California. She didn't want to get ahead of herself. But if he was living in the same state as she was, they wouldn't have to lose touch. The possibilities were tantalizing.

"Sorry about your dad," she said. "I can see why you'd want to go back."

He released a harsh breath. "The thing is—I haven't been home in almost four years."

Four years. Even when her parents annoyed the hell out of her, the longest she'd been away from them was the two months she'd spent in Athens doing research. Despite the miles separating her and Sofia, they talked and texted constantly.

Though she didn't want to pry, she sensed Rick was giving her an opening. "Can I ask why?"

"My dad pretty much disowned me when I dropped out of law school. He said if I didn't go back, I wasn't welcome at home."

There was still so much about Rick she didn't know. "You went to law school?"

He dipped his chin in concession. "Yep. Worst idea ever."

When he didn't follow up, she sat up and stretched out her legs. If he wanted to talk, he'd keep going. If not, she'd respect his decision. She squeezed out her wet hair, letting the drops fall on her thighs as she waited for him to continue.

He eased himself up until he was sitting beside her and placed his hand on her thigh. "The law school thing? One hundred percent my dad's idea. I don't know if you remember, but he runs a law firm with big-money clients. That's why our family's so well-off. Dad wanted me to follow in his footsteps, but I had no interest. So we made a deal. I could take any classes I wanted in college, as long as I got good grades and agreed to apply to law school. Even if I sometimes had *too* much fun, I still made the Dean's List every semester."

She stayed silent, not wanting to rush him. Around them, the waves crashed against the breakwater. A speedboat raced by, loaded with cheering tourists. But they were alone on their own slice of paradise, with no one around to break the spell.

"During my junior year of undergrad, I did a semester abroad in Rome," Rick said. "It was unbelievable. I fell in love with the ruins and all the history."

She'd felt the same way during her two months in Athens. Even if she'd gone there to do archival research, she'd still geeked out when she first set foot on the Acropolis. "I'm not surprised. At Clear Lake, you told me you'd wanted to be an archaeologist since the third grade."

"Good memory. Yeah, I'd always dreamed about it, but that semester sealed the deal. When I got back, I told my dad I wanted to get a doctorate in classical archaeology instead of a law degree. He said it was the dumbest thing he'd ever heard."

Her heart ached for him. Though her parents might not fully understand why she was so passionate about ancient history, they'd never said anything so hurtful. "That's awful."

"Yeah, it was rough. What's worse is that I didn't have the guts to stand up to him. Instead, I backed down and applied to law school during my senior year at Berkeley. I got into three places but ended up choosing Stanford."

Stanford. Her mind reeled. She'd always thought he was smart, but this was next-level. Getting into Stanford meant he'd gotten exceptional grades and crushed the LSAT. "Impressive."

"You'd think so, wouldn't you? But once I was there, I hated it. I begged my dad to let me pursue archaeology or ancient history instead. If nothing else, I could get an MA and teach high school history. He refused to listen."

She wanted to go back in time and console that version of

Rick. Instead, she placed her hand over his, hoping her touch would comfort him. "What happened?"

"I dropped out of Stanford after the first semester. When I went home for Christmas break, my dad was furious, but I held my ground. So he kicked me out and cut me off completely. I bought a ticket to Rome, crashed with friends there, and started looking for fieldwork in Italy. A week after I left, I called my dad to see if we could reconcile. I left messages. Sent emails. He never answered. Eventually, I stopped trying."

"I'm so sorry."

"Thanks. I tried to make him understand. I told him I'd get student loans and pay for school myself, but he didn't give a shit. Not if I wouldn't play his game. My mom still talks to me, and Cassie's been good about reaching out, but I'm worried about losing them forever."

Emotion clogged Olivia's throat. She hated that Rick's father had cut him out of his life because he didn't fit the acceptable mold. A few times, her parents had suggested she consider teaching high school rather than spending years getting her doctorate, since she wasn't guaranteed a job in her field. But they'd never made her feel unworthy.

"I wish there was something I could do to help," she said.

"Just listening is a huge help." He put his arm around her. "It's nice to be able to talk about it."

She wanted to say more but froze when he traced the bridge of her nose with his finger. "You're getting freckles from the sun, princess."

His gentle touch made her tingle all over. "Better than a sunburn, right?"

"Definitely better. Though I'd be happy to rub aloe anywhere you need it."

"Stop tempting me," she grumbled.

"*I'm* tempting you? You're the one wearing the world's smallest bikini."

Maybe Sofia had been right. "You like it?"

"Like it? I can't take my eyes off you. You're so fucking sexy."

A thrill coursed through her, setting off goose bumps on her bare arms. "What are you going to do about it?"

When he cradled her face in his hands, her body responded like she'd been charged by an electric current. Ensnared in his gaze, she couldn't find the will to pull away. He threaded his fingers through her wet hair and claimed her lips. She nipped at his bottom lip, then slid her tongue against his, tasting salt water. Lost in the heady rush of desire, she kissed him back passionately, dizzy from the flood of sensations. But when she reached out to stroke his bare chest, he pulled away with a sigh.

A bemused smile played on his lips. "You're impossible, you know that?"

She bit back a giggle. "Impossible to resist, you mean?"

"Exactly. Thanks to you, I'm trapped on this rock until my hard-on dies down." His swim trunks had tented up in a display unfit for a public beach.

"I couldn't help myself. You can probably get it under control if you get back in the water. Or…"

"Or what?"

"Or you could just keep kissing me." She shaded her eyes toward the beach. "They can't see us, can they?"

"Not if we're lying down." He lay back on the rock and pulled her beside him.

The feel of his sun-warmed body heated her like an inferno. She met his eyes with a sassy grin. "I like the way you think."

And then he was kissing her again, and she gave way to her desire, even if only for a few more minutes. At some point, they needed to talk. Figure out what they hell they were doing, risking temptation like this.

But not today.

CHAPTER SIXTEEN

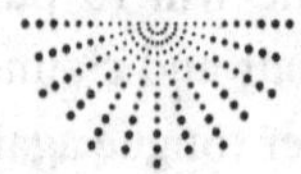

Olivia groaned as her phone alarm went off. Day ten of survey meant waking up early for breakfast duty. No easy feat, considering she'd been up past midnight. She hadn't planned to stay up late, but when Rick brought out his guitar, she couldn't resist joining him. After everyone else drifted away, she spent another hour talking to him. She loved hearing about the projects he'd worked on and the people he'd met. Though her life seemed dull in comparison, he'd listened eagerly to her family anecdotes and tales of academia.

When she got to the camp kitchen, no one was there except Rick, who whistled as he filled the kettle with water. Even at five thirty in the morning, with his hair still mussed from sleep, he looked as devilishly handsome as ever. For a moment, she watched him from the doorway, freely ogling his broad shoulders and sturdy biceps.

When he turned to face her, his smirk suggested he knew exactly what she'd been doing.

She bit back a grin. "Um…hi. TJ's not here yet?"

"I didn't wake him. I figured we could handle breakfast on our own."

Her heart rate kicked up a notch. "So, we're alone?"

"For the moment." He moved in closer and caressed her cheek. "I've been dreaming about you every night."

His gentle touch sent shivers through her. "Same here. But I want more."

"Me, too."

A thought came to her. "Didn't you say Dr. Roth was really excited about my Geometric site? Do you think we could convince him to send us back there?"

He grinned. "Are you hoping to find more artifacts or trying to be alone with me?"

"A little of both, maybe?"

He brushed his finger across her lower lip, making her tingle with anticipation. "I think we could make that happen."

Her breath caught. "Soon?"

"The sooner the better."

The kitchen door burst open. "Hey, guys, sorry I'm late for—" TJ stopped short. "Oh, shit."

Rick pulled away from her quickly, but their intimacy was impossible to miss.

Olivia cleared her throat. "Sorry, TJ. That was totally unprofessional."

"Like I care?" TJ said. "I kind of wondered about you two, anyway. On that first day, you were giving off serious enemies-to-lovers vibes."

Despite Olivia's discomfort, a laugh tumbled out. "Enemies-to-lovers? I didn't realize you were that familiar with romance tropes."

"My sister loves all things romance, so I've watched my share of rom-coms." He glanced around furtively. "I won't tell anyone, but you shouldn't let Grant get wind of this."

"That was the plan," Rick said. "You don't mind keeping things quiet?"

"Hell, no. I love a good secret. You want me to leave, or—"

Olivia blew out a long breath. "No, you can stay."

Not only had the mood passed, but TJ's appearance had made her realize how careless they'd been. Anyone could have woken early and walked into the kitchen.

At least now Olivia had a plan. After today's survey, she'd approach Dr. Roth during lab and ask if she and Rick could dig more test pits at her Geometric site. Then they'd be guaranteed some uninterrupted time together.

WITH THE SECOND WEEK OF SURVEYING ALMOST OVER, THE TEAMS had moved from the coastal plain to the hilly areas around Kouklia. Although Olivia's success in finding a site had given her a boost of confidence, the hill country was a huge challenge. Today's drive took them a half hour from camp, past tiny villages and farms. At one point, they waited patiently as a shepherd crossed the road with a large flock of sheep.

Earlier in the week, Brynn had switched to Grant's team so she could work with Courtney. Knowing that Grant was now responsible for the two most demanding members of the field school filled Olivia with a malevolent glee. In return, Rick's team had gotten Alisha, an easygoing Black woman who took delight in one-upping TJ's stories. Though she'd only worked on one other dig, she'd traveled extensively due to her father's job in the foreign service.

At the moment, she and TJ were going toe to toe over their experiences in Italy. "I still think Rome is overrated," TJ said.

"Oh really?" Alisha demanded. "Hello? Get me the Pope on the line. Listen, Your Eminence, but your city is highly overrated."

"That's Vatican City, not Rome."

"Are you telling me I don't know my geography? I lived in Italy for two years, you fool."

"But Rome's full of tourists," TJ said. "So's Florence, for that matter. Venice, too. If you want to explore the country, you've got to go deeper than that."

"I don't need deep. Not when I have the world's best gelato and a kick-ass plate of pasta."

Olivia nudged Rick. She rarely missed a chance for physical contact. A nudge here, a touch there. "Don't you want to jump into the debate?" she asked. "You spent a semester in Rome."

"Yeah, but I don't need either of them getting pissed off at me. Better to stay out of it."

He pulled over beside a dilapidated wooden fence that stood above a valley. The area around them was composed of rolling hills, covered with scrubby bushes, olive trees, and terraced vineyards. Flocks of sheep and goats grazed at random intervals. Small stone houses dotted the landscape, but the region was sparsely populated. They were truly in the backcountry of Cyprus.

Rick gathered them around. "This area is tricky. Steep inclines and narrow goat paths mean surveying will take longer than usual. The reception sucks, so your phones might not get a signal. Watch out for the ravine on the way back, and keep in mind the terraces might throw you off. Since you won't be able to walk in a straight line, you'll need to rely on your GPS more than ever. Does everyone have enough batteries?"

Olivia checked her pack. Since the Greek brand of batteries they used didn't last long, they always carried spares with them. "I'm good," she said. The others nodded.

"You've all been crushing it this week," Rick said. "I'm impressed we've beaten Stuart's team three days running, but I still need you to be careful. I wouldn't want anyone to break an ankle."

Olivia shuddered. Frida had mentioned how painful her break was, and she'd only been ten minutes from a major hospital. Getting treatment in such a rural part of Cyprus could take much longer.

Despite Rick's warnings, Olivia had no difficulty navigating her first transect. But her second one took her through uneven terrain as she crossed terraced slopes and navigated vineyards filled with twisted vines and thick grapes that gave off a cloying, musty smell.

Though she tried to stay focused, her mind wandered as she imagined returning to her Geometric site with Rick. After the passionate kisses they'd shared at Coral Bay, she'd been dying to get him alone. She would have paid serious money to spend the night in his arms, preferably at a beachside hotel with a comfy bed and room service. But she couldn't imagine Dr. Roth condoning such unprofessional behavior.

"Kalimera."

Olivia backed up. She'd been so lost in thought she'd almost bumped into an old man making his way through the vineyard. He appeared harmless, his face lined and weathered with age. Even so, she didn't want to be alone with him. Her first instinct was to take off running, but he offered her a wide smile, displaying crooked teeth.

She returned his smile. "Kalimera."

Waving a wrinkled hand, he gestured for her to come closer.

She shook her head. "No, thank you…ah…óchi, efcharistó."

When he beckoned again, she backed away hastily. Her heel caught on a tree root and threw her off-balance. As she stumbled backward, the GPS unit flew from her hands and smacked against a rock. She fell onto her tailbone. The pain was so sharp it made her eyes water.

He offered her his hand. Swallowing her fear, she took it.

Don't panic. He's just being friendly.

Once she was back on her feet, he motioned for her to wait. After retrieving her GPS, she clutched the straps of her daypack, prepared to bolt at any moment. She almost laughed out loud when he returned with an enormous bunch of red grapes and thrust them at her.

Her paranoia now seemed a tad extreme. She took the grapes and gave a little bow. "Sas efcharistó."

Though she suspected he wanted her to stay and chat, she needed to get going. She edged backward, smiling and waving. Most of the grapes went in her pack to save for the drive home, but she kept a handful out. They were sweet and delicious.

Ahead of her, a flock of goats blocked her path. *Not docile, remember?*

Rather than approach them and risk getting head-butted, she decided to go down to a lower terrace and reorient herself after she passed the herd.

Her route took her though another vineyard. The thick, tangled vines cast a dark shadow, making her feel like a character in a fairy tale with enchanted trees and a witch lying in wait. Heart pounding, she hurried her pace, only to trip over her shoelace. As she bent down to tie it, a piece of chipped stone caught her eye. She unearthed it, revealing a jagged rock. The stones around her feet were equally unimpressive. Not artifacts— just boring old rocks.

When she righted herself, a wave of dizziness sent her reeling. Around her, the rows of vines appeared so similar she couldn't recall which direction she'd been facing earlier. She made her way out of the vineyard, blinking as she emerged into the bright sunlight.

Feeling thoroughly disoriented, she fought off a surge of fear. As soon as she got back on track, she'd be fine.

She checked her GPS, but the screen didn't light up. Her fall must have dislodged the batteries. She opened the unit and wedged them back into place. The GPS stayed dark, even after she turned it off and on again. She swapped out the batteries and tried a third time. Still nothing.

Her dread grew as she recalled the noise it had made when she'd dropped it on a rock. This was bad. No GPS. No clue which way to go. No one else in sight.

As her panic accelerated, her breath caught in a strangled gasp. She grabbed her inhaler from her pocket and took a quick puff.

Calm down. If you freak out, your asthma will get even worse.

Before doing anything else, she needed to call Rick and let him know her GPS wasn't working. She took out her phone, but the screen didn't show any bars. When she tried calling him, she couldn't connect.

Come on, technology. You're seriously letting me down.

Time to bring out her topographic map. She regarded it like a long-lost friend. "You won't fail me, will you?"

Based on the contour lines of the map, the path of her transect dipped down to a lower elevation. If she followed it correctly, she would reach a ravine with a small stream flowing through it.

Within ten minutes, she came upon the top of the ravine, but the incline was steep and scary looking. She sat on the edge and scooted down on her butt but slid too quickly. Flailing her hands in desperation, she grabbed onto a shrub. Sharp thorns stung her palm, making her cry out in pain. Her heart hammered wildly. If she wasn't careful, she'd end up like Frida. Her hand trembled as she let go.

Inch by inch, she made her descent, but when she reached the bottom, there was no stream. She was in the wrong place.

Her throat tightened. Hands on her knees, she bent over and took slow, steady breaths.

Straightening up, she walked until she found a spot that wasn't as steep. Clutching thorny bushes, she scrambled up the hill, scraping her knees on the rough ground. By the time she reached the top, she was gasping for breath and still had no idea where she was supposed to go.

I'm such an idiot.

Why had she panicked when the old man had approached her? If she'd behaved calmly, she wouldn't have fallen and dropped her GPS. Frustration burned inside of her, but she forced herself to think rationally. There had to be a familiar landmark somewhere.

In the distance, goats grazed on an upper terrace. The flock looked like the one she'd seen earlier. The tightness in her chest eased as she made her way toward them.

Once she reached the goats, she reviewed the map again. The contour lines were helpful when she took the time to decipher them properly. Coming out of the spooky vineyard, she'd headed south instead of east. She'd descended the wrong hill, which was why she hadn't seen a stream.

She followed the map heading east, her confidence growing. No GPS? No problem. Her map-reading skills had saved the day. When the ground sloped and revealed another ravine, she offered up a quick prayer. *Please let me be on track.*

The hill was slight compared to the last one, allowing her to descend it painlessly. A small stream flowed at the bottom, the burbling water soothing her frazzled soul. She walked over to it and splashed cool water on her face. Much better.

Then she made the mistake of checking her watch.

No. She should have been at the car twenty minutes ago. This wasn't a "little late." It was a five-alarm catastrophe.

If she hustled, she could make up for lost time. She took off speed walking, ignoring the tight rasp in her lungs.

Faster. Hurry.

Her chest tightened in a vise grip. She plopped down and sucked in air but couldn't get enough. Time to bring out her inhaler. With another hit, she'd be good to go in a few minutes. She jammed her hand into her pocket, but it wasn't there. A growing sense of alarm crept over her as she checked her other pocket. Nothing.

She dumped out her daypack, but her inhaler didn't magically appear.

The last time she'd used it was when she'd emerged from the

creepy vineyard. But it could have fallen out anywhere after that, including the first ravine she'd descended.

Still seated, she braced her hands against the hard ground and took slow, measured breaths. Gasping for air was the worst thing she could do, but she couldn't relax. Her chest felt like it was trapped under a huge weight.

She couldn't make it to the car on her own. She couldn't walk, couldn't cry out for help. All she could do was gulp in air. No matter how hard she tried, she couldn't get enough.

Her head spun with dizziness. Black spots blurred her vision.

She couldn't pass out. What if no one ever found her?

She could die in this ravine.

CHAPTER SEVENTEEN

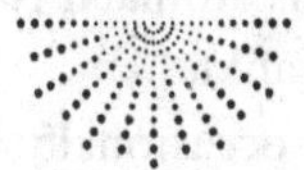

Rick sat in the shade of an olive tree, writing up his notes from the day's survey. He was so engrossed in his work that he startled at the sight of TJ, Alisha, and Marisol standing over him. "What's up?"

"It's close to one," Alisha said. "And we haven't seen Olivia."

"We've been waiting for twenty minutes," TJ added. "I'm worried something happened to her. I tried to call her, but I couldn't get a signal."

Rick's heart constricted. Olivia hadn't slowed them down for over a week. There was no reason for her to be this late. He stuffed his notebook into his pack and got to his feet.

"Maybe she found a site," Marisol said. "That would explain why she's not here yet."

It would, except the hilly area they'd been covering had barely yielded any pottery. His pulse spiked, but he kept his voice calm so as not to alarm the others. "I'll go look for her. TJ, keep an eye on things here. If she shows up, try to call me, even if you have to drive down the road to get reception." He tossed him the car keys.

TJ put them in his pocket. "Got it. Should we do anything else?"

"Nope. I'd rather have the rest of you in one place." Rick grabbed his topo map, scanning it to see where Olivia's transect should have taken her. The ravine or the terraces could have thrown her off, but her GPS should have worked, regardless. Something was wrong. His stomach twisted as he imagined her in pain, felled by a broken ankle.

He took off running, occasionally stopping to call out her name. When he came upon the crest of the ravine, he yelled again and got a weak reply in return.

Scrabbling down the incline, he reached the bottom and jogged alongside the stream. Olivia sat beside it, hunched over and gasping for breath.

"Olivia!" He ran toward her. "What happened? Are you hurt?'

She shook her head and clasped her chest, like she was too winded to speak.

He squatted beside her. "It's your asthma, isn't it?" She'd had an attack at Clear Lake once, but she'd gotten it under control. "Do you have your inhaler with you?"

"Lost...fell out." Still straining to breathe, she clenched her hands into fists.

He brought out his phone and tried calling Dr. Roth. Nothing. He felt so fucking useless.

"You had your inhaler earlier, right?" When she nodded, the tension in his shoulders eased. "I can go look for it. Did you lose it in the first transect or the second?"

"The second."

"Okay." He took a deep breath. At least he had a plan of action, providing Olivia could hold out a little longer. "If I retrace your steps, will I be able to find it?"

"Not sure. I was...off track."

"That's okay. I'll comb the general area. It shouldn't take me too long." Offering her a reassuring smile, he stood up. He didn't want to leave her alone when she was scared and vulnerable, but her asthma wouldn't go away on its own.

He scaled the ravine quickly and headed toward the terraces, half walking, half jogging, as he kept his eyes on the ground.

She'll be fine.

But if she couldn't get enough oxygen, she might pass out. The thought of her lying unconscious was more than he could bear.

How was it that she'd captured his heart again in such a short time? That day when they'd been alone, excavating her newly discovered site, the pull between them had been too strong to resist. It had only strengthened as they worked together each day. Sharing stories during the drive, bantering and flirting, using the smallest excuses to touch each other. At night, he fantasized about whisking her off to a hotel room and making love to her all night.

But as much as he wanted her, he hated the thought of hurting her. After this gig ended, he didn't know where he'd end up. Even if he went back home, he couldn't make any promises. He hadn't committed to anyone in over four years.

You could if you wanted. Why not let someone in for once? What's stopping you?

Catching sight of a large flock of goats, he reared back abruptly. Enough brooding. He needed to focus.

Below the edge of the terrace, something gray and plastic caught his eye. He knelt and scooped up Olivia's inhaler. Rather than stash it in his pocket, he clutched it tightly as he turned and ran back to her.

When he returned, she was still bent over. He placed the inhaler in her hands, then waited as she took a puff. After two minutes, she followed it up with another. No matter how long her recovery took, at least now she was out of danger. Relief washed over him like a tsunami.

"We're not in a rush," he said. "Take as long as you need." He gave her a quick grin, hoping to provide some levity. "Or I could carry you the rest of the way. We're less than fifteen minutes from the car."

She glared at him and shook her head emphatically.

Good. If she could scowl like that, then she was doing a little better.

"We'll wait until you're able to stand." He pulled out his phone. "Maybe I'll get a signal when we're closer to the car."

He sat next to her, keeping quiet while she got her breathing under control. Goat bells jingled in the distance. The breeze cooled his skin, bringing the smell of dried grass and sage. He would have appreciated his surroundings more if he hadn't been so worried about her.

When her wheeze turned into a deep, rattling cough, he startled. "You okay?"

She thumped her chest and cleared her throat a few times. "Almost there. Thanks for finding my inhaler."

"No problem. I'm glad one of the goats didn't take it. They eat everything."

"Speaking of eating…" A hint of a smile crossed her lips. She opened her pack and brought out a huge bunch of grapes. "Want some? An old guy gave them to me when I wandered through his vineyard."

"Sure." He grabbed a handful and tossed them in his mouth. A little squished and warm, but otherwise sweet and delicious.

After a few more minutes, she put the inhaler in her daypack. "We can go now."

He helped her up, catching her when she stumbled. As their eyes met, he wanted to take her in his arms and hold her, just out of sheer relief. But he turned away, not wanting to reveal the depth of his feelings. "Let's get moving."

They followed the path of the stream at a steady pace. When Olivia spoke, her voice was strained and hoarse. "Thanks for coming to get me."

"I'm sorry I didn't look for you sooner. Were you in that ravine the whole time?" She must have been terrified, worrying no one would ever find her.

"No. I got lost, and then I panicked, and my asthma kicked in."

"You got lost? Wasn't your GPS working?"

"I…sort of freaked out when an old villager approached me. I fell backward and dropped it on a rock. I think I might have broken it. Sorry." As she said it, she ducked her head like she was afraid to meet his eyes.

He groaned in frustration. Even if the mistake was an honest one, Grant would be livid that she'd ruined a piece of the school's survey equipment. If they couldn't fix it, they'd have to find another one for her to use during the rest of the survey.

"Rick?" Her voice wavered. "I don't want you to get in trouble because of me. I'll take the heat, I promise."

Regardless of whether she took the blame, he was still the team leader. Now he looked terrible, returning to camp almost an hour late with nothing to show for it. But he got his exasperation in check at the sight of tears glistening in her eyes. Screw Grant and his fucking schedule. All that mattered was getting Olivia out of danger and bringing her back to camp. He placed his hand on her arm.

She met his gaze with a fearful expression. "Please don't be mad."

"I'm not. I was really worried about you. From now on, take a backup inhaler, okay? I don't want anything like that happening to you again."

Saying the words made him realize how deep he was getting, but he didn't care. He didn't want to experience that fear again.

She sniffed and wiped her eyes. "You're being way too nice about this. But thanks."

He drew her close and hugged her tightly, feeling her tremble under his touch. Letting out his breath in a ragged exhale, he held her until he'd gotten his emotions under control. He kissed the top of her head and inhaled her familiar scent—a mixture of sweat, sunscreen, and lavender-scented shampoo. When he released her, the relief in her eyes made his heart soar.

By the time they reached the car, she'd fully recovered, other than the occasional cough.

TJ ran toward her. "Olivia! You're all scraped up. What happened?"

"I headed in the wrong direction, fell into a ravine, and had an asthma attack," she said. "Not my best day of surveying. Sorry I'm so late."

"It's okay," he said. "We were more worried about you than the stupid schedule."

"We walked all over the place trying to get a signal with our phones," Alisha said. "We thought if we could reach someone at camp, we could let them know what happened, but we didn't have any luck."

More than ever, Rick was glad they'd off-loaded Brynn, who would have bitched about being late. Instead, Alisha and Marisol offered Olivia the rest of their water. He hustled all of them into the Kia and barreled along the sharp roads at a furious clip, but there was no way to make up for the time they'd lost.

When they walked into camp, lunch was over, but no one had started their lab work. Instead, the staff and students sat at the picnic tables, waiting for the inevitable showdown. Grant stood beside them, arms crossed, making no attempt to hide his rage.

They were in trouble.

CHAPTER EIGHTEEN

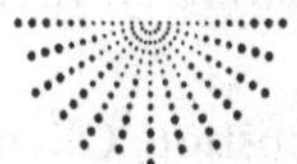

Though Olivia was no longer struggling to breathe, her prolonged asthma attack had left her shaky and light-headed. Now that she was back at camp, all she wanted to do was retreat to the sleeping quarters and collapse on her cot. But she couldn't leave until she faced down Grant. She needed to make him understand that Rick wasn't to blame for their delay.

Their confrontation would have been slightly less nerve-racking if the entire field school hadn't been present, still seated at the picnic tables.

Grant approached them, boiling over with fury. "This is completely unacceptable. Your team was almost an hour late."

Rick held up his hands. "We had a few problems but nothing to worry about. Everyone's fine."

Olivia spoke up quickly. "It's my fault. I got lost because I dropped my GPS and it stopped working. I'm hoping it's just a temporary glitch." When Grant's scowl deepened, she offered up a weak smile, hoping to win him over. "Thankfully, I used the map to orient myself. Funny thing about maps—they might be low-tech, but they can still prove surprisingly useful."

Wasn't that what archaeologists had relied on fifty years ago? If anything, she was being resourceful.

"If you were able to find your way back, then why are you over an hour late?" Grant glared at Rick. "I'm not surprised this blunder happened on your watch."

Why did Grant have to be so petty? And why waste time scolding them when they were all tired, thirsty, and ravenously hungry?

Fighting back her exhaustion, Olivia put strength behind her words. "Rick didn't do anything wrong. When I was rushing to finish my transect, I had an asthma attack. Somewhere along the way, my inhaler fell out of my pocket. If Rick hadn't found it, I could have died."

The shocked expressions around her served as validation. Despite her mishap with the GPS, it was her asthma—not her terrible sense of direction—that had caused the lengthy delay.

Grant pinned her in his gaze. "So, you broke your GPS *and* lost your inhaler? Very careless on your part. I'll need to report this incident to Dr. Roth."

Her shame vanished, replaced by a surge of anger. "I didn't mean to lose it! Do you think I wanted to have an asthma attack in the middle of nowhere?" She was crossing a line, but she didn't care. Not after everything she'd been through.

Dusty hopped off the picnic bench and strode toward them. "Dr. Nilsson! Are you writing up Olivia because she has asthma? What kind of ableist bullshit is that?"

Grant stepped back, as though unnerved by the force of her words. "I'm reporting her because her carelessness made her team unacceptably late."

"She was sidelined by a medical condition," Dusty said. "That wasn't her fault."

Even if she appreciated Dusty's support, Olivia didn't need anyone fighting her battles. "Thanks, Dusty, but Grant's right. I wouldn't have gotten lost if I'd been more careful. But if anyone should be punished, it's me, not Rick." She turned her focus back to Grant. "You want to report me to Dr. Roth? Fine. But I'm coming with you. I don't need you twisting the truth or blaming Rick for what happened."

Her stomach churned. If challenging her immediate supervisor wasn't bad enough, now she was doubling down by demanding an audience with the dig director. She'd be lucky if Dr. Roth didn't send her packing immediately.

Goodbye, dissertation committee.

With a heavy heart, she addressed the students. "I'm sorry you had to see this. It won't happen again."

Grant glared at them. "Why are you still here? If you've finished lunch, you should be starting your lab work. *Now.*"

The students scattered, as though afraid his wrath might settle on one of them next. Olivia turned back to Rick, who hadn't moved from his spot behind her. "I'm not sure what's left of lunch," she said. "Maybe you could take the team into Kouklia to get a bite to eat. I can pay you back later."

Rick kept his voice low. "And leave you here? I don't want you to face Dr. Roth alone."

His supportive words lifted her spirits, but she didn't need his protection. She could handle Dr. Roth on her own. "Thanks, but I've got this." She gave Grant a cloying smile. "Should we head over to the field house?"

"There's no rush. We can wait until Dr. Roth arrives for the afternoon lab session."

No. She wouldn't let Grant shame her in front of the students again. "I'm not waiting. Let's do it now, before I pass out."

AFTER REFILLING HER WATER BOTTLE AND GRABBING A HANDFUL OF figs from the kitchen, Olivia followed Grant out of camp and down the road that led toward the village. The ten-minute walk felt twice that, what with Grant glowering at her the entire time. The field house was a small, picture-perfect bungalow made of cream-colored stone, tucked at the end of a quiet side street. A large lemon tree bursting with plump yellow fruit shaded the front yard. The bright blue door displayed a cast-iron knocker in the shape of a lion's head.

Grant unlocked the door with his key. "I let Dr. Roth know we were coming, but he wasn't pleased. He doesn't like being disturbed while he's working on his research."

She refused to let him saddle her with guilt. "I would think he'd want to know if there were any problems with the staff or the students."

"He doesn't. That's my job. I prefer not to involve him unless it's a serious issue."

Like Rick's team coming in last? Hardly something she'd consider "serious," yet Grant had deemed it worthy of the professor's attention last week.

Compared to the harsh conditions at Camp Kouklia, the field house felt like an idyllic vacation retreat. The inside of the home was old and rustic, with thick wooden beams, arched doorways, and whitewashed walls. Woven rugs in muted blues and grays covered the stone floors. Along the walls, ceramic plates and tiles provided vibrant splashes of color.

Dr. Roth called out to them. "I'm in the kitchen."

Despite the traditional design of the house, the kitchen was tricked out with gleaming appliances and granite countertops. Dr. Roth stood beside a shiny Italian coffee maker, holding a ceramic cup. "Would either of you like some coffee?"

"That's not necessary," Grant said. "We don't want to waste your time."

Dr. Roth turned to Olivia. "Are you sure? It's no trouble."

So far, the professor didn't seem upset that she'd invaded his solitude. She flashed him a grateful smile. "Thanks. I don't suppose you have any iced coffee? Or anything cold to drink? I'm still kind of dehydrated."

"You poor thing. Of course." He opened the fridge and brought out a glass pitcher. "Vietnamese iced coffee. My housekeeper makes it for those mornings when it's too hot for cappuccino." He poured her a glass.

Olivia took it with shaky fingers. The first sip was a taste of heaven, the bitterness of the coffee cut by the splash of sweetened condensed milk.

"Let's go onto the back patio," Dr. Roth said. "Then, Olivia, I'd like you to tell me what happened."

Grant sputtered. "But I—"

Dr. Roth shook his head. "If you insist on involving me in the day-to-day drama, we'll do things my way." He led them out the back door to a paved stone patio. A vine-laden pergola shaded a wicker table and four matching chairs. Beside it, a worn stone fountain burbled softly, adding to the tranquil ambience.

After a few life-giving sips of iced coffee, Olivia told Dr. Roth what had happened on the survey. At first, her voice shook with nerves and exhaustion, but she gained strength as she went on. In describing her ordeal, she didn't downplay the mistakes she'd made. If she hadn't overreacted to a harmless greeting from a local villager, she wouldn't have dropped her GPS. And if she'd placed her inhaler in her daypack after using it the first time, it wouldn't have tumbled out of her pants pocket.

Even as she admitted her failings, she also emphasized the physical peril she'd been in. Had Rick not found her inhaler, the afternoon could have taken a dark turn. Recounting the story, however painful, allowed her to paint Rick in a heroic light.

When she was done, Dr. Roth regarded her with compassion. "Are you sure you're all right? There's a clinic in Paphos if you need medical attention."

His concern eased the stress weighing on her shoulders. "I'm fine. A little dizzy, but I'll take it easy this afternoon. I'm sorry for all the trouble I caused."

Dr. Roth stroked the end of his beard. "You found your way with just the topographic map?"

"That's right. I love maps."

His smile crinkled the corner of his eyes. "When I was a student—back in the Dark Ages—we didn't use anything except a map and a compass when we were surveying. It was more of an adventure then. I place more value on an archaeologist who can read a map than one who relies solely on technology. You never know when you'll need your map-reading skills."

She released a pent-up breath. Who knew Dr. Roth was as passionate about maps as she was? "I still use one when I have to drive long distances."

"As do I." Dr. Roth fixed Grant with a cool gaze. "Quite honestly, I don't see what the fuss is about."

Grant's mouth gaped open. "Are you serious? After all the times her team has disrupted the schedule by coming in late? Not that Olivia is entirely to blame. Most of the problem lies with Rick's inability to keep his group on track."

"From what I understand, his team only lagged during the first few days of the survey," Dr. Roth replied. "Obviously, we want to make sure the students are back in time to do their lab work, but this incident wasn't Rick's fault. If anything, he went above and beyond in his determination to help Olivia."

His praise made her heart swell with happiness. She couldn't wait to share it with Rick.

"That's it?" Grant demanded. "No one gets to be punished? If nothing else, Olivia should pay for the GPS unit she broke. It belongs to the school and cost over three hundred dollars."

"I'm not convinced we can't fix it. Juno's remarkably good at salvaging troublesome tech. At this point, Olivia has been through enough already, and Rick did nothing wrong." Dr. Roth stood, effectively dismissing them. "If you don't mind, I've got work to do. Olivia, make sure to rest this afternoon. If you're still dizzy tomorrow, I'd suggest you stay back at camp and work in the lab. We don't want to take any risks."

"Thanks," she said. "I'll see how I feel in the morning."

Even if she was weak and bone-weary, she felt vindicated. Not only had she defied Grant, but she'd also told Dr. Roth *her* version of the story, and he'd supported her. As long as she stayed on his good side, she still had an excellent chance of securing him for her dissertation committee. She couldn't wait to tell Frida. Her friend would be proud as hell that Olivia had stood up for herself.

As they left the field house, she slowed her pace, hoping Grant would go on ahead. She wanted to bask in her moment of triumph without him stewing beside her. When he didn't leave her side, she decided to push him a little further. For over two weeks, she'd tolerated his dismissive behavior without fighting back. That ended now.

"Grant? Can I ask you something?"

He made no attempt to hide his irritation. "What is it?"

"Why do you resent me so much? You criticize me constantly, and you rarely treat me with the respect I deserve. You don't treat Stuart this way. Is it because I'm a woman?"

"Of course not. How dare you accuse me of being sexist?"

She rolled her eyes. "That's not what I said. I asked if you're treating me differently because I'm a woman."

"I suspect your emotions are clouding your judgment."

On any other day, she might have backed down, but Dr. Roth's support had gone a long way in boosting her confidence. "Are you gaslighting me right now? I know what I've heard. Dusty and Stuart have noticed it, too."

He drew to a halt. "You want the truth? You don't deserve to be here. You have no field experience, you've never surveyed, and you're not prepared for the grueling physical challenges involved."

"Because I have asthma? Or had an allergic reaction to some plants? I've still gone out on the survey every day, and I'm the only one who's found a site worth investigating."

She no longer cared that he ranked above her on the academic ladder. She wanted answers.

Grant's jaw tightened. "Did Frida tell you what happened last year when she was a TA here?"

She called you a joyless control freak. "She said…you two clashed at times."

"That's putting it mildly. From the day she arrived, she questioned my authority constantly. Supervising a field school isn't an easy job, and she made it much harder. More than once, she challenged my orders in full view of the students."

"She didn't mention that. I assumed you two had different styles of leadership."

He gave a short laugh. "We couldn't be more different. I'm a stickler for rules, but Frida didn't respect that. Rick's the same way. It was bad enough when I found out he was going to be working here, but I was dreading Frida's appearance even more. I was extremely gratified to learn she wouldn't be coming."

Never mind that she broke her ankle and all.

As if sensing Olivia's judgment, he frowned. "I wasn't happy she was injured, but I was relieved I wouldn't have to deal with her. Once I found out she wasn't coming, I sent Dr. Roth a list of names, all of whom had plenty of experience. Instead, he chose you, based on Frida's recommendation."

Though she didn't owe Grant an explanation, Olivia felt the need to defend herself. "When my graduate adviser asked me to fill in, I wasn't her first choice. But those other students you mentioned? They already had jobs lined up."

"Even so, Dr. Roth gave Frida's suggestion more weight than mine. Assuming you were anything like her, I wanted to assert my authority immediately. It was the only way to make sure I retained full control."

A plaintive meow caught Olivia's attention. A tabby cat had wound its way around her ankles. She bent down to pet it. "Have you ever considered you might be going overboard in trying to control every aspect of field school?"

He sucked in his breath. "I'm going to chalk up your naiveté to your lack of experience. Obviously, you have no idea what can go wrong on a dig."

Believe me, I do. "I'll admit sometimes students break the rules, but—"

"This isn't just about breaking the rules. It's about students behaving recklessly and putting themselves or the site in danger. My first year as a TA, the dig director was too busy chasing women to supervise the undergrads. He didn't care what they got up to or whether they broke the law. Imagine his surprise when two of them were pulled over for drunk driving. *In Greece.* It took a lot of finessing to make that go away."

She shuddered. At least when she and Rick had committed their offenses, they'd been in the US. "Did you get in trouble?"

"No, because I wasn't the one in charge. But in the ten years I've been in the field, I've seen all kinds of stupidity, as well as errors that could have been avoided if the students followed the rules and stuck to the schedule."

As the tabby left, Olivia straightened up. "I get it. But so far, I haven't broken any rules. I'm not sure how Frida undermined your authority, but that's not my intent. So, in the future, I'd appreciate you judging me on my own merits rather than on my friendship with her."

He nodded. "Fair enough."

If this was his version of a concession, Olivia would take the victory, however slight. She was about to suggest they keep walking when Grant nailed her with a flinty gaze.

"What about your friendship with Rick?" he asked. "Can I pass judgment there?"

Her stomach dropped. Had she gone too far in painting Rick

as a hero? "I…I'm not sure what you mean. I was grateful he came to my rescue, but that's it. He would have done it for anyone on his team."

Grant gave a snort of disbelief. "Hardly. You think I don't see what's going on? Rick angling to put you on his survey team. The two of you going off together to explore that site you found. You joining him at night when he brings out that god-awful guitar. I may not condone relationships in the field, but that doesn't mean I'm oblivious."

She clenched her hands. "Nothing's happened between us."

"Not yet. But Rick's a serial womanizer, so he'll try to make a play at some point." He smirked. "Have you heard what happened at Palaikastro? The real reason he was fired? It wasn't just because of his drinking. He seduced the dig director's daughter."

She was grateful she'd heard the real story from Rick. "That's not my concern. We're just colleagues. I enjoy working with him, but that's the extent of it."

"Good. Because I'd hate to imagine how Dr. Roth would react if he learned today's carelessness had been brought about by *distraction*. That you were so caught up with your 'colleague' that you couldn't focus on your job." He gave her a nasty smile. "I doubt he'd approve. If anything, he'd want to distance himself from you academically, and he certainly wouldn't want to serve on your committee. If you value your career, I suggest you steer clear of deadweight like Rick."

Fuck. She should have known Grant wouldn't concede so easily. She steeled her expression, not wanting to reveal how much he'd upset her. "Don't worry about me. I'm too serious about my future to get involved with some shovel bum."

Even as she said it, she cringed inwardly. Rick was so much more than that. But she couldn't let Grant know the extent of her feelings. He'd twist her relationship with Rick into something sordid and spread the word all over camp.

"Then perhaps you're more mature than I thought," Grant

said. "That being the case, wouldn't you prefer to work with someone else for the last week of the survey?"

His words crawled up her spine like a spider. Was he challenging her? Testing her to see if she'd choose Rick, no matter what the consequences? Her throat lurched with a hard swallow as she weighed the choice that lay ahead of her. Even if she wanted to be with Rick, she couldn't risk it. The stakes were too high for both of them.

She had to stop this train before it went off the tracks and derailed their futures. "Sure. Why don't you put me on Stuart's team?"

The more distance she put between her and Rick, the better.

CHAPTER NINETEEN

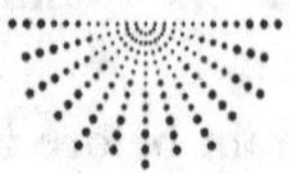

For the last hour, Rick had busied himself preparing the topographic maps for next week's survey, but he couldn't concentrate. His mind kept flashing back to Olivia, alone in that ravine and struggling to breathe. He couldn't forget the way she'd trembled when he held her in his arms. She should have been resting at camp with a cold drink instead of pleading her case to Dr. Roth.

When Grant returned to the lab alone, Rick's fear escalated. Where was Olivia? Had Roth decided to let her go? If he sent her packing, she'd be devastated. Worse yet, she might never venture into the field again.

He couldn't let that happen. If he could catch Roth alone, he'd speak on Olivia's behalf.

Leaving TJ in charge of their team, he took off, intending to jog over to the field house. But when he walked past the women's sleeping quarters, he stopped short. Olivia sat on the porch, staring out into the distance with a vacant look. Though she'd taken off her socks and hiking boots, she hadn't yet changed out of her survey clothes. "Olivia?"

"Hey, Rick." Her voice lacked its usual cheerful enthusiasm.

"Are you okay?"

She gave him a slight smile. "I feel like you ask me that a lot."

He sat on the porch next to her. "Sorry. But you almost died today. Then you took on Grant in full view of the field school and insisted on an audience with Roth. I've been waiting to find out what happened, especially after Grant came back looking smug as hell."

Rick had spent the last hour envisioning worst-case scenarios —something he rarely ever did. More proof he was getting in too deep with Olivia.

"It's all good," she said. "Roth wasn't even mad at me. In fact, he was pleased at my ability to use a map. I also told him this incident wasn't your fault. You scored major points by rescuing me from imminent death."

"That's such a relief. Thank you." He reached over and took her hand, stroking her palm gently. "I was so proud of you for standing up to Grant."

"Thanks. It wasn't easy, but on the walk back, I found out why he doesn't like me. Maybe he'll ease up now since I…" She pulled her hand away, looking uneasy.

"You what?"

"Grant asked me if you and I were involved. Not asked as much as hinted. He's been paying attention."

Of course he was. He couldn't wait for Rick to screw up again. "We haven't done anything wrong."

"I know, but we need to be careful. He already has it out for you. And if I get in trouble again, Dr. Roth might not be as forgiving. Especially if…"

"If what?" An iron band tightened across Rick's chest.

"If he thought I got lost today because I was distracted. Because of us. *Together.* I can't mess things up with him."

"But—"

"Let me finish. When Grant asked me if I wanted to switch teams, I said yes. I'll be working with Stuart next week." Her gaze sank to her feet. "I think it's for the best. The less time you and I spend together, the safer we'll be."

Her words stunned him. How had they gone from furtive kisses to this? "That's it? You're going to ignore the connection between us?"

She wouldn't meet his eyes. "What connection? I fell in love with you when I was nineteen. I'm not that person anymore."

As the frustration built up inside of him, he made no attempt to hide it. "Then who exactly was I kissing when we dug that test pit? It sure seemed like you. If memory serves me correctly, you were as into it as I was. The same with that day on the beach."

When he placed his hand on her thigh, she turned to face him, anguish swirling in her deep brown eyes. "We just can't. Okay? It's too risky."

"Tell me those kisses meant nothing."

Her bottom lip trembled. "They meant everything. I wanted you to keep going. I wanted *you*. But we can't break the rules again and hope we don't get caught. Didn't you learn anything from Clear Lake?"

Her stubbornness was maddening. "This isn't the same. We're not breaking any laws. We're two consenting adults who want to spend time together."

"Two adults with targets on our backs. Don't you get it?"

"I don't. Because these aren't actual rules we're talking about —they're Grant's attempt to control us. And he's full of shit if he thinks Roth cares about any of it." At her wounded look, he softened his tone in the hope of persuading her. "We still have almost four weeks left. Don't you want to enjoy them together?"

"And then what?" Her voice shook. "We'd be risking our futures on a *fling*. I'm sorry, Rick. I really like you, but it's not worth it." She got to her feet. "I need to lie down. Can you tell the others I'll see them at dinner?"

As she left, he stayed where he was, too devastated to move, as her words echoed in his head.

It's not worth it.

Like a fool, he'd almost convinced himself that it was.

~

WHEN THE THIRD WEEK OF THE SURVEY STARTED, GRANT HANDED out an updated list of the teams. Though he claimed a few students had asked for the chance to work with different leaders, Rick knew the truth. Olivia had left his team because Grant had pressured her into it. Now that she was working with Stuart, Rick had gotten Logan, a laid-back college junior with a reputation for being a slacker. Even if he exerted minimal effort, his easygoing attitude was preferable to Brynn's whining.

Rick tried not to dwell on Olivia's absence. He had enough to worry about, just keeping his team on track during the hardest part of the survey. But he missed the way she'd livened up the drives by chatting about random topics or singing along to cheesy pop tunes on Viva FM. He'd tried seeking her out in the evenings, but she was always with Dusty or Stuart, making it impossible to catch her alone. When he'd brought out his guitar, she hadn't joined him.

Screw that.

If she didn't want him, he was better off without her. Maybe she'd been right about the risks involved. For all he knew, Roth might not condone casual hookups in the field. If Rick hoped to snag a recommendation from him, he didn't want to come across as unprofessional.

By the time the last day of the survey unit rolled around, Rick had convinced himself he'd moved on. Their final drive took them deep into hilly territory. Whether due to their cumulative exhaustion or the twisty roads that played havoc with their stomachs, the group stayed silent for most of the trip.

When Alisha emerged from the back seat of the Kia, she

groaned. "I call shotgun on the return trip. Those roads are making me queasy."

"This drive was the worst," Logan muttered. "I'm sick of surveying."

"Not me," Marisol said. "I like exploring these hills. It feels like an adventure."

Rick was pleased by how far she'd come. At the start of the week, she'd gotten the courage to stop shadowing him and now covered her own transects with little difficulty.

He motioned for his team to gather around. "Like Logan said, today's our final day of the survey unit. I know these last few drives have been rough, but I appreciate all of you not puking in the rental car." For that, he got a few chuckles. "You've done a great job, so let's finish up strong. Your transects will cover the usual terrain—a mix of goat paths, terraces, and hills. Is everyone's GPS working? Anyone need spare batteries?"

"I'm okay," Marisol said. The others agreed with her.

"Let's get going. If we finish early enough, we can grab some ice cream in Kouklia on the way back. My treat." As Rick said it, he thought of Olivia and their perfect day together, but he thrust the memory from his mind. He didn't need any distractions.

Despite the uneven terrain, his team finished the first transect in decent time. He was almost done with the second one when he crested a ridge overlooking the Xeros River. Knowing this was his last day to hike in the hills, he slowed his pace. He wanted to commit the scenery to memory in case he never got a chance to explore this part of Cyprus again.

When he stopped to take a photo, a piece of chipped stone caught his eye. He knelt and held it up. The brittle black stone had a translucent appearance, like obsidian. He set down his daypack and combed the area. His excitement grew as he unearthed a few more artifacts: a worn, round stone with a hollowed-out center, a broken projectile point, and a harvesting knife. Around his feet were pieces of chert, a hard gray stone that produced sharp-edged pieces when it was broken. It was often used to make cutting tools and weapons.

If he wasn't mistaken, he'd stumbled upon the remains of a prehistoric site. The location was perfect—decent view, close to the river, near a large grove of olive trees.

He pulled a whistle out of his pocket. After Olivia's incident, Grant had decided all the students needed to carry whistles in case of emergency. Rick blew on it a few times, hoping one of the others might hear him.

TJ came running, his oversized pack banging against his back. "Rick! You okay?"

Rick waved him over and handed him the obsidian flake. "Check this out."

TJ smoothed the black stone between his fingers. "Looks like imported obsidian. This could be a sign of an Aceramic Neolithic site. Maybe ninth or tenth century BC." He picked up the piece of chert. "Clear signs of flint-knapping. Do you know what this means? You've struck gold!"

Rick laughed. Only an archaeology geek would react this way over a few stone tools.

As TJ examined the other pieces, Rick checked his watch. If they bagged up the samples now and hustled back to camp, they wouldn't be late. But he wanted his team to share in the excitement. "Can you track down the others? I'd like them to see this."

"Sure. But first, can you call Roth and let him know what's up? I'd prefer not to get our asses chewed for coming back late."

"The reception's crap, but I'll try." Once TJ took off running, Rick grabbed his phone and punched in the professor's number. To his relief, the call connected. It went straight to voicemail, but he was able to leave a message.

When TJ returned with the others, Rick showed them his finds. "Sorry to make you put in extra steps, but I wanted you to see a Neolithic site—or at least evidence of it. These sites are a lot less common on the island, so finding one is a big deal."

"Does that mean the win goes to us?" Logan asked. "Stuart said there's a prize for the best find during the survey."

"I think so," Rick said. "Right now, I could use more photos and samples. Can you spread out and give me a hand? The more artifacts we find, the better."

They fanned out, pawing through the dirt. Letting out a joyous cry, Marisol held up an intact projectile point. "This looks like an arrowhead I saw in a museum."

"Nice job," Rick said. "Set it in your finds bag."

The entire team worked with enthusiasm, even Logan, who let out a Keanu-like "whoa" when he found another arrowhead. Alisha circled the area, taking pictures. When she was done, she gestured for them to stand next to her. "Team shot! We need one with all of us together."

They crowded next to each other, sweaty, dirt-streaked, and happy, as Alisha took the photo. For a fleeting moment, Rick wished Olivia could be present to share in the thrill, but he pushed her out of his mind.

He'd made a major find on his last day of the survey. He'd redeemed himself and brought his team a little joy.

He didn't need Olivia.

CHAPTER TWENTY

After her painful incident in the ravine, Olivia worried her carelessness had jeopardized her chances of succeeding as a TA. Even though Dr. Roth had supported her, she'd been so afraid of messing up again that she'd spent the following day sorting pottery in the lab. However, the work was so tedious she longed for another chance to prove herself on the survey. Once Juno fixed her GPS, Olivia was determined to get back out there.

Rather than let her mistakes sideline her, she'd learn from them and move on. That was what she should have done seven years ago instead of becoming so risk averse.

Despite her apprehension, she'd gotten through her last week of surveying without any issues. Since her topo map had proven so useful, she'd been relying on it more. Before each day's outing, she studied the contour lines to determine what the hill country had in store. Knowing where she was going heightened her confidence.

Olivia's final transect took her up a steep hill, but she made the climb without needing her inhaler. Standing on a ridge overlooking a valley, she took a moment to appreciate the view:

the rolling green hills, the vineyards, the small stone cottages, and the gnarled olive trees. Thanks to the survey, she'd gotten to explore a part of Cyprus most tourists never saw. She'd even used her Greek when she'd crossed paths with local villagers.

The breeze ruffled her hair. The sun warmed her skin. Though she'd found surveying to be a challenge, she wasn't afraid of it anymore.

She wished she could tell Rick how she felt. At first, he would insist that he'd been right all along. But more than anything, he'd be proud of her.

Nope. Not going there.

Even if she'd grown more comfortable with surveying, the past week had held other challenges. She'd made sure Rick never caught her alone. Every time she heard his guitar, she resisted temptation by holing up in the research library and helping the students with their site presentations. But at night when she lay on her cot and looked up at the stars, she couldn't get him out of her mind.

She told herself it was better this way. Neither of them could afford to fall out of favor with Dr. Roth. But it didn't stop her from desperately wanting Rick. She missed him so much it hurt like a physical ache.

When she reached the car, Stuart sat beside a scrubby bush, reviewing his field notebook. Getting to work with him was the sole upside of joining his team. Their easy friendship didn't leave her heart in a tangle of raw emotions.

"First one back," he said. "Anything good out there?"

Brushing aside a few dried branches, she sat beside him. "Not a thing. Trust me, I was looking." Her stomach rumbled, reminding her she'd skipped breakfast. She rooted through her daypack until she found a squished granola bar at the bottom. Not ideal, but it would tide her over until lunch.

"These hilly areas are tough. Usually, it's a whole lot of

nothing unless you hit the exact right spot." Stuart set down his notebook. "Last day of survey. What's your final verdict?"

"I like it. I'm glad I got to see this side of Cyprus, and I'm in better shape than when I started." She glanced at her bare forearm. "Even my sunburn turned into a tan."

Stuart chuckled. Because of his fair complexion, he always wore long sleeves, pants, and a hat. "I wish I could tan like you, but I can't risk it. I've had my share of agony-inducing sunburn." He took a bunch of grapes out of his pack and handed her a cluster. "Grapes?"

"Thanks. I thought California grapes were good, but these are the sweetest I've ever had."

"Yeah, they're great." He spat a seed into the bush. "You looking forward to the party tonight? Gotta admit, I'm kind of surprised we're having a party halfway through field school. Every dig I've been on, we didn't celebrate until the project ended."

"Maybe Dr. Roth does it because the survey unit is so intense? Either way, it should be fun. I guess."

She wanted to drum up more enthusiasm, but she didn't feel much like celebrating. Avoiding Rick had been stressful enough during the workweek. How was she supposed to act around him at a party? Should she keep shutting him out? Treat him like a colleague? Neither option held much appeal.

Stuart cocked his head to the side. "That doesn't sound like a ringing endorsement. Did you and Rick have a fight?"

Damn. Why was she so transparent? "Wh…what do you mean?"

"Last week, you guys were together constantly. Now you avoid him at every chance. I asked Dusty if she knew anything, but she clammed up. Normally, she doesn't keep secrets from me."

"Rick and I aren't together. Not anymore. It was a bad idea."

"Because of Palaikastro? He didn't do anything wrong."

"I know." She stared at the ground, too ashamed to meet Stuart's eyes. "We...we have a history together. Sorry I never mentioned it before. I met him seven years ago—back when I went on my first dig."

"The one that shall-not-be-named? You were so excited about it before you left, but when you came back at the start of sophomore year, you wouldn't tell me anything."

A rush of heat traveled up her cheeks. During their second-year Latin class, Stuart had tried to pry a few details out of her, but she'd remained tight-lipped. "I didn't want to talk about it because it ended badly. Rick and I were totally irresponsible and broke a ton of rules. When we got caught, we were both expelled from field school."

"Olivia Sanchez got expelled from a class? You've got to be kidding me."

She put her head in her hands. "I'm not. That's why I never talk about it. I can't afford to make the same mistakes again. No matter how I feel about Rick, I need to act like a professional. Especially if I want to impress Dr. Roth."

Stuart barked out a laugh. "You're kidding, right? You think Roth's going to care if you hook up with someone? The guy's all about field rules."

She met his gaze with an incredulous look. "I thought he was married."

"He's been divorced for about ten years. From what I've heard, he hooks up on every dig. He hasn't tried to hide it, either."

"Even here? I haven't seen him with anyone."

Then again, why would she? Dr. Roth didn't spend much time at camp and always went back to the field house after dinner. He could easily indulge in a passionate affair without any of the students taking notice.

Stuart shrugged. "I'm not sure who he's with this year. Last summer, he fooled around with his housekeeper. The year before that, he was with a paleo-ethnobotanist who joined the team for a few weeks. None of his flings ever last longer than a season."

Though Olivia wasn't in any position to judge, she still found the revelation somewhat unsettling. Dr. Roth gave off such a paternal vibe that she didn't want to envision him as a serial womanizer.

"If you want to be with Rick, then go for it," Stuart said. "As long as you're not breaking any laws, Roth won't care about your after-hours behavior."

As the rest of the team came into view, he switched gears and waved them over. "All right, everyone, let's pack it in. If I can beat Juno back to camp, she'll owe me five euros."

During the drive, Olivia mulled over Stuart's words. Since Grant had worked with Dr. Roth last year, he was clearly aware of the senior professor's womanizing. That meant Grant had deliberately misled her, making her think Dr. Roth wouldn't approve of her and Rick. No doubt Grant had done it to keep her in line.

Knowing she'd pushed Rick away based on Grant's lies made her feel even worse than she had before.

To Stuart's dismay, they pulled into camp only seconds after Juno, making her the victor in their daily wager. Olivia washed up and found a spot at the picnic table beside Stuart and Dusty. As they regaled her with a story about Egypt, she got so caught up in the conversation that she didn't notice Rick's absence until Juno brought it up. Olivia's apprehension grew as she checked her watch. His team should have been back by now. Had something happened to them? Given the steep terrain they'd been traversing, one of them could have been injured.

After they finished lunch, the entire group waited in uneasy silence. With each passing minute, Olivia's anxiety escalated. She checked her watch, then her phone, then her watch, flitting between the two.

When Rick's car pulled into the parking area, she released a tight breath. No matter what had delayed them, they'd made it back to camp. Rick led the way, with his team following close behind. None of them looked injured. If anything, their walk had an air of bravado.

Grant sprang from the table and marched over to them. Olivia tensed up, anticipating an unpleasant confrontation. She wanted to leave but couldn't make herself pull away.

Before Grant could utter a word, Dr. Roth strode over to join them. Olivia stared in shock. Apart from the first day of lectures, the professor had never shown up at camp before two.

"Rick!" Dr. Roth exclaimed. "Just got your message. I can't wait to see what you found."

Rick grinned. "Thanks. Our team uncovered evidence of a Stone Age site—possibly early Neolithic."

Our team. Olivia swallowed back a lump in her throat. If she hadn't distanced herself from Rick, it would have been her team, too.

Rick passed Dr. Roth a large Ziploc bag filled with obsidian flakes and chipped stone tools. The professor took out a perfectly formed arrowhead made of light brown stone and held it up. He let out a low whistle. "Marvelous. Looks like a Neolithic projectile point."

"The site was in a prime location," Marisol said, glowing with pride. "Lots of trees, nice vantage point, overlooking the Xeros River."

"We're talking a serious lithic cache," TJ added. "I'd say it's worth investigating."

Alisha held out her phone. "Here. Have a look."

Dr. Roth examined the pictures. No one else spoke, though Olivia caught a few of them smiling. Grant had to be seething. He couldn't yell at Rick—not when this site trumped everything else they'd found on the survey.

"We took a little longer than we should have," Rick said. "But we wanted to make sure we gathered up enough artifacts."

"Excellent work." Dr. Roth clapped him on the shoulder. "Let's not waste any time. After you grab a bite to eat, you should head back and get more samples."

Rick nodded. "TJ, you want to help? You're the lithics expert."

TJ pumped his fist. "Hell, yes. I can't wait to see what else is out there."

Olivia pasted a bright smile on her face. She couldn't let anyone know how disappointed she was to have missed out. "Great job, you guys."

"Who's going to supervise your team during lab?" Grant asked.

"I'll do it," Olivia said quickly. "That okay with you, Stuart?"

"Go for it. I'm just a little jealous." Stuart aimed a mock glare at Rick. "Curse you, Langston, for claiming tonight's prize."

"Just got lucky, that's all." Rick flashed Olivia a quick smile. "Thanks. I appreciate it."

She wanted to praise him for his amazing find, but she couldn't do it now. Not when she was perilously close to losing control of her emotions.

Tonight, at the party, she could congratulate him. Instead of avoiding him, she'd treat him like a colleague. Someone she liked and respected. She owed him that much.

If she put him firmly in that compartment, maybe then she'd be able to move on.

CHAPTER TWENTY-ONE

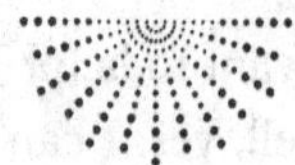

Olivia tried to approach the survey party with a festive attitude. She was going to have fun. Live for the moment. Channel her inner Sofia.

Above all, she was not going to obsess over Rick.

She was the last to arrive since she'd spent an extra hour in the lab making sure all the finds from the day's survey had been processed. After she'd showered, she wasted valuable time agonizing over what to wear. Most of her clothes were disgustingly grungy or hopelessly wrinkled. She settled on a purple sundress with embroidery on the bodice, purchased during a family trip to Baja. Maybe no one would notice the wrinkles once it got dark outside.

When she reached the picnic tables, the students were milling around and talking. After three weeks of field school, they'd attained a palpable level of comfort around each other. Teasing and in-jokes had become the norm, especially during their nightly dinners at Spyros.

Dusty waved her over. "We clean up nicely, don't we?" Like Olivia, she'd swapped out her work clothes for party attire. She was wearing a sleeveless green sundress embellished with white polka dots. Around her neck was an engraved pendant displaying Egyptian hieroglyphics.

"I love that dress," Olivia said. "Mine is all crumpled from spending three weeks in my backpack. I could have used an iron."

"What are you—my grandma? No one irons anymore." Dusty gestured to the picnic tables. "What do you think? Do they look sufficiently festive?"

Though the rest of Camp Kouklia appeared as bare-bones as ever, the eating area had gotten a makeover. The long wooden tables were covered with blue-and-white checked cloths; atop them were flickering candles set in mason jars, vases filled with scarlet lilies, and pitchers of water and lemonade. Twinkling party lights adorned the olive trees above them.

"Looks great," Olivia said. "Did you do this?"

"Me and Juno. She set up the music, too." Dusty pointed to a soundbar playing a tune that sounded suspiciously like the theme from *Zorba the Greek*. "Grant insisted on the traditional stuff, but we'll break out the bops once we're done eating. Though I wish there was booze. More chance for shenanigans that way."

"No shenanigans for me. Not tonight." *Or any night.*

"You sure?" Dusty cast a glance toward Rick, who was talking with Marisol and Alisha. "He'd probably love to celebrate his big find."

Olivia followed her gaze. Why did he have to look so good? Bad enough that he was sexy as hell when he was sweaty and dirty. He was even harder to resist when he was all cleaned up, wearing a light blue chambray shirt that brought out his tan.

Juno approached them. "Greetings, party people." She whipped out a small silver flask and took a sip.

"Is that booze?" Olivia asked.

"Of course not. It's cough syrup. For my ticklish throat." Juno gave an exaggerated cough. "Kidding. His royal grumpiness is not here yet, so I have time to imbibe." After taking another swig, she tucked it into the pocket of her long peasant skirt. "Lucky for me, tonight's ensemble has ample pockets."

Dusty snorted. "Nice. Just don't get caught."

At the sound of Rick's laugh, Olivia snuck another peek at him. Not as discreetly as she'd hoped, since Juno raised her eyebrows.

"Were you scoping out Rick?" she asked. "For a little fun later tonight?"

"What? No!" Olivia gave an emphatic shake of her head. "I need to congratulate him for finding that site. I wanted to tell him sooner, but I was too busy in the lab. That's all."

Juno shrugged. "If you like him, then go for it. Like TJ said, when we're out here, field rules apply. Why not let loose and have a little fun?"

Because my heart can't take it.

Olivia was saved from further discussion when a cohort of women from the village arrived, bringing bountiful trays of Cypriot specialties—moussaka, kleftiko, stuffed grape leaves, and grilled chicken souvlaki. Her mouth watered at the sight of her favorite appetizers: bowls of tahini and tzatziki with peasant bread, grilled halloumi cheese, spanakopita, fried zucchini, and olives. She'd always preferred appetizers to entrees, and Cypriot appetizers did not disappoint.

Dinner was more fun than she expected. Not only was the food delicious, but everyone was in good spirits. With three weeks of surveying behind them, the field school was at the halfway point. The next three weeks would focus on the excavation unit, which offered a welcome relief from the unpredictable nature of surveying. Instead of hiking through uncharted territory, the students would work at one location for the entire time.

At Olivia's table, the students took turns sharing their favorite —or least favorite—experiences on the survey. Dr. Roth joined them and told a few tales from his younger days. Even Grant appeared to be enjoying himself. He spent the entire party seated next to Dr. Lidia Bouras, a striking woman who was visiting the field school as a representative from the Department of Antiquities. From the way Grant hovered over her, Olivia couldn't tell if he was trying to schmooze with her or hoping to win her affection.

After dinner, Stuart gave out the survey awards, Juno's team performed a humorous song entitled "Somewhere Over the Transect," and Stuart and Dusty blew everyone away with their rapid-fire version of "The Model of a Modern Archaeologist." But even as Olivia joined in the teasing and good-natured jokes, her gaze kept wandering over to Rick. He sat with his team at the other table, his laughter so boisterous she couldn't ignore it.

Clearly, he wasn't missing her one bit.

When Juno switched the music from traditional Greek tunes to pop, the students held back as if hesitant to let loose. This wasn't a dark nightclub where they'd have some degree of anonymity but a camp where they lived and worked with each other every day.

"What are you waiting for? This is a party." Rick stood and gestured for Marisol and Alisha to accompany him. They followed his lead, imitating his exaggerated attempts at Greek dancing. Stuart and Dusty joined in next. Olivia longed to lose herself in the music and have fun. But as she watched Rick, a lump formed in her throat.

She wanted to be the one dancing with him. Not just dancing, but flirting and laughing and not holding anything back. Even if she could pretend he was merely a colleague when they worked together, she couldn't do it now.

She caught Dusty's attention, shouting to make herself heard over the music. "I'm going for a walk. I'll see you later."

"You want me to come with you?"

Though Olivia appreciated the offer, she didn't want to drag Dusty away from Stuart. Maybe tonight, things would finally click between the two of them. "Thanks, but I'm good. I just need a break. Have fun."

As she left the camp, the strains of music faded into the distance. She headed down the road toward the village, stopping to pet a few of her favorite stray cats. The tabby always made a beeline for her legs. She scratched its sleek head, suddenly wishing she was back at home in San Diego, curled up on the couch with the family cat, rather than stuck in Cyprus battling her uncontrollable emotions.

Without giving much thought to where she was going, she ended up at Spyros Taverna. The restaurant was bustling with customers, but she snagged a small table in the corner of the patio. The abundance of couples enjoying a romantic summer night made her all too aware of her solitary status.

After she ordered a brandy sour, she pulled out her phone to text Sofia. Her little sister was probably out partying somewhere. On a yacht. Or at a nightclub. But she was never too busy to text back.

Olivia composed her message, only to delete it. Why bother asking Sofia for advice? She knew damn well what her sister would say.

She'd order Olivia to have fun and stop worrying about the consequences. To go after Rick and tell him exactly what she wanted.

Why couldn't she do it?

You know why. The last time you followed your heart, you paid for it.

But this scenario wasn't remotely similar. She wasn't nineteen, sneaking away from camp with a hot guy, a stolen truck, and a bottle of contraband booze. She was twenty-six. If she kept things with Rick discreet and didn't break any laws, no one should care. Certainly not Dr. Roth, who seemed to live by field rules.

What's it going to be? Three more weeks of longing?

Or three weeks with Rick, savoring every moment alone with him?

Even if he couldn't promise her any more than that, they'd have a great time together.

She tossed back the rest of her brandy sour. The sweet cocktail flowed through her, loosening the tightness in her chest.

I'm going to do it. March back to camp, take Rick aside, and tell him how I feel.

Providing he still wanted her. She'd rebuffed him so many times he might not give her another chance.

Maybe a second drink would give her an extra dose of courage. She was about to wave the waiter over but froze at the sound of Rick's voice.

"Olivia? What are you doing here?"

She stared up at him, stunned that he'd suddenly materialized. "I…needed a break. A drink. Not that I'm a lush or anything, but I couldn't unwind. I mean, I should have been having fun because it's a party…but…" Unnerved by his scrutiny, the words caught in her throat.

"Can I join you?" When she nodded, he pulled up a chair and gestured to her empty glass. "Want another?"

"Sure. A brandy sour."

He waved over the young server. "Hey, Kostas, can we get a couple of drinks?"

"Sure, Mister Rick. Two beers?"

"Make it two brandy sours. Thanks."

How was it that Rick always knew everyone's name? That he seemed so comfortable everywhere he went? As he leaned back and assessed her, she flushed under his gaze, ashamed he'd caught her in such a pathetic state. What kind of loser left a party to go off and drink by herself?

"Were you looking for me?" she asked. "Or were you craving a break, too?"

"I tried to find you earlier, but Dusty told me you went for a walk. There aren't many places to go around here, so this was my first guess."

When the server set down their drinks, she focused on stirring hers with the swizzle stick, too nervous to meet Rick's eyes. "Why'd you come after me? You looked like you were having a good time."

"I was. But I'm sick of this." He gestured at the space between them.

Her heart sank. Why had it taken her so long to have her epiphany? Now she'd ruined her chances with him. "You're sick of me?"

"No." He raked his hand through his hair. "Of you avoiding me. Acting like I don't exist. If you don't want to get involved, that's fine. And if I came on too strong before, I'm sorry. But I'd like to be friends. It killed me that you weren't with me when we found that Neolithic site."

An ache built up inside of her, knowing he'd felt the same way she had. "I would have given anything to be there. Impressive find, by the way."

"Thanks." He sipped his drink. "So, can we try being friends again?"

His smile was so endearing it broke down the last of her defenses. Taking another swig of her cocktail, she looked him in the eye. "What if I want to be more than friends?"

He let out a long breath. "Don't mess with me. I already like you more than I should."

"Even after all this?"

"I can't stop thinking about you." He groaned. "You're a huge pain in the ass, you know?"

A silly grin broke across her face. "But you like me anyway?"

"Of course. Because I'm a complete idiot. Even if you cut me off for seven years, I'm still not over you."

She flinched. "Sorry. In my defense..." *Shit*. She didn't have one. She pivoted and flashed him a flirty smile. "If it helps, I feel the same way. Not that you're a pain in the ass. But I think about you constantly. I want what we had at Clear Lake, but more. A *lot* more." She held his gaze, hoping to convey the longing she felt.

He brushed his hand across her cheek. "I do, too, but I don't want you to hate me again if things go sideways."

His touch sent butterflies spiraling through her. "This time, we won't be breaking the law. Like you said, we're two consenting adults. As long as we do our jobs during the day, our late-night activities shouldn't matter."

"What about Grant? Even if we're discreet, he'll figure it out."

The young server popped over to their table to check on them, but Olivia waved him away with a brief smile before turning her attention back to Rick. "Forget about Grant. Dr. Roth is the one who matters. Right now, he thinks you're a superstar. Not only did you save my life, but you also found a Stone Age site. You're kicking ass."

"Thanks, but that's not the issue." A furrow cropped up between Rick's brows. "What if he's not okay with us together? You've got a lot riding on his approval."

"About that…?" She cleared her throat, uneasy at the thought of spreading gossip. "He has a reputation for fooling around in the field. He can't punish us for doing the same thing."

"I'd heard as much, but I'm never sure how much stock to put in rumors."

Her heart went out to him, knowing he was thinking about Palaikastro and the way his reputation had suffered, all because of the lies spread by his former employer.

"Stuart told me, and he's been working with him for years," she said. "So, Dr. Roth's not in a position to judge us, and even if Grant doesn't approve, he doesn't have the power to do anything about it." A wave of regret washed over her. "I'm sorry I let him get to me."

"Don't be. I understand. He can be extremely intimidating."

She twisted her hands together. "Are you up for it? I don't

want to put you at risk, so I'll understand if you say no." Her heart beat in a jagged rhythm as she waited for his verdict.

A tender smile played on his lips. "You think I can resist you? Not a chance. But I have to be honest. I can't promise you anything—not when my future's so uncertain."

She reached across the table and placed her hand over his. "Let's not worry about the future. For the next three weeks, let's just indulge our steamiest fantasies."

In an instant, all traces of uncertainty vanished from Rick's face. He leaned in closer, pinning her with a wolfish smile. "What kind of fantasies?"

She looked down at her drink. "You know…"

"Look at me," he growled. "I asked you what you fantasized about."

She clenched her thighs as a surge of desire raced through her. "Us…together…and um…"

"And what? Are we naked? Am I touching you? Kissing you? Tasting you until you beg for more?"

The low timbre of his voice sent her pulse racing. She met his gaze, her whole body trembling. "I…yes?"

His eyes dilated with hunger. He looked as though he was ready to strip off her clothes right there in the taverna. "Are you sure, Olivia?"

Her breathing quickened. "*Yes*. Definitely. But where—"

"Finish your drink." He tossed back his brandy sour.

She downed the rest of her cocktail, shivering as the powerful brandy hit her system. He placed a couple of bills on the table and took her hand. She stood to face him, slightly light-headed but still in control. "We aren't going back to camp, are we?"

His mouth curved up in a devilish smile. "I've got a better idea. Somewhere quiet and romantic. Want to give it a try?"

Now she was intrigued. And more than a little turned on. "Yes, please. Lead the way."

CHAPTER TWENTY-TWO

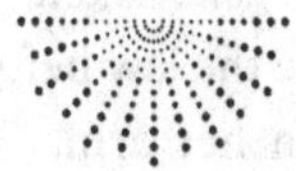

Olivia followed Rick along the road leading through the village square. They'd only walked two blocks when he turned down a street bearing a sign pointing to the Sanctuary of Aphrodite.

They'd visited the site during the first week of field school when the students had toured local monuments in the area. As far as ruins went, the sanctuary wasn't that impressive. Though it had been important during its heyday when it had served as a temple dedicated to the goddess Aphrodite, all that remained now were a bunch of broken columns, some faded mosaics, and a few rectangular areas marked by low stone walls.

Rick led them past the ticket booth—now closed for the night —to a section of the chain-link fence with an iron gate. To Olivia's surprise, he pushed it open with little effort.

"Shouldn't the gate be locked?" she asked.

"It should be, but the caretaker's not that diligent. Most nights, he's at Leda Taverna, getting drunk."

"You've…been here before?" Though she had no right to be jealous, she didn't want to imagine him here with anyone else.

"Nope. This is my first time. Juno told me about it.

Apparently, it's a popular spot for couples." He gestured to the gate. "Shall we?"

Olivia hesitated. Given that the site wasn't open to the public after dark, if they went any further, they'd be trespassing. As in, committing a crime.

Wasn't that precisely what she was trying to avoid?

"What if we get caught?" she asked. "Think how much trouble we got into when we broke the law before."

He placed his hand on her arm. "We don't have to go any further. But it's not like we're stealing a vehicle. If it makes you feel any better, Juno said the last time a couple was caught here after hours, they had to pay a fifty-euro fine."

She could handle fifty euros. She was more worried about the potential humiliation if anyone found out.

"Whatever you choose, I'll respect your decision." He gave her a roguish smile. "But sometimes the best things happen when you break the rules."

Was he referring to Clear Lake? Even if the consequences had been disastrous, they'd made some unforgettable memories. Here was a chance to make more of those memories, with a lover who genuinely cared about her. For years, she'd let her fear and anxiety stop her from following her passion. She couldn't keep living that way.

Besides, how could she pass up the chance for intimacy in an ancient temple dedicated to the goddess of sexual love?

"Let's go," she said. "Hopefully, Aphrodite will watch out for us."

The site was bathed in darkness, the only light coming from a slim, crescent moon. As Olivia made her way around the ruins, she stumbled over a large rock. Rick grabbed her arm and pulled her back.

"Careful. Next time I'll bring a flashlight."

Next time? Her pulse raced. Sneaking into the sanctuary for one night was bold enough. But making a habit of it? That was the mark of a true badass.

With no large structures to hide behind, the area around them was fairly exposed. Fortunately, the darkness provided ample cover. But when Rick almost tripped over a broken column, he took out his phone and turned on the flashlight app. Using the faint light, he led them to a rectangular area, walled in on three sides. The low stone walls provided enough of a barrier to shield them from anyone who might walk past the site. Beneath them, the ground was paved with smooth, flat stones.

Rick eased himself onto the stones and pulled Olivia toward him. "Sorry the ground's so hard. I had no idea we'd end up here, so I wasn't prepared."

She sat next to him and rested her head on his shoulder. "We can bring a blanket next time."

They sat together in the stillness. Even if the site was little more than rubble, it had lasted for centuries, playing host to thousands of steamy encounters. Back in the day, when religious pilgrims had come to worship Aphrodite, the temple priestesses offered up their bodies as part of their duty to the goddess.

Now I'll be adding to that history. The thought made Olivia shiver with delight.

When Rick whispered her name, she turned to face him. Though she was craving the taste of his lips, she let him take the lead. He started slow, placing feather-soft kisses on her eyelids, her cheeks, and the curve of her chin. His lips grazed the sensitive spot behind her ear and the hollow of her collarbones, sending flickers of desire through her. When his lips caressed her bare shoulders, she quivered with anticipation, wanting so much more.

"Should I keep going?" he asked.

"Yes. Please." She glanced at the hard ground beneath her. "Though I wish we had that blanket."

He unbuttoned his shirt, eased it off his shoulders, and passed it to her. "Here. You can lie down on this."

She took it from him but couldn't pull away. Now that her eyes had adjusted to the darkness, she could make out his well-defined figure. Reaching toward him, she stroked his chest, letting her hands graze the firm muscles. "How the hell did you get so ripped?"

He chuckled. "Lots of hard work. Digging, swinging a pick, hauling buckets of dirt. I'm glad you approve."

"I do. Very much so." She spread out the shirt behind her, then turned to him with a sultry smile. "There. All set."

With gentle hands, he pushed her back until she was lying flat. Even with his shirt to serve as a blanket, the ground felt cool beneath her. Leaning over her, he lowered the straps of her sundress and pulled it down around her waist. She shimmied her hips, allowing him to remove it completely. He unclasped her bra and tossed it aside, leaving her in nothing but a tiny pair of panties. As he gazed down at her in awe, she flushed with pleasure.

When was the last time anyone had looked at her with such undisguised rapture?

"You're so beautiful," he murmured. "Even more beautiful than I remembered."

He cupped her breasts, rubbing his thumb over one nipple and then the next until they hardened into tight buds. Though she desperately wanted his mouth on them, she wouldn't beg for it. But when she gave an involuntary whimper—the tiniest hint of submission—he lowered his head and ran his tongue along one of the buds before sucking on it. She groaned and threaded her fingers through his thick hair, wanting him to do more than just tease her. She wanted him to plunder her.

As he sucked on each nipple, she writhed underneath him, the delicious sensations coursing through her. But as sweet and tender as his seduction was, she wanted it a little rougher.

She pulled him up to face her, clasping him tightly until his bare chest was pressed against hers. When she captured his mouth with a demanding kiss, he responded with equal passion. He tasted of brandy, sweet, warm, and delicious. He ground into her, pressing his hard length between her thighs. She ran her fingers along his bare back, kneading strong muscles. Breaking away from his kiss, she nibbled his shoulders and ran her tongue along his neck until he brought his mouth to hers again.

She could do this for hours. *Days.*

Eager to feel him, she reached between his shorts, but he pulled away and flopped onto his back. "You're killing me, Olivia."

She rolled onto her side and ran her fingers along the thatch of soft brown hair covering his chest. "Killing you in a good way, right?"

He turned to face her. "In the best way. I'm so glad you didn't accept my stupid offer. 'Just friends.' What the hell was I thinking?"

She giggled. "It was a noble offer, but it wouldn't have worked."

"Agreed. Even so, I want you to know I respect you completely. I'm amazed at how far you've come in the field."

His words filled her with an unexpected pang of longing.

Don't you dare make me catch feelings. This is just a fling.

She adopted a teasing tone, hoping to defuse the powerful well of emotion building up inside of her. "You don't have to flatter me. I'm practically naked, lying with you in Aphrodite's sanctuary. I'm a sure thing."

He ran his hand along her shoulder. "I'm not flattering you. It's the truth. You belong out here."

"Thanks." Before he could say any more, she scooted closer and placed soft kisses on his chest, inhaling the scent of his spicy aftershave. When she slid her hand under his shorts to stroke him, he pulled it away again.

"None of that, missy. I might explode if we go any further." He gave a rueful sigh. "In my rush to find you, I didn't think to stick a condom in my wallet."

"We can put it on the list for next time—a flashlight, a blanket, some condoms."

Because there would definitely be a next time. Even if they only had three weeks, she wanted to take advantage of every second.

She undid the button on Rick's shorts. "Why don't I take care of this for you? To ease the pressure." A naughty thrill surged through her. "I seem to remember you enjoying it quite a bit."

When he didn't protest, she tugged on his shorts. He pulled them off, and his boxers followed. Naked in the moonlight, he looked like a Greek god come to life. Except bigger than she remembered.

"Oh my," she whispered.

He gave her a grin that was entirely too smug. "You up for the challenge?"

Hell, yes. She'd have him reduced to putty in no time.

Wanting to have complete control, she pushed him onto his back. After brushing her hair against his chest, she leaned in closer and ran her tongue along his rigid length. She took her sweet time, teasing, licking, tasting, making him want her even more.

When she took him fully into her mouth, he groaned and tangled his fingers in her hair. The feel of his hands tugging on it brought forth a rush of heat that shot straight to her core. She ran her hands along the curve of his butt, cupping it and bringing him deeper. She'd forgotten how much she enjoyed giving pleasure this way.

He groaned. "Olivia, I'm going to come."

She let him finish, not breaking her hold until he'd emptied himself completely. With a final sigh, he released her hair from his grip. She pulled away and lay back on the stone, feeling immensely pleased with herself.

She expected him to bask in the afterglow, but he sat up and leaned over her with a wicked gleam in his eye. "Your turn."

"You…you don't have to." Even though her whole body ached with need, she didn't want him to feel like he owed her anything.

"Oh, I want to. It's only fair." When he tugged off her panties, she was embarrassed by how drenched they were. But he only grinned. "I can't wait to taste you."

Her heartbeat sped up in anticipation. "Rick…"

He pressed one finger inside her, and then another, making her gasp with delight. "You're so wet. You loved doing that, didn't you? Naughty girl."

"Yessss." Her words dissolved as he bent down and placed soft kisses on her stomach and hip bones, while his fingers sought out her sweet spot, stroking and teasing.

When he parted her legs and laved her with his tongue, she let out a throaty moan. Her body tensed up, so close to release she could hardly stand it. She was vaguely aware that she was begging—pleading—for him to keep going, but she was so far gone she would have said anything to make him continue. As she reached her peak, she cried out as the sensations crested over her in a powerful wave. He didn't stop until her gasps subsided and her body collapsed in relief.

As he took her in his arms, she melted against him, her muscles loose. Like she could fall asleep this way, despite the hard stone beneath them. A cool breeze wafted over her bare skin, but he sheltered her in the warmth of his embrace.

She was so grateful he'd given her another chance. That he'd made her feel sexy and wanton and beautiful. Even if that was all he could give her, she'd take it.

Right now, she didn't need any promises.

She'd enjoy the moment, however long it lasted.

CHAPTER TWENTY-THREE

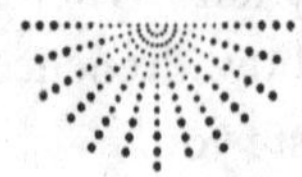

Rick knew he was grinning like a fool, but he couldn't help himself.

As they walked back to camp, he squeezed Olivia's hand. Already, he was fantasizing about their next encounter. He'd bring a pack loaded with supplies—condoms, a blanket, a flashlight, and a towel. Maybe a pillow so Olivia's head wouldn't have to rest on the hard stone.

Around them, the narrow road was quiet. No one was out, save for the usual stray cats. Naturally, Olivia stopped and petted each one. But he wasn't in any hurry to get back to camp. He liked having her to himself for a little longer.

"You're so quiet," she said. "What are you thinking?"

"About next time."

She laughed. "Next time? You're already plotting ahead?"

"Aren't you?"

"Definitely. Though a bed might be nice." She sighed. "A king bed with a comfortable mattress and big, fluffy pillows."

Even if he agreed, he couldn't resist teasing her. "Aphrodite's temple didn't do it for you? She wouldn't be pleased to hear it."

"Okay, but if you're going to be pounding into me next time, I could use a little more cushioning."

Pounding into her? The words conjured up a steamy image that flooded his brain. Olivia lying underneath him, naked and willing, moaning with pleasure as he thrust himself into her. If he wasn't careful, he'd end up with another hard-on.

As he tried to get his dick under control, an idea came to him. "After Cyprus, are you flying straight home or stopping along the way?"

"I'm staying in Athens for a week. My graduate adviser got me approved for library access at the American School of Classical Research. Since the residence hall is full, I need to book a room at a student hostel. Which reminds me, I should get on that."

Yes. He couldn't have planned a better setup. "Would you be willing to spring for a private hotel room? Preferably one with a king bed? I'd pay for half of it."

"You'd come to Athens with me?" Her voice rose in excitement. "That would be fantastic."

"Sure. The Larnaca airport is such a small hub that I need to fly out of Athens anyway, whether I go home or move on to my next job."

"Have you decided where you'll be going yet?" Her voice had a slight hitch to it, like she wasn't sure she should be asking.

Though he wanted to offer her reassurance, he couldn't comfort her with false promises. "I don't know. Either way, it wouldn't be a problem to spend a week in Athens with you."

"Then I'd love it. But…I *will* have to do research. Only during the day, though."

"If you save the nights for me, I'll be fine." He'd have no problem occupying his time in a city filled with world-class ruins. Even if he lazed around and read, he'd be happy. He couldn't remember the last time he'd stayed in a decent place. When he was between jobs, he usually crashed on someone's couch or found the cheapest hostel available.

"Then yes, please," she said. "I'll find a room with a big bed and a decent shower. But I don't want to wait until then to have sex. Like you said, it *is* Aphrodite's temple. She might be disappointed if we don't follow through."

"No argument from me." If she didn't want to lie on the cold stone, she could be on top. At the thought of her riding him, her gorgeous body illuminated by the moonlight, his dick sprang to life again.

Down, boy. We're almost at camp.

He'd have to get his libido under control when they worked together. He couldn't let his steamy fantasies distract him.

She let go of his hand. "If we're trying to be discreet, I should go on ahead. Is that okay?"

He wished he could parade back into camp with her by his side to show everyone what a lucky bastard he was. But flaunting their status in front of Grant would be like poking a beehive. "No problem. You might want to grab a brush and tackle your hair before you face the others. It's kind of wild."

Grinning, she ran her fingers through her curls. "That's your fault, but I'll take care of it." She leaned forward and placed a quick kiss on his lips. "Good night, Rick. Sweet dreams."

They wouldn't exactly be sweet. More like extra spicy. "'Night, Olivia."

He waited for ten minutes, letting his mind wander back to their encounter in the temple, replaying every blissful minute. The feel of her smooth skin beneath his fingers. The taste of her lips. The mind-blowing orgasm she'd given him. The way she'd cried out in pleasure when he'd gone down on her.

Damn. Now he needed a cold shower, but he didn't want to brave the camp shower this late at night. Plus, it wasn't exactly private.

He ambled toward camp, listening for the sounds of music and laughter, but didn't hear anything. As he reached the parking area, he came face-to-face with Grant, who was returning to the field house for the night.

Rather than scowl at his nemesis, Rick gave him a friendly nod. "Hey, Grant. Did you have fun at the party?"

"I'm not one for parties, but I enjoyed meeting with Dr. Bouras from the Department of Antiquities. I'm impressed with how much she's accomplished in the field."

Impressed with her accomplishments or her voluptuous figure? Rick hadn't missed the way Grant had clung to the woman's side. But he knew better than to bait him.

Grant gestured to the road. "Where were you coming from?"

"Just out for a walk. I needed a little break."

"I thought you'd want to enjoy the spotlight for as long as possible, given that you were in your glory after finding that site."

He made Rick sound as though he'd been boasting to anyone who would listen. True, he'd been proud of his find, but he'd given his team plenty of credit. The only one who'd veered into braggadocio was TJ, and everyone expected that of him.

Rick shrugged. "It was a group effort. I had a good team." If Grant was going to be his usual dickish self, he didn't have to put up with it. "The party must be over by now. I should see if they need help with cleanup."

As he said it, he caught sight of Olivia and Dusty dragging their cots onto the field. He wondered if Olivia was sharing secrets or keeping things quiet. Either way, he wasn't concerned since he could trust Dusty.

"Cleanup's over," Grant said. "I noticed Olivia wasn't around to help, either. Was she with you?"

Shit. He turned his attention back to Grant. "No. Wasn't she at the party?"

"According to Dusty, she went for a walk. I find it odd you were both absent at the same time. Surely the backstreets of Kouklia aren't that enticing?" His words were laced with acid.

Even if Rick no longer worried that his fling with Olivia would get them in trouble, he wasn't about to divulge anything in front of Grant. He feigned an air of casual indifference. "Didn't see her."

"You didn't happen to run into her?"

"Nope. Besides, she's not into me. Not that way."

"She said as much, but I wasn't sure whether to believe her." Grant gave a nasty smile. "She told me she was far too serious about her future to get involved with a lowly shovel bum."

Ouch. Even if she'd said the words to throw Grant off the scent, they still stung. Though Rick tried to hide his reaction, Grant saw through him immediately.

He regarded Rick with a smirk of satisfaction. "The truth hurts, doesn't it, Langston? That's all you'll ever be. Just a grunt, screwing your way through the Mediterranean. I'd call you a disgrace to the profession, but you're not at that level."

Without caring about the consequences, Rick unleashed the rage building up inside of him. "What the fuck is your problem?"

"Excuse me?" Grant blanched and took a step back.

"Are you still pissed about the field school in Crete? You need to get over it."

"Seriously? You tried to destroy my career."

Rick clenched his hands, battling the urge to shake some sense into Grant. "Bullshit. All I did was refuse to back you up because you acted like a dick. There was no excuse for the way you treated that kid."

"I'm sure he got over it. But that incident affected my entire career. Did you know the complaint stayed in my file? When I interviewed at Northwestern, the head of the Classics department brought it up. Same with my interview at UC Irvine."

You deserved it, you controlling prick. "You did just fine. Aren't you teaching at UCSD with Roth?"

"I'm an adjunct at UC Riverside. Do you know what that means? Of course not, because you don't know a thing about academic hierarchy. It doesn't matter how many articles I've published or how many talks I've given. I'm on a two-year contract with no job security."

Rick knew more about academia than most people, having worked with archaeologists at all levels. Grant's status took him by surprise. As ambitious as the guy was, Rick had assumed he'd landed a cushy, tenure-track position.

"That's not because of one incident," he said. "I'm sure there are other reasons. It's hard to get a teaching job in this field."

"It shouldn't have been. Not for me." Grant said. "My father is Dr. Olaf Nilsson. Not that the name should ring a bell with you, but he's a noted scholar of classical literature."

"I've heard of him. Distinguished professor at Princeton, right?"

Grant's sour expression curdled even further. "Exactly. His reputation is unparalleled. And here I am, teaching at a second-rate school, without a hope of tenure. Not exactly the future he imagined for me."

Rick felt a twinge of pity. He'd been there four years ago, when his father had berated him for dropping out of Stanford. "Look, I get it. I'm not living up to my father's expectations, either, but—"

"You and I are *nothing* alike. Understand? At least I've got a doctorate. You're just the pathetic nobody who tried to screw me over. So I'm not going to 'get over it.' Ever."

Rick threw up his hands in frustration. "You want to keep being an asshole, then have at it. But karma's a bitch. One day, it'll bite you in the ass."

In his opinion, it already had. Grant had no doubt assumed he'd follow his dad's footsteps and end up teaching at an Ivy League school.

Before Grant could get in another word, Rick took off. His earlier buzz was gone, replaced by a mixture of resentment and anger. He shouldn't have to suffer just because he'd called Grant on his shitty behavior.

When his phone buzzed, he checked it with apprehension. What now?

Olivia had sent him a text. *Tonight was amazing. Only 22 days until Athens.*

Followed by another. *Can't wait for that king bed!*

Forget Grant.

Rick knew what was important, and it wasn't the intense one-upmanship of academia. What mattered was making the most of life, having adventures, and connecting with people who got him, like Olivia.

CHAPTER TWENTY-FOUR

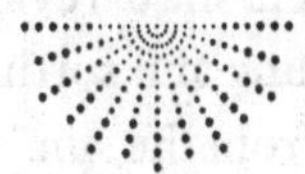

Brynn dumped a wheelbarrow load of rocks into a huge pile. "This job sucks. It's like being on a chain gang."

"The whole dig can't be this way," Courtney grumbled. "I'll die."

Olivia could relate to her team's frustration. All of them were covered in a thick layer of dirt and sweat. They'd been moving boulders and pulling weeds for hours.

"Like I told you before, this is only the first day," she said. "We're prepping the site for excavation."

"The school couldn't afford a few laborers to do this shit work?" Brynn asked. "Our tuition should have covered it."

For once, Olivia agreed with Brynn. The field school was more expensive than it should have been, especially for students outside the UC system. But Olivia couldn't admit that. "Dr. Roth wants you to experience every aspect of excavation. I promise it will get better."

Brynn plunked down next to their pile of rocks and fanned herself. "It has to be break time by now. I'm dying in this heat."

"Not yet. Make sure to drink water whenever you need it." Olivia pointed to one of the gallon jugs she'd brought from camp.

"That water's already warm," Brynn said. "We should have brought a cooler full of ice and stocked it with water bottles. Or Diet Coke."

"When do we get to do the real archaeology?" Courtney asked. "Like, with trowels and stuff?"

"Soon, I promise," Olivia said. Clearly, Brynn and Courtney hadn't been listening when she'd reviewed the process earlier. "After lunch, we'll be washing and sorting our finds in the shaded area, so you'll get a break from the sun."

Now that she and Rick had made up, life had thrown another wrench in her path. For the three-week excavation unit, the students were divided into three teams, each one assigned a different trench on the dig site. Rather than getting to work with Rick, Olivia was supervising a trench that included Brynn and Courtney, which meant she had to deal with their whining.

If that wasn't enough, TJ had decided to spend a few hours each day digging with them. As the resident lithics expert, he was meant to be working with the stone tools they'd found on the survey, but—as he put it—he couldn't resist getting his hands dirty. Though Olivia no longer minded his stories, he and Brynn sniped at each other so constantly even Courtney was fed up with them.

The students had begun excavating this morning after three days of touring Cyprus, visiting ruins and monuments, and giving their site presentations. Today, when they'd first arrived at the Nea Paphos Archaeological Park, their morning had gotten off to a deceptively easy start. They'd toured the Roman ruins of Paphos, which included three villas, an ancient theater, and a building displaying beautifully preserved mosaics.

Their dig site was located a quarter mile from the ruins in a fenced-off area that contained the remains of another Roman villa, discovered two years ago. Dated to the third century AD, the expansive villa was known as the House of Heracles. So far, it was more like the House of Giant Boulders.

Even if the first day wasn't living up to anyone's expectations, Olivia wasn't disappointed. Based on her experience at Clear Lake, she knew the excavation would get more interesting once they dug past the modern layer of dirt. Though she'd never led her own crew before, she could easily ask Rick or Stuart for help if need be, since they were supervising the other two trenches.

Juno jumped down into their trench. "Kalimera. I'm ready to rock and roll." The sleeves of her t-shirt were rolled up, revealing impressive muscles and a skull tattoo. She grabbed the shovel Courtney had set down. "Are you using this?"

"You take it. *Please.*"

Olivia regarded Juno with amusement. "What are you doing here? I thought you were supposed to be processing finds with Dusty." Earlier that day, Rick and Stuart had set up a makeshift lab consisting of four long tables shaded by a series of canopies on the other side of the site. "It's much cooler there."

"I got bored. I can only sit still for so long." Juno shot a glance at Courtney and Brynn. "I figured things might go more quickly with some real muscle." She grinned and flexed a bicep.

TJ stopped digging. "Some of us aren't slacking off. You think this is hot? When I worked in Jordan, it got up to a hundred and ten in the shade. People were dropping like flies."

"Yes, you and your Jordanian adventure," Juno said. "Sometimes I wonder if it happened or if it's an elaborate story in your head."

"It's true! Do you want to see pictures?" TJ grabbed his phone out of his back pocket.

At the sight of Grant approaching their trench, Olivia tensed up. "No pictures. Get back to work. Dr. Nilsson's on his way."

Though the assistant director wasn't participating in the physical labor of excavation, he made a point of conducting periodic inspections, in which he'd comment on their work. He'd already snapped at her team for taking too long during their morning break.

"On it, boss." TJ winked at Juno. "Remind me to show you my photos during lunch."

She rolled her eyes. "Can't wait."

Olivia dabbed at her forehead with a wet bandanna, bracing herself for Grant's inspection. While she appreciated the extra level of responsibility she'd been given, supervising her own trench wasn't going to be easy.

Still, no matter how exhausting her day, she had a sweet reward waiting for her tonight. Sneaking out to Aphrodite's temple would be a breeze since everyone would be focused on the poker tournament taking place at Camp Kouklia. Dusty had set it up after hearing TJ brag about his prowess as a card shark. Naturally, all the students wanted in on the challenge. For Olivia, it was the ideal chance to slip away with Rick. This time, they'd bring a pack full of supplies.

AFTER LUNCH, THE TEAMS SPENT THE AFTERNOON PROCESSING their finds, splitting their time between pot washing, sorting, and labeling. Rick was pleased his trench included most of his survey team—Logan, Alisha, and Marisol—who'd bonded after they'd helped him discover that extraordinary Neolithic site overlooking the Xeros River. He wished he could have worked with Olivia, but she'd learn more by running her own trench.

Besides, he'd have plenty of time with her tonight during their rendezvous at the temple.

During the afternoon break, while the others made a beeline for the table laden with grapes and cookies, Marisol continued sorting, examining her potsherds with meticulous care.

Rick came over to her. "You can take a break if you want."

She looked up at him with a shy smile. "I'll go in a minute. I just got so immersed."

He glanced down at the pile of pottery. "Kind of dull, right now, but it'll get better. Since this was a Roman villa, we might find household goods, like terra-cotta lamps or jewelry."

"It's not dull. Not to me. I still can't believe I'm touching pottery that's almost two thousand years old." She gave a short laugh. "My family's going to be so amazed when I tell them everything I've done."

He pulled up a chair next to her. "Didn't they think you could handle it?"

"Hardly. I'm the youngest of four. The baby. So they don't have much faith in me. I've wanted to be an archaeologist since middle school, but they've always acted like it was a big joke. This summer, I decided to show them how serious I was."

"This is your first dig, right?" When she nodded, he grinned at her. "You took a bold leap. Most people start with a project closer to home."

"Thanks. I could have signed up for a field school in California, but I wanted to go somewhere exciting. I love ancient history. When I was little, I was obsessed with the Percy Jackson books. Greek gods, adventures, the whole deal." Marisol tugged on her braid. "Kind of silly, I guess."

"Nah, I love those books. I've read all of them."

She twisted a piece of pottery between her fingers. "I'm kind of worried about my grade, though. I've always been an A student, but this course has been more challenging than I expected. Do you think I'll get docked points because I waited four days to go on the survey?"

"I doubt it. I'll tell Dr. Roth how you turned into a kick-ass surveyor and helped us uncover that Neolithic site. If TJ and I go back to dig more test pits, do you want to join us?"

She beamed. "Sure. I'd love to. How come we're not doing our excavation unit there? Not that a Roman villa isn't interesting, but Dr. Roth was so excited about the site we found."

"It takes a long time to set up a proper excavation—you need to get permits, consult with the Department of Antiquities, that kind of thing. You also have to prove the site's worthy of a full-scale dig, and we haven't done that yet. But maybe next year. Would you want to come back here and work on it?"

"If I do well in this course, then I'd love to. I'm having such an exciting summer."

Her enthusiasm filled him with a warm glow. This was why he loved working with students. He didn't have to be teaching in a classroom to do it, either.

Olivia approached their table with a stern look on her face. "Langston," she snapped. "What's this I heard about a poker tournament tonight?"

He put up his hands in submission. "Just a little innocent fun. That's it."

"Not for you. I'm supposed to work on the survey report, and I have questions about the Neolithic site you found. I'll need to confer with you after dinner."

He resisted the urge to grin at her ridiculous attempt at subterfuge.

Marisol's brow pinched together. "Is there something wrong? Did we make a mistake when we entered our data?"

"Don't worry about it," Olivia said. "You're doing a great job. I just need a word with your team leader. Got it, Langston?"

"Absolutely, Miss Sanchez." As he watched her walk away, he reminded himself to stay focused. No ogling her cute little ass, no matter how good it looked in her faded cutoffs. No steamy fantasies—not until they were alone in Aphrodite's temple.

After Olivia had left, Marisol spoke up. "When I first got here, I was worried about having Olivia as my TA. She seemed a little anxious. Like she wasn't sure she could handle everything. But she's way stronger than I gave her credit for."

"What do you mean?"

"The day she had that terrible asthma attack, she stood up to

Grant without crying. Then she demanded to talk to Dr. Roth. She's more of a badass than I thought."

He grinned. "Yeah, she's something."

A badass.

He'd tell her tonight. She'd be over the moon.

CHAPTER TWENTY-FIVE

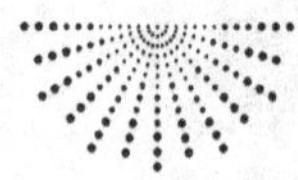

"Where's my bra?" Olivia patted the ground as she tried to find it in the dark. "Why'd you have to fling it so far?"

Rick laughed. "You're the one who insisted I take it off immediately. I had no choice but to comply."

"Too true." She couldn't suppress the contented grin that crossed her face. Perhaps she'd been a little too demanding, but Rick had responded with equal fervor. Their first time had been so passionate it had left her breathless. They'd made up for it during their second round when they'd taken things more slowly.

Rick stood and cast his flashlight around the stone walls. "Found it, along with your panties." He tossed them down to her.

She put them on reluctantly. She wanted a few more minutes to bask in the delicious afterglow of sex with Rick. Finally getting to consummate their relationship—after *seven years*—had exceeded her wildest expectations.

The only problem? Now that they'd shared more of themselves, her feelings for him had grown even stronger. She was afraid she might not be satisfied with just a fling. But she refused to let her anxiety dampen their evening. She could worry about the future later.

Once she was dressed, she folded up the blankets Rick had brought and stuffed them in his pack. He'd come prepared with two camp blankets, a flashlight, a small towel, condoms, and a large bar of Cadbury's chocolate.

As she got to her feet, she was so unsteady she almost careened into one of the walls.

Rick took her arm. "Are you all right?"

"Yeah. Just a little giddy. I mean dizzy. I mean…you know…" She smiled up at him.

"I do." He leaned over and kissed her forehead.

She slipped her bare feet into her sandals and took his hand. "All ready?"

"Ready. Though next time, we should add a brush to our supplies. Your hair is wilder than ever."

"You know whose fault that is?"

"Yours. For being so irresistible."

A giggle burst out of her. Even if his response was cheesy as hell, it made her light up like a firecracker. As they approached the gate, he opened it and led her out, only to stop short at the sight of another couple walking toward the temple.

She almost laughed at the thought of someone else coming to take their place until she recognized one-half of the couple. *Dr. Roth.* Beside him was a Cypriot woman who looked vaguely familiar.

Olivia froze like a deer in the headlights, too stunned to speak. Rick tightened his grip on her hand but remained equally speechless.

Dr. Roth approached them with a benevolent smile. "Rick? Olivia? Is that you?"

"Um…hi, Dr. Roth." Her voice came out as a squeak. "Nice evening, isn't it?"

"It is indeed." He gestured to the site. "Nice to see Aphrodite's sanctuary is still being put to good use."

Oh God. Her face flamed. She couldn't imagine anything more embarrassing than her boss knowing exactly what she'd been doing.

"Ah…nice to see you, Dr. Roth," Rick said. "Olivia and I were just headed back to camp. Right, Olivia?"

"Right. Have a good night." She didn't wait for the professor's reply but followed Rick's lead. His pace was so brisk she struggled to keep up with him. She could have sworn she heard Dr. Roth chuckle as they left.

Once they reached the road leading back to camp, she stopped and wiped her forehead. "That was mortifying. He must know what we were up to."

"I'm sure he does. But, like you said, he probably doesn't care. It looked like he was headed there himself."

She tried to shake off the mental image of Dr. Roth and his partner going at it. "But he has a house to himself. With an actual *bed*."

As much as she'd delighted in the sheer romanticism of making love in Aphrodite's sanctuary, she would have traded it for a private bed in a heartbeat.

"Yeah, but Grant's there," Rick said. "And…"

"What?"

He barked out a laugh. "I was trying to figure out where I've seen that woman. She's Dr. Lidia Bouras from the Department of Antiquities."

Olivia gasped. "No way. The one Grant was sitting with at the party? I couldn't tell if he was schmoozing or flirting."

"Knowing him, probably both, but he definitely seemed into her."

For a moment, she almost felt sorry for Grant. Given Dr. Roth's reputation, he could probably have his pick of women, but he'd chosen the one Grant wanted.

Rick squeezed her hand. "Sorry about all this."

His apology surprised her. "About what? We both enjoyed it."

"Not about the sex. That was incredible. But we almost got caught. Isn't that what you were afraid of?"

She appreciated his concern but didn't want him to feel guilty. She'd been just as willing as he had. "It's okay. Even if I'm a little embarrassed, I don't have any regrets. Do you?"

He grinned. "Nope. Though we should probably cool it with the temple for a while. Good thing we have Athens coming up in a few weeks."

She squeezed his hand in return. "Good thing."

WHEN OLIVIA WORKED AT THE HOUSE OF HERACLES THE NEXT DAY, she worried Dr. Roth might take her aside to talk to her about Rick. Or chastise her for breaking into an ancient site, even though he'd been poised to do the same thing himself. But he treated her as respectfully as ever. During the afternoon lab session, he inquired about the progress she'd made with her trench but didn't mention Aphrodite's temple.

After nearly getting caught, Olivia knew better than to push her luck. She spent the next few nights with Rick hanging out at camp and talking. The promise of Athens eased a little of her frustration.

By the fourth day of excavation, she'd hit a wall of tiredness. Even if digging at the site didn't stress her out the way surveying did, it was more physically taxing. When she'd woken that morning, her need for coffee had been so intense she'd been tempted to sprint over to the field house and beg Dr. Roth to make her an espresso. Why did he get to start his mornings with cappuccino while the rest of them endured Nescafé?

Standing outside the chain-link fence enclosing the House of Heracles, she fought back a huge yawn. She turned to Juno, who stood beside her, rubbing the sleep from her eyes. "You know what I miss, Juno? Good, strong coffee. Preferably Italian or French roast."

"Bah." Juno waved her hand in dismissal. "Greek coffee is the best. None of this cream and sugar crap. Pure caffeine, right to your veins. That's what we should have at camp."

"I'd be up for it." Olivia usually drank her coffee with a splash of cream, but she'd be willing to adjust. She checked her watch. "I wish Grant would let us unlock the site ourselves. I hate wasting time like this."

Ever since the excavation unit had started, they had to wait until Grant arrived and unlocked the tall metal gate at the entrance of the property. Control freak that he was, he insisted the morning's work couldn't start without him. However, he had no such qualms about leaving early, especially if given the chance to schmooze. Like yesterday, when he'd cut out at three to meet with a couple of archaeologists working near the village of Polemi. Since Olivia's team had been the last to leave, she'd been charged with locking up the site and dropping off the keys at the field house.

When she'd stopped by, she'd been tempted to ask Dr. Roth if she could have a glass of his delicious iced coffee. But since no one had been home, she'd left the keys in the mailbox.

Around her, the other students sat under a clump of olive trees, trying to avoid the blistering sun for as long as possible. At least today, they'd get some relief from the heat. After listening to everyone complain for three straight days, Grant had relented and asked Rick and Stuart to set up canopies over the trenches.

When Rick approached them, Olivia perked up. He brushed his hand across her shoulder, making her quiver with longing. They hadn't been intimate since their last visit to the temple, and she was craving his touch.

"Good morning, Olivia," he said. "Morning, Juno. How are we doing today?"

"Tired and craving coffee," Juno grumbled as Grant advanced toward them. "Here he comes—Mr. Sunshine himself. Why is he so surly? He gets to drink real coffee instead of shitty Nescafé. If I were him, I'd be in a perpetually good mood."

Grant strode forward until he reached the gate. When he put the key in the lock, he frowned. Without turning it, he pushed at the gate until it opened wide.

Olivia's heart seized up. She'd been certain she locked it. A twist to the left until it clicked into place like Grant had shown her. Her drowsiness vanished, replaced by a growing dread. This was *her* fault.

Grant's rage was immediate. "Who locked up last night?"

Shit. She cleared her throat. "It was me. But I locked it the way you demonstrated."

"You must have missed a step. If you'd locked it properly, I wouldn't have been able to open it. A huge mistake on your part."

Logan ambled over to join them, looking like he'd rolled out of bed, his white-blond hair sticking up in spikes. "I don't see why it's a big deal. All we've dug up so far is old pottery and shit. It's cool and all, but we haven't found anything worth stealing."

Grant's face reddened. "It doesn't matter what we've uncovered, you idiot. The site was left vulnerable. Anyone could have broken in and vandalized it."

"Whoa," Logan said. "Does that actually happen?"

"More than you think," he sputtered. "Even with our tools locked up in the caretaker's shed, a determined thief could easily clip the lock." He turned back to Olivia, "I'm going to have to report this to—"

"Hang on." Juno pushed past Grant until she stood in front of the gate. "First of all, maybe you shouldn't be calling the students idiots. Second, I don't think everyone knows how tricky this lock is. May I?" She pulled the key out, then inserted it back in. Like Grant had shown, she turned it to the left until it clicked, then kept going counterclockwise, whereupon it clicked again, and she pulled it out. "People forget to do the last part because it's not obvious."

Olivia stared at Juno in admiration, stunned at how easily she'd put Grant in his place. Then again, she didn't need his approval for anything. She'd built up such a solid reputation in Cyprus that she wasn't intimidated by his bullying.

Juno motioned to the rest of the students. "Gather round, people. I'm going to show you the magic of locking up this troublesome gate. This way, none of you needs to fear the wrath of Dr. Grant Nilsson."

Olivia almost laughed until Grant intruded on her personal space. The scent of his citrusy aftershave was so strong it made her eyes water.

"This wouldn't have happened if you'd been paying attention the first time I showed you. I think you've let yourself get distracted." He cast a none-too-subtle glance at Rick.

Rather than cower in his presence, she maintained her composure. "I disagree. Like Juno said, it's tricky. If you report me to Dr. Roth, I'll tell him you called one of the students an idiot just for asking a simple question."

He stared her down for a moment, then walked off in a huff. For now, she'd take it as a victory, though she wished she hadn't made such a glaring error in full view of the students. At the time, she'd thought she'd locked it, but she hadn't double-checked to make sure. She'd have to work extra hard today to redeem herself.

At least she'd begun to feel more confident about supervising a trench. Unlike surveying, excavation was a skill she'd learned before. Now that they'd been digging at the House of Heracles for four days, the site had become less about grunt work and more about discovery. Having cleared the weeds, rubble, and modern dirt, they'd reached the Roman level of the site, which was dated to the third century AD. Trowels and small whisk brooms replaced shovels and picks as they uncovered paving stones and delineated the outline of a room. Along with the ever-present potsherds, they'd found mosaic tiles, coins, and small terra-cotta figurines. Though it was a slow process, Olivia liked watching how the site gradually revealed itself.

For most of the morning, Olivia worked with TJ, excavating near the west wall of the trench. When her trowel hit something solid, she combed through the dirt and revealed an object with a curved shape. Using a small paintbrush, she cleared the dirt away.

"Hey, TJ," she said. "Check this out. The slope's kind of uneven. Do you think it's a broken pot?"

He crouched beside her and ran his fingers along it. "That's not pottery. It might be bone."

"Bone? Like human bone?" A thrill ran through her.

"Maybe. Let me take over for a sec." When she passed him her paintbrush, he continued the process until the curve of a skull became visible.

"I'm going to get Rick and Stuart," she said. "I need them to take a look."

She clambered out of the trench and found them relaxing in the lab area. Having finished putting up the canopies, they were taking a much-needed break. "No rush, but I could use your help when you're free. I think we uncovered a skull."

Stuart set down his water bottle. "A skull? This I've got to see."

He and Rick followed Olivia into the trench and stood over TJ as he continued brushing. Within minutes, they agreed the object had to be a skull. Though it was bashed in on one side, it appeared human.

Olivia watched in awe. "I never thought we'd find a skeleton. This wasn't a burial ground, was it?"

During her field school at Clear Lake, she'd learned about the rules pertaining to burials, particularly those found at Native American sites. She wasn't sure if the same rules applied to archaeology outside of North America.

"We're in the clear because this structure was definitely a

villa," Rick said. "Based on historic records and the wall fragments we've found, we assume it collapsed in the earthquake that destroyed a lot of Paphos. Whoever's skull this was, they were probably killed in that earthquake."

"You mean the house collapsed on top of them?" TJ said. "That's wild."

"With any luck, there might be more than one skeleton," Stuart added.

While Olivia called her students over and explained the situation, Rick went to get Juno. She hopped in to join them and knelt next to TJ. After she brushed more dirt away from the skull, she looked up at Olivia. "Have you ever uncovered a skeleton before?"

"Nope," she said. "TJ probably has, though."

She waited for him to launch into a story, but for once, he didn't seem too eager. "I have, but I wasn't in charge. It's a tricky process."

"Juno, you want to help us out?" Olivia asked.

"With pleasure." Juno motioned for the students to come closer. "This is a huge opportunity. You'll need to work at a slower pace, but you'll learn how to document human remains."

Brynn shuddered. "But there's no curse or anything. Right?"

"Curses are stories created to scare children," Juno said. "Since you're adults, you should have no such worries." She clapped her hands together. "We'll need the right tools. Someone should also notify Mr. Sunshine. Not me since he's still furious that I took him down a peg during this morning's Gategate." She grinned. "Get it? Gategate? Like Watergate? Or Gamergate? You Americans add the word 'gate' to every scandal, right?"

Olivia resisted the urge to snort. Though she understood the reference, most of the students stared at Juno in confusion.

"I'll let Grant know," Stuart said.

"I need to get back to my team," Rick said. "But good luck. I'm sure you'll do a great job." He flashed Olivia an encouraging smile.

Once Rick and Stuart had left, Olivia grabbed toothbrushes, dental picks, and tiny brushes from the lab area. She set her work gloves on the edge of the trench since she'd get a better feel for the bones with her bare hands. As she and TJ crouched down to work together, excitement bubbled up inside of her. Uncovering a skeleton was more interesting than digging up endless buckets of broken pottery.

When Grant came for his inspection, her shoulders tightened as she waited for him to criticize her. Instead, he favored her with a rare smile. "Well done. I expect you'll be using extreme caution as you go along?"

"We will," she said. "Juno's excavated human remains before, so she'll be helping us with the entire process. We don't want to make any mistakes." It was one thing to slip up with the gate, but if she screwed up this skeleton, she'd be on Grant's shit list forever.

"You'll be in good hands with Juno," Grant said. "I'll also notify Dr. Roth and the Department of Antiquities."

"Thanks." With Grant so focused on the skeleton, surely he'd forget about Gategate.

For the next two hours, she and TJ worked carefully. When they needed a break, they let the other students take their place. The process was incredibly slow: brush, scrape, brush, sweep, take photographs, and repeat. Each time they uncovered another intact bone, she considered it a victory.

Dr. Roth showed up at one, examined Olivia's trench, and conferred with her team, praising them for their diligent work. They were so motivated that they continued digging until they'd exposed the entire skeleton. Juno photographed it, and then she and Stuart helped remove the bones. Once the skeleton was safely extracted, Olivia's team was given leave to take a break.

She sat at the sorting table, guzzling water in a stupor of heat exhaustion.

Dusty drew up a chair next to her. "Killer find. I'm so psyched I get to draw a skull."

"You get to draw it?" Olivia asked.

"Yep. I love that shit." Dusty grinned. "You lucky thing. Juno told me about Gategate or whatever she's calling it, but now you're a rock star. Finding a skeleton is a huge win. Plus, you get bonus points for not bashing in the skull with a trowel or breaking any of the bones. I've been on digs where that's happened."

"That would suck." Olivia cast a glance at Brynn, remembering her earlier question. "What about curses? I'm sure your parents worked on burials when they were in Egypt. Anything terrible happen?"

"You've watched *The Mummy* too many times. I've seen my share of real mummies, and none of them have ever come to life. Plus, Stuart said this isn't even a burial. More like the house collapsed in the big earthquake and the victim was buried under the rubble." She grimaced. "Kind of creepy if you think about it."

Rick joined them and placed his hand on Olivia's shoulder. "How's it going?"

"Good, thanks. This has been quite a day. I realize it's pure luck that our team happened to get this trench, but—"

"None of that. Whether it was a lucky find or not, you handled it like a pro. That's what matters. You've got the makings of an archaeological superstar."

His words filled her with a swell of pleasure.

A superstar? Her?

Why not?

Right now, she felt like she could do anything. Be anything.

It was a glorious feeling.

CHAPTER TWENTY-SIX

When Rick arrived at Spyros Taverna for dinner, he grabbed the seat next to Olivia before anyone could claim it. His pulse skyrocketed when she snaked her hand under the table and caressed his thigh, all while maintaining an innocent expression. He liked this naughty version of Olivia.

Focusing on dinner was almost impossible while her hand traced sensual patterns on his thigh. Thankfully, the tablecloth hid her wandering hand and his growing erection. The only way to get over his hard-on was to focus on TJ's lengthy story about the camel excursion he'd taken when he visited the site of Petra.

Once Rick had finished eating, he was about to excuse himself when Grant's voice stopped him cold. "Rick, you need to head into Paphos tonight to get groceries."

"I just went three days ago. The kitchen's fully stocked."

"I would disagree. We need more yogurt and melon, as well as a few more snacks. The students have been particularly ravenous."

Since the grocery run was a nice break from camp, Rick usually enjoyed doing it, but he was hoping to sneak away with

Olivia. Even if they couldn't risk visiting Aphrodite's temple, they could walk into the village and find somewhere discreet to kiss.

"Why don't I go tomorrow afternoon, once we're done at the dig site?" he said.

"Nonsense. Papantoniou Supermarket is open until ten, so you'll have plenty of time, providing you don't dawdle. Make sure you get a receipt. And no more sugary cereals. They're nothing but empty calories."

The last time Rick had shopped in Paphos, he'd brought Juno, and she'd convinced him to purchase four boxes of unhealthy, off-brand cereals, like Frooty Flakes and Honey-Os. Naturally, Grant hadn't approved.

"Fine. I'll go tonight," Rick said.

After they got back to camp, Grant handed him a fully itemized shopping list, complete with notes, as though Rick was a ten-year-old who'd never been to a grocery store. Admittedly, he'd been pushing things by purchasing unauthorized cereal, but the students had raved about it.

While grabbing his wallet from the men's sleeping quarters, his phone buzzed. He stared at the screen in astonishment. Dr. Kaplan, the director of the Institute for Nautical Archaeology, had texted him. *Not sure how often you check your email when you're in the field, but I sent you an offer. Start date is September 1.*

Heart pounding, Rick sat on his cot and pulled up his email. Last fall, he'd worked with Dr. Kaplan on the southwest coast of Turkey, where he'd participated in the underwater excavation of a shipwreck from the third century BC. Not only had the project allowed him to use his scuba diving skills, but it had felt more like a true adventure than anything he'd ever done. In between dive sessions, the crew had lived in Bodrum, a Turkish harbor town with a lively nightlife.

He scanned the email. The professor had invited him to return to Bodrum in September to continue working on the shipwreck. The job would last until mid-November and involve a mix of diving and lab work. He'd be paid enough to afford life in Turkey with a little extra to set aside. If he took the job, he'd be covered for the next few months.

Either Dr. Kaplan hadn't heard about Palaikastro, or he didn't care. Maybe he just remembered how hard Rick had worked. How he'd put in long hours, proved himself responsible, and bonded with the rest of the crew.

Coming on the heels of this morning's news, Rick was in a better place than he'd been a few weeks ago.

For the tenth time that day, he reviewed the text Cassie had sent him: *Turns out Dad's OK. Guess he's too stubborn for cancer. I still think you should come home. I miss you, and so does Mom.*

Sure, he missed them, but with his dad out of immediate danger, he could accept the job in Turkey without a shred of guilt. Put off the big family reunion for a few more months.

But was that what he wanted?

He'd already told Olivia he was considering going back to California. How would she feel if he delayed his return for another few months?

It doesn't matter. You didn't promise her anything.

Normally, when he came to the end of a project, he was ready to move on. No matter how much fun he'd had, he cut his ties without a backward glance. Given his nomadic life, he didn't want to be tied to one place or one person. And—if he was being honest—he'd never allowed himself to let down his walls long enough to consider a real relationship and the trust it entailed. All he wanted was a fun, sexy diversion for a few months.

But Olivia was more than a diversion. He cared about her. Though they hadn't been back together for long, the thought of never seeing her again filled him with a physical ache.

Even if he wanted more, she'd given no hints she felt the same way. All she'd asked for was three weeks of fun. Understandable since he didn't fit into her life. Unlike him, she had actual career plans. In a year, she'd have her doctorate and be on her way in the academic world. He was just a shovel bum without a fixed address, which meant his goals didn't exactly mesh with hers.

"Rick?" Olivia's voice startled him back to the present.

He pasted on a quick smile, hoping to hide the confusion churning inside him. "Hey. Everything okay?"

"The question is—are you okay? You look unsettled. Did you get bad news from home? About your dad?"

He hadn't told her Cassie's news yet. They'd both been so busy at the excavation site that they hadn't been able to squeeze in a moment alone. Now would have been the perfect time to unload his news, but he wanted to process everything first. In the space of twenty-four hours, his options had changed dramatically.

"Nothing yet. What's up?" he asked.

Placing her hand on her hip, she flashed him a flirtatious smile. "Grant might have assigned you to get groceries, but he didn't prohibit you from having company."

Even if he appreciated her eagerness, he didn't want to disappoint her. "It's just a trip to the supermarket. Nothing sexy."

"When I'm with you, everything's sexy. Even shopping for yogurt."

How could he resist an entreaty like that? If they sped through Grant's list, they might have time for a pit stop.

Since the Jeep was parked at the field house, they made do with one of the rental cars. Olivia adjusted the dial to Viva FM and started singing along to an old Madonna song. Though the drive to Paphos was part of their daily routine during the excavation unit, Rick's car was always crammed full of students. Driving alone with Olivia was a rare delight. He liked being with her, and not just during their stolen moments of intimacy. He liked working with her, talking to her at dinner, and teasing her over the course of the day.

He parked outside Papantoniou Supermarket, a giant grocery store located in downtown Paphos. When they got inside, Olivia grabbed a cart and pushed it forward with a surprising amount of enthusiasm.

"Why are you so excited?" he asked. "Don't you shop for groceries at home?"

"Of course. But this is way more fun than going to Safeway. First of all, the signs are in Greek. Second, there are products I've never seen before. My sister's the same way. Whenever she visits a new country, she looks for a local supermarket."

To him, grocery shopping was more of a chore, but Olivia's cheerful energy was impossible to resist. As they passed the produce area, he grabbed four honeydew melons and two pounds of apricots, as per Grant's list.

When they got to the dairy section, Olivia gushed over all the different cheeses. "Ooh. Look at this delicious feta. Can we get some? Or how about this yummy halloumi?"

He tossed in six packages of Laughing Cow cheese. "Sorry, but this is all Grant allows. Makes for an easy snack."

She made a face. "We're in Cyprus and we're getting processed-cheese food? Not cool." As they moved to the bakery section, she grabbed a box of artisanal Greek butter cookies. "How about these for our afternoon break? Buttery goodness."

He consulted the list. "Petit-Beurre cookies only."

"*No*. Everyone hates Petit-Beurres. Same with Morning Coffee biscuits. They're worse than graham crackers. Which are only acceptable when used in s'mores."

"Hang on. Here's what Grant's note says: *In the event no Petit-Beurre or Morning Coffee biscuits can be located, Papadopolous sandwich cookies are an acceptable substitute. Lemon filling only. No chocolate.*"

"He said that?" She snatched the list away. "Damn. He really is picky. I vote for the lemon creams. Pretend we never saw the Petit-Beurres."

"Fair enough." He tossed four packages into the cart.

As Olivia rushed over to examine the yogurt display, he had to admit he was enjoying the odd domesticity of cruising through the supermarket with her. Like they were a real couple out shopping together.

When was the last time he'd thought that about *anyone*? Pretty much never.

Once they'd purchased the groceries and placed them in the trunk, he checked his watch. They could still squeeze in a short detour. The opportunity was too good to pass up.

When he drove past the turnoff to Kouklia, Olivia placed her hand on his thigh. "Rick? Where are we going?"

"You'll see." He continued along the coastal road until he reached a small parking lot, empty save for two other cars. Next to it was a tourist pavilion containing a café and restrooms, now closed for the evening.

"What is this place?" Olivia asked, as they got out of the car.

Without answering, he took her hand. He wanted to see the look on her face once he revealed where they were. If she'd had a better sense of direction, she might have guessed where he'd taken her. But this was Olivia.

He led her along a covered walkway that took them under the coastal road. They emerged onto a pebbled beach facing the Mediterranean. Huge rock formations, illuminated by the moonlight, stood out near the coastline. They reminded him of the rocks he'd seen along the Oregon Coast during a road trip with his sister.

The beach was silent, save for the steady crashing of the waves. Olivia gasped. "It's so beautiful."

"It should be. It's Petra Tou Romiou—the birthplace of Aphrodite."

"I didn't realize it was this close."

"The beach is usually packed with tourists during the day, but I wanted you to see it at night, when it's quieter."

She squeezed his hand. "Thank you."

They walked along the rocky shore, listening to the soothing rhythm of the ocean. When they reached a spot with no one around, Rick sat against a large rock and pulled her onto his lap. She leaned against him and let out a sigh. "This is so romantic. We had sex in Aphrodite's temple, and now we're visiting her birthplace. This must be a sign, right? Maybe the goddess is trying to tell us something."

"Maybe she is."

Was it a sign? Was Aphrodite trying to get through to him? To tell him he needed to stop running and stay with the one woman he'd never been able to forget?

He held her in his arms, breathing in the bracing salt air as they watched the waves crest onto the shore. Though he wanted to disclose his offer to work in Turkey, he was reluctant to spoil the moment. For now, he was content to sit with her and enjoy her presence. With two weeks of field school left, he still had plenty of time to tell her.

When Olivia's phone buzzed insistently, he startled as though coming out of a dream. "Do you need to get that?"

"Let me see." She peeked at it. "It's my sister. I can tell her to call back later."

"You can talk if you want. We should head back soon anyway."

She swiped at the phone. "Sofia. Hey. How's it going? Yes, I'm with him. No, I'm fully clothed. Why? Because I'm at a public beach." She rolled her eyes and whispered, "She wants to use FaceTime. She insists on seeing you for herself."

"Sure." Rick couldn't help but grin. The more he heard about Olivia's little sister, the more he wanted to meet her in person.

Sofia's face appeared on the screen. "Hey! It's you! Mr. Hottie, in the flesh."

"Is that what Olivia calls me?"

"No, that's *my* nickname for you," Sofia said. "Because I kept hearing how hot you were. It's hard to judge by looking at a screen, but I think you're the real deal. My sister didn't lie about your hotness."

"Thanks for the vote of confidence," Olivia said dryly. "Is something up, or did you want to chat about Rick's masterful physique?"

"Ooh, you're a little snippy. Did I interrupt you? Don't give me that crap about being on a public beach. You were in bed, weren't you?"

Olivia laughed. "There are literally no beds at camp. No bedrooms, for that matter. Here." She turned the phone so it was facing the waves. "Petra Tou Romiou—the birthplace of Aphrodite."

"That's so romantic. Didn't I tell you Aphrodite would come through for you? It's truly the island of love." She gave a dramatic sigh. "I'm so glad I get to visit."

"When are you getting here?" Olivia asked.

"In a few days. Just wrapping up things in Greece, then flying to Larnaca. I'm gonna be staying at the Aphrodite Gardens. It's a fully loaded resort about ten minutes from Kouklia. Mouflon Tours is putting me up in exchange for some sweet promo content. Isn't that the best? Maybe if you're extra nice, I'll invite you over for a swim. You, too, Mr. Hottie."

He laughed. "I'd like that."

Olivia didn't look quite as comfortable. "Umm…Sofia? If you come here, can you please call him Rick? We're not supposed to be flaunting our relationship."

"Why? Because of Mr. Grumpy Gills? No worries. I won't say a word." Sofia squealed. "I can't wait to see you. It's been too long. But right now, I've gotta go. The nightlife calls. Catch you on the flip."

When she was done, Rick stared at the screen, dazed by Sofia's exuberance. "Wow. Your sister is—"

"A lot? She's always been like that. At first, I was worried about her coming here because she isn't shy about speaking her mind. We're talking zero filter. But I think it'll be okay. I can't wait to hear all her stories." She grinned. "I used to get so jealous of her, but for once, I have some scandalous stories of my own."

"Like sneaking out to the Sanctuary of Aphrodite?"

"Exactly." Olivia waggled her eyebrows. "Even Sofia's never had sex in an ancient temple."

More than ever, Rick wished they could go back there, but he wasn't willing to risk it—not unless Olivia was fully on board. He stood and offered her his hand. "We should get going."

She took it and rose beside him. "Thanks for bringing me here. Can we come back again some night?"

"We can try." He didn't know if they'd be able to finagle it, but he was glad his gesture had meant so much to her.

You're getting in awfully deep. What the hell are you going to do?

A question he could save for later.

He didn't need to make any decisions. Yet.

CHAPTER TWENTY-SEVEN

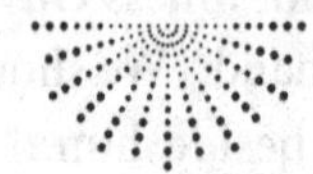

On Sunday, the students and staff were given the opportunity to spend their free day on a six-hour tour of the Akamas Peninsula. Olivia declined since she wanted to visit Sofia, who'd just arrived in Cyprus. She'd invited Olivia to join her at the Aphrodite Gardens Resort and told her to bring "Mr. Hottie," along with anyone else who wanted to come. Since Grant was on the tour with the students, Rick had no trouble snagging one of the rental cars. Stuart, Dusty, and TJ joined them. The resort was a ten-minute drive up the coastal road, then another mile inland.

As they passed through the security gate, TJ let out his breath. "Holy shit. Your sister must be loaded."

Stuart gaped as they drove by a gigantic pool. "No kidding. This place is wicked."

"Sofia isn't paying for it," Olivia said. "It's part of a deal she made with the tour company. She'll be promoting the resort on all her social media platforms."

"Must be nice," Dusty said. "I wish my life were that easy."

Thanks to the image Sofia presented, everyone thought she glided through life with little effort. Olivia was one of the few people who knew how relentlessly her little sister hustled. She pursued every angle, reached out to sponsors, created nonstop content, and worked her charm whenever possible.

Aphrodite Gardens was the size of a small town, with winding streets, sumptuous villas, huge swimming pools, a golf course, and a faux-village square with shops and restaurants. Sofia's rental unit was located inside a three-story building made of cream-colored stone with spacious balconies. Potted plants and bougainvillea livened up the front of the property. Behind the villa was a large pool shared by the complex.

When they went up to Sofia's apartment on the second floor, she greeted them at the door, engulfing Olivia in a giant hug. "Liv! It's been too long!"

Olivia hugged her tightly. Though she rarely went a week without talking to her sister, seeing her in person kindled a rush of euphoria.

After Sofia finally released her, Olivia introduced the others. "You already met Rick on FaceTime. These are my fellow archaeologists—Dusty, Stu, and TJ."

"Nice to meet you! And *so* nice to see you in person, Mr. Hottie."

Dusty raised her eyebrows at Rick. "Did she just call you Mr. Hottie?"

He flashed her a shit-eating grin. "Suits me, doesn't it?"

Olivia cringed. "Sofia, remember what I said about Rick's nickname?"

Her sister beckoned them inside. "Sorry. I'll behave. At least Mr. Grumptastic isn't here to ruin the party. I hope you brought your suits because the water's perfect. We can hit the pool first and eat after. I've got beer, wine, and hard seltzer, and I ordered appetizers from the taverna in the village square."

"Thanks," Olivia said. "This is great."

Sofia squeezed her arm. "Anything for my big sis. We have to take some pics together for the fam. When I called Mom last night, she was so jealous she couldn't be here."

Olivia followed the others inside. The apartment was light and open, with floor-to-ceiling windows that looked onto the golf course. A blast of air-conditioning made goose bumps rise on her arms. She'd been living without central air for so long it felt unnaturally chilly. Though the kitchen was small, she caught sight of a Nespresso on the counter and a compact washing machine tucked into one corner. She was more envious of the coffee maker than anything else in the apartment. Except the washing machine. For weeks, she'd been washing her clothes by hand in a pottery bucket.

Once they got down to the pool, Olivia dove in right away, relishing the feel of cool water on her skin. Sofia grabbed a couple of bright pink pool floats and tossed her one. They drifted across the water together, catching up on family gossip while the others engaged in a fierce game of volleyball. Whenever Olivia got too warm, she slipped off her float and dunked herself in the water again.

Cocooned in her state of sun-warmed bliss, she had no sense of time passing until her sister's phone buzzed. Sofia hopped out of the pool and grabbed it from a chaise lounge. "The food's here. I'll go get it. You all can stay in a while longer."

Olivia paddled her float to the edge of the pool. "I'll come help you."

After changing in Sofia's bedroom—and drooling over the enormous king bed—Olivia met her sister in the kitchen. Sofia was opening containers of appetizers and setting them on colorful ceramic platters. The savory smells made Olivia's mouth water.

"There's wine in the fridge if you want to get started," Sofia said. "Glasses are in the right-hand cupboard."

"Perfect." Olivia opened a bottle of rosé and poured them each a glass. Crisp and delicious, tasting slightly of raspberries, the first sip made her sigh in contentment. "This is unbelievable. I'd give anything to stay in a place like this."

"No, you wouldn't. You're perfectly happy right where you are."

"Seriously? You know I'm not the outdoorsy type." Olivia grabbed a green olive and ate it in one bite. The sour taste made her mouth pucker.

"You used to be. Remember? When we went on those camping trips with our cousins, you always got *so* into it, with your star charts and hiking maps."

Olivia thought for a minute, recalling how she'd pore over the maps to find the best hiking trails. Even back then, she'd been a sucker for maps. "I forgot about that. I guess I changed after I messed up at Clear Lake."

"But now you've fully embraced it?"

"Maybe not fully. Those camp cots are uncomfortable as hell. I'm not a fan of cold showers, either, but…" She snitched a slice of halloumi cheese. Salty and delicious.

"But what? You're into it, right? You know how I can tell? Because you're literally glowing right now." Sofia grinned. "You haven't done that in years."

Olivia opened a container of fried calamari and arranged it on one of the platters. "To be fair, you haven't seen me in person for years."

"You know what I mean, though. Is it because of Mr. Hottie?"

"Sort of? But also because I really like working at the field school. I forgot how much I love archaeology. Did I tell you I found a site? Dr. Roth thinks it might date back to the eighth century BC."

"Awesome. And you're having fun with the students? Not crushing their dreams or telling them Indiana Jones is a poor excuse for an archaeologist?"

"Technically, he *is* a poor excuse for an archaeologist, but I still love those movies."

Sofia tossed an olive at her. "You know what I mean, silly."

"I do. I like working with the students. Maybe I'm not as fun as Rick, but I was able to help most of them with their site presentations."

All the hours she'd spent with them had paid off, as they'd shone with confidence when they delivered their talks in front of Grant and Dr. Roth. Even Marisol had outdone herself, infusing her speech with her passion for ancient history. Olivia had been so damn proud—not just of them, but of herself, as well.

"That's fab," Sofia said. "Have you found anything interesting yet?"

Olivia flashed her a cheeky grin. "I dug up a skeleton. How's that for interesting?"

"A human one? Wow. Was it freaky?"

"No, it was totally fascinating. We had to be super careful, and we used dental picks and toothbrushes to reveal the bones."

"I told you it would get better. Does this mean you might go on more digs?"

If anyone had asked her at the beginning of the field school, Olivia would have said no. But now that she'd had another taste of archaeology, she wanted more. "I still need to get my doctorate and land a teaching job. But once I do, there's no reason why I couldn't assist on excavation projects in the summer or eventually lead my own dig. Classical history isn't just about archival research."

"Did those words come out of your mouth?" Sofia lifted her glass. "Let's toast. To archaeology, love, and more digs with Mr. Hottie."

As Olivia clinked her glass against Sofia's, an uneasy feeling spread through her. "I don't think that last one's going to happen. This is just a fling."

Sofia snorted. "You don't do flings. None that I've heard about. Or do you have a wild side that you've been hiding?"

"Well, Rick and I *did* have sex in the ruins of a temple

dedicated to Aphrodite." At her sister's wide-eyed look, she laughed. "It was amazing. But after field school ends, Rick isn't sure what he's doing next. He's talked about going back to California to work in rescue archaeology, but—"

"That's perfect. Then you guys could stay together."

"Let me finish." Olivia topped up her wine. "He also might go on another dig. Or work on a shipwreck. Right up front, he said he couldn't promise me anything, and I agreed to it."

At the time, she'd thought she could have fun without getting her heart involved. But the longer she spent with Rick, the more she realized that wasn't possible. She was falling just as hard as she had at Clear Lake.

"You want more than a fling, don't you?" Sofia asked.

Olivia let out her breath in a rush. "I'm such an idiot."

"No, you're not. You're following your heart."

"I'm being unrealistic. Like, I'm already imagining this made-up future where we're working together on other digs. Or sharing a cozy apartment in Santa Monica. Or planning more adventures. But it's a complete fantasy."

"It doesn't have to be. Can't you talk to him about it?"

Not wanting to meet her sister's gaze, Olivia focused on arranging the mini spanakopita triangles into a pyramid. She knew she was being a coward. At the very least, she should ask if he'd heard anything from his family. Depending on the news, he might be headed back home. But even if he was, he hadn't said he wanted an actual relationship.

"You need to tell him how you feel," Sofia said. "Guys can be so freaking oblivious."

"It's not that easy. For now, I'm trying to live for the moment. That's what counts, right?"

"Maybe for me. I think you deserve more than that."

When Olivia's phone buzzed, she wiped her hands on her shorts and picked it up. "Rick just texted. Should I tell them to come up?"

"Sure. If they need towels, there's a stack of them on a shelf next to the pool entrance."

Olivia was relieved to set the subject of Rick aside. Talking about him roused too many feelings. If she admitted she was falling in love with him, she wouldn't be able to take the words back. They'd be out there, reminding her of how badly she'd misjudged her heart. And how much it would hurt when she left Cyprus with no guarantee she'd ever see him again.

For the rest of the evening, she put the conversation out of her mind. She had fun with the others, swapping stories, drinking wine, and feasting on delicious appetizers. Only when she was back at camp, lying on her cot, did her thoughts return to her talk with Sofia. She glanced at her sister's last text, sent after the group had left.

Remember how worthy you are. Never be afraid to ask for more.

Though it sounded like one of Sofia's feel-good Instagram quotes, the words lodged in Olivia's brain. She wished she could be that brave. But if she pushed too hard, she might drive Rick away.

If a few more weeks were all she'd get, then she'd take them.

Better that than nothing at all.

CHAPTER TWENTY-EIGHT

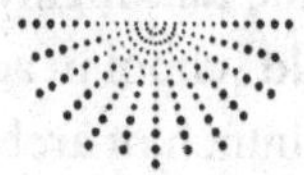

After a long day excavating at the House of Heracles, Rick's energy was flagging. Not only had his team uncovered the eastern wall of the villa, but they'd also unearthed a bounty of artifacts, including fragments of gold jewelry, broken pieces of a large terra-cotta plaque, numerous utensils, and a cache of mosaic tiles. Impressive finds, to be sure, but they'd taken hours to process.

Though Rick was eager to return to camp once the workday ended, he wouldn't get the chance for another few hours. Instead, the students and staff were expected to attend a site presentation at Polemi, a village twenty minutes north of Paphos, where a team from Yale was excavating an Iron Age settlement. Missing the presentation wasn't an option, since the speaker was none other than Dr. Lidia Bouras, Grant's crush from the Department of Antiquities.

By the time Rick's team finished their lab work, they were the last ones left at the excavation site. Rick hustled them out to the Kia. "Everyone ready? We need to get cranking if we're going to make it to Polemi by five."

"Why are we going to another site?" Alisha grumbled. "Haven't we done enough archaeology for one day?"

Rick had to agree, especially since this visit was just another opportunity for Grant to schmooze. "Dr. Bouras is an expert on Iron Age sites in Cyprus, so she agreed to meet with the crew working at Polemi and give them a presentation on her research. Grant thought we'd find the talk highly informative. As a bonus, we'll get to see another field school in action."

"We're meeting with a bunch of archaeological *rivals*?" TJ said. "I'll bet you ten bucks their conditions aren't as hard-core as ours."

Alisha scoffed. "They probably have tents."

"They might even have beds," TJ said. "How cushy is that? We could take them in a fight."

Rick was about to tell TJ to cool it with the trash talk when Marisol reached over the back seat and tapped him on the shoulder. "Can you wait another minute? I left my pack at the sorting table."

"We can get it after if you want," he said. "Remind me on the way back."

"Please? My phone's in there. If my parents try to call me and can't get through, they'll worry."

More than once, she'd mentioned how overprotective they were. He handed her the keys. "Fine. Grab it and lock up after. But hurry. If we're late, Grant will have my head. I'd rather not get reamed out in front of a rival gang of archaeologists."

As they waited, TJ and Alisha argued over the best weapons to use in an archaeological rumble. Assuming such a thing existed.

Rick rubbed his forehead as the first inkling of a headache bloomed in the back of his brain. He wished they could go back to camp. For the past few days, he'd been trying to catch Olivia alone so he could tell her about the offer he'd gotten in Turkey. He'd considered mentioning it during their day off at the Aphrodite Gardens Resort, but he hadn't wanted to share the news with anyone else until he talked to Olivia privately. Each time he saw the message from Dr. Kaplan in his inbox, guilt crashed over him. He needed to make a plan, but he wanted to discuss it with her first.

For once in his life, he didn't know if he could cut and run. Not if it meant losing Olivia again. But he wasn't sure she felt the same way.

Marisol hopped back in the car, red-faced and breathless. "All set. Sorry if we're late."

"Nah, we can make it if I speed," he said. "TJ, keep an eye out for cops."

As he pulled away from the House of Heracles, Marisol let out a cry. "Good thing I got my phone. My mom sent me a bunch of texts about my Tía Carmen's surgery."

"Is she okay?" he asked.

"She's fine. But now I can respond right away, and she won't think I got lost or bitten by a scorpion."

"For the record, there are no scorpions in this part of Cyprus," TJ said. "Though if you went up to the Troodos Mountains, you might find a few."

"She meant it as an example," Alisha said. "She wasn't talking about a literal scorpion."

Rick tuned them out as he picked up speed, swerving around the twisty roads. When they arrived, he fought back a surge of uneasiness at the sight of the other cars lined up at the base of the hill. He hoped they could sneak in without drawing attention to themselves. He hurried his team past the excavation site, mindful of the scattered buckets and dig tools. Four sections of the site were roped off, with rectangular trenches dug into the earth.

The collective group was already seated atop the hill under a grove of trees, with the "rival" field school at the front. Rick's team made their way to the back and sat down quickly. Fortunately for them, Grant was still conferring with Dr. Bouras and a bearded guy in his forties, whom Rick assumed was the dig director.

Was Grant aware that Dr. Bouras was Roth's current hookup? Probably not, otherwise he wouldn't have such a doting look on his face.

Whatever. If Grant didn't know, Rick wasn't going to be the one to tell him.

TJ nudged him. "Do you know who that guy is? It's Dr. Tom Ferrante. He's from Yale, which means this is an Ivy League dig. We're doomed."

Alisha snickered. "You realize we're not going to throw down with his crew, right? Aren't you all about making connections? After the lecture, you should go talk to him."

"Besides, you're getting your doctorate from Harvard," Marisol said. "I thought that was more prestigious than Yale."

"Debatable, but you make a fair point," TJ said.

Dr. Ferrante called the group to attention, welcomed the visitors to the site, and introduced his staff—four graduate students and one junior professor. Grant went next, thanking him effusively for allowing them to attend Dr. Bouras' presentation. When Dr. Ferrante asked him to introduce his staff, Grant called Stuart, Dusty, Juno, and Olivia up to the front.

"These are the graduate students helping run the field school this year. Stuart Carlson, Olivia Sanchez, Dusty Danforth, and Juno Kalavos. They're all working toward their doctorates in classical history and archaeology. So far, they're doing an excellent job with this year's crop of undergraduates."

Though it stung not to be included, Rick wasn't surprised at the omission. To be honest, he hadn't expected Grant to praise *anyone*.

"Um…Dr. Nilsson?" Olivia said. "I think you forgot someone." She caught Rick's eye and flashed him a quick smile.

He mouthed the words "thank you," grateful at her attempt to include him.

"Right. How foolish." Grant craned his neck, seeking out the back row. At the sight of Rick, his lips curled up in a poisonous smile before he turned his attention to TJ. "There he is—way in the back. TJ, will you stand up?" When he did so, Grant gestured to him. "TJ Mayer is from Harvard, and he's our lithics specialist. His expertise has come in handy, given the impressive Stone Age site his team found on the last day of the survey."

His team? What the hell? Rick burned with anger. If nothing else, he should have been credited with finding the site.

Beside him, Marisol spoke softly. "That's not true. You're the one who led the team. Why isn't he acknowledging you?"

Because I'm just a shovel bum. "It's okay," he said. "We can all share the credit."

Even so, he found it hard to concentrate during the lecture, still smarting over the way Grant had put him in his place. To make things worse, after the presentation concluded, Dr. Ferrante asked Grant if he and his staff would like to stay for drinks at the local taverna. Grant accepted for them, no doubt pleased to continue networking.

As the students prepared to leave, Rick sought out Olivia, who was talking with Dusty. She gave him an apologetic smile. "Sorry about Grant's introduction. When I told him he was forgetting someone, I meant *you*, not TJ. But I didn't want to harp on it."

"It's fine. Are you going for drinks or heading back to camp?"

"I should stay since Grant's in a decent mood for once. I met Dr. Ferrante last year at the AIA meetings, and I'd like to jog his memory. It wouldn't hurt to flash my credentials, seeing as how I'm now a legit archaeologist and all." She laughed, no doubt hoping to lighten the mood.

He wasn't feeling it. "Well, have fun. I'm guessing Sofia's busy for the night?"

"She's meeting up in Paphos with the guys from Mouflon Tours. At least you get to relax at camp. I'm wiped."

Then why are you going? She didn't owe Grant anything. But he also understood why she didn't want to miss out. In academia, making connections mattered.

"I'll see you later, okay?" she said. Without a backward glance, she and Dusty walked over to Dr. Ferrante, where they were joined by TJ and Stuart.

Feeling less than worthy, Rick gathered the rest of his team together. "All right, folks. Let's head back to camp."

The drive seemed endless. No one spoke or made their usual off-color jokes. Even the radio stayed silent.

After washing away the day's grime in the shower, Rick's mood improved, but he still wasn't up for socializing. While everyone else headed to Spyros, he stayed back at camp, claiming he needed to work on his section of the survey report. But an hour after dinner ended, his night took an unexpected—and disgusting—turn, when Marisol came to him in tears because she'd thrown up in the bathroom. And she'd missed the toilet.

Rick offered to take care of it. He should have waited, because ten minutes later, Brynn did the same thing. Either the crew had eaten something nasty at Spyros, or they'd caught a stomach bug. Either way, he was glad he hadn't joined them for dinner.

As he scrubbed the tile floor of the bathroom, he felt lower than he had at the site presentation. He wasn't out drinking or networking. He wasn't impressing anyone with *his* academic credentials. Instead, he was on his hands and knees, cleaning up vomit.

By the time he crashed out on his cot, Olivia still hadn't returned. He lay awake for a long time, trying to decide what to do about Turkey.

As he and Olivia had grown closer, he'd almost convinced himself their differences didn't matter. He might not be working toward a graduate degree, but she didn't seem to care. Whenever they conferred at the excavation site, she never treated him like he was inferior. If anything, she came to him for advice.

But he'd been fooling himself. Even if she wasn't as fixated on getting ahead as TJ or Grant, she cared about her place in academia. She'd worked hard to get this far in her career and wanted to keep going. How could she ever respect him when his goals were far more modest?

Even if he wanted to be with her, he'd only drag her down.

He picked up his phone and composed a quick email to Dr. Kaplan, accepting his offer. It was for the best. Instead of trying to fit in where he didn't belong, he'd be doing work that he loved, on a job where his skills would be appreciated.

He'd almost drifted off when a car pulled into the lot. The sound of voices, laughing and talking, carried over to him, making him feel even worse.

His phone buzzed with a text from Olivia. *I missed you tonight. I wish you could have been there. Can I make it up to you tomorrow night? Maybe we could go for a walk?*

For a moment, he felt so peevish he almost didn't respond. But shutting out Olivia wouldn't solve anything. It wasn't her fault he was feeling inadequate. If he met with her, then he could explain why he'd chosen to work in Turkey rather than returning home.

It's a date, he texted back.

But he couldn't shake the uncertainty that haunted him as he drifted off to sleep.

CHAPTER TWENTY-NINE

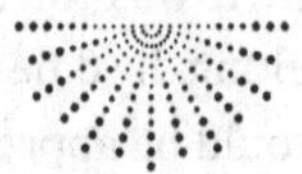

Upon waking the next day, Rick was determined to cast off the misery and self-loathing that had tormented him the night before. But he encountered his first setback during breakfast prep when his team discovered ants had invaded the kitchen. Naturally, Grant charged them with cleaning out the pantry. As a result, they left long after the others. Halfway to Paphos, Marisol begged him to pull over. She bolted out of the car and threw up on the side of the road.

Once she was done, she apologized. "I'm better now. If I sit in the shade and do lab work, I can make it through the day."

Rick ushered her into the car. "Nope. You need to rest and stay hydrated. I'm taking you back to camp."

"But—"

"No arguments." He turned the car around and headed toward Kouklia. "Brynn's at camp, too. She's got the same bug as you. Just take it easy for the rest of the day."

Marisol sniffed back tears. "But Grant said if we missed any of the excavation unit, he'd dock points off our grade."

What an asshole. "I'll talk to him. You shouldn't be punished for taking a sick day." He turned to TJ. "Can you text Grant and tell him we're running late? If he doesn't respond, try Stuart."

"Sure," TJ said. "I hope the rest of us don't get this bug. Usually, I'm immune because I've got an iron stomach. I've eaten more weird shit than Anthony Bourdain, and I've never gotten sick."

Once Rick returned to camp, he got Marisol settled with a bottle of water and some Imodium tablets. He also set two buckets inside the women's sleeping quarters for her and Brynn in case they needed to vomit. He'd rather empty out a bucket than scrub the floor again.

By the time he parked at the House of Heracles, his team was forty minutes late. He braced himself for a blistering lecture on responsibility. Even if he was putting the students' needs first, he'd made the cardinal sin of messing with Grant's schedule.

As they got out of the car, Logan stopped short. "Whoa. What are the police doing here?"

Two Cypriot police cruisers were parked next to the open gate. Rick's heart stuttered in fear. Had someone been injured?

Olivia.

He and his team ran to find the others. The rest of the field school stood at the edge of the excavation area, watching as Dr. Roth and Grant conferred with two police officers. When Rick approached the students, the look they gave him plunged a knife into his heart. Even without asking, he knew he was in trouble.

"What the hell's going on?" Alisha said.

As Rick got closer, his stomach churned. Inside the nearest trench—*his team's trench*—were two empty beer bottles, some cigarette butts, a soda can, and a pile of broken glass. Red swirls of graffiti had been sprayed along the section of wall they'd been excavating.

"Looks like someone vandalized the site," TJ said.

When Rick got the courage to look up, he locked eyes with Grant and Dr. Roth, who stood on the other side of the trench.

Before he could move, Grant thundered over to him. "Langston! This is your doing."

Logan spoke first. "We didn't do this, man. We weren't even here last night."

Ignoring him. Grant kept his gaze laser-focused on Rick. "You were the last to leave, right? The last to lock up?"

"Yes, but—"

Time stood still as he replayed the events in his head. He *had* locked up. He'd done it just like Juno had shown him. But when he'd been about to leave, Marisol…

Fuck. She'd screwed up.

"Well?" Grant demanded.

He couldn't say it. Not when Marisol was back at camp, sick with a stomach bug. Not when she was more passionate about field school than any of the other undergrads. Not when she was terrified of getting anything less than an A. He had a sudden callback to Clear Lake and the way Olivia had suffered after she'd messed up. But unlike Olivia, Marisol hadn't broken any laws. She'd just made a simple mistake.

He could take the heat, but she might not be able to handle it.

Well aware everyone was watching him, he choked out the words. "I'm sorry. In my hurry to get to Dr. Bouras' presentation, I must not have locked the gate properly."

Grant gestured to the trench. "Look at this mess. You put the entire excavation in jeopardy. Now we can't do anything until the police finish investigating the area. We've lost hours of work, all because of you."

Alisha nudged Rick. "It wasn't your fault," she hissed. "Marisol went to get her pack. Remember?"

He shook his head. Now that he'd accepted the blame, he'd take the consequences. No matter how bad things got, they couldn't be worse than Palaikastro.

"Was anything stolen?" TJ asked Grant.

"Fortunately not," Grant said. "I don't think these were expert thieves. Just a bunch of teenagers out for a wild night. We got very lucky. But all this could have been avoided." He leaned in closer, addressing Rick in a low voice. "And to think, I almost felt guilty because I didn't introduce you yesterday."

Rick flinched but maintained a stoic facade. He'd be damned if he let Grant break him. "Again, I apologize. Is there anything I can do to help?"

"Once Dr. Roth is done with the police, he'll want to talk to you. I hope he fires you." Having said his piece, Grant turned to the students. "For now, we'll work at the lab stations. With any luck, we can resume excavating in a few hours."

Rick stood rooted in place, feeling helpless, as the others split up. He wanted to talk to Olivia, but she was busy herding her team over to the pot-washing station. When Dr. Roth approached him, he forced himself to meet the professor's eyes, hating the disappointment he saw. "I'm so sorry."

Dr. Roth sighed. "I know this gate is tricky. It's not the first time this has happened. But Juno said she showed everyone how to lock it."

"She did. It was my fault for being in a rush. If any tools were stolen, you can deduct the cost from my salary." Even if the offer would eat at his meager savings, it carried more weight than a mere apology.

"Looks like we got lucky this time. Everything's accounted for. But it could have been so much worse. You know that."

"I do." No matter what anyone else thought of him, Rick had always taken his responsibilities seriously. That was why the rumors from Palaikastro had been so devastating. For all the times he'd cut loose or hooked up, he'd done it after hours. He'd never let his personal life interfere with his work life.

He swallowed, trying to clear the painful knot from his throat. "If you want to let me go, I'll understand. I'd rather stay for the last two weeks of field school, but it's your call."

Dr. Roth kicked a stray rock out of the way. "I don't want to fire you. Not when you've done such a great job with the students. So, I'll keep you on until the end of the project." He paused. "But I can't recommend you to my colleague. Not in good conscience. I'm sorry, Rick."

Rick's stomach clenched. Even with his job in Turkey on lock, he'd still wanted that reference from Dr. Roth. Without it, he'd have a harder time finding work if he returned to California. Maybe this was a sign he was meant to keep traveling.

"That's fine. I appreciate you letting me stay until field school ends."

Dr. Roth clapped him on the shoulder. "For now, you should head back to camp. Given how tense things are here, your presence might not be appreciated. Olivia told me a couple of students are resting there because they're not feeling well. You can keep an eye on them. If you have time, finish your survey report. I still need a full write-up on that Neolithic site you found."

How humiliating. Instead of working at the excavation site, he was being asked to babysit. He dredged up a semblance of a smile. "Sure. No problem."

"You can return tomorrow," Dr. Roth said. "By then, everything should be back to normal."

The thing was—nothing would ever be back to normal.

Now that his reputation had taken another hit, Rick wasn't just back to square one; he was worse off than he'd ever been.

NO MATTER HOW MANY TIMES OLIVIA CHECKED HER WATCH, SHE couldn't make time go faster. With each hour that passed, she grew more worried about Rick. Though she'd known Dr. Roth was upset with him, she hadn't expected the professor to kick him off the site.

She still didn't understand how Rick could have messed up.

He'd been there during Gategate. Like her, he'd paid attention when Juno had shown them how to finesse the lock. But yesterday, he'd been in a rush to make it to Polemi. His team had arrived so late they'd had to sneak into the back row. Maybe he didn't think anyone had noticed, but she'd been aware of it.

During her first break, she sent Rick a series of texts. She sent another one at lunch and one more during her mid-afternoon break.

He didn't respond.

She could only imagine how awful he must feel. Though he hadn't been fired, he'd probably lost his shot at gaining Dr. Roth as a reference.

As the teams made their way back to the parking area, they had to reconfigure their usual seating since Rick had taken one of the cars. Olivia ended up riding with Juno, Logan, and Alisha. Seated up front with Juno, she was so tense her stomach ached. She tried to calm herself by focusing on the scenery. Anything to avoid obsessing over Rick. But her ears perked up when Alisha mentioned him.

"It's not fair. Rick always gets the shaft. First, Grant didn't give him credit for his big site, and then he blamed him for the gate."

"Gategate Two," Juno muttered. "Rick should have been more careful. He was there when I showed everyone how to lock it."

"But he didn't lock the gate," Alisha said. "Marisol did."

Olivia whipped around to face her. "What are you talking about?"

"Remember?" Alisha said to Logan. "You were there. Rick wanted us to hurry because we were running late for that boring-ass presentation at Polemi. Then Marisol had to go back and get her pack because she can't go anywhere without her damn phone. Her parents are super-protective, and they freak out if she doesn't text them back immediately."

Olivia tried to process what she was hearing. "If Rick wasn't at fault, then why did he take the blame?"

"Dunno," Logan said. "He's been looking out for Marisol since the survey unit."

"He talks her off the ledge when she stresses out," Alisha added.

"Yeah, she's always worried about failing," Logan said.

Alisha uncapped her water bottle and took a long drink. "Maybe Rick figured she had more to lose than he did?"

But Rick had a *lot* to lose. What about Dr. Roth's recommendation? And that job in California? How could he throw that away?

Olivia's emotions churned in a stew. She needed answers.

CHAPTER THIRTY

When Juno pulled the car into camp, Olivia scrambled out quickly. She was desperate to track down Rick and talk some sense into him. Even if Marisol was young and anxious, he shouldn't have to take the fall for her. Not if it put his future in jeopardy.

She didn't find him in the sleeping quarters or the lab classrooms. When she texted him, he replied immediately. *I'm in the library.*

She ran into the library and shut the door behind her. He was seated at one of the tables, leafing through an old volume of *The Odyssey.* He'd once told her it was one of his favorite books because he often felt as unrooted as wandering Odysseus.

"What are you doing?" she demanded.

Frowning, he set down the book. "Nice to see you, too."

Damn. She was going about this all wrong. But her heart was pounding so violently she couldn't think rationally. "Alisha told me what happened with the gate. Why'd you take the fall for it?"

He gestured to the chair opposite him. "Have a seat. And relax. It's going to be okay."

How could he act so calm when he'd just torpedoed his future? "No, it's not. Dr. Roth was furious with you."

"I know. It sucks because I've worked really hard. But I couldn't throw Marisol under the bus. She's come such a long way since she started. She actually reminds me of you, back when we were at Clear Lake. If she failed the class or got expelled, I was afraid she might give up on her dreams the way you did."

Why was he so fucking noble? "That was different. We deserved to be expelled. She screwed up once, and it was totally by accident. At worst, Grant might make her life miserable for a few days, but he's not going to fail her."

Irritation clouded his features. "Don't count on it. We both know how vindictive he can be. Right now, he's super pissed. Even if this incident wasn't his fault, the vandalism happened on his watch. I'm sure he hated having to report it to his crush at the Department of Antiquities."

Rick's desire to protect Marisol might be understandable, but it was still frustrating as hell. "What about Roth's letter of reference? He's never going to write it now. I thought you wanted something lined up when you went back to California."

When Rick didn't respond right away, her stomach bottomed out. "You're not going back to California, are you? What about your family?"

"I'll deal with them eventually. For now, I'm staying in the Mediterranean. I got another offer. Two and a half months in Turkey, starting September first. I figured that could tide me over for a while."

What? Her heart skittered in shock. "Why didn't you tell me?"

"Because I wasn't sure if I was going to take the job. Now that my dad's okay—"

"What the fuck, Rick? I've been asking you about your dad all week. I thought you trusted me, but somehow, your entire future changed, and you never thought to tell me about it? How could you hide this from me?"

Even as the words tumbled out, the demanding tone in her voice made her cringe. He'd only promised her three weeks. She had no right to insist on any more than that. But the fact that he'd withheld this information stung like hell.

"I wasn't hiding anything." His voice rose in frustration. "I was trying to figure out what to do. It wasn't easy making this decision, but this is *my* future, not yours."

Tears welled up in her eyes, but she blinked them away. "So your future doesn't include me?"

"We never talked about it. I'd like to go back to California at some point, but let's be honest. It wouldn't work in the long run. You're obviously going places. Networking with professors and making a name for yourself. I'll never be at that level."

"Is this about that stupid presentation at Polemi? I just went out afterward to stay on Grant's good side. I don't care about any of that!" Indignation rose inside her, setting her blood boiling. How could he lump her in with people like Grant and TJ?

"Of course you do. It's your career. You've been working toward it for years. Let's face it, I'm nothing but a shovel bum. You even admitted as much to Grant."

She flinched, remembering her conversation with him. It killed her that he'd thrown her words back at Rick. "I didn't mean it. I was trying to convince Grant I wasn't involved with you. And honestly? You use the term more than anyone else, including him. If you hate being called a shovel bum, then why don't you do something about it?"

"What would you suggest?"

Ignoring the sarcastic tone in his voice, she plowed on ahead. "Maybe you *should* consider grad school. You're so good with students. And you're too smart to waste…" Her words trailed off as she realized what she was implying.

His expression darkened. "Too smart to what? To waste my life dicking around in the field?"

"I didn't mean it that way. But you might have gone on to grad school if your dad had supported you. Right? You could still pursue it if you wanted."

"Academia's not my thing, remember? But that's not enough for you, is it? Not when you've got your future all planned out. There's no room in it for a guy like me."

She'd never said that. Not once. All she'd been trying to do was get him to consider his options.

Don't you get it? He's pushing you away. Trying to cut and run like he always does.

He'd just made it painfully clear that his future didn't include her. Once she flew home, she'd probably never hear from him again.

Even if she wanted more, she wouldn't beg for it.

Time to cut her losses while she still had an ounce of dignity left.

"You're right. Clearly, our lives aren't headed in the same direction." Her throat was so dry it hurt to swallow. "Which means there's no reason for us to stay together."

"Isn't that what we said from the beginning? That we wouldn't worry about the future?"

"I'm talking about now." She gritted out the words. "I'm done, Rick."

"You're ending things *now*?" His voice was ragged with pain. "Just like that?"

If she took it all back, they could still enjoy their remaining time together—ten days in Cyprus, followed by a glorious week in Athens. But the longer she was with him, the more it would hurt when he left. And he *would* leave. It was inevitable.

"I'm sorry. I can't do this anymore." Fighting back the sting of tears, she turned and left the library. She couldn't cry in front of him. She'd already made herself vulnerable enough.

Wanting to put some distance between them, she kept walking until she'd reached the road leading to the village. When the sobs finally came, they racked her entire body. Her heart ached at the way Rick had deliberately pushed her away. After the intimacy they'd shared, she'd secretly hoped he might want more than another two weeks together.

She was wrong.

What did you expect? He never promised you anything.

Right from the start, he'd told her his life was uncertain. Even when he'd talked about returning to California, he never said he wanted a relationship. But that hadn't stopped her from dreaming about it or imagining a future where they ended up together.

But clearly, he didn't share her feelings. If he had, he would have asked her opinion about Turkey. But he didn't need it because he'd always planned to move on without her.

She'd told herself she could handle a fling.

But somewhere along the way, she'd made the terrible mistake of falling in love with Rick Langston all over again.

CHAPTER THIRTY-ONE

Olivia set down her book. She'd read through the last paragraph three times, so apparently, her mind wasn't on the history of Anatolian trade during the Hellenistic era. After talking with Dr. Roth at dinner the other night, she'd considered adding more source material to her dissertation. Usually, when she got on a new research tangent, she couldn't wait to dive in. She loved finding evidence to support her theories. But tonight, she couldn't focus.

Alone in the research library, she could hear the strains of Rick's guitar. She wanted to join him but knew she wouldn't be welcomed. He'd barely spoken to her since she'd broken things off two days ago.

More than anything, she longed to seek him out and apologize. Even if he'd blindsided her with his news about Turkey, that didn't justify the demands she'd made. Or the way she'd dumped him as if he wasn't worthy. If she'd been brave enough, she would have told him the truth—that she was in love with him and was hurt he hadn't considered her in his plans.

But she could only imagine the pitying look he would have given her. The humiliation she would have felt when he let her down gently. She'd rather leave him feeling angry and frustrated than guilty that he couldn't reciprocate her feelings.

With only eight days left of field school, she should have been taking pride in how far she'd come. Considering her lack of experience, she'd accomplished a lot—finding a site, leading her own trench, and uncovering a skeleton. She'd also enjoyed working with students beyond the confines of a classroom. But she was finding it hard to take pleasure in any of it. If anything, she wanted the time to pass as quickly as possible.

In a little over a week, Rick would be gone. Out of her life, possibly forever. Though the heartache would linger once she was back home, she wouldn't have to see him every day.

How ironic was it that she'd warned the students about the consequences of hooking up, only to deal with it herself?

"Olivia?" Marisol's soft voice broke the stillness. She hovered in the doorway.

"Hey, Marisol," Olivia said. "Everything okay?"

"Not exactly. Can I talk to you?"

"Sure." She shoved the book aside. "Would you rather go outside? It's cooler out there."

"I'd rather talk in private if that's all right." Closing the door behind her, Marisol slowly advanced toward the table.

"We can talk wherever you feel the most comfortable." Olivia gestured for her to sit. "Did something happen with one of the students?"

"No." Marisol perched on the edge of her seat and twisted her braid between her fingers. "It's about the other day—when the site was vandalized. I didn't hear about it right away because I was back here with a stomach bug."

"Right. I remember." Olivia suspected Marisol had come to offer up a confession, but she didn't want to push her.

"Yesterday, Alisha told me Rick took the blame for not locking the gate properly," Marisol said. "But it wasn't his fault. I was the last one out. I thought I locked it the way Juno demonstrated, but I messed up. I should have said something as soon as I found out, but I didn't want to get expelled."

Olivia could only imagine how tormented Marisol must have felt, torn between admitting her mistake and keeping it hidden. "Alisha and Logan told me the truth. It's okay."

"It's not. Rick got in trouble with Dr. Roth, didn't he?"

From outside the window, Olivia caught the first few bars of Elton's John's "Goodbye Yellow Brick Road"—one of Rick's favorite songs. An ache spread through her, making her wish nothing had changed between them.

Clearing her head, she focused on Marisol. "Rick will be fine. He's already got another job lined up. Don't worry about it."

"That's the thing—I can't stop worrying. I wanted to tell everyone what happened, but I knew Grant—I mean Dr. Nilsson —would be furious with me." She twisted her braid again. "If it wasn't for him, I would have confessed right away. But he's made me so scared of messing up that I don't want to upset him."

"That's awful. I'm sorry you feel this way."

"It's not just me. We're *all* scared of him."

The revelation hit Olivia like a body blow. This wasn't just about Grant targeting her or Rick. It was about him intimidating the students and making them so afraid that they'd rather lie than face his wrath.

Why hadn't Frida told her Grant was such a bully? She'd called him a joyless control freak, but there was a difference between being hypercritical and blatantly abusing his power. Maybe Frida hadn't realized how much he'd bullied them when she wasn't around to see it. But now that Olivia was aware of it, she needed to take action.

"I apologize for not tackling the Grant issue sooner," she said. "Would you be willing to talk to Dr. Roth about it? You'd need to tell him the truth about the gate, but you could also explain why you were too afraid to come forward immediately."

Marisol's eyes glistened with tears. "Will I get expelled? Or fail the class? If that happened, my parents would never let me forget it. I had a hard enough time convincing them I could handle this course."

"Believe me, I know how you feel, but Dr. Roth won't fail you. And he won't blow up at you, either." When Marisol hesitated, Olivia pushed a little more. "I'll go with you if you want."

Marisol wiped her eyes. "That would make me feel better. When should we tell him?"

The longer Olivia waited, the harder it would be. "As soon as possible. I'll call and see if he's available. We can walk down to the field house to talk to him."

As she picked up her phone, her hands trembled. Grant had instructed them never to use Dr. Roth's personal number, except in case of an emergency. What if she told the professor the situation and he didn't believe her? What if he thought she lacked the proper respect for authority? He'd never want to serve on her dissertation committee.

But as she glanced at Marisol, who sat hunched over, her hands wrapped around herself, she summoned up her courage. Hadn't she been hired to look out for the students? No matter how nervous she felt, she needed to put them first.

That was why she'd wanted to go into teaching. Not for the networking or the connections, but to share her passion for ancient history with students and encourage them. If she let someone like Grant tyrannize them, then she wasn't doing her job.

To her immense relief, Dr. Roth answered her call. After a quick conversation, she and Marisol were on their way to the field house. Once they got there, Marisol hung back, forcing Olivia to step up and ring the bell. As she waited for someone to answer the door, she tried to control the ragged beat of her heart. Up until this minute, she hadn't considered the possibility that Grant might be there.

When he opened the door, his scowl was so menacing she

wanted to turn tail and run. She forced herself to speak clearly. "I'm here to see Dr. Roth."

Grant made no attempt to move aside. "I don't think so. It's after nine."

"I called ahead. Marisol needs to talk to him."

"If there's a problem at camp, she should be coming to me." He crossed his arms. "I told you not to bother Dr. Roth with your petty concerns."

"It's not petty." She whipped out her phone. "Are you going to let us in, or do I need to call him again?"

To her relief, Dr. Roth appeared in the doorway. "Good evening, ladies. Thanks for coming."

"I apologize for the intrusion," Grant said to him. "Whatever the issue, we could have dealt with it tomorrow during regular work hours."

"I don't think so." Olivia gave Dr. Roth a generous smile. "May we talk alone, sir?"

"Certainly." He gestured for them to come in. "Would either of you like a drink? Perhaps a beer or a gin and tonic?"

Olivia followed him into the house, with Marisol trailing behind her. "Thanks, but Marisol's underage. Maybe something else?"

Dr. Roth chuckled. "Of course. I always forget. Ridiculous thing, this American drinking age. No other country is so draconian." He led them to the kitchen and opened the fridge. "I'm sure you're sick of lemon squash by now. How about a soda?"

After getting a beer for himself and a couple of Sprites for them, he led them out to the back patio. It was even more blissful in the evening, the pergola decked out with twinkling fairy lights, the fountain glimmering with illumination.

Olivia sat on one of the wicker chairs, letting the patio's calming ambience wash over her. "Marisol has something to tell you. Before she does, I assured her you wouldn't erupt in anger. Do you think you can agree to that?"

"Well, I suppose." He cast Marisol an inquisitive glance. "You didn't break any laws, did you? Stash valuable artifacts in your pack or smuggle drugs into the country?"

"Really, Dr. Roth?" Olivia said.

"Trust me, I've seen it all." He turned to Marisol with an avuncular smile. "Tell me what happened. Even if I'm disappointed or angry, I promise not to yell. It's much too late in the day."

"Okay...thanks." Marisol's voice trembled at first, but the longer she spoke, the stronger it grew. She told the professor how she'd screwed up, how Rick had covered for her, and why she'd waited to come forward with her confession. A few times, her eyes misted with tears, but she kept going.

When she was done, Dr. Roth handed her a cloth handkerchief. "Here. Take a few deep breaths, all right?"

She wiped her eyes. "I'm so sorry. Please don't send me home early."

His voice was gentle. "I'm not pleased you let someone else take the blame, but I admire your bravery. You risked a lot by coming to talk to me. I'm also glad to learn Rick wasn't at fault. I was torn over whether to recommend him for a job in California, but—"

"*Please* recommend him," Marisol said. "He's been a wonderful teacher. He's patient and understanding, and he never gets upset with us."

"That's good to hear," Dr. Roth said. "Knowing all this, I'll have no problem telling my colleague about him."

Olivia's heart flooded with relief. No matter how much she'd hurt Rick by ending things, at least she'd helped him repair his reputation.

"I'm not the only one who feels this way about Rick," Marisol added. "Alisha likes working with him. Logan, too. The only reason Brynn complained during the survey was because our team came in last those first few days. She was terrified of getting a bad grade."

"I told her our pace wouldn't affect her grade," Olivia said. "So did Rick."

"I know," Marisol said. "But Dr. Nilsson didn't feel the same way. This one time, he pulled a bunch of us aside and warned us not to mess up his schedule. He said we'd be docked points if our team kept coming in late."

"He did?" Dr. Roth chuffed out an aggravated breath. "I never asked him to set standards like that. What else did he say about your grades?"

"It was the same with excavation. If we screwed up anything, we could lose points. When Olivia didn't lock the gate properly the first time, he yelled at all of us. Said if anyone messed up like that again, they might get sent home. He likes to run a tight ship." Marisol straightened up, as if gaining strength. "If you want my opinion, he's the worst teacher here."

Dr. Roth frowned at Olivia. "Why didn't you mention this before?"

Despite the guilt tugging at her conscience, Olivia reminded herself she'd been equally intimidated. "Grant told us never to bother you. That day I came to see you after my asthma attack? I was terrified you'd be angry that I interrupted your research. Grant's made it clear you're off-limits unless you're at the field school." She swallowed, afraid of what her honesty might cost her. "You're not there that much, so you've missed a lot."

She cringed inwardly, waiting for him to reprimand her, but he let out a pained sigh.

"You're right. The fault is mine. I have a book due to the UC Press this fall, and I needed to make inroads. But I shouldn't have prioritized my own work over the students." He smiled at Marisol. "Thanks again for your honesty. Your grades won't suffer in the least. They'll be based on your work on the survey, the lab, and the excavation, and they'll be submitted by the grad students. Their opinions are the ones that matter."

Marisol folded up his handkerchief and placed it on the patio table. "Thanks, Dr. Roth."

Olivia stood up. "Thanks for hearing us out. We'll let you get back to your research."

Dr. Roth's eyes met hers. "Thank *you*, Olivia, for bringing all this to my attention. You've been a real asset to this field school. I look forward to reading your dissertation when it's completed."

Of all the outcomes she'd expected tonight, Olivia never imagined receiving such powerful words of validation. "Thanks for taking a chance on me."

"Before you go, can you ask Grant to come out here?" he said. "I need to have a chat with him."

As Olivia left with Marisol, she could barely contain the happiness bubbling up inside her. Though she didn't imagine Grant would get fired, maybe Dr. Roth would call him on his shitty behavior. For now, that would be enough.

On the walk back, Marisol recounted the conversation with glee. Olivia joined in, elated that Grant might finally be getting his due. By the time they reached Camp Kouklia, she was coasting on a wave of positive energy. When Marisol went to look for Alisha, Olivia sought out Rick at the picnic table. To her relief, he was alone, with his guitar resting on the bench beside him.

Heart pounding, she walked over to him, unsettled by the look of disinterest on his face.

"What's up?" he asked.

No smile. No warmth. No gesture for her to sit down. He was still mad, and for good reason. But his mood might change once she shared her news.

"So…Marisol came to talk to me tonight. About the gate. She said the only reason she didn't admit the truth earlier was because she was afraid of Grant. Did you know he threatened to fail the students if they screwed up?" Her voice rose in indignation. "He's been intimidating them so much they're terrified of doing anything wrong."

Rick scowled, but his anger wasn't directed at her. "What an asshole. I didn't realize he'd taken things that far."

"Me neither. Apparently, he did it when we weren't around to intervene. But I convinced Marisol to talk to Dr. Roth about it. She told him everything. He was upset but not with us. He also acknowledged he'd been pretty oblivious."

Rick favored her with a hint of a smile. "I can't believe she spoke up like that. Or maybe I can. She reminds me a lot of you."

He'd mentioned that before, but hearing it again filled her with remorse. By sticking up for Marisol, his heart had been in the right place. Olivia had just been too focused on her own needs to appreciate his enormous act of generosity.

"Marisol didn't get in trouble?" he asked.

"Nope. Dr. Roth was very understanding. He said the incident wouldn't affect her grade."

"Good. She deserves an A. She's worked really hard."

Olivia gnawed on her lip. "Anyway…now that Roth knows the truth, he'll have no qualms about recommending you to his friend who runs the rescue archaeology firm." She forced a bright smile on her face. "Isn't that great? If you want, you could go back to California."

A part of her—an extremely foolish, optimistic part—thought Rick might jump at the opportunity. If he so much as hinted at choosing California over Turkey, then maybe she could drum up the courage to tell him how she really felt.

I'm sorry I hurt you. I didn't want things to end. I just wanted more.

But he merely shrugged. "Good to hear, even if I don't need it right now."

Her heart plummeted. "Your plans for Turkey are set?"

"Yep. Since my dad doesn't have cancer, I'm not needed at

home. And unlike you, I'm not trying to get ahead in the world, so it doesn't matter where I end up, does it?"

"I'm sorry if I made it sound like you were wasting your life." Her voice was raw with regret. "I shouldn't have said that."

"Don't be. I'm not ashamed of the way I live. But obviously you are, so it's just as well you ended things. I wish you the best with your academic career, but like you said, we're not headed in the same direction."

She'd done this to herself. Shut him out rather than confess her true feelings and expose herself to more hurt.

Speak up for yourself. Tell him you're in love with him.

But she couldn't do it. "I'm sorry."

"Me, too. Athens would have been a blast." He got up, taking his guitar with him.

She watched him go, feeling more miserable than ever.

She'd won him a victory. But not getting to celebrate with him was the worst feeling of all.

CHAPTER THIRTY-TWO

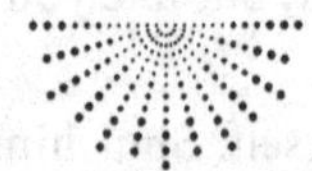

Though Rick was grateful Olivia had helped clear his name, it didn't change anything between them. The damage had been done. Not only had she dumped him when he was at his lowest, but she also considered him so unworthy that she didn't even want to spend her last week of field school with him.

He set his guitar on his cot and strode away from camp, wanting to put some space between himself and Olivia. When his phone buzzed, he removed it from his pocket grudgingly.

Dr. Roth had texted him. *We should chat. How about a drink at Spyros?*

Despite his sullen mood, Rick wasn't about to turn down an invitation from his boss. *Sure. Be there in ten minutes.*

By the time he reached the restaurant, he'd calmed down a little. Dr. Roth was seated at a table on the patio, drinking a beer. Rick joined him and ordered one for himself, but he was unsure of how to start. Should he apologize for lying about the gate? Bring up the Grant issue?

Fortunately, Dr. Roth took the lead. "How are you doing?"

Heartbroken, but I'll survive.

Rick managed a weak smile. "Better, now that Marisol came to you and confessed." He looked up as the server set down his beer. "Thanks, Kostas."

"No problem, Mister Rick," the boy said. "Nice and cold, the way you like it."

Dr. Roth waited a minute before speaking. "Why'd you do it?"

"Cover for Marisol, you mean?" Rick asked.

"Yes. You put your reputation on the line for a student you've known for all of five weeks. Why bother?"

Rick took a pull of his beer. The cool, refreshing ale went down so easily he could have drained it in a few swallows, but he needed to pace himself. "What I did wasn't just about her. It was about every student who's been intimidated or felt like they weren't good enough. I didn't want her to leave this field school feeling like she'd failed, just because she made a mistake."

Like Olivia, back at Clear Lake.

"That's a noble gesture, but what about you? What about *your* future? And don't say it doesn't matter because we both know that's not true. What do you want?"

Rather than make up some bullshit about considering a graduate degree, Rick opted for the truth. "Honestly? To keep doing fieldwork until I'm too old to lift a shovel. Either here in the Mediterranean or back in the States. My plans might change at some point, but for now, I feel like that's enough."

His shoulders tightened as he waited for a response, hoping Dr. Roth wouldn't think less of him for not going the full academic route.

But the professor merely shrugged. "It's more than enough. If you wanted to get a doctorate, I'd tell you to go for it, but I sense your heart wouldn't be in it." He gave a rueful smile. "Besides, academia has its own burdens. I wouldn't recommend it to anyone unless they're sure it's the path they want."

Rick might have wanted it when he was nineteen, but his life had followed a different course. It was time he started respecting himself for the choices he'd made. "Thanks. I appreciate your take on things." He cleared his throat. "Given the job I've done this summer, I'd also appreciate it if you could recommend me to your colleague in California. I have a lot to offer."

"Indeed you do. Can I ask you, though—what really happened at Palaikastro? From what I've seen, you're not the type to go on a drunken bender and show up for work hungover."

An unexpected laugh broke free of Rick's throat. "You're right. I've never done any of that—not when I was on the clock. My only mistake was chasing after the wrong woman and pissing off her father."

Dr. Roth chuckled. "Ah yes, I can relate. I've been there myself."

I'm sure you have.

"I'd like to help you out however I can," the professor said. "So, I tell you what—not only will I call my colleague, but I'll also write you a letter of reference for any job you'd like to pursue in the future. Finding someone with your integrity is rare indeed."

His words boosted Rick's confidence even further. "Thanks. For what it's worth, I'd jump at the chance to work with you again."

"I'd be glad to have you on board. Unfortunately, I can't say the same for Grant. Olivia and Marisol told me he's been bullying the students. But when I spoke to him about it just now, he claimed the two women were overreacting."

Rick frowned. "They were being honest. Grant's attitude has been toxic from day one. I'm sorry I didn't bring it up sooner."

"Don't apologize. I should have paid more attention. I'd like to meet with the students and get their feedback—maybe one night after dinner. They deserve to be heard."

"Great idea. But what about Grant?"

Dr. Roth rubbed the back of his neck. "That's a tough call. He hasn't had the easiest path. Have you ever met his father?"

"Dusty told me about him—some academic big shot at Princeton?"

"He's a brilliant scholar. Fluent in six languages. A huge name in the Classical world. And—if you'll pardon my French—a complete asshole."

The professor's unexpected profanity made Rick laugh so hard he almost spit out his beer. "Really?"

"Trust me. I had the misfortune to take a couple of his classes when he was a visiting lecturer. The man could bring a student to tears with a few well-placed words. Following in his footsteps couldn't be easy."

Rick nodded. "I got that impression. My dad's not much better. He kicked me out four years ago, after I dropped out of law school. At the time, it hurt like hell."

"I'm sorry to hear it. But you still turned out to be a decent human being. Someone who treats students with respect and patience. Grant—not so much."

Rick didn't want to feel sorry for Grant—not after everything he'd done. But he couldn't hate the guy either. Anyone that toxic had to be dealing with a lot of internal pressure. "Maybe you could try talking to him again? Not that he deserves another chance, but if he doesn't change, he's not going to have much of a future."

"I suppose it couldn't hurt." He smiled at Rick. "Now tell me about this law school business. I have to say I'm very intrigued."

Now that he was back in Dr. Roth's good graces, Rick was given another chance to take his survey team—TJ, Alisha, Logan, and Marisol—back to their Neolithic site to investigate it further. When Roth suggested it, Rick almost asked if Olivia could join them since he knew she'd love the opportunity. But he was still smarting over the way she'd ended things.

Our lives are headed in different directions. Code for "I'm going places, and you're not."

After his talk with Dr. Roth, Rick had no regrets about the path he was on. If Olivia couldn't respect his choices, then so be it. He didn't need her.

To be fair, she wasn't the only one who'd fucked up. Instead of telling her about Turkey sooner, he'd thrown it at her when she was already upset. Even then, he could have smoothed things over by admitting he cared about her. He should have told her he'd struggled with his decision to stay in the Mediterranean. Not because of his family, but because he didn't want to lose her. But when she accused him of wasting his life, his walls went up, and he pushed her away.

They'd barely spoken since. Yet another reason he was grateful that he didn't have to spend the day excavating at the House of Heracles. He and his team had been digging at the Neolithic site since early morning, but he'd been so immersed he hadn't noticed the time passing. He straightened up, his body stiff from crouching for so long, and walked over to the pit where Alisha and Marisol were working.

"Time for lunch," he called out.

Marisol peered up at him, her face smudged with dirt. "Do we have to stop now? I think Alisha and I found part of a wall. Or maybe a structure. Does that mean our site could be a settlement?"

"Why didn't you tell me sooner?" Hopping down inside their pit, Rick scraped his towel along the row of stones. They were packed too tightly to be a random assortment of rocks. "Yep— you've definitely found something. Great job. We'll need to expand out from this area."

TJ dropped his sieve and loped over to them. He gazed down at the stones lining the far side of the pit. "Sweet! If we could find a structure, Roth would be pumped. Maybe he'll mention us in his survey report. I already have a few publications to my name, but I'll take whatever credit I can get."

"Of course you will," Alisha said. "You want to be as famous as Dusty's parents. Did you know they were on last year's season of *Ancient Histories—Ancient Mysteries*? They did six episodes about Ancient Egypt. I have to watch it when I get home."

"It's a great show," TJ said. "Maybe a little dumbed down for the masses but still entertaining. I wouldn't say no if they asked me to do a guest appearance. Not that I want to go all Hollywood or anything. Gotta keep it real. None of that Indiana Jones bullshit."

Alisha stood and stretched out her back. "Nothing wrong with Indy. I wouldn't turn him away from my bed. The young Indy from *Raiders of the Lost Ark*, not the cranky old guy from that whack movie about the aliens."

"Yeah, the fourth one really sucked. Aliens? That's the biggest cop-out of all time."

While TJ and Alisha continued debating the merits of the Indiana Jones franchise, Rick retrieved the team's cooler and brought out their lunch—peasant bread, cheese, tomatoes, hard-boiled eggs, oranges, cookies, and more of the ubiquitous grapes. After everyone had cleaned up with the wipes from the dig bag, they sat together in the shade.

"Rick, are you doing okay?" Marisol said. "Dr. Roth spoke to you, right?"

He was grateful she cared enough to ask. "He did. Thanks for telling him the truth."

"I'm sorry I didn't confess right away, but I was afraid of Dr. Nilsson." Her eyes brimmed with tears, but she swiped at them with the back of her hand. "Olivia gave me the courage to speak up. When we talked to Dr. Roth, he wasn't even mad. Not at me, anyway. And not at you, either."

"Thanks. I'm glad it all worked out." Even as Rick said it, guilt nagged at him.

Olivia had stuck her neck out—not just for Marisol and the other students, but for him as well. If not for her, he wouldn't have gotten a second chance with Dr. Roth. Had he actually thanked her for what she'd done?

No. He'd been a jerk. Still smarting from the way she'd dumped him, he'd frozen her out and refused to accept her apology.

Alisha's voice grounded him. "Rick. You still with us?"

He nodded. But as he unwrapped a piece of Laughing Cow cheese, he recalled Olivia joking about it during their trip to the supermarket in Paphos. He pushed the memory away.

TJ popped a handful of grapes into his mouth. "So, Rick, now that we're almost done here, what's your next gig? Have you got something lined up?"

Trust TJ to ask if he was thinking ahead. But looking forward was far preferable to brooding over Olivia.

Rick tapped a hard-boiled egg against his knife and started peeling it. "I was considering a couple of options, but I decided to go back to Turkey to work for the Institute of Nautical Archaeology. I'll be doing a mix of underwater excavation and lab work like I did last fall."

"That's so exciting," Alisha said. "I lived in Istanbul for a year and really liked it. If you visit the city, hit me up for recs. I know some killer restaurants."

"Just out of curiosity, what was the other choice?" Marisol asked.

"I was thinking about going home to California to see my family," Rick said. "I haven't been back in years. I was going to look for work in cultural resource management." At Marisol's curious look, he added, "Rescue archaeology—conducting surveys or excavating sites threatened by construction or land development."

Alisha unpeeled an orange and broke it into segments. She passed a few to Marisol. "Let's see…uncovering an underwater shipwreck versus digging up the site of a future high-rise. Sounds like you made the right choice."

"Except if you went back to California, you could be with Olivia," TJ said. "Isn't she at UCLA?" At the stunned looks Alisha and Marisol gave him, he clapped his hand over his mouth. "Oh, shit. Forget I said that."

Marisol giggled. "Seems obvious to me. I've seen the way Olivia looks at you."

"Yep, the girl's got it bad," Alisha agreed. "Are you two an item?"

Rick released a tight breath. "We were, but not anymore. It wouldn't work out in the long run."

"Why not?" Marisol said. "You're both archaeologists. You both love what you do. I think it's so romantic."

"Yeah, but by next spring, she'll have her PhD and be looking for teaching jobs. I'll never be at that level." Rick's gaze fell on TJ. "Like you said, it's all about connections, right? I'm not a very valuable one."

"Shit, man, I shouldn't have said that," TJ said. "I was talking out of my ass. When I saw you at the airport in Larnaca, looking so jacked, I had to compete somehow. Unlike you, I'm not exactly built like a superhero. I don't have half your experience, either."

"But you've battled scorpions in the desert heat," Alisha teased.

"Rick's done more than that," TJ said. "The guy's been living without a safety net. That's super ballsy." He grabbed the last two cookies from the pack and crumpled up the wrapper.

"You honestly think Olivia cares whether you get a PhD?" Marisol asked. "That might be her dream, but it doesn't mean she expects you to do the same thing. Unless you want to?"

Even if he'd been stung by Olivia's words, their argument had forced Rick to think about what he really wanted, as had his conversation with Dr. Roth. "Nope. As much as I like working with students, academia's not for me. I'd rather be out in the field, but it's hard to teach without a doctorate. Or a master's, at least."

"Maybe you could figure something out," TJ said. "Like, if you did the rescue archaeology thing, you could teach high school students about it. Run weekend courses where they could learn about preserving our cultural heritage. They won't care if you're from an Ivy League school. They'll just want to hear about all the stuff you've done in the field."

True. A kid fascinated by archaeology would be more impressed by Rick's adventures than his credentials.

"Thanks," he said. "I'll consider it, though I'm not sure when I'll be heading back to California."

"What about Olivia?" Marisol asked. "Are you just going to let her go? If you really want her, I bet you could make it work. She knows you care about her, right?"

Does she?

When she'd told him it was over, he hadn't asked if they could talk things out. Instead, he'd let her walk away. He hadn't even tried to stop her.

"No. I never told her. Because I'm an idiot," he muttered.

"Don't beat yourself up," Alisha said. "Most guys are idiots. But it's not too late to fix this. We've got—what—a week left? That's still time to win her back."

"Yeah, man," TJ said. "First rule of rom-coms—it's never too late for a grand gesture."

Rick wasn't sure what a grand gesture entailed, but he sure as hell wasn't going to ask. Knowing TJ, there was a lengthy story behind it.

Once lunch was over, he and TJ staked out two more test pits. With any luck, they might learn whether the stone feature Alisha and Marisol had uncovered was part of a larger structure, like a wall or a building. Rick secretly hoped they might find the remains of round stone dwellings, like the type seen at Choirokoitia, a well-known Neolithic settlement located an hour east of them. Discovering a similar site would be a huge accomplishment.

As his team continued working, he watched them with pride. Despite the dust and heat of the day, they were just as invested as if they'd uncovered a Pharaoh's tomb. What had started as a chance find—a handful of stone tools—might turn out to be a seven-thousand-year-old settlement. This was the part of archaeology he loved—being at the forefront of new discoveries and sharing his excitement with the students.

A twinge of sadness pinched his heart as he imagined how much Olivia would have enjoyed being here with him.

For the rest of the day, he couldn't get her off his mind. She'd risked a lot when she'd gone to Dr. Roth. She'd had the courage to speak up against Grant, regardless of the repercussions. And she hadn't done it to get ahead. All she'd wanted to do was help the students.

But Rick had shut her out. He'd been so defensive about graduate school that he'd forced her hand. Then he'd put up walls so high she couldn't get in.

Could he risk lowering them? Could he try to win her back?

The only way to do it was by being completely honest. He needed to tell her how he felt.

Battling scorpions in the desert heat might be easier.

CHAPTER THIRTY-THREE

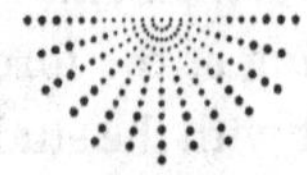

Seated on the balcony of Sofia's apartment, Olivia watched the sun make its descent, painting the sky with a rose-gold glow. Sipping her wine, she released a contented sigh, thankful for an evening out. Her day had gotten off to a rough start at breakfast when Rick had announced that his team would be digging at the Neolithic site they'd found during the survey. When Rick had locked eyes with her, she could have sworn his expression softened. For a tantalizing moment, she thought he might ask her to join them.

But if he'd felt a connection, he hadn't acted on it. Instead, he rounded up his team and left. Olivia went about her normal duties at the excavation site while trying to ignore the growing ache in her heart. When Sofia had texted her with an invitation for a girls' night in, she jumped at the chance and brought Dusty with her.

Dusty joined her on the balcony, carrying a can of Pellegrino. "This is a sweet setup. Whenever I traveled with my parents, we never stayed anywhere like this."

"Were you mostly in army tents?" Olivia asked.

"Sometimes. Either that or a field house, but they weren't as nice as the one Roth is renting. We're talking bunk beds, communal bathrooms, and a shared kitchen. Not exactly the height of luxury."

Sofia bustled out to the balcony and set a ceramic tray on the wrought-iron table; on it were clippers, nail files, cotton balls, and bottles of polish. "Manicure time. You two have the worst nails I've ever seen."

Though Olivia usually wore work gloves while excavating, she preferred using her bare hands when uncovering smaller artifacts. As a result, stubborn bits of dirt remained lodged under her fingernails. "It's kind of a waste, seeing as how we have another week of excavation left."

Dusty examined her hands. Though she didn't spend her days digging, her fingers were streaked with ink. "I'm willing to go for it."

Sofia passed Olivia a bottle of crimson polish. "Here. This will look good with your tan. Dusty, your skin tone's a little paler, so the rose polish is a better match."

Olivia had never been one to fuss with her nails, but she appreciated her sister's effort. "Thanks. Pass me the clippers. The first thing I have to do is trim these suckers."

"Before you start, do either of you want anything else to drink?" Sofia asked. "More wine?"

"I'm good for now, thanks." Olivia's second glass had smoothed over the day's rough edges, but a third might make her too sleepy.

Dusty held up her can of sparkling water. "I'll stick with this. I have to drive us back to camp."

"You can crash here if you want," Sofia said. "Isn't tomorrow your day off? Why not sleep in and wake up with real coffee? Olivia can bunk with me in that giant bed, and you can take the couch. I'm sure it's nicer than those ratty camp cots. Plus, the shower here has hot water."

Like the place where I'll be staying in Athens. Olivia had been so pleased when she'd found an affordable hotel room with a big bed, a private bathroom, and a balcony with a view of the Acropolis. Except now, she didn't have anyone to share it with.

"I'd love to take advantage," Dusty said. "But we've got an early morning tomorrow. We're going to the Troodos Mountains."

Olivia winced as she clipped off a hangnail. "I'm not sure whether I should go. I don't need to be stuck in a car with Rick for two hours."

As soon as she spoke, she wished she'd kept quiet. She hadn't told Dusty or Sofia exactly what had happened, only that she and Rick were over. She hadn't planned to bring him up, either. Tonight was for having fun, not for agonizing over her failed love life.

"Back up a sec," Sofia said. "Because you still haven't told me the whole story. One day, you were all, ohmigod, we're having sex in a temple dedicated to the goddess of love, and the next, you're telling me it's over."

Dusty's eyes went wide. "You and Rick had sex in the Sanctuary of Aphrodite? That's unbelievable."

"And romantic," Sofia added. "You said the sex was amazing."

A rush of heat warmed Olivia's cheeks. She shot Dusty an apologetic glance. "Sorry you had to hear that. I'm not the type to brag about—"

"About what? Your amazing sex life? At least someone's getting a little action. Stuart still treats me like I'm his sister."

"Stuart? The hot blond guy?" Sofia asked. "I can see why you'd be into him. TJ's sorta cute, too, in nerdy way. But we're getting off topic. I want to know what happened with Rick."

Keeping her eyes downcast, Olivia focused on buffing her nails. "Fine. That okay with you, Dusty?"

"Absolutely. Spill."

Since Dusty didn't know what had happened at Clear Lake, Olivia had to backtrack. Then she had to explain the long and frustrating path she and Rick had taken before they'd finally gotten together. Though she didn't go into detail, she *did* mention the temple. She still found it hard to believe she'd had sex out in the open. She finished by explaining how Gategate Two had led to their big argument.

Dusty blew on her nails to dry them. "You want my advice? Go apologize. I don't blame Rick for being mad, but he's had time to cool off."

"But after the way I dumped him, what makes you think he wants me back?"

"He might not," Dusty said. "But you also got him off the hook for the gate fiasco. He owes you for that."

"Hardly. He wasn't even grateful."

"He was probably still pissed at you," Sofia said. "But before you go after him, you have to decide whether you want him back, just as he is. Even if he forgives you, he's not going to change his lifestyle. Can you accept that?"

Olivia had given the issue a lot of thought. "I wouldn't want him to change; he's a wonderful guy. But I'm not sure if there's room in his life for me."

"There might be," Dusty said. "But you need to be honest. Put yourself out there."

Sofia gestured with the nail file. "No wimping out. Look him in the eye and tell him how much you love him."

"I never said I *loved* him," Olivia sputtered. "I..."

Why was she denying it? She loved him as much as she had at Clear Lake. Or more because she wasn't that same inexperienced nineteen-year-old. By now, she'd dated enough guys to know Rick was the real deal. Not only had he treated her with patience, respect, and kindness, he'd helped her rediscover her love of archaeology.

"You're not fooling anyone," Sofia said.

Olivia released a long, drawn-out breath. "Okay. But even if I admit I'm in love with him, I don't think he feels the same way. All he wanted was a few weeks of fun. Nothing else."

Sofia began brushing a clear coat of polish over her nails. "Maybe he's changed. You won't know unless you ask."

"Even if he just wants a fling, wouldn't you rather spend your last week in Cyprus with him?" Dusty asked. "Sure, it'll hurt when he leaves, but you're already hurting anyway. Why not go out with a bang?"

Sofia grinned. "A literal bang. Am I right?"

She always was.

If Olivia wanted a shot at happiness, she couldn't let her fear and anxiety get the best of her. For years, she'd been so afraid of taking chances that she hadn't really lived. Even if she'd be opening herself up to more heartbreak, she needed to be honest with Rick. Because a life without risk was no life at all.

CHAPTER THIRTY-FOUR

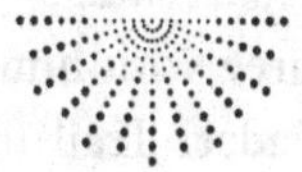

When Olivia woke the next morning, still groggy from her late night at Sofia's, she regretted her decision to return to camp. Why hadn't she slept over at her sister's place? Then she could have spent her day swimming and sunbathing. Instead, she was dragging her sorry butt on a group outing led by Rick, who was still freezing her out.

Though she needed to find the courage to confess her feelings, she couldn't do it with the others around. Maybe tonight, she could catch him alone. For now, she'd endure his silence.

The drive to the mountains took them an hour inland along winding roads, past steep hills and small villages that looked lost in time. At TJ's urging, they stopped at Lofou to indulge in Greek coffee and delicious pastries. The cobblestone streets and open-air shops gave the village a more traditional feel than a touristy harbor town like Paphos. They took another break at Monagri, where they visited a twelfth-century church decorated with vibrantly colored frescoes. After five weeks in Cyprus, Olivia appreciated seeing something other than ruins and beaches.

When they got to the town of Platres, near the base of the Troodos Mountains, Rick parked the car in a public lot. The group clambered out and gathered by the trailhead.

TJ glanced up from his phone. "Our best bet is the hike to the Caledonian Falls. It's not too steep and should give us some sweet photo ops."

"Sounds good to me," Stuart said.

Olivia was about to agree with him, but Rick spoke up first. "I'm going to take the Madari Trail up to Mount Adelphi. It's challenging, but the views are supposed to be spectacular."

"Surprisingly enough, the term 'challenging' isn't doing it for me," Dusty said. "Not on my day off. I'll do the falls hike, too."

"How about you, Olivia?" Rick asked. "You up for a real hike in the mountains?"

His question caught her off guard. She assumed he'd chosen the arduous hike as a way of avoiding her. Was he trying to get her alone? She tried not to read too much into his question for fear of getting her hopes up.

"Are you sure?" she asked. "I might slow you down."

He fixed a steady gaze on her, like she was the only person there. "You haven't yet."

Goose bumps pebbled her arms. Maybe he *did* want her to himself. "Okay, I'll go with you."

At this point, what did she have to lose?

TJ grinned. "A tough hike might be fun. I don't want to wuss out. Ow!" He rubbed his side and glared at Dusty. "Why'd you hit me?"

She grabbed his arm. "You're going with me and Stu. Got it?"

Her expression was so ferocious that TJ nodded. "Sure. Whatever you say."

As their group split up, Dusty smiled at Olivia and mouthed the words "good luck."

She was going to need it.

At the outset, Rick kept quiet. He led her along a rough dirt trail, past pine and cedar trees. The scent reminded her of hiking in the High Sierras, during a trip with some friends from grad school. Unlike her hiking buddies, Rick's strides were ridiculously long. Though he occasionally stopped to let her catch up, she was forced to bring out her inhaler after twenty minutes.

When his brow constricted, she shook her head. "I'll be fine."

He waited patiently until her breathing resumed an even cadence. But once they started up again, the steep incline made her legs scream for mercy. Though the air was cooler, the sun was as fierce as ever, making the back of her shirt dampen with sweat. Maybe she'd misjudged Rick. Instead of wanting to get her alone, he'd planned this hike as a way to torture her.

At the first viewpoint, she leaned over, braced her hands on her knees, and took a few deep breaths.

"Do you need to stop for a while?" Rick said. "We're not in a hurry."

"I'm good. No problem." The words came out as more of a gasp.

She would have been happy to stay where she was, looking over the hilly terrain and enjoying the gorgeous blue-sky day, but Rick only nodded and resumed climbing.

What was his game? Why had he invited her if he planned to stay silent the whole way?

Maybe he wasn't ready to open up to her yet. Or he wanted her to make the first move.

Dusty's words came back to her. *You need to put yourself out there.*

The second overlook was outfitted with a bench. Giving a sigh of relief, Olivia plopped down on it and drained half her water bottle. Rick went to the edge, brought out his phone, and took photos of the valley below.

This is it. If she didn't speak now, she'd be too winded to say anything by the time they got to the top of the mountain.

When she stood, her legs wobbled. She inched closer to Rick, but he didn't turn toward her, which was just as well. She'd have an easier time confessing her feelings if she wasn't looking him in the eye.

"Rick?" Her voice hitched, but she willed herself not to cry. "I'm sorry about the other day. I had no right to question you for helping Marisol. And I shouldn't have gotten so upset about Turkey. I was just hurt you hadn't told me about it earlier. I'm also sorry that I implied you're wasting your life. You're not— you're following a path that's right for you. I should have respected that."

When he didn't speak, she swallowed, her throat too dry to continue. Taking another swig from her water bottle, she found the strength to keep going.

"I also should have been honest with you. The real reason I was so mad about Turkey was because I wanted you to come back to California, but it was for selfish reasons." She forced herself to push the words out. "I wanted you to come back because of *me*. I told you I'd be happy with three weeks together, but I started wanting more. I was too scared to admit it."

"So you broke up with me instead?" His ragged voice hinted at the depth of his pain. "What kind of messed-up logic is that?"

She was screwing this up again. *Be honest, you coward.*

"I knew the longer we were together, the more it would hurt when you left," she said. "Because this ended up being more than just a fling. I'm in love with you. But it was too hard to stay with you, knowing you didn't feel the same way."

She crept forward, one step at a time, until she was standing right behind him. She placed her arms around his waist and rested her head against his shoulders, finding comfort in the warmth of his body. "I've probably ruined any chance of us being together, but if you ever wanted more, I'd be willing to wait for you."

His body shuddered as he drew in a breath. "Olivia…"

"I was hoping we could still enjoy our last week in Cyprus together. One final trip to Aphrodite's temple? I promise not to ask for any more than that."

"What if I want more?"

Her breath caught. The sting of tears prickled her eyes. "Do you?"

He turned to face her and placed his hands on her shoulders. "Yes. I'm sorry I didn't tell you about Turkey sooner, but I was still trying to figure things out. I wanted to discuss it together, but when you got upset, I...pushed you away and acted like a jerk. It didn't help that you treated me like I wasn't good enough. That hurt like hell."

Anguish cut into her, burning a painful trail to her heart. "I'm so sorry. I didn't mean any of it."

"I get it. We both said things we didn't mean. But that doesn't resolve the bigger issue. I'm not planning to go to grad school, which means I might not belong in your world."

Her voice trembled. "You belong more than anyone I've ever met. I love that you're so passionate about what you do and that you're so good at sharing your passion with students. That's what counts, not some degree. You're an incredible guy, and don't let anyone convince you otherwise. Not Grant, not your father, and certainly not me. You're more than enough."

"So are you." With a gentle touch, he brushed his hand across her cheek. "I love you, Olivia."

Her heart swelled with affection. "I love you, too. Even if you did force me to climb a giant mountain."

He gave a wry chuckle. "That's why I wanted you to come on this trail—so I could get you alone and tell you how I felt. TJ told me to go for a grand gesture, but I wasn't sure if I could do it. I was trying to work up the courage, but you beat me to it. You're braver than I am."

"Maybe a little more desperate. But I love that you considered making a grand gesture." She put her arms around his neck and pressed up against him, but the movement sent him stumbling backward. As his feet scrabbled against the edge, she pulled him back with a rush of panic. "Sorry. I don't want to send you tumbling over a cliff."

"Let's take this somewhere safer." He led her to the bench and drew her onto his lap so she was facing him.

She brushed a strand of tawny brown hair from his forehead. "I couldn't stop thinking about you. I wanted to go back and undo all the hurtful things I said."

His hazel eyes fixed on hers. "Same here. I shouldn't have hidden so much from you."

"We can do better. I want to make this work."

"It will." His lips traced a path down her throat, lingering on her collarbone. When he slid his hand under her shirt and cupped her breast, she whimpered with desire. She leaned closer, nuzzling his neck with her lips. As his thumb found its way under her bra and rubbed at her nipple, she gasped in pleasure. She squirmed against him, delighting in the feel of his hard length pressing into her. She claimed his lips, going for a soul-searing kiss, oblivious to everything but the taste and feel of him.

Until a clipped British voice broke the stillness. "Excuse me."

Olivia startled. Standing beside them were two elderly British women dressed in athletic gear. The taller of the two carried a walking stick. She nailed them with a withering glare. "That sort of display is highly inappropriate for a public walking trail. Please take it elsewhere."

She sounded so formal that Olivia stifled the urge to giggle. She rolled off Rick's lap, then immediately regretted it when she saw the bulge in his shorts. "Sorry, ma'am," she said.

"We're very sorry," Rick agreed.

The woman gave a loud harrumph, then walked with her companion to the edge of the ridge, where they began taking photos.

Rick stood and tugged on Olivia's hand. "We should get going."

"Do we have to keep climbing? We're good, right?"

He squeezed her hand. "We're better than good, but the hike will be worth it. The view is supposed to be stunning. I know you can do it."

She loved that he had so much faith in her. "Okay. But can you slow down a little?"

By the time they reached the summit, she was shaky and sweaty. Her water bottle was nearly empty. But the view was magnificent. Spread out below them were valleys and dense pine forests. The sky was a brilliant shade of blue. For a long time, she stood beside Rick, taking in the scenery, her heart light with joy.

After taking pictures, they found a secluded area under a thick grove of pine trees. Rick pinned her up against a tree and kissed her until she was breathless. Though she wanted to keep going, she was afraid the scary British women would catch up to them. There would be time for real intimacy later.

On the walk down, they slowed their pace, teasing each other and taking a ridiculous number of photos together. Olivia sent one to Sofia and got a series of heart-eye emojis in return. They'd almost made it back to the car when Rick's phone buzzed.

He peeked at the screen. "TJ said they're done hiking and ready to go. I'll tell him we'll be there in about fifteen minutes." Grinning, he plucked a pine needle out of her curls. "Sorry about your hair. I don't think it's salvageable."

She didn't care if everyone knew what they'd been doing. She was done with secrets. Now that she and Rick were together, she had nothing to hide.

CHAPTER THIRTY-FIVE

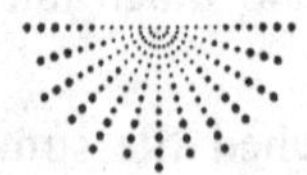

If the end-of-survey party had been fun, the end-of-excavation party was *epic*. Rick was so full he could barely move. After feasting on a delicious Cypriot meal full of mezes, salads, souvlaki, and stuffed grape leaves, they'd celebrated with a cake. Not just any cake, but an enormous chocolate cake Juno had purchased in secret to celebrate Rick's twenty-seventh birthday. Seated at the crowded table with Olivia at his side, he couldn't remember a better birthday. Especially since she'd promised to continue the celebration once the party was over. They'd both decided to risk one last visit to Aphrodite's temple. Hopefully, no one else would choose tonight to pay tribute to the goddess.

The past week had gone by in a blur. Rick had gotten another chance to dig at his Neolithic site, and this time, Olivia had come with him. Based on the evidence they'd uncovered, the site was likely to be the subject of a full-scale excavation next year. Back at the House of Heracles, the students had finished the excavation unit and turned in their field notebooks. As promised, Dr. Roth had fully committed himself to the field school. He'd shown up early every morning and stayed at the dig site until the day's work was done.

Amid all the activity and bustle, Rick was grateful for his rare moments alone with Olivia. Now that he had her back, he had no intention of letting her go, even if their paths were about to diverge for a while. Or were they? A few days ago, he'd come up with a way to keep them together. It was the only secret he'd hidden from her, but he wanted to wait until they were alone before he revealed it.

When Juno cranked up the tunes, Sofia roused everyone to start dancing. She'd joined them for her last night in Cyprus and had fully embraced the party spirit.

Olivia stood over Rick and motioned for him to get up. "Let's go, old man."

"Old man?" He pressed his hand over his heart. "You cut me deeply. I'm only two months older than you."

"It's not the years, it's the mileage. And you've had plenty of mileage."

"Give me a second and I'll sweep you off your feet." He smiled at the sight of TJ twirling Sofia around in a wild attempt at ballroom dancing. "TJ's doing pretty good with your sister. Any chance for sparks there?"

Olivia laughed. "I doubt it since she's leaving tomorrow. Off to Athens for two days, and then she's flying to Cairo. Dusty's stopping there to see her parents, and she asked Sofia to join her. Naturally, Sof's planning a full week of Egyptian-themed content."

"Sounds like fun." He'd grown to like Olivia's younger sister, who still referred to him as Mr. Hottie. "Are you psyched for Athens?"

"Of course. The Acropolis. The Agora. The National Archaeology Museum. And that delightful king bed."

He couldn't wait. The ruins in Athens might be world-class,

but he'd seen them all before. He was more excited about making love to Olivia in a real bed.

When Grant approached them, Rick's shoulders tightened. Over the past week, the assistant director had barely been a presence at the House of Heracles. Instead, he'd spent his time at camp working in the lab. Rick had been hoping to avoid a final confrontation with him.

Grant gave a curt nod. "Rick. Olivia. I assume you're enjoying the party. When do you leave Cyprus?"

If Grant could be civil, then Rick could follow suit. "We're flying to Athens the day after tomorrow. How about you? Are you headed back to Riverside?"

"The fall quarter doesn't start for a few more weeks, so I'm staying in Paphos until mid-September. Lidia—I mean, Dr. Bouras—asked me to conduct a series of test excavations at the Cypro-Geometric site that we found during the survey."

Olivia grinned. "You're digging more test pits at my site?"

"It's hardly *your* site, Miss Sanchez, but yes, it's the one you discovered. Given my expertise in that era of Cypriot prehistory, Dr. Roth suggested I pursue it further." A sour expression clouded his features. "I suppose it's his form of consolation since he informed me that I won't be welcome back at the field school next summer. In fact, it may be a while before I work with students in the field again."

Under normal circumstances, Rick would have expected him to unleash a tirade, ranting about the unfairness of Dr. Roth's decision, but Grant's words had a resigned air. Like he knew he'd screwed up and was dealing with the consequences.

An awkward pause followed until Olivia spoke up. "Well, good luck with the site. I hope it turns out to be an Iron Age settlement."

"Dr. Bouras seemed to think so. In any case, I'm sure to get a publication or two out of it." He gave another nod. "Good night."

Rick watched him leave. In an ideal world, Grant might have

apologized for the way he'd treated them all summer. For all the insults, the intimidation, and the gaslighting. But at least he wasn't simmering with anger. That was a start.

Olivia waited a minute before bursting into laughter. "Was it my imagination, or did Grant seem sort of human?"

"I'm not sure, but it's a nice change. The question is—will he get a chance with Dr. Bouras once Roth's out of the picture?"

"Who knows? What happens in the field stays in the field." Giving him a flirty smile, Olivia reached for his hand. "Speaking of which, there's a sweet reward waiting for you later if you dance with me now."

How could he resist a proposition like that?

For the next hour, Rick lost himself in the music, jamming with the field school students. They'd all be headed back home soon, but for one last night, they bonded together over their shared experiences. Life in the field had that effect. It was one of the reasons Rick loved it so much.

By the time he and Olivia crept away from camp, the party was winding down. When they reached the temple, the moonlit ruins were as quiet as ever. He led her to their favorite spot and laid a blanket over the smooth stones. Taking another one out of his pack, he folded it up to serve as a pillow.

Without a hint of inhibition, Olivia pulled her sundress over her head. Her bra and panties followed. She stood before him, naked, radiant, and sexy as hell. He stared at her in breathless awe, wondering how he'd gotten so lucky.

She placed her hands on her hips. "Well? Aren't you going to undress?"

"You're incredible. You know that?"

"I know." Her laughter pealed across the ruins. "Come on. I feel silly being the only one naked. Or would you like me to undress you?"

He shot her a cocky grin. "Would you? Since it's my birthday and all?"

With a toss of her hair, she sashayed over to him. Her nimble fingers quickly unbuttoned his shirt and tossed it aside. After running her hands along his bare chest, she placed soft kisses on his neck and shoulders. He groaned, torn between enjoying the buildup and wanting to plunder her gorgeous body.

She kissed the hollow of his throat. "I need to be on top. I know it's your birthday, but I want to be in control."

If he wasn't already as hard as a rock, her request would have pushed him over the edge. "Whatever you want, princess."

She unbuckled his shorts and pulled them down around his ankles. He kicked them to the side and stripped off his boxers. Then he was as naked as she was, in a temple dedicated to the goddess of sexual love. He pulled her closer, pressing his bare skin against hers, and captured her mouth with a passionate kiss. Her tongue tangled with his, tasting of chocolate.

When she pulled away, her breathing was ragged, her voice husky. "Lie down."

He eased himself onto the blanket and lay on his back. Even with the cloth beneath him to serve as padding, the stone was hard and chilly. But once Olivia straddled him, his body heated up, the warmth rushing through him like an inferno. When she leaned forward, her full breasts close enough to touch, he tweaked her nipples, eliciting little gasps out of her. He pulled her closer until she was caging his body and licked slow circles around each taut bud. She moaned with pleasure, her voice carrying across the quiet site. Her noisy, passionate response made him ache with need, but he wanted to make tonight last.

He reached between her legs and dipped a finger into her slick, wet folds, seeking out her sweet spot until she gasped again.

"Yes," she murmured. "Like that. *Please.*"

She moved her hips as he stroked her, her breath coming faster. Seeing her caught up in ecstasy turned him on even more. He was desperate to bury himself deep inside her, but he wanted to satisfy her first. She tightened her grip on his shoulders and arched her back. As her body shuddered atop his, she cried out his name in abandon, like she didn't care who heard them, even the goddess Aphrodite herself.

She pushed her messy curls from her face and let out a rush of air. "Ohhh. That felt so good."

He grinned at her. "Want me to do it again?" Even if he was craving a little release, he loved watching her come.

A saucy smile crossed her lips. "This time, I want you inside me." Reaching for the condom, she tore at the foil and took it out. "May I?"

"Yes, please."

She sheathed him slowly after taking her time to stroke him first. Then she guided him inside of her, angling her hips until she'd settled on the perfect position. "Is that good?"

"The best." For a moment, he kept still, gazing up at her in a mixture of lust and admiration.

And then she was moving against him, thrusting her hips in a steady rhythm. He grabbed her ass and pulled her even deeper, losing himself in the feel of her. She leaned closer and kissed him fiercely, her tongue dancing against his. As the pressure built up inside of him, he was close to exploding, but he stayed in control, wanting Olivia to come first.

His entire body tensed up as she flung her head back and cried out again. With a groan, he gave into sensation, shuddering as he came inside of her. The powerful orgasm rushed through him, so intense it almost made him light-headed, the sheer bliss more incredible than anything he could remember.

She collapsed on top of him, still breathing heavily. "Oh… wow. That was unbelievable."

He stroked her hair, not wanting to break the connection between them. When she finally eased off him and lay down at his side, he brought her closer, cradling her in his arms.

She let out a contented sigh. "Best ritual sacrifice *ever*."

"I agree. Aphrodite would be pleased at how well we used her temple."

"You think she was watching over us the whole time?"

"With Aphrodite, you never know," he said softly. "But I'd like to think so."

CHAPTER THIRTY-SIX

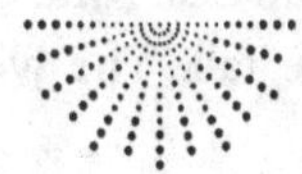

Olivia lay next to Rick on the blanket, still coming down from her sex high. Maybe because it was their last night in the temple, or because they weren't hiding their feelings, the sex had been incredible. Whether it was luck or fate or Aphrodite, they were meant to be together.

She traced a finger across his lips. "I'm kind of sad we won't have any more chances to worship the goddess."

"Me, too. But that hotel's going to be sweet. We can wake up together every morning."

"Mmm." She shivered. "Morning sex. We've never done that."

"Don't forget about shower sex."

"Yes, please. Preferably with hot water." Though she was excited for Athens, she didn't want to dwell on what came next. After they parted, the earliest she'd see him would be December. But he'd promised to keep in touch. If they stayed open and honest, they could make it work.

He pushed a stray curl out of her face. "I love you."

"I love you, too. I'm so glad we didn't miss this last week of field school. Or Athens. Or whatever our next adventure might be."

He grinned at her. "Speaking of which, I had a brilliant idea. Hear me out, okay?"

"Brilliant? You sound like TJ. But since it's your birthday, I'll allow it." Though she kept her voice light, her heart leapt in anticipation. Had he changed his plans?

"This Turkey gig is based in Bodrum. It's a harbor town like Paphos, right on the Aegean Sea. Kind of touristy in the summer, but it quiets down in the fall. The weather in September and October is perfect."

She poked him in the shoulder. "Stop making me jealous. Fall in Los Angeles means Santa Ana winds and wildfires."

He still had a gleam in his eyes. "You're ABD, right? Not on the hook for any classes?"

"Nope. I don't even have to work as a teaching assistant next year. I got a research scholarship, but I'll probably be done with my research after I leave Athens. Once I get home, I need to start writing. Why?"

"Could you do this writing in Turkey? Or add to your research there? This shipwreck is from the same era as your thesis. And it held an enormous cache of wine bottles."

Her breath caught. Go to Turkey? With Rick? She'd never considered it. "Well…my dissertation *is* about Hellenistic Greece, but I could expand my thesis. Dr. Roth suggested it when we were talking at dinner one night. I started researching the trade activity in Turkey when I was holed up in the camp library."

The more she thought about it, the more exciting it seemed. Even if she didn't add to her dissertation, she could get enough material to write an article. Maybe present it at next year's AIA meetings. If she went to Turkey, she'd get to visit a new country. Work on a new project. And she'd be with Rick.

"What do you think?" His voice rose in enthusiasm. "I'd love it if you joined me."

She cast him a playful smile. "You realize you're throwing me off-kilter? I usually plan things months in advance."

"That's not what happened with this field school. You got asked at the last minute, and look how well it turned out."

"True." Even if she'd struggled at first, her life had changed for the better, all because she'd taken a risk. "It sounds like a great opportunity, but I can't just show up uninvited, can I?"

He gave her a sheepish grin. "Don't kill me, but I might have paved the way. I asked Dr. Kaplan if I brought my girlfriend—who also happens to be an archaeologist—whether he could find room for her on the project. Once I wowed him with your credentials, he was on board."

The words filled her with a swell of happiness. "You called me that?"

"My girlfriend? Sure. It's true, right?"

"Not that. Of course I'm your girlfriend. You called me an *archaeologist*."

"Because that's what you are. Even if you never go back in the field again, you proved yourself this summer."

"I'm definitely going back into the field. Just try and stop me." The thought of it was a tantalizing lure. The world was wide-open, with opportunities waiting to be taken. The boyfriend thing was pretty sweet, too.

"If you came to Turkey, Dr. Kaplan said you'd be welcome to help out in the lab as a paid assistant. But if you wanted to focus mainly on writing, that would work, too. Even if you don't get a ton of writing done, the project only goes through mid-November. You'd have the rest of the academic year to finish your dissertation."

When he put it that way, the idea sounded doable. Not just doable, but a lot more appealing than flying back to LA. She could easily change her ticket home, and it wouldn't cost much to fly from Athens to Bodrum.

"What about after?" she asked. "You think you'll want to go back to California?"

"Definitely. Dr. Roth's recommendation will be good

whenever I need it. But first, I have to visit my family. Last night, I called my mom and told her I'd be home for Thanksgiving. She said I'd be welcome, no matter what."

"That's wonderful. What about your dad?"

"Maybe she stood up to him? I don't know. But I'm excited to see her and Cassie again. After the holidays, I'll start looking for a place in Southern California. Near my *girlfriend*."

"That would be perfect." She'd have to tell her parents she was going to Turkey, and she'd need to notify her academic adviser. But those were minor details. The thought of more archaeology, more travel, and more time with Rick was too good to pass up.

Her future was unfolding like a wonderful map, full of mysterious islands and uncharted waters. She couldn't wait to experience all of it.

"When we're in Turkey, could we visit Ephesus?" she asked. "And Aphrodisias? They're two of the most important sites in the ancient world."

"We can do that." He gave her an indulgent smile. "Don't forget the city of Troy. I know how much you love *The Iliad*."

"*Yes*. And maybe check out Istanbul? I've always wanted to go there."

He leaned over and kissed her forehead. "Of course. This is just the beginning."

Thank you for reading *Field Rules!*

I hope you enjoyed Rick and Olivia's story.

If you did, please consider leaving a review wherever you purchased this book.

Thanks! Your support is much appreciated!

Want more Sofia? Check out her novella in *Fiesta Nights*, a Latinx romance anthology releasing in September.

The Romancing the Ruins series will continue in 2023. Stay tuned for Book 2, a friends-to-lovers romance featuring Dusty and Stuart.

Website and Newsletter Sign-up:
carlalunabooks.com

AUTHOR'S NOTE

Of all the books I've written, *Field Rules* is the one closest to my heart because it's based on my own adventures. When I was twenty, I participated in my first overseas dig—an archaeological field school in Cyprus like the one in this novel. The six weeks I spent there were challenging and exhilarating. The experience changed my life, in that I ended up pursuing archaeology in graduate school and spent the next seven years participating in digs all over the world. The *Romancing the Ruins* series is my attempt to turn these adventures into stories.

Though I took a few liberties in this book in terms of modern geography and ancient sites (e.g. the House of Heracles is a fictitious Roman villa), most of the places mentioned are real, such as the village of Kouklia (and the Sanctuary of Aphrodite), the Nea Paphos Archaeological Park, the Minoan site of Palaikastro in Crete, the Institute of Nautical Archaeology in Bodrum, Turkey, and the Jordanian excavations at Humayma that TJ mentions.

Speaking of Turkey, in June 2022, the country began the move to change its internationally recognized official name to

Türkiye. However, to avoid confusion, I opted to use the familiar spelling of the country's name.

Please note that the archaeological methodology in this book is based on my own experiences, combined with reports gathered from recent surveys and excavations on the island of Cyprus. However, the range of digital technology, lab work, and hands-on procedures often varies from project to project, depending on the budget, staffing, and resources available. The field school in this story isn't meant to encompass every aspect of archaeology but to give the reader a snapshot of life in the field.

ACKNOWLEDGMENTS

To say this book has been a long time coming is an understatement. After all my adventures in the field, I've been wanting to publish "the archaeology book" for years, and I'm so grateful I can finally share it with the world. I wrote the earliest version of this story many moons ago with the help of Karma Brown, a talented writer who served as my mentor.

Along the way, *Field Rules* went through many different iterations before taking on its final form. Among the generous writers who read those earlier versions and offered feedback are Barb Britton, Mia Jo Celeste, Liz Czukas, Liz Lincoln, Michelle Mason, Kip Wilson, Mona Shroff, and Shaila Patel, as well as my former agent Erin Niumata. My brother, John Luna, also deserves a hearty thank-you for listening to all my long-winded archaeology stories.

For this current version of *Field Rules*, I owe a debt of gratitude to my team of professionals: Bailey McGinn for her wonderful cover design, April Bennett at The Editing Soprano for her copy-edits, and Sandra Dee at One Love Editing for proofreading. I'm also very grateful for the writers who served as beta-readers for this book: Jennifer Rupp, Jenn Ficcara, Laura Luna, Gail Werner, Michelle McCraw, Charlene Groome, Susan Keillor, and Liz Czukas.

I couldn't have gotten this far without a ton of support from the writing community. Thanks to my long-standing writing group, the FITWIGS (Lolly Rzezotarski, Jennifer Motl, Lisa Minneti, Virginia Small, Shlomo Levin), for our monthly get-togethers featuring wine, delicious food, and heaps of encouragement. I'm also very grateful to the "Class of 2021" indie author squad: Michelle McCraw, Ofelia Martinez, Kristin Lee, Brandy Shaw, and Jazz Matthews.

Thank you to all the readers who bought, reviewed, and supported my *Blackwood Cellars* books. I'm so grateful you took a chance on a new romance author, and I hope you'll continue to stick with me.

In addition to the writing community, I want to thank the friends who have stood behind me on my journey. Thanks to the spice crew (Byron, Cheri, Gayle, Deanna, and Shari), for being the most encouraging coworkers ever. Thanks to my coffee cohort, Jackie Dhein and Andrea Wallus, for laughter, gossip, and constant enthusiasm; and to my friend Mindy Makinster, the most supportive fan any writer could want.

Thanks so much to my fellow romance authors Liz Lincoln and Liz Czukas for listening to me whine, helping me brainstorm, and cheering me on. Thanks to my long-standing critique partner, Tricia Quinnies, for reading endless versions of this story and never giving up on it.

Since this book was inspired by my archaeological adventures, I'd like to give a shout-out to some of the professors who encouraged me in the field: Dr. David Rupp (Cyprus), Dr. George Bass (Turkey), Dr. John Oleson (Jordan), Dr. Rafael Azuar Ruiz (Spain), and Dr. Jeanne Arnold (California). Thanks also to my good friend, archaeologist Dr. Robert Beardsell, who answered my questions early on in the writing process.

As always, I'm incredibly grateful for the support of my loving family—Mike, Tasmine, and James. Finally, I want to thank my late parents, Dulcie and Mario Luna, who encouraged me to follow my dreams of being both an archaeologist *and* a writer.

ABOUT THE AUTHOR

Carla Luna writes contemporary romance with a dollop of humor and a pinch of spice. A former archaeologist, she still dreams of traveling to far-off places and channels that wanderlust into the settings of her stories.

When she's not writing, she works in a spice emporium where she gets paid to discuss food and share her favorite recipes. Her passions include Broadway musicals, baking, whimsical office supplies, and pop culture podcasts. Though she has roots in Los Angeles and Vancouver Island, she currently resides in Wisconsin with her family and her spoiled Siberian cat.

For sneak peeks, giveaways, recipes, and free short stories, sign up for Carla's newsletter:
www.carlalunabooks.com

ALSO BY CARLA LUNA

The Blackwood Cellars Series

Blue Hawaiian

Broke, single and jobless, Jess Chavez feels like the family screwup when she flies to Maui to attend her *perfect* older sister's wedding. But sparks fly when Jess reconnects with her roguish ex, Connor Blackwood. A secret fling offers the ideal escape from family drama, as long as Jess can keep from falling in love again.

Red Velvet

When April Beckett's plus-one bails right before a big family wedding, her best friend, Brody Blackwood, offers to take his place. Now they have to convince everyone they're lovers—while sharing a cozy cottage in the Northwoods of Wisconsin. But what happens when the fake relationship starts to feel real?

White Wedding

When Victoria Blackwood is tasked with planning her ex's Christmas wedding, she doesn't think her life could get any worse. Until she discovers the caterer , Rafael Sanchez, is the lover she ghosted five years ago after a steamy fling in Baja. To pull off the perfect wedding, they'll need to keep things professional. But it won't be easy, not when the fire between them burns hotter than Christmas in July.

* 9 7 8 1 7 3 6 8 6 6 1 7 7 *